T0196456

THE HIDDEN HISTORY OF
JACK QUINN

MIKE ROBERTSON

authorHOUSE®

AuthorHouse™
1663 Liberty Drive
Bloomington, IN 47403
www.authorhouse.com
Phone: 1 (800) 839-8640

Published by AuthorHouse 07/14/2017

ISBN: 978-1-5462-0024-6 (sc)
ISBN: 978-1-5462-0023-9 (e)

Print information available on the last page.

MUSINGS AFTER THE FACT

Detective Robert Neeson was leaning back in his chair behind his desk in the Truscott Police Department pretending to smoke a cigarette. After years of surviving the appeals, if not the demands of most of the people he knew, including most particularly his wife, Neeson had finally surrendered to the inevitability of giving up smoking. His only comfort now was the faint illusion provided by holding a cigarette and remembering the experience that he had had so much difficulty forsaking. Like the four other officers in the Truscott Police Department, Detective Neeson was a seemingly gruff, profoundly overweight man in his forties. Unlike his colleagues, however, he was unusually intense for a peace officer protecting the citizens of a relatively small rural community. Much to the consternation of his fellow officers, Detective Neeson was in the habit of approaching every infraction committed in the borough as a major crime. He would employ the kind of analysis usually reserved for homicides in television crime dramas. In fact, Police Chief Casper was often forced to order Neeson not to pursue small time robberies, petty vandalism, and domestic commotions as if terrorism was involved. He was always looking to solve the big case, even though Truscott hardly ever offered any detective such opportunity. The historical evidence of significant law-breaking in Truscott was scant --- the murder of a local man named Quinn back in the 1950s, a couple of suicides, automotive accidents, repeated robberies of the only bank in the town, suspicious fires, and drug arrests. Fact was that the main criminal activity involved minor domestic disputes and disturbances.

So when an amateur gumshoe named Mark Purchell raised the murder conviction of a man named Williams Boggs, a man who had killed himself decades ago rather than face life in prison, Neeson was more than interested. He was happy to recommend that Mr. Purchell speak to his father, a former police officer, also named Robert Neeson. His father, who was deeply involved in the original investigation that led to the conviction of Mr. Boggs, later told him that he would be willing to talk to Mr. Purchell.

BACKGROUND RECOLLECTIONS

More than sixty years later and 1,500 kilometers away, a man unknowingly connected to the murder of a man named Quinn by a Mr. William Boggs in the small town of Truscott, Nova Scotia, an Ottawa man named Jack Quinn awaited his own demise. He was profoundly sick and almost fatalistically resigned to the coming end. He was a collection of curious character traits and personality quirks that would excite most students of psychology. He was moody and amusing at the same time, a man with the classic chip on one shoulder and hilarity on the other. He was sentimental but cynical, charitable but selfish. He had always wanted to be a bad guy but usually ended up a good guy. He tried to be pugnacious. He tried to be aggressive. He venerated tough guys. He wanted to become one himself but he turned out to be too decent. Fact was that for most of his life, despite all his efforts to the contrary, people regarded him as a good guy. He was blessed with epic dreams and tormented with epic nightmares. Though he eventually resigned himself to both, none of which were real.

He passed away on a Thursday night in the middle of the month of October, neither the day or month memorable. He was found maybe several hours after he expired, laid out in regrettable repose in a dingy apartment on the third floor of a dingy apartment building, found the next morning by a neighbor, a congenial but noisy guy named Danny who sometimes dropped into Jack's place unannounced. Aside from Danny, who was admittedly a casual visitor but did live next door, Jack had two regular visitors, one a friend of almost four decades named Mark Purchell, the other a former wife of short duration, the latter presumably the last person to have seen him alive. That was debatable, the prospect of an unknown visitor having been briefly discussed by two police detectives on the scene, the neighborhood hardly a safe vicinity. Both detectives surmised, if a stranger was involved, Mr. Quinn would hardly be able to put up much of a fight, his physical condition so poor that he would probably drop dead before an intruder could land a second blow. There was no evidence, however, of any time of a struggle. It was no surprise then that the case, if a case could actually be made of his death, was closed with a shrug of some bureaucratic shoulder, vanishing into a file with a click of a computer mouse.

The deceased man's narrative had been predictable. The beginning was the end, not only for the ex-wife, who had invested only a couple of years in their union, but also for his old friend Jack, who was to figure prominently in Jack's life after death. Both of them might well have anticipated that Jack would pass away long before either of them would have expected. The departed was virtually housebound. He was a gravely ill man with irredeemable health problems. He was in his mid-fifties but looked much older. He was painfully thin with a graying beard and a stringy ponytail hanging to the middle of his back. He had been found dead in his customary outfit of perpetually unwashed sweatpants, a dirty t-shirt with an unidentifiable inscription across the chest and a classically tattered dressing gown. He had been stricken for several years with an assortment of serious medical ailments, the most crucial of which was emphysema, two packs of cigarettes a day since he was barely in his teens, making that practically an inevitability. He was also afflicted with a barely functioning liver, thirty five years of hard drinking another obvious culprit.

Mr. Quinn did not deny his fate. In fact, he celebrated it, in a predictably strange, dark way. He had been expecting, if not seemingly planning for his own death for some time, a certain existential flourish being the main feature of his approach to his unfortunate future. He had started to actually take a certain perverse delight in discussing the macabre enterprise of his own departure. During his last few months, he would mention his wretched fate pretty well every chance he got, so often that the rapidly dwindling circle of those who had any involvement in his destiny started to lose interest in it. To them, Quinn's complaints about his evident destiny had started to seem more like melodramatic self pity than anything approaching the true tragedy he imagined. Fact was that the dramatics pursued by Quinn became almost operatic in dimension, so much so that his friend Mark had sarcastically suggested that he might consider taking his act on the road, retirement and funeral homes obvious audiences for such theatrical expressions of existential angst.

As a consequent of his behavior, most of his so-called friends, mainly former co-workers or guys with whom he had played beer league hockey years before, had stopped visiting Quinn, their irritation with his act having gone past a point of exasperation. That left only one old friend Mark. He had met Quinn over forty years ago when they both were working at an automotive parts warehouse. He had maintained a close friendship with Quinn ever since. Over the past months of that life, it was Mark Purchell who visited Quinn practically every day as he waited to pass away, his old friend's discomfort with the latter's dramatics fading with the latter's physical condition. Purchell had simply gotten accustomed to, if not bored with his friend's madness, variations of which had bedevilled him for years. When they first met, all it took was three or four quarts of *Molson's Export* and Quinn would be suggesting that some authority figure, usually but not limited to his mother Eileen, of conspiring to ruin his chances of success in a variety of ambitions.

He would sometimes even claim that he was adopted, usually when he was inebriated, intimating that there was something tragically commendable about such circumstances. When he was sobered up, however, he would come clean so to speak and admit that he like to pretend to be adopted. Having grown familiar with his new friend's rants of misfortune and regret, Purchell had started to invariably compare Quinn to Marlon Brando emoting in *On the Waterfront*. Quinn himself seemed to take a certain misguided pleasure in that observation, any reference to a moody role model, particularly one who was famous, being of definitive, almost whimsical value. He almost become an actor himself. Or so he wanted to think. None of it was true of course.

As their friendship developed --- they had become best friends within months --- Purchell could predict the ebb and flow of the Quinn melancholia with the precision of a meteorologist. Fact was that their relationship had evolved, like a lot of relationships, into an exchange of common interests, life's disappointments being one if not the prevalent theme. Both of them enjoyed discussing their own misfortunes, their own depressions, their own despairs, of which there were supposedly many. They ridiculed them, they made light of them, they were sarcastic about them. For years, they had transformed their own failures, some real, some imagined into something approaching entertainment, histrionics that eventually grew tiresome to anyone unlucky enough to catch their act more than once. Now, after forty years, with Quinn staggering toward the most significant dashed hope of all, Purchell was still around, sharing his friend's feeling for failure with a sort of feigned responsibility, his interest long ceasing to be in any way sincere. Regardless, Mark Purchell was there practically every day, waiting for the end with his old friend, an obligation to a palliative friend his sole motivation.

With Purchell covering the morning shift, it was left to his ex-wife Deborah Inkster to take up visitation duties for the late afternoon/early evening. Despite their forgettable years together, she repeatedly tried to convince her ex-husband to forgo his affinity for, if not his dependence on pessimism and other addictions, Ms. Inkster, who sometimes seemed to have the disposition of a nun, felt a predictable obligation to nurse him, a compulsion that she continually defended, always denying that it was a character flaw. She habitually reminded herself, as well as reminding Purchell, with whom she often discussed Quinn's situation, of the importance of their visits, comparing it to visits to the hospital. Mark and Deborah often exchanged tales of dreary days spent in hospital rooms with their ailing parents, desperately pretending to stay awake and staring at the various medical monitors beeping quietly above the patient's bed. They agreed that the undeniable tedium of sitting in the hospital was the principal characteristic of the obligation. Purchell had to struggle through his daily meetings with Quinn, without benefit of such moral self-assurance. As for the good Sister Inkster, she was sympathetic enough with Purchell's plight not to criticize the latter's lack of empathy. Purchell sometimes but not often wondered, however, whether he should have felt guilty about not being as charitable about his obligation toward his sick friend as the man's ex-wife. He felt like it was just another job. To be honest, his real job, a mid-level management job with an insurance company, was a helluva lot better, no matter from which perspective one employed. He had grown to regard his daily meetings with his old friend as almost a family obligation, perhaps penance for some past transgression, like a plenary indulgence. He was an old friend. He had no choice, like family.

Quinn's apartment was familiar to Purchell, the frequency of his visits there making a close acquaintance with the surroundings unavoidable. It reminded him of his first apartment in the city, a small furnished bachelor on the first floor of an old Victorian house that had been converted into six separate units. There was very little difference, at least to Purchell, between that old apartment, which was likely still occupied by a young tenant like he had been, and the rooms that Quinn had inhabited until he passed away. Quinn's place was situated in what could be accurately be described as a row house, a dwelling in an unremarkable brick building. It was situated up from an unmarked wooden door, which was never locked and upon which brass numerals were once attached. It was a sparsely furnished flat at the top of a flight of stairs that was missing several steps. The place consisted of a grimy bathroom, a kitchen counter with a sink, a barely functioning refrigerator, and a stove that appeared to have been installed some time in the 1950s. There was a small living room in which the housebound occupant sat on one of the two old sofa chairs in the room or laid on the narrow wooden bed situated under one of the two windows that faced the street from that second floor. The room also featured an old television set that was seldom turned off, two night side tables, a coffee table that was always covered with old newspapers, magazines, books, coffee cups and beer bottles, an intermittently functioning floor lamp, a disconnected telephone on the wall near the stove, a large tin can that was normally used as a spittoon and, most dramatically, several oxygen tanks. There was no bedroom. It was a bachelor. Jack called it the "beauty of decay" while most people, including Mark, called it a dump.

Jack Quinn was estranged from any suggestion of family. Both his parents were dead, his siblings lost somewhere on the map. He said that he thought that his brother had moved to California. He was a musician and was by nature rootless. He had neither seen nor heard from him in decades. His sister, who was younger and with whom he never did have any significant relationship, had married a man, whose name he could not recall, and moved away as well, to where he did not know. That was maybe twenty years past. He could not even remember her married name. So it was left to Mark Purchell to make any arrangements, Deborah apparently being too upset to participate. There was neither a church service nor a burial ceremony. Jack Quinn was buried in the ground on a slight incline beneath a small metal disk in the Royal Cross Cemetery. There was no name on the disk, only a number.

Not surprisingly, Jack left no will. Institutional arrangements had to be made nonetheless. A couple of government departments had to be advised as in a couple of pensions to be discontinued, a police report completed and filed, and the cost of his burial paid. Mark Purchell and Deborah Inkster split the cost.

A PRELUDE

Aside from a number of other common behaviors, sarcasm, interests, alcohol and other assorted intoxicants being principal curiosities, Quinn and Purchell both pursued the pretense of poetry. However peculiar, both had convinced themselves, a fantasy vocation which originated in high school, that they were poets, dark, brooding and sensitive as hell, personaity traits they carefully played out like they were characters in unwitten dramas. Decades ago, during their spectacularly irresponsible post-university years, they continually wrote verse, free form doggerel that impressed no one but each other, their initial objective being the seduction of young women foolish or naive enough to be impressed by amateur poetry. Their ambition was hardly ever realized, the few exemptions being women who were disposed to being persuaded anyway. Regardless of whether anyone ever read their poetry, they had a limited audience to be sure, most people being convinced that they were intellectuals, no longer the smart alecs they had been in adolescence. In fact, one of their mutual university friends, an acknowledged wit who always seemed to have too many female friends, once remarked that all smart alecs eventually turned into intellectuals unless they ended up in jail. For Quinn and Purchell, that exalted status had evaporated along with their prospects as the years wore on.

Despite their best efforts to affect an acceptable level of melancholy temperament, Quinn having a particular talent for feigning depression, they could not maintain that act forever. Fact was they could be fairly congenial when they wanted to be, even avid and sometime entertaining conversationalists as well, as least between each other. When they weren't playing the thespian role, they would be rehearsing for roles as comedians. At such times, it seemed that they attempted to inject humor, or what they thought was humor, into practically everything. So they told predictable stories about predictable personalities and predictable experiences, sometimes shared, sometimes not, in school, both having graduated with Bachelors of Arts from different schools. Regarding the latter, Purchell would refer to his high academic achievements as a degree in drugs and rock music. They would talk sports, they both having invested considerable time and effort in various athletic endeavors. They would talk about their succession of dull and tiresome jobs, a myriad of which had bedeviled them since they were both in high school. And of course, they would review, with appropriate comic asides, their efforts to attract women. They exchanged cynical observations, past and present, sometimes dark, sometimes absurd, sometimes appropriate, sarcasm seemingly being the main if not only emollient of everything they said. They threw barbs around like they were exhaling cigarette smoke about the room. As long as they were in a crowd, the introspective poet persona did not appear. No one was interested in that kind of thing anyway.

It was doubtful that neither Quinn nor Purchell ever knew that their exasperated audiences did not always appreciate their repartee. Many years later, long after their shows had closed for good, they were surprised, if not astounded, when Purchell was told, by an acquaintance who may have had some old grievance or other to ponder, that their entertainments were usually not that funny. This acquaintance also confided, in a purportedly confidential aside --- the veracity of which was doubted for a time by Purchell ---- that several of their male acquaintances contemplated making their point physically. In fact, it was later recalled that one of these individuals had specifically suggested that he had wanted to eat Purchell's glasses, an image that was mildly entertaining in itself, an irony about which Quinn and Purchell were to ruminate for weeks. Purchell also admitted, at least to himself, to being a little frightened. Fact was that Mark Purchell was preoccupied with the possibility that he was not as well regarded as he thought he was. It worried him for much of his life. On the other hand, his friend Jack Quinn never seemed to care about such matters. Mark Purchell could never explain his friend's apparent lack of concern about what people thought of him. On the other hand, he remained convinced that Jack Quinn cared about what his friend Mark Purchell thought of him.

That was the basis he guessed for his unexpected acceptance of Jack's occasional sincerity. Maybe his almost constant cynicism made any expression of sincerity from Jack all the more credible. Mark could only remember several instances in which Jack offered anything even remotely confidential to his supposed best friend. Early in their relationship, maybe a few months after they first met, Jack informed Mark, after more than several hours of hardcore drinking at a joint across the street from the automotive parts place where they were both working, that he had fathered a child while both he and his girlfriend at the time were just out of high school. Jack said that Alison was likely four or five months along when he escorted her to the graduation dance. By the fall, her parents had moved Alison out to the west coast to live with her aunt and her husband. She eventually gave birth to a girl named Phoebe, a curious name of which Jack was unaware until one of Alison's old school friends confided it to him when Jack ran into her in a downtown club several years later. The old girlfriend just knew the name, nothing else she said. No city, no address, just the name. Jack pressed her but to no avail.

After that one exchange with Jack, during which they had discussed Alison and their lost daughter, the subject never re-emerged. Despite his silence, Mark had always suspected that at some point his friend would ask him to assist him in some sort of search for the lost daughter. He didn't know why, he just had the feeling that he would eventually enlist his help in such an endeavor. In fact, Mark had developed the impression, based on something Jack had casually said about adoptions that Jack had somehow hoped that Phoebe had been adopted. But he never did ask for his help in searching for his lost daughter. In fact, Jack Quinn never mentioned it again, a curious development for a man who often liked to wallow in his own despair, extenuated now that he was edging towards his own demise. Mark thought that it would have been a dramatically impeccable denouement, a variant of a death bed request.

After his second or third quart of beer that evening, Jack confessed to another regrettable act that he quietly admitted was something that he would rather not discuss, at least while he was sober. In fact, he said that he had kept his participation in a truly deplorable event that he had kept hidden for at least the decade. It wasn't like the birth of a child out of wedlock, an accident of a romantic relationship gone wrong, but more like a criminal transgression that, if the authorities had been involved, would have resulted in an arrest, if not a jail sentence. Jack, whose voice was practically down to a whisper while he was testifying to the particular act, explained to Mark how he and two of his adolescent friends, he gave their names as Jimmy and Pete, used to break into neighborhood houses while the people living in them were away on vacation, the information on the vacancies courtesy of another boy who had a paper route and therefore was able to report on the families who had discontinued their newspapers while they were away. The gang would use the information to identify the houses they would ultimately burglarize. They would then steal the usual worthless junk that always seem to appeal to adolescent males: liquor, money, dirty magazines, records, and stereo equipment. As a final act of felonious imbecility, the boys would invariably signal their escape from the house by ransacking it, for no apparent reason other than any reason that adolescent boys have for doing anything.

Mark reacted predictably. He shrugged his shoulders and quietly snickered, acknowledging that he could remember engaging in similar adolescent hi-jinks although he admitted to less serious transgressions, like serial shoplifting, stealing cigarettes from the old lady, and occasionally chucking stones at trucks and cars going by on the highway. But Jack moved closer to Mark, almost as if he was kneeling in a confessional, and told him, almost whispering now, that there was an incident during one of their break-ins that effectively ended their crime spree. Jack said that the three erstwhile cat burglars were provided with faulty information on one of the houses they had planned to invade. The newspaper route informer had said that the Fagans, two elderly readers, had discontinued their newspaper subscription for two weeks during which they were not actually away on vacation. Apparently, the Fagans had wanted to terminate their subscription, not to suspend it. Consequently, when the three boys entered the Fagan home, breaking a basement window as they normally did, both Mr. and Mrs Fagan were sitting in the living room watching television in the dark, there being no lights on in the rest of the house. Although they tried to be quiet, the boys naturally made some noise in sneaking into the house. By the time Jack, Jimmy and Pete reached the top of the basement stairs, Harry Fagan was standing in the kitchen holding a wooden broom, his wife Doris cowering behind her husband. All three boys weren't wearing masks ---- after all, they didn't expect anyone home to identify them. Harry made a feeble motion with his broom and Doris shrieked, immediately collapsing.

According to Jack, all three of them immediately scrambled out the backdoor, which ironically enough was unlocked, and disappeared into the night. They ran across the Fagan backyard and stood shivering behind the hedges at the rear of the property. They hid out long enough to witness the arrival of an ambulance, apparently for the suddenly stricken Doris Fagan. Jimmy, who was the boldest of the three, crept around the house by the driveway and saw the ambulance leave. Jack, Jimmy and Pete sat behind the hedge for maybe fifteen minutes before they sneaked home, still trembling from the fear of being arrested. The three of them soon ascertained, based on neighborhood gossip picked up from their respective parents, that Doris had suffered but had eventually survived a stroke. Although there was a short discussion as to whether they should continue breaking into houses, Jimmy being the most persistent advocate of further thievery, they decided to discontinue their felonious activities before they went home that evening.

Jack told Mark that they all sweated that incident for at least a month after it happened even though Doris was released from hospital four or five days after she had been admitted. He also admitted, an admission that he did not make to his other partners at that time or since for that matter, that Jack was anxious for more than three months. While he was frightened of being arrested, an arrest that was never made, Jack was also guilty about Mrs. Fagan. Sure, she had been discharged from the hospital but he was worried that she would eventually suffer from long term affect from the stroke. Jack said that the three of them seldom spoke about the incident afterward. Fact was he said that they seldom spoke at all afterward. Jack told Mark that he still thought about Mrs. Fagan even though she likely died maybe twenty years ago. Mark wondered whether Jack still thought about Mrs. Fagan.

His last admission, a confession of an action for which he sometimes conjured up some guilt involved a comparatively minor childhood prank which Jack may have thought had inflicted permanent psychological damage on one of his classmates in the sixth grade. Jack had no way of knowing that but he had managed to convince himself that falsely accusing another boy of stealing a fountain pen belonging to the class teacher, an earnest young man named Mr. French, would have developed into anything of any significance. The caper was as simple as it was fateful. For reasons he had long forgotten, Jack had lifted Mr. French's fountain pen on a dare, the challenge being proposed by a classmate named Peter Walters, a mischievous little miscreant who liked to get other kids in trouble. This time, it wasn't Jack who got in trouble but another student, Ronald Barnes, who didn't even know that Mr. French had a fountain pen to steal in the first place. Once Mr. French discovered that his fountain pen, a prized possession that had been a gift from his father was gone, he accused pretty well every student in his grade six class of theft. When that approach didn't work, Mr. French having spent a week staring meanacingly at his grade six charges, he threatened something a little more tangible, that is, more homework for the entire class until the pen was returned. For reasons that he could never really recall, Jack removed the pen from his own locker, where it had been hidden since he lifted it from Mr. French's desk when Jack was alone in the classroom, having crept in early from recess, and then placed it in the desk belonging to Ronald Barnes. As Jack related the story, he said that he had forgotten, if he had ever known in the first place as to the reason they had concentrated their mischievous evident scorn on Ronald Barnes, a boy that neither he nor Peter Walters knew very well. Jack did say, however, that he thought it more his friend Peter's plan than his own but he could not be certain. In any event, Jack repeated his confusion regarding the basis for the identification of Ronald Barnes as the target of their prank.

The story went on as they both ordered another beer. The next day, he slipped a note into Mr. French's mail slot directing the good professor to the desk behind which poor Ronald Barnes sat. Just to ensure anonymity and avoid detection, Jack had thoughtfully typed the note on his old man's Underwood. It suggested that Mr. French inspect Ronald Barnes' desk. That day, in fact that morning, Mr. French asked Ronald Barnes up to the front of the desk where he told him to stand facing the chalkboard. There were a low hissing sound coming from the kids in the class. Mr. French stared them into silence. He went back to the desk, three desks down in the row nearest to the window, lifted the desk lid, and found his fountain pen. He then slammed down the lid, it sounded like a casket closing, and returned to the front of the class where every student in the room thought that he was about to hit the incriminated Ronald Barnes. Mr. French told Ronald Barnes, whose repeated denials began immediately after Mr. French lifted his fountain pen out of Ronald Barnes' desk, to turn around. There was a frozen moment and then the entire grade six class erupted into laughter. It was almost uncontrollable. Not only was Ronald Barnes crying but he had peed his pants, a large wet splotch having spread across the front of his dungarees like an expanding shadow. Most of the student witnesses thought the pee spot looked like a bad drawing of the province of Ontario. The poor Barnes boy looked like he was in shock. His classmates expected Mr. French to bring out the strap.

Mr. French just stood there waiting for the laughter to subside. After waiting for a minute or so, Mr. French took one step toward Ronald Barnes, not surprisingly the dreaded strap already in his hand, stopped and then stood. His back to the class, Mr. French put his arms out like he was about to orchestrate the class, lowered them to his sides, his shoulders sloped, and then audibly sighed. He then raised his arms, lowered them to his sides again, turned around to face to the class for a moment, and then ordered Ronald Barnes back to his desk without further comment. His classmates looked at each other in stunned silence, mesmerized by this unexpected expression of mercy. Ronald Barnes and his stained trousers shuffled back to his desk like his feet were shackled, the thought of a man walking to his execution later occurred to Jack. It seemed strange. In retrospect, Jack wondered why Ronald Barnes did not walk back to his desk with a relieved smile on his face. Maybe he didn't believe that he had just been blessed with clemency from a merciless bastard like Mr. French. Ronald Barnes returned to his desk, sat down and continued to weep, a state which prevailed for several minutes.

Strangely enough, aside from that moment, Ronald Barnes did not make or continue with any protestations of innocence, even to Mr. French or anyone else for that matter. While he was never a particularly exuberant boy, he was sociable enough. No one thought he was odd in any specific way. He was thought to be average, conventional, blending into the fabric of the class like most of his normal classmates. But, at least according to Jack and his partner in crime Peter Walters, the fountain pen incident had changed Ronald Barnes. Of course they never shared their psychological assessment regarding Ronald Barnes with anyone else, their fear of discovery overriding any desire to discuss the change in his behavior with their classmates and friends. On the other hand, maybe their own paranoia, which did not last that long, explained any concern that might have evolved. Peter Walters thought that Ronald Barnes had become a loner. Jack could not disagree. And he was guilty about it, guilt he carried into the seventh grade. His friend Peter, who did not seem similarly afflicted, suggested that he should have been more worried about getting caught for their little act of foolishness than guilty about the effect it may have had on poor Ronald Barnes. By the time everybody had graduated to high school, any guilt suffered by Jack Quinn had faded into the oblivion.

To satisfy Jack's drunken insistence on fair exchange, Mark would only provide two examples of guilty misbehavior. Mark could have invoked, if he concentrated hard enough, maybe three or four other incidents about which he would rather not discuss. Unlike Jack, he did not have anything particularly dreadful to conceal, an aborted homosexual encounter with a stranger in a campground washroom as close as Mark could come to any incident worth concealing. In any event, he told Jack about an unfortunate office affair with a woman who eventually left, or was left by her husband, a tale that so interested Jack that he seemed to sober up a bit to actually pay attention to the details, domestic tragedies he noted were often worth recounting. The other story that Mark was willing to share involved a refund scam at a department store that had employed him for a summer just after he had graduated from high school. While Mark should have felt a certain degree of remorse after embezzling from the store several hundred dollars by providing confederates with cash refunds for merchandise that was never purchased, he was more proud than guilty, having amused many of his associates with the entertainment value of the caper.

TWO DAYS BEFORE THE END

It was a Tuesday morning in October. Mark approached the stairs to Jack's apartment. He carried two medium cups of Starbucks and three oatmeal cookies in a paper bag. He climbed the stairs and then sat down in one of the sofa chairs. Jack was sitting up in bed. He was holding an unlit cigarette in his right hand, a perpetual threat of resuming one of his many unhealthy habits. The weather channel was playing on the television as it always did. As usual, Jack was staring blankly at the screen, a mysterious habit since he never went outside. Mark handed Jack a cookie and put one of the medium coffees down on the nightstand. Jack looked at the cookie and put it down on the nightstand, right beside the coffee and the tin ashtray that was always close to overflowing even though Jack swore he wasn't smoking again. The customary exchange of absurdity ensured.

Mark: "I see you just woke up."

Jack: "I was awake. I'm always awake."

Mark: "You're not always awake. Sometimes you're still asleep. Don't forget, pal, I would know. Fact is that I'm here practically every day, so is Deborah. Everyday but Sunday when you're on your own, unless Danny drops by."

Jack: "Never on Sunday, right? Just like the movie."

Mark: "What movie?"

Jack: "It was a movie from the early '60s. About a prostitute, it took place in Greece."

Mark: "Was Anthony Quinn in the movie?"

Jack: "No. That was Zorba the Greek."

Mark: "I don't think I ever saw that one."

During their brief conversation about the two movies, Jack continued to stare at the weather channel. Meanwhile, Mark stared at the cigarette in Jack's hand.

Mark: "Don't tell me you're smoking again." Mark nodded at the cigarette in Jack's hand.

Jack: "Not really. Okay, so I had a butt last night, one lousy butt but I'm not going back to smoking, not that it matters. Danny dropped by with groceries. He stayed for a few minutes. We both had a smoke and he left me one in case I got the urge later. But I didn't have a drink, even though he had one, maybe more than one. The bastard had a bottle with him, like he usually does."

Danny lived in the apartment adjacent to Jack's place. He had recommended the apartment to Jack after they met in Alcoholics Anonymous. Danny also attended two other self-help groups, his addictions to various street narcotics and to gambling were explanations for his penchant for such groups. In addition, while he acknowledged the groups could help him, he also thought the meetings were fertile grounds for meeting women. While Mark thought that Danny was a useful neighbor for Jack, providing him with groceries and companionship, Deborah Inkster disliked and distrusted him. He was always on the make it seemed, indications being a cheap gold medallion hanging over greying chest hair and under a spectacularly tasteless polyester shirt unbuttoned almost to his waist. While Mark was favorably disposed toward Danny, he could not disagree with Deborah's assessment that Jack's next door neighbor was a classic hound dog, a cad of undeniable reputation, his biography so slandered by almost everyone he knew.

Mark: "Have you gotten the urge since?"

Jack: "No. Look, I was coughing for about an hour after he left and I'm still just holding the smoke, aren't I?"

Mark: "Congratulations. Another achievement for you to contemplate. On the other hand, do you plan to smoke it today?"

Jack: "Maybe, maybe not. I don't know."

It was curious, at least to Mark and Deborah, the two people who were the most familiar with his medical condition, that Jack was being surprisingly nonchalant about his impending doom, his death seemingly inevitable. Jack thought he had less than a week to live, an estimate that he had disclosed to Deborah but not to Mark, another one of Jack's choices that seemed curious. Nevertheless, with maybe less than a week to live, his imminent passing did not seem to concern him at all. He was relatively casual, willing it seemed to discuss his illnesses --- he had several problems, any of which could probably kill him eventually. He would actually make fun of his condition, referring to its causes, the drinking, the smoking, the street pharmaceuticals, without regretting his excessive participation in any of them. To Mark and Deborah, Jack seemed to delight in using his declining health as a significant talking point, if not some sort of boast.

On that Tuesday, which would turn out to be his last Tuesday with Jack, Mark decided to prompt a conversation that was more interesting than the damn weather channel. Most of the time, during those tiresome mornings when Mark was making his palliative visits to Jack's dreary apartment, their discussions were usually limited to the news of the day, a subject that interested Mark much more than it interested Jack. He would listen to Mark editorialize without comment. Mark decided to bring up the matter of his friend's impending demise directly, if for no other reason than to relieve his boredom.

Mark: "Care for some cyanide with that coffee"
          They both laughed and then there was another
          silence.

Jack: "Very funny."

Mark: "Well, do you want to discuss it?"

Jack: "Discuss what?"

Mark: "You know what."

Jack: "You mean the end."

Mark: "Yes, that."

Jack: "No thanks, I'm not in the mood."

Mark: "Why not?"

Jack: "I think I already told you."

Mark: I don't think you did but tell me again anyway.

Jack: "Why?"

Mark: "Because I don't think you're facing your future. You may not have much time."

Jack: "I know I don't have much time. I know but I don't think I'm up to discussing it."

Mark: "Why not? Christ, if we were having this conversation forty years ago, you'd be all over it. I remember when you liked to talk about it all the time. We thought it was – you know – heavy."

Jack: "Shit. All that existential stuff. Who was that guy who was wrote that book about death --- the one we used to talk about all the time back then, you know when we were both pretending to be intellectuals?"

Mark: "You mean pseudo-intellectuals? Anyway, the guy's name was Kierkegaard and the book... anyway, I think the book was called "Sickness Unto Death" or something like that."

Both Mark and Jack started to shake their heads, then snicker and then laugh. It was an obvious acknowledgment, recognition that only the two of them could appreciate. Despite their excessive use of the title of Mr. Kierkegaard's most acclaimed work in those barely recalled conversations, neither of them had ever read the book. Here they were --- one of them facing death forty years after talking about it so enthusiastically --- unsure as to whether they were being sarcastic or were still pretending. In any event, they still thought they were being clever, in a smart aleck sort of way.

Mark: "So do you think about the possibility that you may not have much time?"

Jack: "Possibility? You're kidding, right? It's not a possibility, it's a damn fact. I'm going, maybe not tomorrow, but soon, damn soon."

Mark: "So any thoughts?"

Jack: "Maybe."

Mark: "And..."

Jack: "Nothing really. I try not to think about it much... which seems kind of strange when you think about it."

Mark: "Strange, you can say that again."

Jack: "Okay, it's strange."

Mark: "Surely, you must have some thoughts on the matter of your own demise."

Jack: "My demise? You mean, my death."

Mark: "Right, your death."

After a casual shrug, Jack sat in silence for several minutes staring at Mark who momentarily returned and then averted his friend's gaze by looking about Jack's hovel like he was thinking about following Jack as the tenant. He noted, for the first time he thought, that there was a faded sepia photograph of a young man in a military uniform on the wall behind Jack's bed. He had not noticed it before, a curious oversight given the frequency of his visits; he had been in that apartment on dozens of occasions over the past year or so. He stepped around Jack and his bed. He examined the photograph and asked Jack to provide details.

Mark: "Who's this?" He was standing next to the wall and pointing to the photograph.

Jack: "You mean him?"

Mark: "Yes, him!" Mark's exaggerated his gesture toward the portrait.

Jack: "That, my friend, is my old man's older brother. It was a photograph of him just before he was shipped overseas in World War II. Anyway, that's what the old man told me when he gave me the damn thing."

Mark: "Where were you living then?"

Jack: "In a place called Truscott, in Nova Scotia. All the relatives lived there, including my parents, my brother, my sister and me."

Suddenly, Jack went quiet, looking down at his hands, which were clutched together like in prayer, a pose that seemed a trifle peculiar for a man who was seldom given to emotional affect. For a moment, as he regarded him with a certain sympathetic regard, Mark thought Jack was about to cry, a development that would seem to be even more startling that catching Jack in prayer. Mark was hoping that even mentioning his family wouldn't prompt Jack to go into one of his sorrowful monologues about his pathetic upbringing.

Minutes went by. There was an eerie silence in the room, all Mark could hear was the sounds of traffic outside Jack's two front windows. Above that noise, Mark could hear someone yelling at someone. He turned his head toward the windows. He could not make out anything the person was saying. Fact was that Mark could not even make out whether the screamer was a man or a woman. He looked back at Jack. He was now looking at the ceiling, as if he were contemplating something important, like his family, maybe even his relationship with his father, including his fantasies about him being adopted. Both of them sat in that silence for a few more minutes before

Mark tried to reinvigorate the conversation. As usual, Mark knew there were always mysteries worth exploring.

Mark: "You know, I've heard a lot about your mother but you're never talked much about your father."

Jack: "Well, he died early. Not much to say. He was okay I guess. All I can say is that he left me alone with that bitch Eileen."

Mark: "You mean your mother of course."

Jack: "Yeah, my mother."

Mark: "Sure, you've told me about her before." Another silence fell over the two like a momentary shadow. Jack shrugged.

Jack: "I know I told you. I probably told everybody. She was one tough woman and she often seemed as demented as hell. No wonder the old man died before he hit fifty. Living with her was like doing time in jail. She always seemed pissed about something, like she had been robbed of something when she was younger. To me, the woman was more like an extremely strict prison warden than a mother."

Mark: "I think you already made that delightful comparison to me --- a prison warden! Don't you remember those nights she used to call me to find out where you were and some of them were long distance calls for god's sake. Hell, I never met the women but based on those few calls, I'd have to agree ---- she was a piece of work."

Jack: "She was more than that. She was evil."

Mark: "Evil? Hey, a little metaphysical, wouldn't you say. Okay, so she was difficult to live with but you survived, at least until now."

Jack: "Barely but my father didn't."

Mark: "So you think."

Jack: "So I know."

Mark: "I suppose you do or at least you should."

Mark starts to get out of his chair. "I have to get going now. I'll see you tomorrow, usual time. Okay?"

Jack leans forward and holds both hands up as a gesture to delay Mark's departure. "Why don't you stay for a while. When you brought up my father, it reminded me of something I have wanted to tell you for a long time. And the time is certainly right."

Jack: "Remember my drunken confession about those two incidents that I made to you like forty years ago or so."

Mark: "Huh. You told me about a lot of things in those days."

Jack: "Yeah, and some of them might have been true."

Mark: "Not that it mattered." They both started to laugh. After less than a minute, Jack then held out his hand again.

Jack: "Look, I'm serious. You remember when we used to go to that joint across from that auto parts place we used to work. And we were drinking one night, like we did a lot of nights, and you managed to get me to tell you about a couple of things I did that I wasn't particularly proud of."

Mark leaned forward, his left hand holding up his chin. He had a brooding look on his face, obviously searching his memory for those unfortunate events reported long ago. They were both staring at each other for a moment, the noise of the traffic outside breaking the silence.

Mark: "Can you give me a hint?"

Jack: "I told you about my old girlfriend Allison and a baby girl she had named Phoebe."

Mark: "Wait a minute. I remember now. You also told me about how you framed some kid back in grade school for stealing a fountain pen from some teacher. I remember thinking at the time that, at least compared to the story of your girlfriend, a stolen fountain pen doesn't seem all that terrible."

Jack: "I suppose but, as I may have told you, I felt damn guilty about it. I still do --- I don't know why. I've done worse, much worse but I still think that it was a terrible thing to do."

Jack stopped talking and looked at Mark with a curiously blank look on his face. Again, he was pondering.

Mark: "But there is something else, isn't there?"

Jack: "Yes, there is."

Mark: "And you're going to tell me about it now, aren't you?"

Jack: "I don't know. I really don't know."

Mark: "Why the hell not? I mean, you don't have much time, not much time at all --- days, weeks, who knows."

Jack: "That I know."

Mark: "So what the hell are you waiting for?"

Jack: "As I say, I don't know."

Mark: "Jesus Christ, Jack, what is the problem?"

Jack: "I can't really say. It's something that I've tried to forget ---- you know, to pretend that nothing happened."

Again, the two of them fell into silence, quickly looking first at each other and then down on the floor. They both started to clench their hands --- they were almost trembling. They were nervously shuffling their feet, and bowing their heads as in pensive prayer. After a couple of moments, Mark leaned forward, slapped his hand affectionately on Jack's knee, and started to get up to leave. He glanced at his watch, frowned and sadly shook his head. He obviously didn't consider further inquiry of his friend Jack of any value. Reluctantly, he stood up and turned to leave. He stopped, bent down and left Jack with a final appeal, at least for the day.

Mark: "I'll be back tomorrow and I want to hear about that third incident, that thing you are so reluctant to tell me about."

Jack: "I told you, I can't say."

Mark: "You mean, you won't say." A pause. "Just think about it, okay?"

Again looking at his watch, he was now almost thirty minutes late for the morning staff meeting, an obligation that he usually dreaded and therefore was secretly grateful for any excuse to avoid it. He descended the stairs, walked out the front door and across the sidewalk to his car. A bedraggled, fearsome looking man in a dirty sweat suit and a torn baseball cap was casually sitting on the hood of his car, as if he had been waiting for a lift.

He was wearing a pair of decrepit sneakers that were evidently manufactured by two different athletic shoe companies. In addition, the shoes did not even appear to be the same size, the left shoe obviously larger. He was attempting to light a cigarette butt that may have had one or two drags left on it. As Mark went around the front of the car to the driver's side, his possible passenger disembarked from the hood of the car, removed his cap and turned it over in the universal sign of the panhandler. Mark wordlessly dropped three quarters into his hat and continued on to open the door to his car. The street guy looked at the three quarters in his cap and mumbled something unkind to his benefactor. Mark ignored him. He looked up at the window of Jack's apartment. He half expected to see Jack in the window. He didn't know why.

Not surprisingly, on his drive to work that day, consideration of Jack's third incident haunted his mind like a song loop. What could it be he wondered? Was it a significant secret ---- like the daughter born out of wedlock, a barely recalled teenage relationship turned complicated ---- or a comparatively trivial matter involving the theft of a fountain pen? Or something in between although Mark could not imagine what that could be? While he was certain there were other secrets that his friend Jack may have wanted to keep confidential,he choose to mention only three, only one of them he continued to keep private. He thought of his own misdeeds, or at least those indiscretions which he might wish to conceal. Although he may have occasionally confided a couple of them, he could not remember which potential embarrassments he admitted and to whom he may have admitted them. But he could not think of any one of them that he would not eventually acknowledge: predictable tales of shoplifting, sophomoric misbehavior, youthful inebriation and a couple of more serious transgressions which occurred during a couple of business trips. All of his indiscretions, however, seemed not as serious, at least compared to one of Jack's transgressions, that is, a child born out of wedlock, a significant social lapse in the late 1960s. Mark finally decided that he should share his indecision with his fellow nursemaid, Deborah. Maybe she would know something.

Deborah and Mark had maintained a shared responsibility for the care of Jack for more than a year. Accordingly, the two of them spoke frequently, almost entirely in fact about Jack, mainly about his declining health but also about the abject complexities of his life, a tangled series of errors that culminated in a lonely existence waiting for the end in a dumpy attic apartment. Mark thought, not unreasonably he concluded, that Deborah might be aware of other unfortunate incidences that Jack might not want to admit. Sure, they had discussed the two episodes that Jack had confided to Mark, both of which Deborah was aware. She shared several other stories about Jack but while Mark had not heard of all of them, they could not have risen to any level of secrecy that Jack was apparently seeking to maintain. In fact, most of the stories that Deborah told Mark usually had something to do with their married life, a subject in which Mark had little, if any interest.

Jack phoned Deborah that afternoon and, in addition to expressing concern about the continued decline in Jack's health, casually mentioned his curiosity about Jack's final mystery. Aside from referring to some of the tales she had already relayed to Mark, she said that she could not think of a secret that Jack may have been concealing. She remarked that she found it odd. She had said more than once that, despite their general marital problems, they were always honest with each other. She sounded disappointed that Jack had not confided everything to her, a failure that Mark thought she might bring it up with Jack when she made her usual visit to his place that afternoon. Mark quietly asked that she not mention the issue of the supposed secret to Jack. He was concerned that Jack wouldn't say anything if Deborah started to bother him about it. It was just a feeling. He knew Jack. He could be sensitive. Deborah acknowledged the request. Mark wasn't sure that she wouldn't attempt to encourage Jack to confess anyway. He was still thinking about that damn mystery.

THE MORNING AFTER THE END

When Mark arrived at Jack's place the next morning, he was greeted by a small gathering of neighborhood types: elderly ladies pushing walkers, three or four may have been male panhandlers dressed in a variety in transgender outfits, a couple of hard eyed street floozies, a woman wearing a leather skirt accompanied by an infant in a stroller, two adolescent boys toting skateboards and a police officer standing in the doorway to the stairs of Jack's apartment. He was surprised that yesterday's fearsome looking man with the baseball cap wasn't in the crowd.

It was evidently a local event of considerable curiosity. Ignoring the interested bystanders, Mark strode straight up to the police officer, his name tag identified him as Officer Joseph Tontini, introduced himself as a close friend of the occupant of the upstairs apartment, and asked him about the circumstances that had prompted all the street interest. The officer shrugged, leaned down and casually informed Mark that the occupant in the apartment was dead, having been found earlier that morning by a local street guy who, at least according to the officer, looked like maybe he should have joined the occupant in the afterlife. The sudden disquiet on Mark Purchell's face was obvious, even to Officer Tontini, who had been guarding the entrance to the building since the body was discovered. That was about all Officer Tontini had to report although he did add that he thought that an ex-wife was the only person who had been informed of the death and had been there earlier to identify Jack Quinn's body. Apparently, her number had been found in his apartment. She was apparently so upset that she fainted and then was driven to a hospital. Hospitalized? Mark thought that Officer Tontini or one of his colleagues might have been exaggerating. Or maybe he wasn't. He also said that police had found his name in the apartment as well.

Before he could turn away from Tontini and the crowd scene that Jack Quinn's death had precipitated, the intrepid officer placed a hand on Mark's arm and informed him, in a clearly conspiratorial voice, that his superior, a certain Lieutenant Ogilvy, wanted to speak to him, down at police headquarters on O'Connor Street. Officer Tontini also said it was important although he did not have any further information. Mark asked whether Lieutenant Ogilvy had any specific time in mind. Officer Tontini shrugged again, a gesture with which he seemed well acquainted. He suggested Mark either telephone Ogilvy, providing the number, or present himself at the police station. Mark also asked about the whereabouts of Deborah Inkster. Officer Tontini didn't know. Mark decided to consult the nearest hospital, Saint Mary's on Percy Street.

Mark was in the emergency room of Saint Mary's within twenty minutes. He wasn't surprised that Deborah, who must have been awaken that morning with the news of Jack's death, would have been so distressed that she would have ended up in the hospital. He immediately consulted a hospital volunteer, an older woman in a white jacket. She informed Mark that Deborah Inkster had been treated, for what she did not know, and was still resting in bed six of the triage room. The woman pointed to the left, smiled and then turned to answer the telephone. Without waiting, Mark went through the doors on the left, past a circular desk behind which several people, presumably doctors and nurses, were contemplating computer screens. He quickly spotted Deborah in a bed above which was a sign identifying it as number six, the curtains around her bed not providing much privacy. Mark walked over to her bed with obvious purpose, not wishing to alert anyone that maybe he didn't belong in the room --- he was uncertain as to the hospital ordinances concerning visits. He swept around the curtains and stood at the foot of the bed. He felt like peeper, an inappropriate eavesdropper but no one paid any attention to him. There lay Deborah, behind whom there were no activated monitors and to whom nothing was connected, not even a pair of humble oxygen nubs. Deborah appeared to be asleep. He was hesitant although tempted to ask one of the staff as to the proper procedure regarding patients in such a state. He stood there motionless.

Mark waited in that state for several minutes and then returned to the desk. He attracted the attention of one of the people behind the desk, a chubby woman in a navy colored nursing uniform with Disney cartoon characters emblazoned on it. The woman acknowledged him and immediately knew what he wanted . She told him that Deborah, sedated since she arrived in emergency, was asleep, her vitals were good. Without any further prompt from Mark, the cartoon festooned nurse reported that poor Ms. Inkster had been quite agitated when the police brought her in, saying that she had reportedly been asked to identify her ex-husband's body that morning. She then said it was unlikely she would be admitted and would likely be released once she woke up. Nurse Cartoon added that it was unusual that anyone with simple anxiety problems would be given a bed. Normally, she said, they would be given a tranquilizer, a prescription for more and a seat in the waiting room. It was obvious, at least to the nurse, that Ms. Inkster was hysterical, not exactly a professional diagnosis but perhaps understandable if you've just been asked to identify the body of a man to whom you were once married.

Mark was unsure as to whether to wake Deborah up. The nurse again noticed his ambivalence, shook her head and suggested that he might wait an hour or so, maybe pull up a chair by her bed and wait. Mark nodded but said he didn't want to bother Deborah in the hospital, his intention to call on her later at home. His plan was to present himself at police headquarters and confer with Lieutenant Ogilvy. He thought that he would likely receive a much more dispassionate, if not more accurate report on the death of Jack Quinn. He was, however, somewhat confounded by the report that a police lieutenant was interested in the circumstances surrounding a death that was almost certainly inevitable.

On the drive downtown, Mark returned to his consideration of Deborah's reaction to Jack's death. She and Jack were married for only a couple of years and they had only dated for a year before that. Mark was hardly any sort of expert in gauging the mysteries of romance, either involving himself or anyone else for that matter. In addition, Deborah and Jack divorced almost ten years ago, which further complicated the enigma of Deborah's continuing attachment. It was not the first time he had contemplated the curiosities of Jack's relationships with women. In so far as he could recall, they were often difficult and sometimes inexplicable. He would sometimes discuss his romantic indulgences, which were not as frequent as most people who knew him would have thought. After all, he was attractive and had an undeniable charm. Invariably, Jack dismissed any problems he had with women as the fault of his partners. Jack would usually characterize any eventually estranged girlfriends, including his ex-wife as somehow disturbed. No wonder they broke up he would confide. But despite all the difficulties every woman Jack had every romanced had with their relationships, despite their breakups, which were often fairly ugly, the women involved continued to have affection for him. This baffled almost anyone who was aware of it. Having recalled this, Mark felt it was understandable then that Deborah would have become so overwrought when she was informed of Jack's death.

When he arrived at police headquarters on O'Connor Street, he could not find a parking spot, practically all of which could have been reserved for alleged felons and their attorneys. Accordingly, he had to park on O'Connor Street itself, a block and a half away from the station. It took him several minutes to arrive at the front desk where he consulted with a Constable Aprille Fuchs, an attractive young woman with partially green hair. Mark was surprised that the police force permitted brightly colored coiffs. He asked for Lieutenant Ogilvy. Constable Fuchs made a telephone call, had a relatively curt conversation, and informed Mark that the lieutenant had an office on the third floor. It was numbered 314 in the northeast corner of the building. He walked over, boarded an empty elevator, pressed a button, disembarked on the third floor, turned right and headed to Office 314, which was less an office than a futuristic pod, a cubicle. Mark noted that the walls around the Lieutenant's cubicle were higher than those of the other police officers in the general area, presumably an indication of her seniority. Mark stood at the entrance to her office and waited. There was no one to greet him. He stood there for a minute or so before Lieutenant Ogilvy, a tall, stern looking women, looked up and motioned him over. The Lieutenant immediately knew who Mark was and why he was there.

Ogilvy: "You're Mr. Quinn's friend, right?"

Mark: "Yes." He was silent for a moment and then asked about the purpose of his presence there. "Why did the police asked me down here?"

Ogilvy: "Sorry for the bother. It's standard procedure in any case involving a suspicious death, like when a person dies at home rather than in a hospital, we investigate." Ogilvy motioned for Mark to sit down in a chair in front of her desk.

Mark: "What can I do?" A second time.

Ogilvy: Just answer a few questions, that's all."

Mark: "Okay. Ask away."

Ogilvy: "Thanks. I assume your name is Mark Purchell, right? We got your name from a neighbor of the decedent, a guy named Danny Beliveau. He said that you visited his apartment every day." Ogilvy had been reading from a computer monitor.

Mark: "That's right. His ex-wife and I .."

Ogilvy: "Deborah Inkster --- I understand she was quite upset by the news."

Mark: "Yes, the officers at the scene told me that she had been taken to the hospital."

Ogilvy: "That's too bad. I hope she's feeling better."

Mark: "Me too. I intend to head back to the hospital from here."

Ogilvy: "Well, I won't hold you up any more than I have to."

Mark: "Thanks."

Ogilvy: "Well, Mr. Beliveau told us that Quinn had been sick for a long time. Exactly how sick was he?"

Mark: "As far as I know, he was pretty well close to the end. He could have passed away at any time. I really wasn't surprised when I was told that he had."

Ogilvy: "Do you know what was the matter with him?"
            To Mark, the question seemed to be more
            conversational as opposed to investigative. She
            sounded personally interested.

Mark: "He had lung and kidney problems which
            was not a surprise since he drank and smoked
            like crazy for years. That must effect a person.
            As far as I know, pretty well everything was
            wrong with the poor guy."

The statement sounded like a eulogy to both of them.
There was then a pause in the exchange.

Ogilvy: "Another reason I had for getting you down
            here was to ask whether you intend to make
            any arrangements. Do you know, for example,
            whether Mr. Quinn had a will?"

Mark: "Not that I am aware."

Ogilvy: "Did Mr. Quinn have any family?"

Mark: "Yes but he hadn't been in touch with his
            mother, his brother or his sister for years. But
            I have no idea where they are but I think Jack
            told me that both his brother and his sister
            moved away years ago. And his father has been
            dead for years."

Mark thought about but did not raise the possibility
that he could have been adopted.

Ogilvy: "So I guess it's you." concluded Ogilvy.

Mark: "I guess."

Ogilvy: "Well, if you're interested, I suggest that you might want to clean out Quinn's place, if you feel you should. We spoke to the landlady of the building --- a Mrs. Tardis. She said that she intends to rent out place as soon as she can. She said that she'll soon be hiring a firm to get it ready for a new tenant. She said that she'll give you a key for the place --- I have her telephone number --- before she changes the locks. She said you have a week or so."

Mark: "Thanks,Officer, I guess I'll get in touch with her."

Mark thanked Lieutenant Ogilvy, said goodbye and left her cubicle. Now he was ruminating about whether he should continue to involve himself in the business of Jack Quinn's passing. By the time he returned to his car, Mark had managed to convince himself that he should, not just out of some sort of continuing responsibility but also out of genuine curiosity. After all, he did recall that he had one secret incident to uncover, at least to himself. He was still fascinated he supposed. There may be a clue somewhere in the now empty apartment.

EXPLORING THE APARTMENT
OF THE DEPARTED

The next morning, Mark spoke to a local funeral home about the most economical method of transporting Jack to the hereafter. Next on his list was Mrs. Tardis, the landlady of the rental accommodation where Jack had spent his last days. It became apparent that Mrs. Tardis was reluctant to allow Mark to explore the apartment. She did, however, finally agree to provide Mark with a key, which she said would be useless within a week, by which time the lock to the front door would have been changed. She told Mark that he could come by the office to pick up the key. Mark was in the landlady's office about a hour after lunch and was climbing the stairs to Jack's former apartment about half an hour after that. He found that he didn't need a key. After all, the door to Jack's place was never locked, meaning of course that he never had to use a key, his reasoning that no one would ever want to break into his place anyway.

Once in the apartment, Mark stood there perplexed, not knowing where to actually look for anything worth finding. He was well aware of the apartment's furnishings, or more precisely the lack of furnishings. Mark was often confounded by the fact that Jack's habitat did not feature few, if any pieces of furniture in which you could hide anything: no dressers, no night stands, no desks, no shelving units, no cabinets. The only place in which anything could be concealed was a top drawer in the kitchen, one of three in the kitchen, the other two drawers having been nailed shut. He went to the drawer and opened it. He pulled the drawer from under the counter and placed it on the floor. He then removed every item from the drawer and spread them out on the floor. He used a notepad and a pen from the drawer to record every item: an old Valentine's card from Deborah; a faded undated note from someone named Sharon; a U.S. dollar bill; a collection of coins of various denominations from a number of countries; a passport that had expired twelve years ago; an assortment of receipts, including several from a dance studio; two plastic cases for business cards and a small red box in which Mark found an unidentifiable medal with an engraving of the profile of Queen Elizabeth II. The contents also included: a number of long expired ID's; his SIN cards; cards belonging to several local businesses; and four expired credit cards. Further investigation uncovered a package of yellow ear plugs; some golf tees; a small digital camera; a lens cleaner and a small screwdriver for glasses Mark did not think Jack ever wore. There were also several prescription bottles; two magnifying glasses; two combination locks; a squash ball; a used movie stub; a computer CD; a rosary, which Mark had to admit to himself was a surprising discovery; maybe a dozen ballpoint pens, some of which were still operational; a small stapler; and a USB flash drive though Mark never saw a laptop or any sort of computer in Jack's place. The most beguiling item was a narrow white envelope on which a tiny number was inscribed on the upper right front corner. It was evident that the envelope held a small thin key. Mark immediately and carefully opened the envelope. It contained, as he had anticipated, a small flat notched thin key, perhaps a key to a chest, a key to a suitcase, a briefcase, a drawer likely in another apartment, or a bank safety deposit box. He carefully placed the digital camera, the USB flash drive and the envelope with the tiny number and notched key in the pocket of his jacket, all three of which could uncover information worth investigating. Regarding the key, he thought that he might need a locksmith. On the other hand, anything worth pursuing on the digital camera and the flash drive would be disclosed rather simply. Mark also pocketed Jack's SIN card. He thought he might need it.

For a reason that was more reflex than consideration, Mark then looked under Jack's bed, the only place that he hadn't actually searched, not that there were too many places to search. Underneath, down towards the end of the bed, a vintage wooden single bed with an antique design on the headboard, Mark located two books with hard, maroon colored covers, and a stack of index cards. Mark had some difficulty in recovering the books and the index cards from under the bed. He had to pull them out from under a bed that was so sagged in the middle that Mark had to lift the bed up about a foot before extracting the books and the index cards. The musty scent of mould and moth balls swept over the room like a storm cloud. Mark, who was working on a headache, then sat down in one of the two old sofa chairs in the room, checking underneath both of the chairs before sitting down in one of the them and started to explore his recent finds. The books were annual reviews for the years 1965 and 1967 for Saint Ignatius High School, one of the city's oldest schools. It had recently moved from one part of the city to another, its previous building having been replaced by a predictably designed condominium. To preserve the school's century old tradition of providing religious education, Saint Ignatius had moved to a recently abandoned Catholic seminary two years ago.

Mark opened the 1965 review. Inside the front and back covers was a black and white photograph of the old Saint Ignatius building, back at a time when the faculty was almost entirely staffed by Jesuit priests and brothers. The exposure, taken in the winter, was a classic, almost iconic portrait of a Victorian era looking building that would not have seemed out of place illustrating a novel by Charles Dickens. Following the title page, which featured a less aesthetic picture of the school, there was a two page spread dedicating the review to a Father Francis Franklin, a priest who reportedly was celebrating fifty years in the Society of Jesus. There was a full page portrait of the good father, who looked like he might have qualified as a man of the cloth during the Spanish Inquisition. This was followed by a religious homily from the school principal, an unidentified and a painfully beatific looking priest. Then came another message, this one signed by the school rector, another officious looking member of the Society of Jesus. Eight pages followed, featuring pictures of faculty members, identified by scholarly discipline and, if relevant, extracurricular activities, e.g. athletics, drama, various school clubs. Mark noted that sixteen of the thirty one faculty members were Jesuits. He thought to himself that if he was to peruse the 2015 Saint Ignatius annual, it was doubtful that he would find more than a couple of faculty members to be Jesuits.

Mark then browsed through thirty one pages of individual portrayals of that year's graduates. He studied the faces --- they were all boys, maybe one hundred and twenty of them, all likely retired now or maybe even passed away. Saint Ignatius had not been and probably would never be coed. Mark flipped through those pages. Everyone of them had short hair, crew cuts and brush cuts were popular, wore thin dark ties, white shirts and suit coats. Mark read some of the personal accounts. Each included four or five pithy and predictable comments, about the individual's personality, his school activities, sports were particular favorites. Comments also included the student's relationship with the teachers or his classmates, and, if applicable, anything uncommon, like if the graduate owned a car, had a lot of success with girls, or had an unusual nickname. Not surprisingly, Mark did not recognize any of the names, they were all unknown to him, no one famous or otherwise accomplished. Mark remembered that Jack had told him that several of his fellow graduates of 1968 were known personages, one a Cabinet Minister, one a Supreme Court Justice, and another an entertainer of some repute, an actor in television.

There came fourteen pages of undergraduates, grades eight, nine and ten. There may have been three hundred boys in those pictures. Mark knew that Jack had gone to Saint Ignatius and surmised that he would have been present in one of the grade eight photographs. It took Mark awhile to locate Jack in the top row in the picture of Class First High D, standing between a boy named Page and another boy named Kusznirecky. Jack was hardly recognizable, which was not unexpected since it was fifty years ago. But Mark could have identified Jack, even without the names listed below the picture. The class teacher, or Master as he was called, was a priest named O'Grady. There were then six pages of "Milestones", anniversaries, including Father Franklin's fifty years as a Jesuit, Jesuits ordained, and deaths. This was followed by nineteen pages reporting on the activities of student council members, the high school newspaper, the yearbook staff, the literary magazine, religious organizations know as soladities, and a multitude of other clubs like drama, science, debating, and art. Finally, there was twenty pages devoted to athletics. Mark spent several more minutes scanning that section, locating Jack Quinn on both bantam football and hockey teams, Finally, there were a number of pages of advertisements by local businesses, random pictures of school activities, and two pages for autographs, of which Jack had managed to gather several dozen.

Mark then put the review for 1965 down and picked up the review for 1967. He checked the classes for grade ten for Jack, located him in Class Third High A, standing again in the top row between boys named Davis and Clement. Mark had lost interest. He now definitely had a headache. He leaned back further into the chair and then rose out it again. He saw the stack of index cards on which were recorded handwritten notes. He leaned forward to pick up the cards and started to flip through some of them. Each card had a specific note on some aspect of or event in ancient history. After reading and then re-reading about events like the the Code of Hamurabi, the Punic Wars, and a host of Roman emperors, Mark picked up the 1965 review again, flipped to the faculty page, and located the head history teacher, his title was Chairman of the History Department. He was a curious Germanic looking guy with a tiny mustache. His name was Dr. Walter Strangle. Mark thought he looked like the type to require students to record handwritten notes on index cards, presumably so that they could more accurately memorize historical details. The man was obviously an academic traditionalist. Looking at his picture in that review, Mark thought that he would not have been out of place in instructing pupils during the days of the Weimar Republic.

Leaning back again in the chair, Mark closed his eyes, remembrances of his own high school days passing over him like a momentary daydream. He went to another local high school, a parochial institution known mainly for its insignificance. Situated in a relatively uninspiring suburban neighborhood, Hilldale High School opened in the mid-1960s in a building that could easily have functioned as a warehouse, hardly an edifice that might have found its way into an illustrated Dickens novel. Although he was certain that Hilldale did publish annual reviews, he could not remember any of them. On the other hand, he could not help but begin to reminiscence about his own high school experiences. While vague, his memories were plentiful, warm and a trifle mawkish: inspiring teachers, memorable teachers, incompetent teachers, and a multitude of fuzzy memories, friendships made, friendships faded, tomfoolery in the classroom, nonsense in the locker room, Friday night sock hops, and playing football for some of the worst teams in the city. Like some of former classmates, Mark remembered or maybe had fantasized his high school days as something out of a Beach Boy song. His ex-wife, whose high school memories were less gratifying, thought Mark was almost delusional about the pleasures of his own adolescence, laughing about his recalled illusions about high school. Over the years, other people have made similar observations about Mark, suggesting, as one humorist bystander once remarked, that his future seemed mainly in his past, his memories almost completely fictional. Oddly enough, Mark had not disagreed with that particular assessment, occasionally observing that as far as he was concerned, the past, at least his past, was more fun than his present or for that matter his likely future.

He admitted an arguably warped perspective may have been a character flaw. On the other hand, Mark also dismissed people who were either indifferent or forgetful about their histories as people who had unfortunate pasts, nerds who did not have a good time in high school. For her part, Mark's ex-wife thought it was just plain foolish, suggesting that his memories, or at least the memories that he used to share with her, were invariably part fantasy anyway and should not be celebrated. She may have been right. Mark admitted, at least to himself, that a lot of his memories weren't memories at all but retrospective wishes, wishes that were sometimes exposed as outright fabrications. For example, he still recalled the instance when one of his old college associates, a short term buddy from whom he occasionally bought mescaline, caught him prevaricating about attending Woodstock. Though he was temporarily humiliated at the time, he never stopped telling people about his entirely fictitious Woodstock experiences. He had memorized the movie by then and the member of the Woodstock Nation buddy wasn't around to correct the record. Besides, he knew at least two guys who actually did attend.

All nostalgic serendipity soon evaporated as Mark was sitting there on his deceased friend's lousy sofa chair, his fanciful recollections of high school obviously having a limit. Mark removed the white envelope containing the notched key from his jacket pocket and examined it. In contemplating its origin, if not its purpose, the key and the tiny six digit number on the outside of the white envelope eventually convinced Mark --- a few minutes of labored consideration led to the conclusion --- that he was holding the key to a safety deposit box in some bank, likely in the city. Mark continued to sit in that chair for another ten minutes, his headache from Jack's stale scented apartment not yet faded. He eventually realized that if he were to explore the mystery of the envelope containing the tiny key, he would need something more than rapt curiosity. He would need something official, something to persuade banks and perhaps other institutions to relinquish their confidences, such as the location of a safety deposit box. He also had the camera and the USB flash drive. Perhaps they had secrets to surrender.

Having relaxed in Jack's sofa chair for maybe fifteen minutes, contemplating his next move in a beckoning investigation into Jack's future, which of course was based on his sudden lack of a future, he made one more sweep around the room, slowly staring, almost as if he was trying to memorize every detail. For a moment, he thought that Hierodimous Bosch might have chosen Jack's now vacant apartment for inspiration. Speaking of painting, he was drawn again to the picture of Jack's uncle that was on the wall above his bed, the portrait that Mark first noticed just before his death. Mark was somehow surprised that it was still there, suspecting that maybe even the police might have removed it. Another thought went through his head. It was possible that nobody but Jack and Mark knew that the picture was there in the first place.

Before pursuing any further evaluation of the envelope with the notched key inside, which surely would have involved more than a simple search, Mark went to investigate the contents of both the digital camera and the USB flash drive. So, when he arrived home, he immediately put in fresh batteries into the camera and pushed its replay button. The result was disappointing to say the least. All the camera held were six pictures, presumably taken during the same sitting, of a barely recognizable Jack staring into the lens at different angles, the usual consequence of a digital camera used for a self portrait, a poorly executed "selfie". Not one of the photographs had any artistic merit whatsoever, hardly a surprising conclusion given the circumstances. Mark wondered about Jack's reasoning for taking the pictures --- were there clues hidden in the photographs, were there mosaic mysteries in those pixels? After staring at the pictures like he was standing in the Louvre rather than in his own apartment, slowly clicking the camera buttons almost like he was treasuring a rosary, he concluded that the pictures meant nothing, nothing just Jack's mindless attempts to battle his own boredom. Maybe Jack had taken dozens of such photographs but had neglected to erase the last six. Before he put the camera down, Mark deleted those last six pictures.

Mark then took the USB flash drive and inserted it into his laptop. There was only four files available on the drive: a photograph of who he assumed was Jack wearing a little league baseball uniform, the team name was somewhat obscured although it could have been the Cubs; an apparently unpublished letter to the editor of a local newspaper concerning local bus service, an ironic issue for Jack since he seldom, if ever left the apartment; the title page of a planned three act play entitled "So Much Older Then"; and a couple of pages of notations entitled "Losing Consciousness: A Leger". As suggested, the latter was a diary or journal recording. The comments were more than two weeks worth of random thoughts, in daily sequence although a couple of days received no entries. There were neither dates nor indications of any dates although from the content of the entries, mainly sophomoric musings, Mark thought that they must have been written shortly before his demise. As for the unfinished play, there was only the title page and nothing else.

Before reading the journal, Mark briefly wondered how the photograph, the letter to the editor, the title page to the play, and the journal all ended up on the flash drive. Mark had not found a laptop anywhere in Jack's apartment and could not recall whether he ever saw one there at any time in the past. Maybe it belonged to Danny the neighbor or Deborah the ex-wife or somebody else for that matter. Mark would ponder that enigma later, after considering the other mysteries that were prompted by Jack's death. He went on to read Jack's journal.

"Losing Consciousness: A Leger

Monday:	*Alive, thanks to Eddie Vedder. Nothing on television but the weather channel. I grow old.*
Tuesday:	*Danny dropped by with some groceries. He smoked a cigarette. I didn't partake though he offered. I grow old.*
Wednesday:	*Felt lousy today. Thought about death, as usual. Deborah was late today. She got serious when I mentioned the death thing. Mark might have laughed. I shall wear the bottoms of my trousers rolled.*
Thursday:	*Went to the window tonight. The street looked scary. I saw two women with bad haircuts across the street. They were smoking cigars. A bus went by. I only saw one passenger. He was eating something. Shall I part my hair behind?*
Friday:	*Deborah asked me whether I had a will. I honestly couldn't remember. I can't remember now either.*

I might write one if I get a chance. Do I dare to eat a peach?

Saturday: *I spent the day contemplating the last time I was out of the house. I thought I had gone to the hospital. Again. I shall wear white flannel trousers.*

Sunday: *Didn't feel like writing anything. Even this and a walk upon the beach.*

Monday: *The oxygen tank guys came by today, after Mark left. Can't even get high anymore. They gave me a couple of new prongs. They felt weird. I have heard*

Tuesday: *Deborah just left. We got into a sort of argument. She said she didn't know why we were married. I never knew why either. The mermaids singing*

Thursday: *It's Thursday. I don't know why. I missed Wednesday. Mark looked tired. Said he was out late with the boys, whoever they are now. I don't think I know or even knew any of them. each to each.*

Sunday: *Was awake most of the night. Staring. Like the daytime I suppose. This is the way the world ends*

Monday: *Like to think about the end of the line. It's sort of invigorating, just like that existential crap we used to talk about in college. This is the way the world ends*

Tuesday: *I woke up this morning asleep. This is the way the world ends*

Wednesday:	*I'm undecided. About what I don't know. Not*
Thursday:	*I'm depressed. I guess. As usual. Don't know but even Mark seemed a little depressed this AM. If not him, maybe Deborah. with a bang*
Friday:	*I thought I might start work on a play. But with*
Saturday:	*I looked out the window tonight. Thought I saw a windmill. A whimper."*

Immediately after reading his apparent diary, Jack had concluded that his friend's ramblings were hardly worth considering further although they did include promise of further clues ---- a play. Mark found the T.S. Eliot references marginally clever, somewhat amusing and remarkably ambitious considering the shape he was likely in when he wrote the lines. He did not, however, see any point in exploring the entries any further. For the most part, aside from quickly spotting the concealed references to the Eliot lines, Jack's journal seemed just as tiresome as his conversations with him often were. In other words, nonsense. Nothing there but a kind of forced cynicism and empty observation, a fumbling attempt Mark thought to plagiarize Samuel Beckett, some sort of literary pretense, maybe an unknown Bob Dylan lyric. Hell, Jack could have written that stuff in university. In any event, his diary read like Jack's life over the last couple of years. Either that or he was trying to impress a professor of English literature, an old girlfriend, or his psychiatrist. But there were only seventeen entries, by days.

THE KEY

Before exploring the camera and flash drive for clues ---- there weren't any --- Mark began to consider the notched key in the envelope. It was obvious, at least to Mark, that the key was intended to open a safety deposit box, a conclusion he confirmed by showing the key to a teller at a local branch of the Bank of Montreal. The teller, a woman named Carol who also happened to be the younger sister of his hairdresser, briefly consulted with a colleague at the bank before returning to assure Mark that the key would open a safety deposit box in a bank. On the other hand, as helpfully emphasized by Carol, she could not tell Mark which bank housed the safety deposit box that would be opened by that key. Again, just to be helpful, a quality that when added to her physical attributes, likely made her the most popular teller at this particular branch, she said that, in addition to all the banks in the city, post offices and hotels were other institutions that housed safety deposit boxes. Mark immediately dispensed with the latter two possibilities, unlikely for someone like Jack.

As expected, Mark was disappointed, walking away from Carol, holding the key and shaking his head while he casually calculated the number of bank branches and the number of safety deposit boxes available to Jack. By the time he was sitting in his car, he had concluded that there were maybe 50 bank branches in the city and in each branch maybe 100 safety deposit boxes. That made for about 5,000 possibilities. Mark thought that he might as well purchase a lottery ticket. It was ridiculous. Period.

On the drive back to his office, Mark was so perplexed by his predicament that he had difficulty keeping his car on the right side of the street. By the time he pulled into the parking lot of his office building, eight floors that used to house the police department before the cops moved downtown to a larger facility, he was so depressed by the possible, maybe even obvious futility of looking for Jack's safety deposit box that he sat in his office staring out its window like he was contemplating a chess game resignation. His first move, if he was to make any move at all, would be to determine if Jack actually owned a safety deposit box. To Mark and presumably anyone else who knew Jack, ownership of a safety deposit box would seem not only uncharacteristic of him but unnecessary as well. Mark could not envisage Jack possessing anything of value to merit such careful safekeeping. Normally, one hypothesis, if not the most likely prospect, was that a safety deposit box belonging to Jack Quinn could contain his last will and testament. Mark thought about that for a time, ruminating about Jack's generally dismissive attitude toward the mundane requirements of normal adult behavior, dutiful responsibilities like families, jobs, bank accounts, and such, and then rejected the possibility that Jack would actually bother with retaining a lawyer to execute a document that would leave his worldly goods, of which there were likely next to nothing, to some unknown beneficiary.

Other possibilities, which went through his mind with all the enthusiasm of someone doing arithmetic, included the usual range of keepsakes: love letters, valuable baseball cards, old photographs, high school report cards, that kind of thing. However, despite his initial reluctance to investigate the safety deposit box possibility, he felt obligated to pursue it anyway, one of the few duties that Mark had with respect to his old friend Jack. In any event, he would have to take up the quest once he completed the other arrangements that he and Deborah Inkster thought were required. Both he and Deborah questioned them though, given the fact that aside from the two of them and maybe the shady but occasionally helpful neighbor Danny, no one would probably care about Jack's demise. They agreed ---- no visitation, no service, just a perfunctory cremation and then interment, likely in the local Royal Cross Cemetery, interment without a stone memorial.

When he told Deborah about the key, she said that she understood his sense of obligation toward the pursuit of whatever that key would open but did not offer any assistance. She said that she was not interested in anything her former husband may have been keeping in a safety deposit box anyway. She must have known or thought, Mark figured, that Jack did not leave anything worth recovering, no last will, no testament, no insurance policy with a big buck payout to some lucky beneficiary, no annuities, no bank accounts, no lines of credit, no registered retirement savings plans, no registered retirement income funds, no non-registered income funds. In short, no nothing. As he had previously thought, Mark suggested that Jack had managed to save some rare coins, stamps or baseball cards. Deborah dismissed that possibility with a wave of her hand, emphasizing that Jack never saved anything in his life, a hypothesis with which Mark could not disagree. Despite there being no grounds to support the fantasy that Jack's safety deposit box held something worth recovering, Mark still felt obligated. No, he thought, it was more than that --- it had developed into a treasure hunt. It might be, it would be more fun than it was sitting around every weekend morning with the man who owned the box. For sure.

Now determined to locate the safety deposit box in a bank --- he had given no thought that the key could open anything else --- Mark thought that he first had to obtain power of attorney for Jack now that he was dead. Otherwise, Mark would not have any authority to even inquire about the box, let alone find and open it. Power of Attorney for a deceased person, as he had been informed after a relatively routine search of the internet, could be obtained, that is if it had not be granted by the person while he or she was still alive, from probate court, a legal term that Mark had occasionally heard on television. He further determined that a probate court, if satisfied that the person applying for power of attorney "is on the up and up", a remarkably casual requirement given the legal implications, would allow the applicant to act as administrator of the departed's estate, usually after issuing something called a "letter of administration" or, as the article on the internet helpfully noted, "something with a similar name that would be recognized by local financial institutions". All he had to do was approach the local probate court, presumably pay a small fee,and Mark could be walking into every bank in the city to ask whether a Jack Quinn owned a safety deposit box in that branch. It was so simple that Mark did not even have to take notes about the procedure.

Again using the internet, he also learned that the power of attorney was only the first step in accessing the contents of a box. Evidently, finding a box was one thing, opening it and removing its contents was another. Once he determined where Jack had a box, that is if his assumption about the key and the box it opened were correct, he would have to obtain some sort of certificate appointing him the estate trustee, officially entitled a "Certificate of Appointment of Estate Trustee", a profoundly bureaucratic term that reminded Mark almost painfully of his occasional positions in the Government of Canada. Once he was issued such a certificate, the details of its pursuit unknown to Mark at this point, he could then presumably open the box, that is once he found it. After discovering that fact, which had required him to research a host of convoluted websites made available by various law firms, he decided to skip the power of attorney step entirely. He had concluded, perhaps correctly, perhaps not, that obtaining power of attorney for anyone was only useful if that anyone was still alive. Fortunately, the ostensibly helpful information available from the internet provided a series of steps that would be required to obtain the certificate. There were seven pages of so-called steps. A flicker of headache threatened. He printed out the pages provided by a law firm that featured six partners on its masthead.

He leaned back in his chair and exhaled in predictable resignation. He then leaned back toward the computer screen. More than a simple headache, a migraine was now menacing, its possible arrival prompted by momentary panic when a sudden thought that it was possible that Jack either did not have a box or had kept his box somewhere else, in a city other than Ottawa. After all, he was born somewhere in a small town in Nova Scotia and grew up in Montreal. He often returned to Montreal, mainly for its recreational possibilities, at least until those possibilities overwhelmed him. He also realized, however, that he would never know the answer to that question unless he pressed forward with a search for a damn safety deposit box, despite the obvious obstacles that its pursuit would entail. He concluded he would need either a tranquilizer or advice. While he did not have access to either form of relief --- neither liquor nor wise counsel was available --- Mark got up from the computer. He headed out the door, got in his car and drove to a bar on Metcalfe Street called, not surprisingly, the Lawyer's Lounge. It was located right across the street from the city courthouse. Perhaps he could get some free advice from one of its denizens, that is if any were available. It was three o'clock in the afternoon.

One of those daytime business shows was silently playing on the large screen above a long bar where maybe thirty spaces were available. The host of the business show, a bland looking man who looked to be awaiting a lobotomy or rehearsing for a role as the Grim Reaper, seemed to be competing with a series of graphs and ticker tape news stories. Both were running too quickly across the bottom of the screen to read. The man, who Mark recognized for some unknown reason ---- he seldom watched such shows --- seemed to be informing whatever audience he had of some catastrophic event.

His expression alternated between grim and a little frightened. Mark took up a spot in the middle of the bar, ordered a draft, and started to read a newspaper, *The Globe and Mail*, that had been abandoned on the bar. Mark surveilled the room. There were a dozen or so other customers; a couple of groups of four who seemed quite jovial, their occasional bursts of laughter competing with the ambient music filling the room. Three groups of three who seemed less jocular but still talkative enough, two couples, two women who seemed to be in discussion about something serious, papers spread out in front of them, and the other looked to be deciding on whether to retain a room for the rest of the day, gripping each others' hands across their table like they were afraid to let go, and three singles, all men, one of whom was sitting at the far end of the bar while the other two were relaxing behind their drinks at tables near the restrooms. Tending to the tables was one waitress, a tall, thin woman who looked like she might have worked at the Lawyer's Lounge for several decades.

Mark had already gone through the sports section of the paper and was part of the way through the editorials when the bartender, a tall black guy with a shaved dome and a small goatee adorning his chin, asked him, in a bored, world-weary tone practiced by years of tending bar, whether he was looking for a lawyer, an inquiry that seemed, at least to Mark, like a jest, a requirement of the job for a barkeep in a joint situated across from the city courthouse. After all, anybody drinking alone in the middle of the afternoon in this place was looking for something, a lawyer being high on the range of possibilities. The bartender, whose name was Jeffrey, according to the small name tag on his chest announcing the fact, was actually cleaning glasses and holding them up to the light, just like in the movies. He was asking Mark the question without looking at him.

"Not specifically but maybe." Mark looked up from his paper with a certain surprise, not expecting, let alone appreciating the interruption. Jeffrey had momentarily discontinued his domestic chores, the glass he was polishing sufficiently pristine.

"Maybe? Maybe?" answered Jeffrey the bartender, feigning surprise. He had heard that response before too. It was a practiced response to almost every potential client that ever came into the Lawyer's Lounge. Most, if not all of them were looking for something, advice, counsel, guidance, anything to reassure them that their legal difficulties were not insurmountable. Unknown to Jeffrey, any possible interest by Mark Purchell in the legal profession was limited to the issue of applying for something called a "Certificate of Appointment of Estate Trustee".

Mark answered in an absentminded whisper, almost a mutter. Jeffrey leaned closer, turning his left ear to Mark who went back to staring down at the newspaper, as if he had regretted saying anything at all. Jeffrey stepped back, unconsciously shrugged, and went back to polishing the glasses, adding a perfunctory eye roll with his back to Mark who would not have noticed in any event. But for reasons unknown to either of them, Mark suddenly reconsidered his dismissal of Jeffrey's mumbled denial, raising his voice loud enough for the group at the table nearest the bar to momentarily discontinue their conversation. All four of them looked up from their discussion, were silent for a few seconds and then went back to entertaining each other. Jeffrey turned back to face Mark a second time. He had stopped polishing the glasses again.

"What's that?" asked Jeffrey, sounding a trifle annoyed underneath the friendly demeanor that bartenders usually affect. Jeffrey occasionally had difficulty retaining any sort of professional detachment while serving drinks to lawyers, some of whom exhibited a certain practiced arrogance, a quality that did not impress either the bar's other customers, specifically those who were not engaged in the legal profession, or in fact the people employed by the Lawyer's Lounge. It was curious, therefore, that bartender Jeffrey, like many of his colleagues, was still employed at this particular bar, given that the majority of its clientele were attorneys at law. On the other hand, they were fairly generous when it came to gratuities. In addition, as was often discussed among Jeffrey's male colleagues, the legal profession now seemed to be populated by more women than men, an evolutionary development that prompted the increased attention of male bartenders, including Jeffrey.

Mark looked up at Jeffrey across the bar. "I'm looking for advice, nothing serious you know --- I'm not in any trouble --- I just need some advice on a legal matter."

"And you think that you should be able to find some counsel in a place like this, right?" asked Jeffrey, a casual, trained smile spreading on his face like a greeting.

Mark looked hopefully at Jeffrey. "That's right and..."

Jeffrey nodded "And you don't want to spend any money."

"Partially. But to be honest, I really don't know where to find the right kind of lawyer." Mark spread his hands out as if he was asking for something, which he was.

There was a smirk from Jeffrey and a semi-flippant comment. "Well, there's always the law society. I'm sure they have an extensive website on the internet."

"Okay, so I'm looking for a shortcut." answered Mark.

Jeffrey offered Mark another smirk, leaned forward, stroked his goatee, and nodded toward the guy at the end of the bar. Mark looked toward the guy. He was sitting behind a glass of soda, seemingly transfixed. To Mark, the man elicited a assortment of observations. He looked gaunt, ghostly, haggard, sketchy, jumpy, nervous, on the edge of rehab, waiting for a cure that was unlikely to come. He looked to be late middle aged but could have been, or most likely was younger, a hard life having taken a toll. While Mark was studying the man, the man stood up, almost stumbled, and started out the door, which was maybe ten feet behind him. Mark had noticed that he was dressed in a rumpled three piece black suit that might have been expensive. He was wearing a white shirt with a frayed collar. He wasn't wearing a tie but he was sporting a nice maroon pocket square.

Jeffrey chuckled a bit and then explained. "Don't worry, he'll be back in a few minutes. Out for a smoke".

He put a couple of the proverbial fingers to his lips. Mark looked up at Jeffrey. He was waiting for a further explanation. He received one.

Jeffrey: "His name is Gore, Harvey Gore. You might want to talk to him."

Mark: "Yeah, is he approachable?"

Jeffrey: He nodded and laughed a bit. "Oh yeah, he's approachable alright. He'll talk to almost anybody who'll talk to him."

Mark: "Is his advice cheap?"

Jeffrey: His laughter grew a little louder. "Sometimes, it's free."

Mark: "Free?"

Jeffrey: "Well, he can't charge with a straight face anymore."

Mark: "Huh?"

Jeffrey: He was no longer laughing. He had suddenly turned serious. "He's not a lawyer, at least not anymore."

Mark: "Not anymore?"

Jeffrey: "No, not anymore. He was disbarred a couple of years ago. Apparently, and no one who knew him was surprised, he was usually drunk, he was stealing from clients, he was insulting judges, stuff like that. People were supposedly surprised that he lasted as long as he did."

Mark: "And now....?"

Jeffrey: "He sits at the end of this bar, drinks club soda and dispenses legal advice to anyone who asks for it. I think he really misses the business or maybe he doesn't but he likes to talk about the law. Pretty weird but not surprising. I think he now wants to be that lawyer who writes bestsellers, whoever he is."

Mark: "I see. And he dispenses legal advice without charge."

Jeffrey: "Well, as far as I see, most of the time."

There was a silence. Jeffrey then shrugged, stood up again and pointed to the end of the bar. Harvey Gore was now back at his post, back at the end of the bar, staring.

Mark thought of buying Mr. Gore a drink but then again, the guy didn't drink. Despite Jeffrey's observations regarding free legal advice from Mr. Gore, Mark was still disinclined to simply approach him. Jeffrey noticed his reluctance and offered him some encouragement. "Don't worry, he may look a little scary, maybe a little crazy but he really isn't. Just go and talk to him. He'd be glad to talk to anyone."

Mark: "Anyone?"

Jeffrey: "Yeah, pretty much. I know that sounds odd but I've seen him talk to a lot of people. But he doesn't bother people. If you don't talk to him, he doesn't talk to you."

Mark: "Does he give good advice?"

Jeffrey: "He is okay. I understand he is pretty well known at the Court House, even though he hasn't practiced there for a couple of years. I don't know why. Some of the lawyers who come in here jokingly say that his old pals like to refer potential clients who don't look like they can pay for legal advice to Counselor Gore. In fact, Gore likes to call himself a recovering lawyer."

Mark: "Okay. I think I'll give him a try."

Jeffrey nodded and turned away to tend to the drinks ordered by one of the tables, the tall, thin waitress standing at the bar with one hand on a hip and another under her chin. She seemed to be looking at nothing in particular and was rhythmically tapping her left foot. Mark got up and slowly started to walk down the length of the bar towards Mr. Gore, unnoticed determination on his face. Harvey Gore was still staring, oblivious to the fact that Mark was approaching him. Mark was maybe a meter away when Mr. Gore suddenly looked up from his stare like he had just been informed that the bar had run out of soda. He was waiting for Mark to initiate the conversation.

Mark did not of course disappoint. "Mr. Gore," Mark paused for a couple of moments, "my name is Mark Purchell. I don't want to be presumptuous but ..... well, the bartender told me that you don't mind giving people legal advice."

Gore: "You mean, Mr. Jackson?"

Mark: "You mean Jeffrey?" asked Mark.

Gore: "Yes, Mr. Purchell. The bartender, Mr. Jeffrey Jackson. He apparently likes to think that he's my agent. As I am sure he's told you, you're probably not the first person he's sent my way." Mark had expected a misanthrope but got a wit.

Mark: "That's true. He told me that."

Harvey threw his head back and let out a chuckle. "Yes, Mr. Purchell, it's too bad that Jeffrey wasn't around when I was actually practicing law instead of sometimes dispensing free advice about it. Maybe I'd still be practicing." Harvey stopped his chortling, paused and leaned forward. "On the other hand, I probably wouldn't be sitting here, or at least not sitting here as often as I do."

He then put out both hands, his elbows on the bar, waiting for Mark to ask for whatever it was that he wanted to ask the former attorney. He still looked amused, an expression on his face that looked a little like a theatrical smirk.

Mark, who had been standing, finally took a stool across the corner of the bar from Gore. He gently placed his beer on the top of the bar and turned, in an almost conspiratorial pose, toward Harvey Gore. He looked nervous, a little embarrassed, hunched over, like he was some sort of penitent. Though he was hardly a confessor, Harvey Gore seemed to be waiting with a gentle, understanding smile. He was still amused.

Gore didn't wait for Mark. He immediately initiated whatever conversation the two of them were presumably about to conduct. "I assume you are having or about to have a legal problem." He looked down at the bar and then back up at Mark ---- a little smile creeping over his face. "Fact is that most everyone that comes and talks to me here has a legal problem, even if they don't know they have one....yet. So what's your problem?"

Mark, who had straightened up to face Mr. Gore across the bar, explained his current search for a safety deposit box that could have been owned by a recently deceased man, mentioning that the only evidence he had that he may have had a safety deposit box was a key that he had found in his apartment after he died. Mark then reached into his jacket pocket and produced the small notched key that he thought would open a safety deposit box owned by the decedent.

"And you want to find the box and open it?" asked Gore with that same small smile on his face. "So why come to me? It seems to me that all you need to do now is to visit every bank in the vicinity, looking for your friend's box. By the way, did he leave a will and do you have any idea as to what's in the box?",

Mark shrugged and let out a barely audible sigh. "No will and I have no idea as to what's in the box or whether there is, in fact, anything in the box."

"So why pursue it?" inquired Gore, a certain level of comic incredulity in his voice. He spread his hands out in a gesture like he was about to end the conversation. Mark noticed that Gore's little smile was still affixed on his face like he was posing for a portrait.

Mark shrugged again and tried to explain his thinking. "You may not believe it, Mr. Gore, but I felt sorry for him and you know, kind of obligated, still do. The poor bastard didn't have much of a life toward the end. He was an alcoholic. For years, he was terminally ill or at least he thought he was. He lived in a complete dump of an apartment, his only friends were me, an ex-wife, and a semi-alcoholic neighbor. Face it, the man's life was sort of pathetic."

Mark regretted almost immediately raising anyone's alcoholism in a conversation with a man who looked like he had had and was perhaps still having his own battle with the bottle. After a short interval, during which Gore began to play with a red swizzle stick, Mark continued his account of his reasoning for pursuing the safety deposit box. "I went over to his apartment after he died, just to clear it out, to finalize his affairs, you know. Aside from some bad poetry and some old photos, the key was pretty well the only thing that he left. As I said, I felt sorry for him, I felt obligated, the key and the box it opens was the only thing he had left to pass on. And ..."

"And you were curious." added Gore.

"I guess." replied Mark, not really surprised that Gore had identified the motive for his search for the key, a treasure hunt based on his hunch that Jack Quinn might be hiding something worth finding. Mark had been reluctant to admit to Gore that curiosity was a more powerful inclination than some sort of posthumous obligation. "Regardless of my motive, Mr. Gore, I need advice as to how I can find Jack's box and if I find it, how I can have it opened." Mark felt he had to come clean.

Gore was still interested. "In the circumstances you describe, you are going to have to go to court. I am not exactly clear on the procedure --- I was mainly a criminal defense attorney. I don't have much in the way of experience with estate law. And if you want to know the truth, it is not very interesting."

Mark nodded. "Well, I researched the situation. I understand that I will probably need something called "A Certificate of Appointment of Estate Trustee". The steps for obtaining that document, which would allow me to find and open the box, look incredibly complicated, at least to me. I gave up after staring at one of those legal websites for what seemed like hours. There had to be ten pages of instructions, everything from what forms you need to where you have to file those forms." Mark paused again, trying to read Gore's expression. He couldn't but went ahead with the narrative anyway, asking the question. "So any advice for me?"

Harvey Gore slowly leaned back on his stool, not too far of course, and then forward again. "Well, all I can tell you at this point is that you will likely have to pay a fee and go to the court to file the documents necessary to obtain that certificate."

Mark slumped a bit and observed, in almost a whisper – lawyer-client confidentiality, a popular television drama issue, crossed his mind somehow -- "It still sounds awfully complicated. I still think I'm going to need some advice."

Gore casually shrugged, agreed with Mark and then offered a surprising suggestion. "I would be happy to help you out but I would have to ask you for a fee."

Mark was momentarily stunned. He understood that Mr. Gore had been disbarred from practicing law, an inconvenience that perhaps he was prepared to overlook for the good of Mark Purchell's judicial treasure hunt. "I thought..."

"You thought that I was no longer able to practice law?" exclaimed Gore.

"It's true, isn't it?"

"Yes, it's true but that's doesn't mean that I can't offer advice and that doesn't mean I can't ask for a fee ---- call it a gift if you like ---- as long as that fee or gift is just between you and me and no one else."

Mark nodded. "You mean, cash? Jeffrey never mentioned anything about a fee, I mean, a gift." Mark immediately regretted mentioning the bartender.

Gore started to laugh, a low, almost mumbling laugh. "Yes, Jeffrey tells everyone who comes in here that you can receive legal advice from me at no charge."

"But you do charge, right?" asked Mark.

"Sure, most of the time. I mean, why shouldn't I? Do you think I'm just sitting here everyday behind a glass of soda water just for the hell of it? People come by, ask for my advice and if I can ask somebody for a financial contribution, well why not?"

"And how do you decide who to ask, you know, ask for payment?" asked Mark.

"If I think a client ---- sorry, I know I shouldn't use that word client, I prefer fellow customers ---- if I think somebody seeking my counsel can pay, then I ask for payment. If not, well, if not, then I'm an off the books legal aid lawyer."

"Legal aid? It doesn't look like too many people who would be looking for free legal advice would come into this place." observed Mark.

"You're right. And if someone like that comes in here, then I can always ask Jeffrey or one of the cooks in the back to deal with them." Again a smirking smile appeared on Gore's face. He then raised his soda water, took a sip, put the glass down and winked, almost theatrically.

"You're kidding, right?" Mark asked. Harvey Gore did not have to agree with him but he shook his head gently.

The two men were quiet for a few moments. Mark took a quick survey of the room, noting that one of the two tables at which a quartet of men had been discussing the events of the day was empty but that the other twenty or so customers who had been in the Lawyer's Lounge when he walked into the bar were still there. For his part, Harvey Gore was staring over Mark's left shoulder, maybe at the television monitor which had been, and likely still was broadcasting breaking business news. No wonder he was staring.

Mark broke the silence with a predictable admission. "And I know which category of client I fit into --- sorry customer ---- and I would be happy to pay you."

Gore nodded. "Well, okay."

"Yes, I would really appreciate it." Again, there was another silence punctuated by another nod, this time from Mark.

Gore slowly nodded. "Well, I can certainly help you with obtaining that certificate. But, as I mentioned to you, I'm not exactly familiar with estate procedures ---- I never practiced in that area which, as I am sure you can understand, is pretty convoluted but I think I still have enough friends in the legal profession to get advice and then master the icissitudes of successfully applying for your certificate." Vicissitudes? Mark wondered where that word came from. "You think so?" questioned Mark, in reflex.

"Yes, it shouldn't be too difficult." explained Gore, "In fact, it shouldn't be too difficult at all.", a self-assured smile was now featured on Gore's face.

Mark went on to the next question. "I hate to be crude but how much is this is going to cost me?"

"We can talk about that and don't forget that there is probably some sort of fee for going to court for the certificate." explained Gore who started to stand up. "You'll have to excuse me. Time to satisfy one of my many shortcomings." He then put two fingers to his lips in that time honored gesture of someone about to enjoy a cigarette.

THE SEARCH BEGINS

It was more than six weeks after Jack Quinn passed away when Mark Purchell received an unexpected e-mail from Deborah Inkster inquiring about his presumed search for Jack's safety deposit box. Mark was mildly surprised to be contacted by Jack's ex-wife. He had not heard from her since they had both buried Jack's cremated remains under a numbered metal disk in the Royal Cross Cemetery. At first, Mark thought that Deborah might want to keep Jack in a vase, while he felt like flushing Jack. Eventually, they both decided on the cemetery route although neither of them were particularly happy about it. Deborah's e-mail did not mention Jack's final resting place, only the safety deposit box, which neither he nor Deborah were absolutely certain actually existed.

After considering his response for most of the day, Mark advised Deborah that he had just been issued a document entitled "Certificate of Appointment of Estate Trustee" by the Estate Registrar of the Ontario Superior Court of Justice. He assumed that Deborah might not be familiar with the workings of the Ontario judicial system, particularly as it applied to wills and estates. He briefly explained that since Jack did not leave a will, an oversight that didn't surprise anyone, he needed the certificate to investigate any mystery that may have been left after Jack's death, clues of which were likely sitting in his safety deposit box. After presumably contemplating the prospective contents of a safety deposit box rented by Jack Quinn, the idea being as curious to Deborah as it had been to Mark, Deborah responded by suggesting that Jack might have used the box to keep all the money he might have saved by living in that dump for the last few years. Either that, said Deborah in a rare witticism, or he was using it for filing his important papers, like medical reports, rehab certificates, or divorce decrees, although they have been very few. Mark ended that particular e-mail exchange with the pledge that if he found a box, he would advise Deborah. Mark wasn't sure that he was being entirely honest about that assurance, although he was sure that unless there was a wad of cash involved, Deborah probably wouldn't be that interested anyway. As cynical as that comment was, Mark was confident that it was accurate. After all, he thought, she had suffered matrimony with the guy, no matter how briefly.

With one relatively minor requirement fulfilled, Mark waited for the next week to begin his hunt for whatever treasure was sitting in Jack's safety deposit box. The first and most obvious step in the search was to determine the location of any box belonging to Jack Quinn. Mark had already found that there were over fifty bank branches in the city. He had also been able to determine that at least half of them had advertised the availability of safety deposit boxes, the other half did not mention safety deposit boxes at all, although he assumed that since they provided safety deposit boxes as well, he would also have to check those branches.

His first step was to contact the largest branch of each of the ten separate banks that were established in the city. His thought that the largest branch of each bank could also function as the de facto headquarters for each bank and would therefore be able to confirm whether each branch under its jurisdiction provided safety deposit boxes to its customers, an assumption that later proved to be inaccurate. He would honesty explain his predicament and ask for assistance. By the time Mark was in touch with the sixth of the ten branches on his list, he was pretty well certain that every bank in the city featured safety deposit boxes. The only information of any value he obtained was that the larger the bank, the more safety deposit boxes were likely to be available to the public, an obvious conclusion. He realized that he would have to call on each individual bank to ascertain whether Jack Quinn had a safety deposit box there. This had been suggested to him by every bank official he had contacted.

He then consulted the list of the bank branches and addresses he had compiled and planned his approach to the investigation. He moved the largest branches moving to the top of the list for each bank. He decided to approach the main office of the Royal Bank of Canada first, wondering whether he needed an appointment with a bank official before proceeding. He telephoned the main branch on Sparks Street in downtown Ottawa. After being referred to a number of different departments, without of course speaking to an actual person, someone named Ben Horvath finally introduced himself and offered assistance. Mark explained his aim in contacting the bank, careful to emphasize that he had been issued "A Certificate of Appointment of Estate Trustee". Not surprisingly, Mr. Horvath hesitated, at first fumbling with the question of whether Mr. Jack Quinn had a safety deposit box at the RBC, and whether the specific branch could be identified. Mr. Horvath, who sounded to Mark like he just graduated from some educational institution, Mark's tendency to identify everyone under the age of forty as barely out of high school growing as he aged, paused and then asked for a moment while he consulted with one of his colleagues.

Within several minutes, an interval during which unexpectedly spirited background music was played, the young Horvath was back on the phone to inform Mark that he could not provide information on Quinn's arrangements with the bank without proving that he actually had the certificate. This obviously could not be demonstrated over the phone. Understandably exasperated, Mark then asked if Horvath could at least confirm or deny whether Quinn had a safety deposit box. He further pointed out that he was not interested in whether he had accounts or any other financial arrangements with the bank. Without a power of attorney, which was supposedly irrelevant in the case of a dead person, or "A Certificate of Appointment of Estate Trustee", Horvath said that he could not provide any banking information about anyone. As politely as he could, Mark hung up without threatening a personal visit. He now understood that he was about to visit every single bank branch in the city, that is of course unless he was to locate Mr. Quinn's box before that search was exhausted.

Mark waited three days before visiting any specific bank branch. He decided to concentrate his search to banks in distinct geographic areas of the city. So on a Monday morning, he was dressed in a business suit that he had not worn for several years. He had difficulty with the waist of the trousers, it was now a couple of inches too small, a look that he had often criticized when it had been sported by others. He headed downtown to visit the largest branches of eight of the ten banks he eventually intended to call on, the other two of the ten banks having chosen to locate their largest branches in the suburbs. The first up was the largest branch of the TD Canada Trust.

He arrived there around ten o'clock in the morning and reported to the front counter, a low slung, modern designed circular counter behind which sat two bank officials, one a young Asian woman in a maroon dress and the other an older man who looked to be having the same trouble fitting into his suit as Mark had had with his, the latter fidgeting with his jacket and the collar of his shirt like he was suffering with some sort of nervous condition. The Asian woman got up and greeted Mark with a dainty smile and a slight forward motion of his hand, like she was about to introduce herself, which she did. For his part, the man with the tight suit leaned back as the Asian woman introduced Mr. Purchell to the TD Canada Trust.

"Good morning, sir, can we help you?" said Ms. Yang, her name emblazoned on the tag on the front of her maroon dress. She then knitted her fingers in front of her, straightened up and waited.

Mark smiled back. "Good morning. My name is Mark Purchell. I am looking to see if a man named Jack Quinn, who recently passed away, has a safety deposit box in this branch." Mark then placed a copy of his "Certificate of Appointment of Estate Trustee" on the counter before Ms. Yang. Mr. Tight Suit suddenly awake from a temporary daze came to the counter and leaned over to inspect the document before Ms. Yang. After looking at the certificate for a minute or so, Mr. Tight Suit leaned back, shrugged his shoulders and then relaxed back into the indolence that he was previously enjoying. He returned to his desk and picked up the telephone. Ms. Yang was examining the document carefully, her head bent over the counter like she was preparing to write an examination. After a suitable interval, maybe a minute or two, Ms. Yang looked up at Mark Purchell and basically avoided the question. She said that she would have to consult with her supervisor. She then asked Mark to have a seat in the lobby, motioning him over to the lobby off to his left. She told Mark that her supervisor, a certain Ms. Markham, would be out to speak to him shortly. Mark, though disappointed and a little surprised that the cautious Ms. Yang could not deal with the issue, dutifully stepped over to the lobby. He immediately noticed that the lobotomized host of the business show he had had the pleasure of watching the other day in the Lawyers' Lounge was still on television. He sat down, picked up one of those glossy magazines that featured the latest in corporate avarice, and waited.

It did not take long for Ms. Yang to return. She sat down beside Mark and informed him that Ms. Markham was satisfied that the certificate he had provided was legitimate and that he did therefore have the legal right to take possession of his friend's safety deposit box. She added, however, that this particular branch of the TD Canada Trust did not have any record of Jack Quinn ever having a safety deposit box. Mark thanked her, as cheerfully as he could in the circumstances. She then wished him good luck, almost as cheerfully as he had thanked her. He got up and left. He had a lot of other addresses to visit.

The next bank on his list was the main branch of the Royal Bank of Canada (RBC) which was housed on the same street as the main branch of the TD Canada Trust. Unlike the TD Canada Trust branch, which was housed in a recently renovated three story Victorian era building featuring miniature gargoyles on the four corners of its roof and a cathedral door entrance, the RBC branch occupied an architecturally unobtrusive structure which was likely constructed in the last ten years or so. To Mark, the place looked like one of the many bland government buildings that populated the city much like the bland bureaucrats who worked in them. It was a little more than a block away on the other side of the street from the TD Canada Trust. Mark walked into the front door of the RBC branch. To greet customers was a middle aged woman sitting behind a large desk off to the left. His first impression of the woman was how presentable she was, how affluent, how attractive, how commanding. Fact was that to Mark, she was stunning: impeccable make-up on a handsome face, hair that looked freshly coiffured, a dark blue maxi-dress that looked more like a negligee, and a necklace and earrings that looked like they was purchased at an expensive jewelry store. She looked full figured, maybe even a bit heavy, but on her, that hardly mattered.

She stood up and addressed him in a voice that could have only emerged from a woman that looked like she did. It had a husky melodic sound, like a jazz singer purring into a microphone in a nightclub. It also sounded somewhat aristocratic, like it had been practiced. Maybe the hearing aids she was surprisingly wearing had some effect on her voice thought Mark, hearing aids that weren't immediately evident. Mark immediately started to wonder about the circumstances through which she came to work at this or any branch of the RBC. She looked like she might have a lot of stock in the bank as opposed to being one of its receptionists. For a moment, he wondered whether he would run into Ben Horvath, the bank employee with whom he had an unsatisfactory telephone conversation several days ago.

"Good morning, sir. Can I help you?" she asked in that voice again, like someone was quietly playing a saxophone in the background. Rather than a name tag, a name plate on her desk identified her as Claire Balfour.

"Yes, you can." Mark must have been smiling. The expression on Ms. Balfour's face seemed routinely courteous. Evidently, she was used to men smiling at her. "My name is Mark Purchell, I am looking for a safety deposit box belonging to a deceased friend that may be located in your bank. His name was Jack Quinn. I have a document here that allows me to take possession of the box, that is if it is here." With that minor legal flourish, Mark held the "Certificate of Appointment of Estate

Trustee" out to Ms. Balfour who leaned forward and took the document in hand. The aroma of Ms. Balfour's perfume was now in the air between the two of them. Mark was suddenly lightheaded. Claire was no more than a foot from him, reading the certificate. After a weird pause, during which Mark continued to contemplate if not fantasize about Ms. Balfour, she looked up at Mark and told him that she would have to check with someone named Mr. Lemieux, an assistant manager. Mark was surprised, as he also had been at the TD Canada Trust branch, that a request to locate a safety deposit box required as much bureaucratic effort as it seemed to. Mark thought there would be a list somewhere that anyone working for the bank could consult without any further consideration.

Mark waited in a chair in front of her desk as Ms. Balfour disappeared into the catacomb of offices behind her to confer with Mr. Lemieux. After several minutes, she emerged from the offices, where she was presumably enlightened by Mr. Lemieux, walked up to Mark, and told him that the bank had no record of any safety deposit box being leased by Mr. Jack Quinn. Mark had stood up when Ms. Balfour approached him. For some reason, he then noticed that, in addition to wearing hearing aids, she was also holding a remote. Mark thanked her effusively, a gesture that she ignored. Mark shrugged and started out of the building. He happened to catch the eye of one of the security guards standing by the main entrance. He turned toward Mark. The guard assured Mark that Ms. Balfour seldom acknowledged salutations from people once "....she was done with them." The guard leaned over and confided a second detail --- about which he was obviously amused --- that Ms. Balfour often used the remote in her hand to turn off her hearing aids, usually in a gesture that ensured that people noticed that she was discontinuing her attention. The guard also told Mark not to feel bad, assuring him that she frequently used the maneuver, particularly when it came to males that did not appear important enough for her attention. He also said that that included a lot of males.

Appropriately disappointed, though hardly dismayed, Mark went to lunch, something he regularly did after he retired several years ago. He thought about heading over to the Lawyer's Lounge for a sandwich, a beer and maybe another chat with Harvey Gore, who he assumed would be available for conversation as always. But he didn't, choosing instead to lunch at a nearby brasserie, one of the increasing number of pubs that featured their own selections of brews, as if beer were now on the same gastronomic value system as vintage wine. He had remembered that this particular place, he couldn't recall the name, had a handy stack of newspapers available for patrons who were there to eat, drink and avoid socializing with their fellow customers. He sat at the bar, a favorite perch, and started to stare at the three monstrous television screens mounted above the bar. Highlights of the previous evening's hockey games were being endlessly replayed on one of the screens while the other two screens were showing cable shows where loquacious newscasters discussed the events of the day as if they were exchanging views on general relativity.

After lunch, a beer, a bowl of soup, and two cups of coffee, he was forced to the washroom three times in the hour he was there, prompting the waiter, a rotund fellow in black pants and a white shirt, to ask Mark if he had a urinary problem. Mark was shaking his head as he went to the can for the last time while the bartender in the tuxedo outfit snickered. By the time Mark returned from the facilities, the bartender was annoying someone else. Mark quickly finished his coffee, placed some cash on the bar, leaving the bartender with an inappropriately generous gratuity, and started out for the head office of the BMO Bank. It had originally been called the Bank of Montreal but now known by its abbreviated, initialed moniker. It was two blocks south.

On the walk over to the BMO office, he recalled that he had maintained an account with that bank for decades, not the specific branch that he was about to visit but one in the city and one in Montreal. He remembered, and he was convinced that the memory was clear, that a Bank of Montreal account had been opened for him when he was in grade one. This was a Catholic school's idea of establishing good money habits at an early age. He also recalled that the Bank of Montreal branch that held his account, into which he had deposited 25 cents every two weeks, had been robbed. The bank sought to compensate itself for its financial loss by removing the funds from every account holder, ultimately resulting in Mark's account being reduced by half of the eleven dollars it held at the time of the robbery. This was prior to the establishment of government backed deposit insurance. Aside from his own disappointment, not that he would have kept the money anyway, he remembered quite vividly that both his parents were as mad as hell, as were most of the parents of the other students whose accounts were looted. Funny thing, however, was that Mark never closed his account with the Bank of Montreal or whatever name it had now. He had simply transferred it to Ottawa when he moved there for university. That was more than forty years ago.

Unlike the two banks that he had previously visited, this BMO office greeted its customers with all the formality of a confused coffee shop. There did not appear to be, at least to Mark, anyone specific to whom he could introduce himself. So he got in line to consult a teller or bank functionary or whatever official title employees who handled customers held. There were three tellers, the line was light and before he could rehearse his request, he was standing in front of a high counter behind which, on a small stool, sat a young man named Benjamin Tyler, or so said a desk template on the counter in front of him. He asked Mark, somewhat nervously it seemed, if he could be of assistance. Mark explained his intention in visiting the bank, showed him his "Certificate of Appointment of Estate Trustee" and asked Mr. Tyler if Jack Quinn had a safety deposit box in the bank. Poor Benjamin looked dazed, as if he hadn't quite heard or understood what Mark had just said. Mark repeated his request, expanding his explanation regarding Jack Quinn's safety deposit box, showing Benjamin the key that he had found in Jack's apartment, placing it on the counter between them. Benjamin seemed to wake up, suddenly interested in Mark and his little notched key.

Benjamin tentatively touched the key, almost as if he was attempting to avoid placing a fingerprint on the damn thing. Mark pushed the key closer to Benjamin's side of the counter. He gingerly touched the key, he looked down at his hand in contact with the key and then picked it up. He smiled, maybe relieved that he had not been struck with an electric shock. Mark was sure that Benjamin was contemplating an appropriate response to Mark's inquiry. He was thinking --- was there a procedure here, a process for dealing with a circumstance that Benjamin had not come across? By the time that Benjamin had put the key back down on the counter, having convinced himself that providing anyone with information on whether some dead person had a safety deposit box was hardly a question of national security. No big deal. Ordinarily, he knew he would have to seek authorization of his supervisor, a miserable little toad of a guy named Morris with whom Benjamin never wanted to speak. To hell with him Benjamin thought. He looked up at Mark and told him that to give him a minute and he would give him an answer. Benjamin then gently slapped his hand down on the counter, got off his stool and walked back into one of the offices behind him.

He quickly returned with a ledger of computer sheets which he placed on the counter between him and Mark. He ran the index finger of his right hand down the columns on the left side of all six pages, these being the columns recording the name of each person who had a safety deposit box with the bank. He looked up and informed Mark Purchell, with a certain disappointed inflection in his voice, that Jack Quinn did not have a safety deposit box in that bank. Benjamin Tyler apologized to Mark and wished him good luck. As he left, Mark picked up one of Tyler's business cards. It was a reflex he guessed. He was fairly certain, however, that he would never have further use for it.

It was almost four o'clock in the afternoon by the time Mark left the BMO bank. He wasn't particularly disappointed, only frustrated, a feeling that he anticipated he would have to become accustomed. He stood by the door to the BMO office and checked his list of bank branches. The next closest bank was the CIBC, the Canadian Imperial Bank of Commerce. It was on the same street, maybe six or seven doors down from the BMO office, in a building that looked like it had been built sometime in the sixties. It reminded Mark of one of those high schools that sprang up like three bedroom bungalows in the suburbs where he grew up, architectural marvels that were first copied and then never replicated. Mark walked into the building. He was forced to hurry, noting with concern that the bank was about to close. On the left side of the lobby was a scattering of plush chairs and circular tables, all appropriately retro. The other side had a long counter behind which was the only bank teller, the other four positions empty. On that right side of the lobby in front of the long counter, seated behind a desk, was a good looking young woman wearing a short violet dress, sporting heavy black eyeliner, maroon lipstick, and exotic serpent tattoos on both forearms. She was just about to emerge from behind the desk, a handbag in one hand and a blue metallic bottle in the other. It was obvious she was leaving for the day. Once she saw Mark approaching, she stood still for a moment, turned to place the bag and the bottle down, turned back and put her hand up as if to stop him from getting any closer to her. Mark stopped a meter from her.

"Sorry, sir, as you can see, I'm just about to leave for the day." she said, a slightly irritated edge to a voice that would have sounded quite pleasant otherwise. Mark also had the impression that the woman did not look like she belonged behind a desk greeting people coming into a bank ----he thought that a hair salon, a clothing store, a nightclub, maybe even a gentleman's club would have been a more appropriate place of employment for her.

After explaining her haste to Mark, she turned back to her desk, picked up her water bottle and her bag and headed out the building a second time. Mark noted that it was a Coach purse, his familiarity with handbags a consequence of having dated a fashion conscious woman named Carole. Mark turned sideways to let her pass and asked if there was anyone else in the bank who could help him, albeit at this late hour. The woman motioned somewhere behind her, half pivoting and pointing at a meek young man, the only staff member standing behind the tellers' counter. He was serving an elderly woman leaning on a walker that was carrying a small tan poodle. She said simply "Try David --- he always stays late." Her tone was not complimentary. After providing Mark with the recommendation, she was gone out the door. Mark watched her leave.

Mark half shrugged, started toward David's post and stood behind the elderly woman with the poodle. The dog looked to be asleep. The dog was wearing a red sweater.

The woman was explaining something to David, a tall kid with big car door ears and fashionably weird hair with side walls, a tint of blue and a requisite man bun. He was smiling patiently. It was now five minutes after closing time. David did not appear to be considering packing it in for the day. He looked up and nodded at Mark, implying that he would be attending to him shortly. He then smiled and went back to serving to the old woman and her dog. Mark found it difficult to believe that David and the woman in the violet dress and the tattoos were working in the same office. Mark was close enough to hear David tell the old woman and maybe her dog that he would be happy to show her how to use the ATM, even though, as he kindly assured the old woman, he and the staff of the CIBC would be happy to continue to serve her personally. She appeared to nod although it might have been a tremor. David smiled and handed her a bank passbook. It took her a minute or so to return the passbook to her purse that she almost dropped. She then hooked the purse on her walker and slowly pushed her way toward the bank entrance, a theatrical smile on her face, characterized in particular by a misapplied slash of bright red lipstick that could have been applied by a small paint brush. As she strolled by Mark, he heard her talking to her dog. He did not hear the dog talk back.

Mark stepped up to talk to David who had modified his smile from one of gracious sympathy to a grin of official cheerfulness, not much of a change but one that was fairly obvious to Mark. David quickly looked at his watch, prompting Mark to assure him that his request wouldn't require much time.

"Don't worry." responded David, "You're the last customer of the day anyway. They've closed the doors." David swept his right arm out like he was showing Mark the bank lobby for purposes of leasing it. Mark noticed a security man walking back from the front doors.

Mark returned David's smile. "Thanks, this won't take long, at least I hope it won't."

"Look, I don't think you could take up any more of my time than poor old Mrs. Banbridge." explained David, a different sort of smile spreading over his face. It was obvious that David was good natured enough to endure customers like Mrs. Banbridge. Maybe it was his specialty.

Mark returned David's smile and continued with his request. "I'm here to see if someone who passed away might have had a safety deposit box in this bank."

Mark then tried to present David with his "Certificate of Appointment of Estate Trustee", slightly leaning over the counter with the document in his left hand. David didn't even pretend to look at it, adding a quick observation that he didn't need to look at Mark's precious certificate.

"I can tell you whether your friend has a safety deposit box in this bank without seeing any sort of official document." David saw the expression on Mark's face.

David continued his explanation. "Don't worry. You'll need the certificate to look in the box, that is of course if we can find it." Another friendly smile. Mark drew the certificate back from the counter and returned it to his jacket pocket.

David held up his right hand and responded to Mark's request. "Let me look to see if your friend has a box here. Give me a minute, will you."

Mark nodded. Before he turned to walk back to wherever the branch's records regarding safety deposit boxes were held, David placed a little brass sign on the counter informing potential customers that another bank teller would be happy to serve them, although Mark doubted that no other bank officer would be happier to do so than David. Besides, there were no other bank officers were available.

As David disappeared down a corridor behind the counter, his footsteps audible on the marble floor, Mark passed the wait by reading a CIBC brochure on retirement investments. He absentmindedly read its first paragraph at least twice before he realized that he had understood neither the purpose nor the meaning of the pamphlet. He was pondering his lack of financial acumen when David returned from his exploration of the bank's files.

David was smiling, understanding Mark's confusion regarding the treatise on investment strategies. He looked at Mark with an amused expression on his face. He explained. "Most people have the same reaction. We all think that the bank should seriously consider dropping it or rewriting it so that people who don't have a MBA can understand it." David continued to smile, sounding a little wiser than he appeared to be. He then returned to character and politely shrugged.

"And....," interjected Mark, hopefully.

David nodded. "Right. I couldn't find any record of a Mr. Jack Quinn as having a safety deposit box in this bank. Sorry." David sounded honestly apologetic. Mark thanked David. For some reason, Mark actually felt like shaking his hand, compensation perhaps for staying past closing to help some man, a man who wasn't even a customer, with a request for information on a man who also wasn't a customer. Even that or Mark had been impressed that, after the unfortunate encounter with the woman with the Coach purse, someone was still tolerant enough to be helpful. Mark turned away from David, walked across the now empty lobby of the bank, and was out on the street again. It was after five o'clock and time to head home, with everyone else. He would start with the Bank of Nova Scotia in the morning.

A VISIT WITH DANNY

Mark was driving home along his usual route, one that he routinely employed when he was working downtown, when he detoured to drive past Jack's old apartment. This was something he had done at least three times since Jack died, a custom that he could not explain. It reminded him of the sort of neurotic behavior he used to exhibit as an adolescent, like occasionally following ex-girlfriends after their breakup or mindlessly calling them and hanging up before anyone could say anything. He would drive by, slow down, and gaze up at Jack's apartment, as if he expected someone or something to appear in the middle window on the second floor. No, he couldn't explain it. Not that it mattered much. He wasn't sure he wanted an explanation anyway.

This day, the traffic was bumper-to-bumper on his street, virtually immobile, the result being that by the time he reached Jack's building, he could survey his apartment at his leisure. Fact was that he had no choice. He was parked in the middle of the street, right behind a black BMW with a *Baby on Board* bumper sticker and right in front of a navy blue mud splattered Ford SUV driven by a bearded man in a battered *Toronto Blue Jay* baseball cap. Both the man in the cap and the person driving the BMW --- Mark couldn't tell whether that driver was a man or a woman --- were talking on cellphones, presumably informing loved ones, friends, and/or business associates of their whereabouts and the delay. An ex-smoker for maybe twenty years, Mark now wanted a cigarette, a yearning that he had not experienced in a long time. He was staring out the driver's side window, hypnotized by inertia, when he suddenly awoke to see Danny Beliveau leaning on a railing in front of the building where he lived and where Jack Quinn used to live. The railing itself was a strange fixture, an architectural artifact that didn't seem to fit with the building before which it stood.

To attract Beliveau's attention, Mark used his car horn, embarrassed as he was with attracting unwanted attention from the other commuters waiting for the traffic to regain its flow. The man in the car behind him responded with a bleat of his own, as did several other drivers. At least one of them added a discourteous gesture to the sound of car horns. Mark's embarrassment turned to paranoia for a moment as he imagined a crowd of angry drivers leaving their cars with imaginary weapons in clenched fists. His paranoia faded always as quickly as it had emerged when he noticed Danny Beliveau actually waving at him, apparently signaling to him. Almost immediately, Mark waved back, prompting Beliveau to beckon to Mark a second time. Beliveau then started across the street, calling out to him. Drivers honked their horns, no telling whether the most recent bleats were a response to Danny Beliveau walking across the street or simply another note in the melody of car horns that had been playing for the last few minutes. Before he knew it, Danny Beliveau was standing by his car and Mark was lowering the window. The driver in the BMW in front of Mark was evidently either annoyed or curious and turned around in his seat to follow Danny as he approached Mark's car. The driver was a woman, maybe in her thirties, long blond hair, wide brimmed hat, and an unpleasant expression on her face. Her face was partly covered by what appeared to be expensive sunglasses. She looked irritated. She had the look of entitlement. She turned back around and went back to presumably torturing one of her associates or friends on her cellphone.

Danny Beliveau was now leaning through Mark's car window. The beard in the car behind them gave them another honk of his horn. Danny looked up and gave him a surprisingly jaunty wave. Danny then laughed and stuck his head back into Mark's car, greeting Mark with his usual lopsided grin. He was mildly high on something or other, booze and some street pharmaceutical the usual cause. He was a street guy, as he often identified himself.

"Hey, man, glad you dropped by." his salutation.

"Dropped by?" answered Mark."I'm not dropping by. Can't you see that I'm stuck in traffic."

"Stuck in traffic, my ass." Danny remarked. He then observed that he had seen Mark driving by this particular address several times since Jack died. "What about that?"

Mark was taken aback, temporarily at a loss. He was searching for an explanation. He looked at Danny and shrugged. "Yeah, maybe you're right. I just... I mean I'm just curious I guess."

"Shit, man, what's with this curiosity stuff?" Danny asked. "Are you expecting Jack to come back from the dead, you know, like a resurrection?" Danny hesitated for a moment and then continued his inquiry and/or his interpretation of the event. "Are you religious? Maybe this is some sort of religious thing, you know, a weird wish fulfillment thing?"

Again, Mark regarded Danny with a dumbfounded look on his face. As he did not know Danny well, he was understandably surprised that someone like Danny Beliveau, a street guy who wasn't sober most of the time, would ask such a discriminating question. Wish fulfillment? Maybe?

Although he had thought about it, he really didn't know the reason for his occasional visits to Jack's erstwhile residence. He admitted it to Danny. "I really don't know why. It's just curiosity I guess." He paused for a moment and then continued with his explanation, as incomplete as it may have seemed, even to Mark himself. "But I never actually stop. I just drive by, maybe slow down a bit but I never stop. But today, I stopped because of this damn traffic, honestly."

"Okay, whatever you say." Danny accepted the explanation with that lopsided smile still on his face. "I don't really care. I'm just glad you stopped by."

"I haven't stopped by, I'm not stopping by." Mark replied. "Like I told you, it's the traffic, like every other car on the block right now."

Danny shrugged, reached into his shirt pocket for a pack of cigarettes, took out one out, and lit it. He was still leaning into the window of Mark's car. He glanced at the beard in the car behind them. The guy was looking increasingly annoyed. Danny didn't look at the woman ahead of them. He took a drag on his cigarette and then announced to Mark, like he was confiding something, that he had come across something in which that Mark might have an interest.

"What the hell are you talking about?" replied Mark, a blank look on his face. He then brought his hand up to point through the front window of his car. Traffic was starting to move.

"You'd better park the car." suggested Danny.

Mark put the car in gear and started to creep forward. Danny started to walk beside Mark's car while he continued to talk. "Come on, park the car. Park around the next corner there. I got some stuff for you." Danny waved him forward.

Mark started to move, the car inching forward about half a block at 15 kilometers an hour or so, Danny Beliveau was walking beside the car. Mark was worried about running over one of Danny's feet. Twenty minutes had gone by since he stopped.

"Okay, what do you have, Danny?" asked Mark. He started to turn right at the next corner onto a narrow little strip of tenements crowded together on street called Lola, an interesting street name for a neighborhood that was primarily populated, at least these days, by Chinese and Vietnamese families.

Encouraged by Danny, who was signaling like one of those ground crew guys with the ping pong bats, Mark was waved into a space right in front of a bright yellow water hydrant. Danny was back to leaning into the window of the car as Mark turned off the engine.

"Are you going to pay for the parking ticket? "asked Mark, hints of exasperation, annoyance, and maybe a little curiosity creeping into his voice.

Danny shrugged. "What ticket? People tell me that cops just aren't issuing them here That's what I hear."

"Whatta you mean, the police aren't giving anybody any tickets?" asked Mark.

Danny laughed. "Hey, nobody pays tickets around here, so the cops just stopped issuing them."

Mark, still sitting in his car, was shaking his head, incredulous as he was amused. "Isn't not paying parking tickets a problem for anyone getting one?"

Danny shrugged again. "I guess so." He was a quiet for a moment, looking down at his feet, like he was considering a witticism. Then his face brightened a bit and he added an observation. "They must have gotten tired of trying to go after people whose names they didn't really know for sure." He then backed away from the car.

Mark got out of his car and look quizzically at Danny. "What the hell are you talking about? Are you sure about any of this?"

"I just hear stuff, that's all." replied Danny. "I just don't know why the cops are so lenient about parking tickets here...maybe its just that there are so many people here with strange names that the cops aren't sure who anybody is."

"So they've just given up giving anyone tickets. That doesn't sound right" replied Mark.

"Maybe not but that's what I heard." repeated Danny with another quick shrug.

"Okay, okay, I'll take the chance." said Mark. He then returned Danny's shrug with one of his own, closed the car door and joined Danny on the street across from Jack Quinn's old place. They both stared at the place for a moment, imagining Jack standing in the window, a pose he hardly ever assumed when he was alive.

Mark wondered whether anyone had moved into Jack's now vacant apartment. He doubted it. It had been almost two weeks since Jack moved out, dispatched on a stretcher down those treacherous stairs from the second floor Into an ambulance on his way to the morgue. He had left behind an accumulation of soon to be discarded possessions, just forgettable junk. Mark remembered meeting the alleged superintendent of the building, a frighteningly gaunt older man who looked like he might have spent time in a concentration camp. Jack had introduced him, not by name of course but by position, one morning six months previously. It had been a strange meeting. Mark was about to depart for the day when the superintendent walked into Jack's place unannounced, no knock on the door, no warning. While Mark thought it likely that the man had a key, he thought it strange nonetherless. The door to Jack's place was always open. Jack never locked the doors to any of his apartments, including this, his last residence. He reasoned that he never did possess anything worth stealing. This was not altogether a strange notion for a man who usually lived in neighborhoods where inhabitants generally directed their larceny to more affluent precincts. Mark couldn't recall the substance of Jack's conversation with the superintendent although he was sure that the discussion had been quite short, no doubt terse, a quick exchange that seemed to annoy the both of them. When the man left, Jack mumbled something profane but did not explain further. That was the only time Mark ever saw the superintendent.

After Mark parked the car, Danny invited him to his apartment, which was located directly adjacent to Jack's old place on the second floor. "I found some stuff in my place that may have belonged to Jack." explained Danny. "I thought you might be....like interested." Danny then reached into his shirt pocket, pulled out another cigarette, made a gesture like he was about to offer it to Mark, withdrew it with a charming little smirk, and fired it up. Although Mark was not that familiar with Danny and his mannerisms, he had always noticed that he had an odd backhanded way of cupping a cigarette when he was smoking it. All three of them were together one dreary morning in Jack's apartment when Mark suggested that Danny, for some sort of theatrical effect, was pretending to smoke like a German officer in the movies. They had all laughed. Danny admitted that he was in fact doing a "James Dean thing", a reference which prompted shrugs from Jack and Mark. Funny thing but Mark never saw Danny actually smoke a cigarette in that fashion. He only affected the pose when he was pretending to smoke a cigarette.

Not unexpectedly, Mark asked Danny why he would be interested in anything that Jack would have left in Danny's apartment. "Look, man, I hope you don't mind but I was awake that day when you came over after Jack died. I heard you going through his place. I don't know why you would be going through that dump --- I mean, what could he have left that would be worth anything?" Danny then spread his arms out in a grand gesture, like there was no way in the world he could conceive of Jack actually possessing anything of value. He then laughed that little street junkie laugh of his, a hollow scratchy sound that suggested that he might be in need of medical attention. He then started to cough, that frightening rasp of his erupting.

Mark provided the explanation. "I was just curious, nothing more than that really. I wasn't checking for anything, nothing in particular. Besides, I just didn't want the cops or the superintendent or the landlord or whomever should collect up his stuff and give it to the Salvation Army, without checking it first, just in case you know."

In response, Danny developed a blank look on his face, an expression that was not entirely unfamiliar to him. Danny often affected the kind of inanity that made people wonder about his mental health. After ninety seconds or so of suspended animation, during which time Danny threw one half smoked cigarette down on the street and then lit another, seemingly in one practiced motion. He looked up and inquired, in a quiet, uncertain voice. "Okay, but what makes you think that Jack had anything worth anything?"

Mark just shrugged. "Hey, look, I told ya. I was curious. I really didn't think I would find anything of value, just some items of interest."

"You mean, like old photographs and stuff like that." offered Danny, another smirk creeping onto his face.

"Yeah, stuff like that." assured Mark, unwilling to tell Danny about the only thing he did find in Jack's apartment that could have been of any interest --- specifically, the safety deposit box key. While Mark did find some items in Jack's place that did interest him --- old letters, high school reviews, a USB drive, an empty memory card from a digital camera, empty liquor and prescription bottles and other inconsequential crap --- only the notched key was of any value. Although Mark was somewhat surprised that Danny would have volunteered that Jack had left anything in Danny's apartment --- Mark had been fortunate or unfortunate enough to have been a guest in Danny's apartment once. It was maybe six months ago when he found Jack on Danny's couch instead of his own bed, no explanation provided. It was possible he guessed that Jack spent enough time at Danny's place to have left something there. In any event, he considered this while he stood watching Danny smoke his cigarette.

"Anyway, why don't you just come up to my place? I think I have something for you." Danny was inviting Mark for a second visit to his apartment. Mark was intrigued and a little worried. Despite his curiously amiable demeanor, Mark always thought that Danny Beliveau was somewhat dodgy, at least to acquaintances from the more conventional world, people like Mark for example. Danny had street credibility. At least, Mark thought that he did. But what the hell Mark thought. He nodded and started across the street with Danny. The traffic, while moving, was still slow, creeping along. They were across the street in thirty seconds and climbing the stairs to Danny's apartment. Like Jack's abode, Danny's place was never locked, the same reasoning being applied ---- nothing worth stealing inside.

His apartment was much larger than Jack's, two actual bedrooms as opposed to the bed sitting room that

Jack had occupied. Fact was that Jack had been Danny's roommate for several months before he moved next door and before Mark had become a regular visitor to his final residence. Mark had been a guest in Danny's place only that one previous time, having had the pleasure of Danny's company on maybe a dozen occasions. This was mostly at Jack's apartment but a couple of times they ate in a Vietnamese restaurant three doors down the street. While Danny's apartment did not have the opulence of a hotel room for example, it was hardly the dump that Jack occupied for the last months of his life. In addition, given Danny's assistance with Jack's declining medical condition, not to mention his general amiability, Mark had wondered why Jack had left Danny's in the first place. Jack had explained that some of Danny's predilections, a constant use of various narcotics and unusual sexual practices being high on the list, disturbed him enough for Jack to consider an alternate living arrangement. This included a move next door --- where he would still retain the convenience of having Danny available for emergencies without having to endure his unbecoming habits. Still, Mark did not share Jack's opinion and tried, albeit briefly, to talk Jack out of moving. After all, as Mark was to explain, it was better for Jack to be living with someone, even someone like Danny, if he needed someone to call the paramedics or pick up his meds. But Jack was not convinced. But still, being next door, Danny was still available to provide assistance whenever Jack needed it. Or so Jack reasoned.

The first thing Mark saw once the two of them scaled the stairs that day and walked into Danny's place was a bright red tubular contraption. It appeared to be a bong, an accurate identification if Mark was current on his knowledge, which was usually fairly shaky, of drug paraphernalia. Danny noticed that Mark had seen the bong and said it was for entertainment purposes only, claiming that he wasn't using much anymore. The expression on his face suggested that Mark was somewhat skeptical with that explanation. This prompted Danny to smile, spread his arms out wide and exclaim, in a raised voice, that he was telling the truth. Mark recalled that Jack reporting that Danny used to be an abuser, an abuser of pretty well any substance he could get his hands on, an abuser of a smorgasbord of street drugs that could anesthetize anyone. But that was years ago, again according to Jack who was apparently Danny's confessor for the several months he was his roommate. While Jack never said that he was regretted his decision to leave Danny's place, he did miss their conversations, particularly the ones in which Danny would relate his adventures on the so-called dark side of the street. Jack would gently accuse Danny of appropriating many of the stories from the police dramas he liked to watch on television. Not surprisingly, Jack invariably regarded anything Danny told him as at least partial fabrication. But Jack was seldom dismayed by Danny's theatrical exaggerations. Fact was that he often looked forward to Danny's stories, many of which were as entertaining as any narrative he had ever heard from anyone else. Most, if not of all of Danny's stories were populated by a range of interesting characters, many of whom would fit nicely in those same police dramas he liked to watch on television --- the hookers, the drug dealers, the street guys, the poor vagrants living in crummy group homes begging for change. All of them lived in Danny's narratives like characters living in the architecture of a hundred screenplays, a hundred novels.

Mark sat in one of the three large plush chairs that had been liberated from neighbors on various garbage days. The chairs, which were pockmarked with burn marks and decorated with stains from unknown sources, formed a rough circle around the coffee table on which sat the bong, some rolling papers, several empty liquor bottles, two glass ash trays containing mountains of cigarette butts and extinguished joints, a few scattered newspapers, and a damaged vinyl copy of the Santana LP *Abrasis* that looked like someone had bitten into it. Danny had disappeared, not announcing his intentions, and then Mark heard some whispered though unidentifiable mutterings coming from one of the bedrooms. Mark was surprised, although maybe he should not have been, when a woman in her underwear, holding her clothes and carrying a plastic shopping bag, was ushered out of the room. She was out the apartment door without a word from Danny, the woman or Mark for that matter. The door was slammed shut, Danny went into the kitchen, and then offered Mark a beer but no explanation about the suddenly departed woman. Mark never asked. He imagined, however, that this kind of event was not an infrequent occurrence, the entire matter open to every kind of prurient interpretation.

Although Mark was reluctant to accept a beer from Danny, fearing that even one beer would prompt some sort of boozy interlude from which it would be difficult to extricate himself, he did anyway. Danny seemed surprisingly pleased to provide Mark with a libation, remarking that he was under the impression that Mark had always thought he had been a bad influence on Jack. Ironically, fact was that Mark was worried that Danny would eventually have a bad effect on him, not Jack who he thought was beyond, at least in that last year of his life, influence of any kind anyway. Despite all his faults, his less virtuous life style, his debatable personal habits and his shady friends, Danny was still a charming individual, personable and eager to please. So Mark sat back in his chair, took a couple of swigs from his beer, and waited for Danny, who had returned to the kitchen after delivering Mark's beer. It sounded like he was going through the kitchen drawers.

Finally, Danny re-appeared in the living room, a half finished plastic bottle of vodka in one hand and a sheath of papers in the other. He sat down, took a healthy gulp from the bottle and then held out some papers in front of him. Referring to the papers, he explained. "Like I told you, I found some of Jack's stuff. You may be interested." Danny paused for a moment and then continued with his explanation. "I don't know why Jack left these papers here in my place. I can't actually remember him dropping them off or having seen them before. I just came across them one day last week. I found them under a set of drawers in the empty bedroom --- Jack's room when he was staying here. He probably just left them here –- you know, from when he was living here with me." Noticing a look of incredulity on Mark's face, Danny expanded on his account of the discovery of Jack's papers. "I know, what the hell was I doing looking through a set of drawers anyway. To be honest, I can't really tell you ---- maybe I was looking for some change for a pizza or something." On that observation, they both laughed.

"Anyway, take a look if you want." Danny handed the papers to Mark who put his beer down, took the papers from Danny and started to examine them. After what seemed like seconds though the interval was likely longer, Mark looked up at Danny with an astonished look on his face. He had the look of someone who had just been informed that he had won some money. "Why the hell would Jack leave a bank statement and some blank cheques with you?" Mark paused for a moment and started to shake his head, like he couldn't believe what he was now holding in his hand. "Hell, Danny, damn it, I've been looking for Jack's bank for..... I don't know, at least a week or so.... and you could have told me where to look."

Danny looked chagrined and a little surprised. "Hey, man, don't get all psycho on me, I didn't know, I never knew what you were looking for. I just heard you going through his place just after he died. I didn't know that you were looking for anything in particular. I just thought you were looking ----- you know, like looking through his stuff for anything you should keep."

Mark came forward in the chair, lowered the bank papers in his hands, and started to explain his thoughts in a calm, even voice, like he was talking to a child. Though he wasn't that friendly with Danny, he had been under the impression ---- maybe it had been advice and/ or an observation that Jack had provided ---- that it was easier to get though to Danny if one didn't get him too excited. According to Jack, an excitable Danny was close to being useless. Again according to Jack, the gallery of drugs that Danny had consumed over the years made him less than emotionally stable. Mark didn't disagree. "Look, Danny, I found something in his place, a key to one of those safety deposit boxes, like they have in banks. That's why it would have saved me a lot of time and effort if I knew what bank Jack was doing business with so I would know where he had a safety deposit box is. But I know you couldn't have known how important the location of his bank was."

"Sorry about that." replied Danny, blankly.

Danny finished off his bottle of vodka and then smiled, that lopsided grin that usually suggested he was somehow under the influence. "Okay, I get it. Hey, any idea what's in that safety deposit box?"

Mark laughed and leaned back in the chair. "Come on, Danny. I have no idea. That's why I need to find the box. But now that I know that it's most likely sitting in the Bank Street branch of the Royal Bank, I'll know where to go." Mark was holding up one of the cheques. Interestingly enough, Mark noticed that the cheques only featured Jack's name, i.e. Jackson Quinn ---- no address, no telephone number. Mark was mildly surprised by the omission although he guessed that when he obtained the cheques, he could have been between domiciles. In addition, he wondered about his given name. He thought that Jack's given name was John, not Jackson. It was likely that few people knew his given name either.

"So this is all good. Right?" suggested Danny, that lopsided grin still on his face like it had been drawn there like a cartoon character. Before Mark could agree, Danny asked him if he wanted another beer. He had been heading into the kitchen. Mark declined. Danny shrugged and went back into the kitchen. Mark assumed that Danny would soon reappear with another vodka. Mark got up for no apparent reason and then sat back in another one of the living room chairs. He started to plan his visit to the Royal Bank that was maybe two hundred meters from the apartment. He removed and started to study his list of bank branches from his pocket. He estimated that, at least at his current pace of investigating bank branches, he would have eventually visited that particular branch of the Royal Bank within two weeks anyway. So Mark concluded that Danny's discovery would at least save him some time. He had been lucky.

Danny reappeared from the kitchen, a fresh bottle of vodka in one hand, another smoke in the other. He noted, however, that Danny's second bottle was only a third full. Maybe Danny liked to limit his consumption of liquor by only imbibing from partially finished bottles. Who knows, thought Mark, maybe it was an acceptable, if not required practice among boozers on the edge of addiction. Anyway, it was eleven o'clock in the morning and Danny could have been half in the bag already. Not that it was unusual, or so Mark had already assumed. Maybe that was one of the reasons, maybe the major reason that Jack had emigrated from Danny's apartment to one of his own. Jack knew, or at least he should have known, that his own problems with booze made close proximity to anyone else with a similar problem a dangerous combination Jack had been an alcoholic most of his adult life, a condition about which he was not only aware but about which he used to boast. But in the last few months of his life, when he knew that his health was failing, he had given up the booze, which he often characterized as "my best friend". He also reluctantly gave up smoking, which he sometimes compared to oxygen. Speaking of which, he had been permanently affixed to his oxygen tank prior to his passing. Jack had also given up on almost everything that could be considered unhealthy, to the point of abstaining from almost all food and drink. Fact was that whatever snacks, mainly coffee, cookies and the occasional donut, that Mark and Jill would bring him every day were pretty well the only nourishment that Jack consumed those last few months. Although he never discussed it with Jack, he had assumed that Danny had provided Jack with some sort of sustenance when Mark or Deborah weren't around, that is on the weekends.

Danny settled back down into his chair, sinking down like he was about to turn in for a nap, brought the bottle to his mouth and took another slug, spilling some on the front of his t-shirt, prompting a snort and a jaunty wave of the vodka bottle. Mark couldn't help but laugh. It reminded him of a skit from a television show. The shared guffaws seemed to re-energize Danny who suddenly leaned forward and looked at Mark with a comically quizzical expression on his face, like he was continuing the skit. His laughter subsided and then an uncharacteristic seriousness suddenly descended over him. He stared at Mark and then asked a fairly obvious question. "What do you think Jack had in that safety deposit box?"

Mark shrugged. "I don't know. I'm just curious, that's all."

Danny shrugged in response himself. "Curious? Hey, I may be an idiot but I know you're not. You must have some idea ---- you know, like a treasure map or something?" Danny laughed again, took another drink and then turned earnest again. "Who knows, maybe he left a will or a stack of cash in that box?"

Mark nodded. "That I doubt." He then looked up at Danny and offered additional speculation, conjecture that he suspected that Danny himself could have been considering. "Look, I thought about it but I still think it unlikely. And, let's face it, there's no way in the goddamn world that Jack had any money. I mean, where would he get it anyway? He didn't have a job --- fact was he hadn't had a job for...what, three years or so. He was on disability for god sake, a lousy $850 a month. That and maybe a $200 a month from some insurance/annuity policy." Mark paused for a moment and then continued his supposition. "And what was the rent on the dump he lived in?"

Danny nodded. "Well, my dump costs me $1,100 a month. I think his place cost him maybe $800."

"And then there's food --- not that he ate or drank much, didn't smoke --- not much there. That wouldn't leave him with much to stash away in a safety deposit box, right?" Mark pointed out with a certain emphasis, a deliberate grin spreading on his face.

Danny nodded, one of his well-known dumb looks on his face. "Right. He never had much money, even when he was living with me and paying only half of $1,100 every month. But he was still smoking and drinking a bit then. He even used to pay for his dope, a little coke every now and then, some meth, you know, this and that, that is before he found out that he was sick. After that, he was still interested in drugs but not the kind that I could get for him."

"I think I know what that's all about." Mark, nodded. Though Mark was generally familiar with Jack's living habits, having reported there every weekday morning for months, he was not aware of Jack's recent drug habits. Fact was he had been under the impression that Jack had been clean for a few months before he passed away, at least according to what Jack had been telling him. Apparently he had been wrong.

Danny was only too happy to expand on his story of Jack's medical problems. He was always ready, if not enthusiastic to provide commentary on the behavior of others, particularly if it was unusual in some way. He often talked, if not boasted about the psychology courses he had audited at Carleton University. And given the neighborhood in which they both had lived, he had plenty of opportunities for observation. He could have written a soap opera with plenty of curious characters.

Danny continued without any further prompting. "Once he knew that he was seriously sick --- I remember he gave me a full explanation; you'd think he was thinking of going to medical school. He used to talk about stuff like white blood cells, blood plasma, platelets, whatever the hell they are or were. He sounded like he was actually proud of being sick and that to me is sick. He started reading books about his conditions ---- I don't remember how many medical problems he may thought he had. The more he read, the worse seemed to feel."

Mark agreed. He too had been audience to a number of Jack's medical lectures although apparently not in the same level of detail as Danny had received. He had occasionally transported Jack to the hospital where he received various treatments. Based on the description of the care he said he had received, Mark thought that Jack probably had cancer and that he was receiving chemotherapy or radiation, not that he actually knew anything about either cancer or its treatments. He never did, however, find out the cause of Jack's passing nor did he ever think about it. He had been seriously ill and that conclusion was enough he supposed. Besides, he thought as he was exchanging medical insights with Dr. Danny Beliveau, what possible difference would that make anyway? He did wonder, however, whether a death certificate had been issued and whether it had been submitted to someone. He didn't think about it for very long.

Danny returned to his inquiry regarding the possible contents of Jack's safety deposit box. "If it wasn't cash and if it wasn't a will, then what the hell could Jack have kept in any safety deposit box? Come on, man, what the hell could it be?" Danny asked, a funny little grin on his face and his hands spread out in curiosity.

"Who knows? Family heirlooms maybe although I doubt it. Could be photographs, baseball cards ---- maybe the guy had an old Mickey Mantle. He was a fan after all, a big fan." theorized Mark, reflecting on the possibility that Jack was a custodian of keepsakes.

Danny shrugged and then, in a rare moment of insight, posed an interesting question. "Maybe the guy was keeping secrets."

"Secrets? What do you mean, secrets?" asked Mark, a trifle stunned by Danny's inquiry. Danny's reference to secrets prompted a flash of a memory of Jack mentioning that possibility, some mystery to which Jack vaguely referred during one of those last conversations the two of them had.

Danny leaned forward and attempted an explanation. "I don't know. Everybody has secrets I guess, even me, even you."

Mark was still contemplating that last discussion with Jack. He hadn't really heard Danny's obvious observation. Maybe Danny had been reading his mind.

Mark feebly responded. "What's that?" he asked.

Danny repeated his previous comment. "I just said that everybody has secrets. Maybe Jack was keeping one."

Mark was left blankly staring at Danny finishing his second partial bottle of vodka. He was still contemplating the question of whether his friend Jack actually had secrets, particularly that one secret that Jack might have been hiding and to which he vaguely suggested that last day Mark visited Jack's apartment.

The two sat facing each other in silence for several minutes. Danny was now holding his third bottle, this one looked like there was maybe three or four ounces left. However, as Danny pointed out almost immediately, the third bottle contained ginger ale, not vodka. He was smiling at Mark. "Hey, look, I have a limit ---- only two bottles a day and they were only half full."

"That's wise I guess." said Mark. There was another pause and then Danny asked. "So what are you going to do now?"

Mark started to get out of his chair. "Well, it's obvious, isn't it? I now know where he probably has his safety deposit box. I see no problem now. I'll find the box and whatever Jack kept in that box."

Danny also started to get out of his chair. "Need a hand with your, you know your investigation? I think it would be quite interesting, you know."

Mark shook his head, leaned over toward Danny, and slapped him on the left arm. "Thanks, Danny, but I don't think I'll be needing any help. But I'll let you know if I find anything". Mark could picture Danny Beliveau, who looked like his only experience with banking was to cash a social services cheque every month, standing at the counter in a bank.

THE SAFETY DEPOSIT BOX FOUND

Mark knew the building. It was the Royal Bank of Canada on Bank Street in Ottawa. It was housed in a local marvel of Victorian architecture, one of the more notable of the few such structures that still graced the city. He had been in the building five days a week in the mid-1970s when he had put in several unfortunate months as an administrative trainee. It was more memorable than that. While he was working there, he was conducting an affair with a married woman named Sharon who was a teller at that branch. They had both been married at the time, Sharon to a hot-tempered bus driver named Norbert and Mark to his first wife, a mild mannered woman named Christine who had two university degrees, a great job and a spectacular bosom. Mark could never quite explain, even to himself, the reasons for his passion for Sharon. She was hardly a knockout, drinking, smoking and recreational drug use having turned her into someone who looked like she required heavier makeup or hospitalization, her only redeeming characteristic an obvious interest in a good time. On the other hand, while Mark's relationship with his first wife was hardly without flaw, it had survived four years without serious incident. They hardly argued, the sex was acceptable to the both of them, or so Mark thought. In addition, Christine seldom complained about her husband's frequent periods of indolence, his aversion to long term employment, the only real source of any conflict between them.

On reflection, aside from her pursuit of a good time, about which Mark was previously aware through office chatter, it had to be Sharon's penchant for frequent sex that had attracted Mark to her. Her promiscuity was another source of office hearsay and had been evident from their first encounter. During his first week on the job, Mark had found himself in the vault with Sharon auditing the day's transactions when she suddenly informed him, in a barely audible, trembling, tearful voice, that she was having trouble concentrating. At first, Mark pretended not to have heard her although he did turn to face her.

"Pardon me?"

"I'm having trouble." Sharon said, "It's affecting my work."

"I'm sorry to hear that. Maybe you should just go home" answered Mark, a trifle formal, not wanting to discuss her personal problems, particularly since he had never actually spoken to her. He started to turn away when she put a hand on his arm.

Sharon looked at him and nodded. "I can't go home. That's where I'm having the trouble."

"What makes you say that?" asked Mark, nervously. He had turned back toward Sharon.

"My husband. I might run into him ---- I don't want to see him right now. He usually goes to work before I get home." Sharon explained.

"Well, why don't you just take a break, have a seat outside in the office. I can finish up here." offered Mark, finding himself looking at Sharon a little more intently.

"Oh, you're sweet." replied Sharon, her grip on his arm softly tightening. He was still a little nervous. The tears were gone. Mark started to fiddle with the papers that the two of them had been examining. His embarrassment was obvious, at least he thought so. Several moments went by as Mark continued to tinker with bank deposit and withdrawal slips and Sharon stood there looking at him. There was a silence for a couple of moments. She hadn't left the vault.

"Maybe I shouldn't mention it but my husband hasn't made love to me in months. I think that's our main problem." Mark looked up from his ministrations, stunned. There was another intermission between the two of them.

It was obvious, too cliched an opening to ignore. In fact, Mark's response to Sharon's pathetic admission was almost unnecessary, so predictable was its intention. "I find that hard to believe." Mark should not have been surprised but was a trifle dismayed when Sharon offered him a look of practiced coyness. It was as if, as Mark was to later conclude, she had heard comparable comments from a number of other men in similar circumstances. She then loosened her grip from his arm, leaned up toward him, kissed him on the cheek, and whispered in a dark purr. "Yes, you sure are sweet." She then walked out of the vault, leaving Mark with the day's paperwork, which may have been her plan all along Mark thought.

Within a week, Mark was committing adultery, the result of a number of flirtatious exchanges between them.

Their first encounter was a surprisingly efficient coupling that had lasted barely five minutes and had left both of them close to fainting. For the next month or so, Mark and his illicit consort Sharon managed to share sex acts two or three times a week, in all sorts of interesting locales --- in the telephone booth on the second floor of their building, in each other's apartments when their respective spouses were out, mainly Mark and Christine's place since Sharon had two kids. There was also the back seat of a city bus, in a taxi cab, in the lunch room at work, and predictably in the vault of the bank. But for reasons that Mark could not completely comprehend, the affair ended as quickly as it had begun, the conclusion of his stint as an administrative trainee likely having had something to do with it.

There was, however, an interesting consequence of the end of the affair. Afterward, sex with the betrayed Christine proceeded with unfamiliar enthusiasm. Mark never knew whether she had suspected something was amiss. It was almost as if he was attempting to imitate passions that he and Sharon had generated, including acts for which Christine had previously shown little appetite. Mark later thought that he and Christine had stayed together for a couple years longer than they might have, if they had not developed that renewed sexual enthusiasm.

Scenes recalled from his sexual autobiography, particularly his trysts with Sharon, were flooding through his mind as he climbed the marble stairs of the Royal Bank. Mark was alone, having avoided a semi-serious discussion with Danny about the suggestion that he accompany Mark to the bank. By the time Mark reached the top of the stairs, he had attracted the attention of a bank official, a tall, statuesque young woman behind a counter. The woman was blessed with a spread of dread locks carefully arranged with colored ribbons on the top of her head, a line of pink rhinestone crawlers on each ear, a single diamond on her upper lip. Her complexion was the color of bronzed coffee. She had vivid brown eyes, makeup that likely required a professional application, and a fluorescent blue design on her nails that belonged in a fashion magazine. Her name was appropriate ---- Jasmine, a fanciful letter *J* emblazoned on the name plate affixed to the right lapel of a maroon blazer with yellow piping, the final feature of her outfit. Mark was no longer even remotely aroused, he was intimidated. It was eleven o'clock in the morning.

She greeted him with a voice that was in line with her persona, a voice that would be more appropriate emanating from a rhythm and blues song, not a voice but a melody, an imperious melody. "Can I help you, sir?" Mark was struck with something close to paralysis, overcome by an inexplicable feeling of anxiety that he had not experienced for years, if not decades. For a moment, maybe more than a moment, he started to search his pockets for a Xanax or an Ativan, the remedies to which he would previously turn when a flash of panic went through him. But he did not have any medication, not even an aspirin. He stood there, almost trembling. He was fighting an inclination to retreat, just like he would have in the old days. He started to breathe deeply, inhaling and exhaling, long past therapy sessions with a psychiatrist named Henry suddenly retrieved.

"Yes, yes." Mark mumbled almost inaudibly. Jasmine had to lean over the counter to hear him. Her perfume was intoxicating, another aspect of her that seemed designed to control almost every circumstance in which she found herself. She could easily have been a model ---- if not a model, at least a sales woman in the cosmetic section of a high end department store. He briefly considered the reason for her career choice. To Mark, it seemed curious. It also seemed a little tiresome, maybe even chauvinistic. He later felt guilty about pursuing such a thought. There were countless beautiful women working in all sorts of occupations, including banking, he thought. After all, she was the second beautiful woman he had encountered working in a local bank over the past few days. Any fleeting observation regarding Jasmine slowly evaporated as she repeated her offer to assist him. She leaned closer. Mark stepped back, concentrating on his purpose. He was still nervous.

"My name is Mark Purcell. I'm here to recover the safety deposit box of a Mr. Jack Quinn who recently passed away." said Mark. "I have a document here giving me access to his box." He held the "Certificate of Appointment of Estate Trustee" up to Jasmine who initially seemed a little puzzled and then annoyed. "A what?" She had quickly developed a look that suggested that she was about to begin attending to the maintenance of those spectacularly stylish fingernails, the classic bored look.

Mark answered, the volume a little louder this time. "It's a legal document that gives me access to Mr. Quinn's bank records, that sort of thing. That includes any safety deposit box he may have. And Jack Quinn has, I mean had a box in this branch."

Jasmine seemed to drop her bored look for a moment. She evidently posed a question. "Do you know for a fact that this man Quinn had a safety deposit box in this branch?"

"Yes. He had a chequing account in this branch. I found a cheque book from this branch in his apartment." Mark reported and further explained. "And I assume that if he did have a safety deposit box, he would have one in this branch, not any other bank."

Jasmine seemed a little more interested. "And how do you know that Mr. Quinn had a safety deposit box at all?" Coming from Jasmine, her question sounded like the beginning of an interrogation.

"He had a key, a key that looks like it would open a safety deposit box." declared Mark, having reached in his pocket for the key, which he then held up for Jasmine's examination. After about ten seconds or so, during which time Jasmine looked to be pondering her next comment, she continued with her interview. "Could that key be to one of those boxes that are available at postal stations?"

"Maybe but I doubt it." replied Mark. "I used to go over to his place practically every day. He used to get mail at his place, not much but mail nevertheless. That was before before the post office had decided to use street post boxes. So you see that he have no reason to keep a mail box." Mark paused and then added a conclusion for Jasmine's benefit. "So I guess that key cannot be for anything other than a safety deposit box."

Jasmine thought about it for a moment and then did what she probably should have as soon as Mark presented himself in front of her at the counter. She told him that she would have to consult her superior, apparently a woman named Ms. Butterworth. She gave Mark another bored look, a theatrical little shrug and then was on the telephone for Ms. Butterworth. She then gestured toward a semi-circle of light blue chairs. He wordlessly walked toward them. He sat down, looked through a fan of magazines that was spread out on a table under a huge wide screen television. Amazingly enough, it was showing a silent *Three Stooge* episode. Someone must have changed the channel from the usual dull business fare. Another man waiting for somebody or another was laughing out loud. Mark noticed that such obviously unusual behavior, at least for a bank, had prompted several bank officials to look up from their computer screens. Mark actually recognized the *Three Stooge* episode that was playing on the television. ---- it was called *Brideless Groom,* an installment that involved Shemp Howard's accidental nuptials to a tone-deaf woman who also happened to be taking piano lessons. Mark joined the other man in laughter.

Mark watched the rest of the episode after which an officious looking woman in an expensive black suit and red horn rims appeared with a converter and changed the channel.

A white haired man stood in front of an array of computer screens displaying stock prices. He looked to be weary, almost close to sleep, a familiar face. The office entertainment was now back to the usual business programming. Mark looked away as did the other man waiting for a meeting. He was thumbing through a recent edition of one of the many business magazines available on the table in front of him when Ms. Butterworth appeared with an outstretched hand of greeting. Mark stood up quickly.

"Hello, Mr. Purchell. My name is Ruth Butterworth. I understand you're looking for one of our safety deposit boxes." She was a tall, attractive looking woman in her late thirties. She was wearing a white blouse under a gold jacket, black trousers, and black pumps with short heels. She wore two rings on her left hand and silver bracelets around both wrists. Mark also noticed that she was sporting a triangular gold and maroon necklace. It looked expensive.

Mark was not nearly as intimidated as he was with her associate Jasmine. She had a calm voice, easily listenable. He was immediately drawn to the woman, so pleasant was her voice. He actually wanted to speak to the woman. "Yes, I have a document, a "Certificate of Appointment of Estate Trustee" ---- I showed it to your colleague. It allows access to any safety deposit box that my friend Jack Quinn may have in this bank." Mark had the certificate under his left arm, transferred it to his right hand and showed it to Ms. Butterworth. She took it from him, little more than glanced at it, nodded and handed it back.

Ms. Butterworth informed Mark that Jack Quinn did indeed have a box on the premises, a box he had rented only six months ago. She said she was prepared to give him the box, provided that he was able to produce a copy of the "Death Certificate" and sign a release form. She held up a master key. Fortunately for the both of them, Mark had been carrying a scrunched up copy of the

"Death Certificate" in his wallet since he had received it. He carefully unfolded the certificate and handed it to Ms. Butterworth who predictably took it from Mark as if it had just come out of an oven or a garbage pail, the expression on her face suddenly and quietly appalled. He immediately apologized. Ms. Butterworth managed a tight smile and then asked him to accompany her to her office. She turned and headed toward the rear of the branch. Mark followed her. He noticed that she had a fine figure. One of her colleagues, a woman with an office to the right of Ms. Butterworth's office, looked at Mark with a funny little grin on her face. He didn't think that Ms. Butterworth saw him looking at her. At least, he hoped not. He felt guilty for some reason.

She led Mark into a large, rectangular office at the end of the hallway. Safety deposit boxes of two distinct sizes had been installed on three of the four gray colored walls of the room, the forth wall blank except for the door. There was a waist high silver aluminum table standing by the door. It was equipped with wheels. As she walked into the room, Ms. Butterworth picked up a clipboard that had been laying on the rolling table and then pushed the table away from the door. She waved Mark into the room and gestured toward the safety deposit boxes. She then picked up the clipboard and, using the forefinger of her left hand, began to survey a list of names on the third or fourth page of the batch of papers that were held by the clipboard. The page had been previously folded over for easy reference. It was obvious that the list had already been checked. Ms. Butterworth quickly found the name she was looking for.

"There's my check mark ---- Mr. Quinn has box number 275." said Ms. Butterworth. "You know, Mr. Quinn has paid for the box for another seven months. I don't know why I'm telling you but it's available, if you want to use it. And oh, can I have your key?" she asked.

Mark, who had been holding the key since they both started down the hallway to the safety deposit box room, handed it over to Ms. Butterworth and moved a little closer. Ms. Butterworth turned around, stepped up to the box Mark had rented and put both the master key and Mark's key into the door behind which sat Jack's box. She pulled out a long rectangular black box which she then placed on the table. She smiled and observed, "Just like in the movies, right?"

Mark smiled back and replied. "And now you're going to give me the box and lead me to a small room where I get to look through the box?" Ms. Butterworth curtly nodded, handed him the box and waved him out of the room. She steered him into a cubicle with a plastic windowed door, a small desk and a folding chair. Mark sat down, placed the box on the desk and watched Ms. Butterworth leave. She slid the door closed and left Mark to his probe of Jack's safety deposit box. Mark sat and stared at the box for a minute or so before he lifted the latch and opened it. Inside the box was a plain white envelope with a simple handwritten caption in block letters: "To My Friend Mark". Inside the envelope was a single page statement and a wallet size black and white photograph of a young boy sitting in the arms of a man who Mark immediately guessed was his father. The boy, who was wearing a pair of tattered overalls over a checkered shirt, appeared to be maybe two years old. The man, who looked to be in his late twenties, was leaning on the fender of a vintage Chevrolet sedan. Mark studied the photograph for a moment. It was faded, yellowed and creased. He carefully put the picture in his wallet.

As for the letter, the more important piece of evidence he assumed, it was handwritten in printed block letters, the penmanship remarkably neat. The tone was surprisingly lucid, considering that the author might well have written it under duress so to speak, as ill as he was. It may have taken him an entire day to draft it. It did not contain a salutation and had not been dated. However, from its opening line and the fact that Jack had rented the safety deposit box only six months ago, it was easy to conclude that it was written within months before his passing. Mark proceeded to read.

> "As I write this, I know that I will soon, like they say, shuffle off this mortal coil. If you're reading this then, buddy, I have already shuffled. You have found the key to my safety deposit box and opened the box. Way to go.
>
> I'm sorry I didn't say anything to you earlier, like when I was still around but I just didn't. Don't know why. Anyway, as you have probably already figured out, I don't have any money or anything else of value to leave. But I do leave you with a mystery that I hope you will investigate. By the way, before you ask yourself, I didn't know there was a mystery until quite recently. So I never had the chance to look into

it myself but hell, in my condition in the last year or so, I doubt I could look into anything.

For almost all my life, all but the last two months or so, I thought that I was born to Robert and Eileen Quinn. I have enclosed a picture of my father, Robert. Even though you may remember that I used to talk about being adopted, mainly because I thought my parents were lousy parents ---- my mother almost admitted it one Christmas when she told me that my father was probably the best she could do in the circumstances. Anyway, I didn't really think that much about the adoption thing until one of my cousins, a guy named Glen Quinn, the son of my father's brother, a guy I haven't seen or heard from in maybe thirty years, showed up at my place one Saturday afternoon a couple of months ago. He said he got my address from somebody at my old office. The crazy bastard said he wanted to visit me because his father thought it was the right thing to do. I don't know why my uncle thought so but that's what he told his son, my cousin. Apparently, my uncle had found out that I was sick and would not be around much longer. Deborah had been in touch with the old man and must have told him of my condition. I don't know why she stayed in touch with him but she did. I asked her about it. She said she had. But I didn't tell her what I am about to tell you. It just didn't seem right.

My cousin told me that his father had wanted me to know that I was actually adopted when I was a little boy, no more than two years old. According to Glen, his father said that there was something funny about the adoption. Glen's father said that he didn't know exactly what was odd but had understood that it was. Apparently, it remains this big family mystery. Again according to Glen, only my parents, my uncle, Glen's father, my aunt, Glen's mother, and Glen himself apparently know the story. Only Glen and his father are still around.

Ever since Glen told me, I have naturally been obsessed with the circumstances regarding my adoption. I have been thinking about it almost constantly. Not much else to think about I'm afraid. I know I should have told you and maybe Deborah but I just didn't. I thought that it would be more appropriate that I wait until I could ask you to grant a dead friend his last wish so to speak. I'm asking you with this letter.

The only physical clue I have is the enclosed photograph of my adopted father Robert Quinn and I, taken sometime in the mid-1950s. I can also tell you that the picture was taken in a little town called Truscott on Cape Breton Island in Nova Scotia where both Robert and Eileen Quinn were supposedly born. That is all I can tell you. Maybe some of the people who still live there can give you a clue. I've been told

> *that people there like to talk, talk about their*
> *history. So they say. Maybe they''ll remember*
> *for you. Good luck."*

The note was signed Jack Quinn, RIP. Mark considered his farewell as Jack's final attempt at sarcasm. Mark sat there contemplating the photograph and Jack's last will and testament. After a couple of minutes, during which time Ms. Butterworth tapped on the door to his cubicle a couple of times, Mark Purchell had decided that he would proceed with the investigation of the adoption of Mr. Jackson Quinn, now deceased. He got up from his chair, left the cubicle, thanked Ms. Butterworth and left the bank, the photograph and the note from Jack now in his possession. That was the first step in his investigation.

A SMALL TOWN IN NOVA SCOTIA

He had to admit it, even to himself. Despite his determination to avoid a sedentary retirement, Mark was unusually indolent after he concluded his career as a government functionary. But he didn't have any hobbies, pastimes or other pursuits by which to occupy his time. Consequently, the prospect of a project as potentially fascinating as a search for the origins of a mysterious adoption changed his disposition. Fact was that Mark was almost excited to be taking on such an investigation. It was a feeling with which he had not been familiar for years, particularly since he retired.

His first decision was to study the town of Truscott. He had assumed that the adoption, if there actually had been an adoption, occurred in Truscott. He thought it prudent to become acquainted with the town if he was to travel there to get to the bottom of Jack's mystery adoption. His initial internet search revealed that Truscot was a virtually a village ---- less than 800 people lived there. Mark thought that if he were to suddenly appear in Truscott and start asking questions, which to him was likely the only way to discover whatever secret laid beneath

Jack's adoption, he would have to at least appear to be acquainted with the details of the town. His strategy was to shade the truth somewhat, to present himself as being intimate with the town, its history having been related to him he would say by his second cousin, Jack Quinn. Mark thought that such a narrative would somehow be more convincing than the actual story. He thought people in small towns were more likely to be cooperative in talking about former neighbors with family members, as opposed to inquisitive outsiders. As an additional cover, he would tell the good citizens of Truscott that he was there to research the family tree, a pretense that would likely be well received given the assumed ethos of the village of Truscott.

According to the Wikipedia entry, Truscott was a village on the northern shore of Brae d'Or Lake on Cape Breton Island in Elizabeth County, somewhere near the bottom of the famed Cabot Trail. According to the village website, some local scholars claim that Truscott was named after its first citizen, a Scottish settler who landed in the area in the 1840s after deserting from a British naval ship. Interest in the village's historical narrative was made noteworthy by the tale that the original Mr. Truscott, his original Christian name Hector, had escaped from the ship with a woman who remained anonymous for reasons that were never explained by the historical record. The most generally accepted myth, however, was that the woman was married to the ship's captain, who also remained unidentified by the British navy for reasons of 19th century propriety. Regardless of the story's actual origin, it was long accepted that Hector Truscott and his female partner had started the village's first family and had lived there for several years before they were joined by other immigrants. Almost all had arrived from Scotland via the then active port of Halifax, Nova Scotia. By 2011, the village had a population of 855, many with assumed Scotch heritage. After coming across that fact, Mark wondered whether Hector Truscott was an ancestor of Jack Quinn. That curiosity would fit in well with his masquerade as a pilgrim researching his family tree.

The remainder of Truscott's history was hardly edifying. The listing of historical dates started from the formal establishment of the village in 1855 in Elizabeth County. It included such momentous occasions as the incorporation of the village in 1908, the construction of the Truscott Psychiatric Hospital in 1875 and the village post office in 1924, the 1933 birth of an Olympic sprinter named Gilbert Gross, and the 1967 visit to the village by Queen Elizabeth II. Like most Wikipedia entries regarding small towns and villages, the entry for Truscott had a list of a dozen notable residents, starting of course with Hector Truscott and including such historical luminaries as Percy Baxtor, a science fiction writer, several federal and provincial politicians, a man named McNabb who served four terms as the reeve of Truscott, a priest named Kelly who eventually ascended to the post of Archbishop of Albany, New York, and an allegedly famous astronomer named McConomy. There was also an entry regarding the only school located in the area, a primary/secondary school, the Truscott Academy. The final entry was a paragraph regarding the local tourist attractions, including the fact that the village featured

200 hotel rooms, a curious statistic given that only 855 people lived there, at least in 2011. The tourist attractions advertised included the lake-front Truscott Bay resort, a golf course, flea markets in the summer, skating on the lake in the winter, small shops, restaurants, and, in a curious reference, the local branch of the Royal Canadian Legion. It was helpfully noted that the Legion was open to the public, provided live music and had long maintained a status as a watering hole.

Mark arrived at the Halifax Stanfield International Airport just after noon on a Monday in mid-October. It was curious he thought. Though retired, he was still conducting himself as if he was still working. That's the reason he decided to leave for Truscott on a Monday as opposed to a Tuesday for example. For Mark, it would be like a work week. He had taken a flight on one of the smaller airlines, a choice that he usually avoided if he could, slight claustrophobia the main difficulty. The plane was filled to capacity, 30 people in ten rows, two seats on one side and one on the other. Fortunately for Mark, he had managed to acquire a single seat on the left side of the plane. As he usually did on most flights, he concentrated on watching a movie on the back of the seat in front of him, hoping that his bowels did not rebel against him. Two hours later, he disembarked from the plane, without any digestive incident to speak of, with the proverbial spring in his step. He headed for the second of the two baggage carousels available. A computer screen indicated that bags from a number of flights would be available on the second carousel, including from destinations as diverse as Newfoundland, Las Vegas and Ottawa. There was a crowd that included a bunch of people dressed in Hawaiian shirts and another group wrapped in ski jackets. He waited twenty minutes surveying the room. Most of the crowd seemed to be desperately manipulating their phones. Maybe he should have gone with a carry-on although he usually avoided troubling his fellow passengers with extraneous luggage, the jostling, the bumping, the straining, the overhead bins opening and closing, a whole theater of annoyance.

Mark was standing next to an older man at the east end of carousel #2. He was dressed in a fairly expensive business suit, carrying an attache case, and seemed to be surgically though uncomfortably attached to his telephone. He was attempting to transmit a message, the stabbing of his fingers on the screen threatening his grip on the telephone, the required dexterity obviously eluding, if not perplexing him. Once he had managed to complete his text, he looked up, scanned the baggage sliding by, audibly sighed, and stood there slumped over like he was about to pass out. Mark was looking at him when the older man started to mutter about the efficiency of the Halifax airport. He was talking to himself, actually whispering. Mark could hear him, albeit barely. "I'll bet Bob Stanfield would have been pissed." Taking a look around, Mark quickly figured that he may have been the only passenger waiting for baggage who might have know who Bob Stanfield actually was. After all, the former Premier of Nova Scotia and leader of the federal Progressive Conservatives was hardly likely to generate much in the way of name recognition, particularly among a generation who spent the majority of its time hunched over a laptop, a tablet or a smart phone. As the bags started to tumble out onto the conveyor belt, the older man almost fell down lurching toward the carousel, starting the race toward collecting one's bags and heading out the entrance. The older man decided to just stand there waiting for his bag, no rush, no anxiety. Mark's bag then appeared. He picked it up, nodded to the older man, and then squeezed past two teenage girls giggling about something on their cellphones. Mark headed toward the car rental counter, where he planned to arrange for transport toward his ultimate destination, the bucolic domain of Truscott, Nova Scotia.

He walked up to one of the car rental counters ---- he had had the presence of mind to reserve a compact from Avis. A young man attired in a white shirt with a red *Avis* badge on the pocket, black tie and trousers, and a red uniform jacket was waiting. A big phony smile was pasted on his face like some sort of cosmetic. There was a form sitting on the counter in front of him. The young man had pushed the form toward Mark.

"Good morning, sir:" said the Big Phony Smile, his hand still on the paper now in front of both them. He tapped the paper and continued. "Mr. Purchell, I see that you have reserved a compact for a week. Where are you headed?"

Mark smiled back, his own effort to match big smile's congeniality too feeble either way to make an impression. He absentmindedly provided a reply. "Truscott."

"Truscott!" his voice suddenly up climbing up a couple of registers, "Truscott, why would anyone want to go up there?" He was kidding of course but to Mark, he imagined that Big Phony Smile was beaming like he was working the carnival crowd in bumpkin city. To complete the fantasy, all he needed was a striped straw boater, a white shirt with ornamental garters and a purple sash situated diagonally across his chest.

Mark thought that he knew what the guy may have been or should have been thinking and should have been moved to annoyance. But Mark didn't show it. He played it straight and simply replied. "I have business in Truscott."

Mr. Big Smile tilted his head to one side and produced what Mark could only have regarded as a smug look, his big smile now a sort of crooked line above his chin. Mark thought Big Smile was going to laugh or more likely snicker but he didn't. He just followed his smug with a shrug, content even though he had not understood the explanation provided by Mark. "Sorry but I've heard that there isn't much business up there anymore."

"Really?" countered Mark, a dismissive tone in his voice. He quickly went back to studying the rental form that Big Phony Smile had placed before him.

Big Phony Smile did not want to let the issue of Truscott's economy drop. "That's what everybody says. There's nothing much there ---- a lot of drinking, abandoned dairy farms, and some sort of junior hockey team --- that's about it."

Mark looked up from the form and offered Big Phony Smile another rebuttal. It was a firmly stated, stern rebuke. "Well, I've got business there." he still insisted.

The big smile started to disappear, shrinking into something verging on the bureaucratic. No longer smiling, the *Avis* counter man returned to business. "I see that you have asked for a compact. Will a *Ford Focus* do?"

"Yeah, sure." replied Mark.

"And how long will you need the car?" asked the *Avis* man.

"At least a week. I've reserved for a week." speculated Mark.

The *Avis* man leaned forward and started to smile again. "A week in Truscott? Boy, for your sake, I hope you have a few good books to read. Either that or maybe you'll be lucky enough to have access to *Netflix* or something like *Netflix*." With the comment, he nodded to the computer bag Mark Purchell had been holding that was now sitting by his feet. At least Mark had a laptop for entertainment.

Mark offered a tight smile. "As I say, I have business there. It will probably keep me busy enough."

"I hope so." He watched Mark sign the rental form and handed him the key fob to a 2016 black *Ford Focus*. "By the way, good luck with Truscott." Mark offered the *Avis* counter man his last forced smile of their encounter. The *Avis* man returned it with his last flash of smile, at least until the next customer, a young woman sporting fashionable spectacles and carrying an ostensibly brand new briefcase.

Within minutes, Mark was sitting in the *Ford Focus* in the parking lot, trying to familiarize himself with another new car instrument panel. He was always worried, those few times he did get behind the wheel of a new car, that he would accidentally activate the wrong function of the car by pressing the wrong device, making a fool of himself and threatening everyone else on the road. He fiddled around with the satellite radio, the telephone, the sun roof and the compact disc player. He inspected the glove compartment, briefly consulted the manual and noticed that the previous renter, a man named Cortland had left a receipt for four nights at the *Hilton Garden Inn Airport Hotel* and a half dozen *Durex Performa* prophylactics. Staring at the receipt and the *Durex Performas*, Mark immediately imagined a scenario involving a phantom business trip and an active extramarital affair. As he continued to ponder, Mark contemplated his own matrimonial histories, recalling the occasional opportunities for similar liaisons that he had been either too righteous or too scared to pursue. He also wondered whether his two ex-wives had ever taken advantage of such opportunities, at least without letting Mark know. In that context, his first wife, a lawyer named Gail whose early success had eventually doomed their marriage, had told him, even though the two of them were still living together, that she was sleeping with one of the partners in her firm, and would soon be requesting that he leave her presence. Mark remembered that he was hardly troubled by their separation, having seen its eventuality for the last two of the four years they were actually together. In fact, he later was told, when he ran into one of her friends, that she had stayed with him for at least a year simply because "the sex was too good to give up even though the guy providing it was a bum." As for his second wife, Mark had no idea as to whether she had ever been unfaithful although he would have been both surprised and indifferent, their mutual interest in sex barely perceptible. Fact was that they were hardly ever intimate, once a month the average frequency.

Although his rented *Ford Focus* was equipped with a GPS, Mark had never knew how such devices worked. He preferred instead to consult a map. Mark had picked up one of a map of Nova Scotia from the *Avis* counter after he had been given the keys to the car. Mr. Avis had winked. It was almost 350 kilometers from Halifax to Truscott, a little less than a four hour trip. He figured he would be checking into the Truscott Bay Hotel by six o'clock that evening, in time for a nice lobster dinner, supposedly the epicurean specialty of the region. As he had previously noted, the car was also equipped with satellite radio. After fiddling around with the dial for a while, Mark settled on a channel that played so-called classic vinyl, basically well known songs from the late 60s and early to mid-70s. Although he was generally satisfied with the playlist, Mark found the DJ annoying. The man had a deep sonorous voice that was constantly suggesting that he was somehow personally engaged in the production of every classic song he played, particularly the more obscure, Mark surmised this implied that the less popular the song, the more likely it would be admired by the truly discriminating, the inclination of those annoying hippies who Mark knew in college. So every now and then, a truly excruciating number by bands with names like Captain Beefheart, Atomic Rooster, Foghat, or Uriah Heep would come booming out of the speakers like tornado warnings. Mark would then change the channel, preferring for example the mindless rhythms of dance music or the innocent tunes of the early 1960s. Nonetheless, it was still strangely coincidental, if not serendipitous that the annoying DJ was playing something by Black Sabbath when a man appeared on the side of Highway 105 just outside of New Glasglow with his thumb out. Mark had been on the road for a hour or so.

Mark had not seen many hitchhikers recently, let alone picked up any hitchhiker for years. It used to be a fairly common practice but no longer it seemed. Sure, hitchhiking was a popular, if not routine mode of transportation when Mark was in his late teens. For a time, particularly among people who considered themselves in the tribe, it was akin to asking for spare change. As for Mark, he often attempted to hitch rides, a common practice. He didn't have access to a car, his father was opposed to him driving any kind of vehicle that had an engine, and hitchhiking seemed preferable to the bus or the train, cost being a primary consideration. In addition, there was the cultural requirement thing. He did remember, however, that the last time he managed to hitch a ride, an unfortunate experience occurred. It was late one Saturday night, early Sunday morning in June, in the early 1970s. Mark was standing on the shoulder of Highway 2 and 20 just west of 40th Avenue in Lachine, the West Island of Montreal, heading home. His thumb was out and he was smoking a cigarette. He was a little high, a little weed and maybe a few beers having done the trick. He had just left his so-called girlfriend of the moment, Diane, with whom he had spent an hour or so amorously wrestling in the basement playroom of her parents' house. He might have been standing out on the highway for about ten minutes when he got an overwhelming need to urinate. With his back to the highway, he was in the process of relieving himself when a police car, its red light and horn fully operational, was suddenly behind him. Mark turned to face a police officer holding a flash light. The officer pointed at Mark's crotch.

Mark stood stock still and mute, his zipper still open, his bowels now rebelling, he felt close to fainting. The officer, shining his flashlight in Mark's eyes, demanded to know what he had been doing, standing there on the shoulder of the highway. He knew that any smart aleck response was out of the question, not that he could think of any. He couldn't speak. He was scared. The police officer wasn't a local cop but a member of the recently established and dreaded Montreal Urban Community (MUC) police force. The cop with the flashlight motioned Mark into the car. Mark noticed the back door of the police car was open. He got into the backseat and the driver, a pudgy middle aged guy who had an unfiltered cigarette stuck motionless in his mug like he was posing for a photograph. The driver grunted, put the car in gear, and took off like the officers had been ordered to pursue a fugitive. Mark sat in the backseat, desperately trying to control his bowels and his anxiety, staring at nothing in particular, like he was riding in a taxi cab on its way to perdition.

The police officers never asked for his name or his address, no identification, no frisking, nothing but a motioning gesture into the backseat of their cruiser. They just continued to drive, the cops speaking to each other in French, the tone congenial, almost jovial, without any apparent interest in their frightened passenger now sitting paralyzed in the backseat. One of them, the cop who had held the flashlight, was drinking from a silver flask. They both continued to smoke. Despite a few mumbled words of almost pitiful complaint, they drove past the exit sign to Valois, where Mark lived. It seemed like they were accelerating past the Valois exit. They had both laughed as the Valois exit sign disappeared into the rear view mirror. They drove for another ten minutes or so, out past Pointe Claire and out past Beaconsfield. They then slowed down and stopped the car, without comment. The police officer who had been holding the flash light turned around, looked at Mark with a smirk on his face and motioned him out of the car. Mark got out of the car like he was escaping, not like he was being released, just escaping. Once out of the car, Mark managed to close the door just before the car sped off. Mark stood at the side of the road, trembling and wondering exactly where he was, maybe five or six miles past his exit, the Valois exit. His trousers were strained with urine and subsequently befouled, an accident that prompted a flash of light from one of the cops and a roar of sinister laughter from the other. He wanted to remove them but didn't. He turned east and started to walk home, retracing his steps. He arrived home around three o'clock that morning. The house was dark and empty. Fortunately, his parents were away on vacation. No more hitchhiking. Never again, he thought, never again. And he could not recall ever going back on that commitment.

The hitchhiker looked like a classic veteran of a cultural war that had started in the mid-1960's, a hitchhiking ragamuffin straight out of a moment in history that took place on a 600 acre farm in Bethel, New York almost fifty years ago. Come to think of it, thought Mark, the man could easily have been an older associate of Jack Quinn's neighbor, Danny Beliveau. Either way, within seconds of stopping the car and motioning him into the car, Mark was unable to explain his decision to offer a lift to the man whom he later came to know as Jacob Fagan. He had been inexplicably inspired and then, almost simultaneously, regretted that inspiration. But by the time any regret had occurred to him, however, the man was already in the car. The moment passed and Mark put the car into gear. Fagan then informed Mark that his destination was Port Hawksbury, a town of little more than 3,000 people on the southwest corner of Cape Breton Island, more than halfway to Truscott. Mr. Fagan apparently would be with him for more than an hour. What could he do now? He was already in the damn car.

"I hope that's cool, chief." said Jake, a big grin on his buffoon face. He then pulled out a cigarette and held it towards Mark . "Is this cool too?" Already regretting one mistake, Mark compounded it by making another. Even then, having given up smoking maybe ten years ago after two heart attacks and resultant surgery, he was still disturbed by proximity to a lit cigarette. But he nodded and rolled Jake's window down. "Very cool, thanks." Jake fired up his smoke and leaned back to inhale. He then immediately informed Mark that while he appreciated transport to Port Hawksbury, where he hoped, as he put it, to re-establish an association with an old girlfriend who owned "a big farm", his ultimate destination was Baddeck. This was an equally insignificant burg that was about a hundred kilometers past Port Hawsbury up through the middle of Cape Breton. He said that his parents were born in Baddeck, a village that he claimed was famous for two things: Alexander Graham Bell, whose family resided in Baddeck in the late 1890's, and a rugby club that he said was one of the oldest in the Maritimes. Jake then added, with a mischievous grin out of a cloud of smoke, that Baddeck was also known for a high level of alcoholism. This reputation he claimed was somehow connected to the many retired dairy farm owners who had sold out over the past several decades, now left with plenty of time and plenty of money. Jake said that the place had more taverns than they needed.

Mark had hoped his passenger wouldn't be too talkative. So, to encourage his passenger's possible silence, Mark turned up the volume on the radio. That was probably another mistake. Classic radio was playing Led Zeppelin. There was no surprise when Jake offered commentary "Stairway to Heaven --- wow, I sure as hell remember that one."

Staring straight ahead, Mark agreed. "Sure, we all remember it, maybe too well."

Jake chortled with a burst of cigarette smoke. "Yeah, I know what you mean. I may have heard the song a thousand times, maybe two thousand times. But it's still a pretty good song, damn memorable, even now after all these years, especially that last guitar solo ---- classic, man, classic. Makes you want to fire up a doobie." He looked at Mark, who appeared to be a little anxious all of a sudden, smiled and shook his head. "Look, I didn't really mean it. Besides, I'm happy just having a smoke." He held up his cigarette and shrugged. Convinced that he had assured Mark that he wasn't about to mire the car in marijuana smoke, Mr. Fagan went into a predictable rhapsody about his experiences with Led Zeppelin. This included most particularly three concerts he had attended in Montreal sometime in the 1970's, at least one of which Jake laughingly said he could actually remember. Mark assumed that the last comment was related to the drug drenched stadium shows when everybody was intoxicated, one way or another, intentionally or not. Not surprisingly, Mark started to plunge into concert reminiscences himself. Historical remembrances were exchanged, some genuine, some imagined.

Predictably, Mark's memories could hardly match, at least in terms of sheer volume, if not excitement, Fagan's recollections. Fagan's narrations described maybe dozens of rock concerts although he said he had participated in a lot more. It sounded like Fagan may have attended hundreds of performances, a possibility that Mark found difficult to believe but the stories were comparably intimidating nevertheless. Fact was that Mark, who at one time regarded himself as an acceptable hippie, now realized that he had been little more than weekend poser, at least compared to a legitimate flower child like Fagan. Sure, he probably took in several dozen rock concerts over the years but his experiences were nothing close to the experiences residing in the resume of Jacob Fagan.

So he listened with some fascination as Fagan related, in unexpected chronological order, his attendance at rock concerts going back to the mid-1960s. Presumably, Fagan chose to cover only some of the highlights, including, fortunately enough, the two days he spent in August 1969 at Woodstock, a stay that would have been longer he confided if he had not got lost somewhere in Vermont. The man turned out to be quite the raconteur, waxing theatrically about an odyssey of musical performances, concentrating on the curious, the drug situation, and the mishaps at a few of the many concerts he had attended. He complained about the inconvenience of terrible weed and potentially harmful junk at some concerts and mishaps at others. His list included things like a broken leg at a concert at the Autostade in Montreal, a fractured skull when someone fell off the stage at an outdoor concert north of Toronto, speakers and other things falling on performers and the audience, countless drug related delays, canceled concerts, and a riot incited by the arrest of the lead singer of a popular British band for something or other.

They were thirty minutes from the exit for Port Hawksbury when it became obvious to the both of them that they had exhausted themselves with his tales of rock concerts going back forty years, maybe even fifty years, if Fagan's attendance at a Beach Boy concert in 1964 was counted. On that point, Fagan basically concluded his series of monologues by bemoaning the fact that one of his greatest disappointments was his failure to procure a ticket to a Beatle performance in Montreal in September in 1964. He explained that it wasn't really a matter of money, most of the tickets having gone he said to people with connections or good fortune. Fagan then threw up his hands, provided Mark with a mischievous wink, leaned his head back and looked like he intended to take a nap.

"Hey, Jake, we're only thirty minutes from Port Hawksbury." Mark pointed out. "No time for a nap." His time with Jake Fagan had gone by so quickly that Mark and presumably Jake Fagan were surprised that they were so close to Jake's destination.

Jake's head came forward. "Thanks." replied Jake. He fired up another smoke and asked Mark about his destination. "Hey, I never asked you. Where are you going? I guess it isn't Port Hawksbury. Right?"

Mark nodded. "Right. I'm going to Truscott. It was about 100 kilometers past Port Hawksbury, maybe a little more."

Like the *Avis* counter man with the big smile, Jake asked Mark an obvious question. "What are you're doing there? Do you have friends, relatives there?"

"No. I have business there?" explained Mark.

"Business? I don't know a lot about what goes on in Port Hawksbury --- I lived in Halifax for years and I've heard that nothing much goes on up there."

Mark shrugged "I don't know what goes on there but I plan to find out."

"Say what?" asked Jake, offering Mark an amusing quizzical look.

Mark nodded demonstratively. "I know, it sounds strange but I'm pursuing a kind of historical research project."

Jake started to laugh, almost snickering. Mark threw his hands off the wheel for a second and started to vigorously nod. "I know, I know. As I said, it's a bit weird but a good friend of mine may have had a family in Truscott that he didn't know he had and he certainly never met."

Jake uttered some noise approximating a low whistle. "So let me get it. You're basically looking for a family for someone else? You called it a historical project, like an academic study."

"Yeah, that's pretty much what I'm doing. But no, it isn't academic but it could be. No, it's personal." replied Mark, an embarrassed smile on his face.

"You've got to admit, that's pretty strange when you think about it. And why are you doing this in the first place?" Jake queried.

Mark was tempted although not overly so to explain to Jake the motive behind his investigation of the origins of Jack Quinn. Maybe Jake Fagan, purportedly well traveled and possibly blessed with the wisdom and perceptions of the road, could offer relevant advice to Mark. But as he was contemplating the prospect of letting his hitchhiking passenger in on the search for the origins of Jack Quinn, a sign appeared on the horizon informing traffic that Port Hawksbury was ten kilometers away. Despite the pleasure he had eventually derived from spending more than an hour conversing with Jake, Mark was still relieved to be on his own again, surprisingly so. The two of them rode in virtual silence for the next ten minutes. Jake smoked his last cigarette, at least his last in Mark's *Ford Focus*, and agreed to disembark by the exit sign for Port Hawksbury.

Mark stopped and Jacob got out of the car. He leaned back into the car, bumped fists with Mark, thanked him for the ride, and wished him luck with his search for the origins of Jack Quinn. Mark was surprised that Jake had not flashed him a peace sign.

Mark was now more than half way to Truscott. He turned east and then north on to the two lane Route 4 toward Dundee, a small community on the south end of Bras d'Or, the main body of water in the middle of Cape Breton Island. He stopped at a gas station just outside Port Hawksbury, filled up the tank. In the process of paying for the gas and a chocolate bar, Mark actually thought about purchasing a pack of cigarettes, a transaction that he had envisaged but not completed in more than a decade. He of course blamed the cigarettes that Jacob Fagan had enjoyed during their drive up from Halifax. He was surprised that he was able to resist so easily, at least until now. It was curiously predictable. He recalled when he first gave up cigarettes, more than ten years ago. He had had two heart attacks and was scheduled for a triple bypass, a procedure for which he was fated to wait for over two months. He had been smoking for almost forty years, a pack a day addiction that he quit every three years or so for a month or so before resuming the dreaded habit. While Mark had had a lot of difficulty giving up the weed between his heart attacks and his surgery, once the surgery was performed, it was easier, particularly with the help of a wife who had threatened a nice cot in the garage if he was caught smoking. His ten year old son would also occasionally look at him with what could have been tears in his eyes. So, despite the temptations afforded by three or four friends who were still using tobacco, he managed to survive the ten years since the operation without taking a single drag from a single cigarette, an achievement for which he was occasionally congratulated, usually by himself. It had become easier as the years of abstinence passed, particularly since the only two good friends he had who had smoked had passed away, their habits not insignificant to their eventual demise. That included Jack Quinn.

He passed through Dundee within thirty minutes. It was a small town, more like a village actually, appreciatively smaller than Port Hawksbury. It consisted of five stores, including a bank, two churches, a low slung brick building which may have been a school, a cemetery and maybe a dozen farm houses dotted along Route 4 around the centre of town. There was a large stone monument standing just past the two churches which were situated on the opposite sides of Route 4. Brass lettering with the town name Dundee and the year 1888 were affixed on the monument. It stood right before the cemetery, beyond which were scattered several dozen headstones in various states of decay, only one looking like it was erected within the last decade or so. As Mark passed through Dundee, he noticed only one person, an elderly woman leaving one of the churches. It was the middle of the afternoon. Mark wondered about the reason for the elderly woman's attendance. He wondered about any person's reason.

Just past Dundee, Mark turned back on Route 105 en route to Truscott. It did not take him long to came across another small town, this one was called Marble

Mountain, the site of a former marble quarry and a long abandoned steel plant, historical facts Mark had gleaned from his internet research. According to a website on Cape Breton, Marble Mountain Village was populated by 879 citizens, most of whom it was assumed hosted visitors attracted by a pristine white beach. The beach was presumably made both pristine and beautiful by the mining of white marble in the quarry that dominated the mountain behind the village. There were two clapboard churches beside each other on the same side of Route 105, one Catholic, Saint Joseph's, and the other United, Saint Matthew's. These two places of worship, regardless of their different denominations, looked almost identical with white clapboard, single steeples with crosses, shingled roofs, tall front doors,and similarly shaped stained glass windows. While Mark wondered whether the capacities of the two churches were similar, he did not consider stopping to inspect the interiors of two churches. He noted there were six stores, the website claimed seven stores, two hotels that had seen better days, something which may have been a fire station and a Royal Bank. On his way out of town, Mark counted at least three dozen farm houses set back from both sides of Route 105. Mark didn't any cemeteries or schools although a huge automobile graveyard sat on the furthest western edge of the town. There must have been hundreds of decaying automotive carcasses scattered across several acres of otherwise empty fields. Mark wondered about the origins of all those abandoned vehicles. It was strange. Mark thought that the story of the auto graveyard might make an interesting book or television documentary.

About twenty minutes outside Marble Mountain was a RCMP detachment, two squad cars and a pick up truck parked outside a small building.

In less than thirty minutes along Route 105, Mark came across another rural community, this one had the curious name of Whycocomagh, some sort of Indian name Mark assumed. A sign introducing the town informed travelers passing through that the town was populated by 525 people. Unlike Marble Mountain, the town had only one church. It was Anglican and looked to be much newer and much larger than the two churches in Marble Mountain. The town had five stores and a small bank, a Bank of Montreal. There was also an apartment building, an actual apartment building strangely situated on Route 105 in the small town of Whycocomagh. It presumably provided flats to citizens who couldn't afford a farmhouse or didn't want to live in one. To Mark, an apartment in a village like Whycocomagh was almost as strange a story as the auto graveyard. He did not see a school, a police station or a fire station. Perhaps there were hidden outside of town somewhere.

Truscott was now about forty minutes away, pretty well straight along Route 105, no landmarks to speak of, almost a Maritime version of the existential ennui of the Prairies. With nothing to see and nobody to talk to, the hour of silence since Jake Fagan disembarked was filled with the classic vinyl radio station, a lazy DJ playing Led Zepplin's greatest hits. Mark started to reformulate his plan to research the origins of the presumably adopted Jack Quinn. His rather superficial research into the town of Truscott and environs yielded several possible sources of information: the Truscott Public Library, the Heritage and Archives Department of the Municipality of Victoria County, two churches, two schools, a Royal Canadian Mounted Police detachment, the Royal Canadian Legion in Truscott and in Sydney. It was easily the largest, if not the only city in Cape Breton. Mark could also consult the Cape Breton Genealogy and Historical Association, and the Victoria County Memorial Hospital. He wasn't sure, however, as to where to begin his research.

As he drove, he reviewed his facts. Robert and Eileen Quinn, ostensibly his friend Jack's natural parents were now actually his adopted parents, apparently born in Truscott, Nova Scotia. Jack had a cousin named Glen and an uncle, Glen's father, name and location unknown. Mark had presumed that Glen's mother, again the name and location unknown, had either passed away or was separated, for one reason or another, from both her husband or her son. So there it was, the only unimpeachable information that Mark could use to prompt his investigation were the births of Robert and Eileen Quinn in Truscott. He concluded then that his first undertaking would be to confirm that Jack's parents, adopted or natural, were actually born in Truscott. His first stop then would be either the Victoria County Memorial Hospital or the Heritage and Archives Department of the Municipality of Victoria County. Both institutions were based in Truscott. Mark thought he would first contact the latter. By the time Mark had made that decision, he was turning off Route 105 on to Turley Road toward the Bras D'Or Lake and the Truscott Bay Hotel and Resort. It was a little after six o'clock in the evening.

The Truscott Bay Hotel and Resort looked more like a motel than a hotel, a rectangular assemblage of two dozen attached units built around an office/restaurant. A large wood sign announcing itself in frayed green lettering with black trim stood out on Turley Road. The Truscott, its presumed qualification for calling itself a resort being a restaurant/dining room, looked like it was built sometime in the 1950s. It evoked the ranch style architecture of the era, its major characteristics being its tan aluminum siding and its sloping orange slate roofs with little lattice work flourishes. Mark parked the car in front of the office and went into the office. A tall, thin man who had looked like he had been out back doing some sort of manual labour appeared at the small counter. Behind him was a large car dealership calendar, two dated pictures of The Truscott, a coffee machine and a dark brown door with an embedded green curtained window. Above the counter was a large fluorescent light illuminating the place like someone was about to perform surgery. To his left was a display stand holding two bags of potato chips. To Mark, the place sure as hell didn't look like a resort of any kind. It looked like a motel that would not have been out of place in an old television show, more like a set than an actual location, the weird decor of a hootenanny. No wonder Mark had been quoted such a reasonable rate, even though it was the highest in Truscott.

The man moved two papers that had been sitting on the counter, managed a vacant grimace and looked up. He addressed Mark with a greeting that he had not heard in years, "What can I do you for?"

Mark almost immediately recalled he had always been annoyed when he had heard that expression. It was usually employed by individuals who either possessed or had liked to feign a rustic charm. The man then immediately displayed a goofy country smile that was almost theatrical. The man was genuine, he wasn't impersonating anyone.

Mark returned the smile although not with the same corn-pone expression that the man behind the counter had offered him. "I have a reservation. My name is Mark Purchell."

The man behind the counter pulled out a ledger book from underneath the counter, laid it out on the counter, opened it to the page that had been marked with a thick elastic and skimmed down the page with his finger, which was curious since there was only one entry on the page, no doubt the page for Monday, October 16. "Yes, here it is, Purchell, Mark. You from Ottawa, eh?"

"That's right. I'm from Ottawa." replied Mark, a little irritated.

"Ottawa, nice spot I hear, my wife Daisy and I have always had plans to go up sometime but never made it." He paused and then asked, in a kind of humorous tone, "Work for the government, do you?" It almost sounded like an accusation to Mark. When Mark did work for the government, he had heard that question many times. He always thought it barely concealed sarcasm, particularly from citizens who lived in places like Truscott.

"I used to." answered Mark. "I'm retired now."

Another ironic smile emerged from the man behind the counter. "A retired government man, eh? I won't hold that against you but maybe I should be charging you double anyway." He paused, seemed to snicker to himself for a moment and then offered his hand over the counter. "By the way, my name is Heller, Tom Heller but you can call me Buster. Everybody does. I run this place."

Mark was mildly amused by Mr. Heller's volunteering his nickname. The moniker itself generally suggested a rotund individual rather than the slim, almost haggard man that stood behind the counter. Mark nodded and shook Mr. Heller's outstretched hand. "Nice to meet you." Mr. Heller then closed his ledger, reached under the counter again and then produced a registration card. He motioned to Mark to fill in and sign the card and then asked for his credit card. Heller announced the daily rate, which Mark already knew, and asked Mark to sign the card. He then looked up and apologized, explaining that the Truscott did not provide baggage porters and he would have to carry his own luggage up to Unit 150, a one bedroom suite, "the best in the house" according to Mr. Heller. He then provided Mark with a key, which was attached to a plastic red tag shaped like a fish. With an exaggerated exaggerated wink, he waved him out the door, telling him to park his car in the lot. He was sort of surprised that Heller had not asked him to park his car in front of Unit 150, just like the old days when family vacations almost invariably involved staying in chintzy motels. That was until Mark's old man decided that it was cheaper to force the family to holiday in tents rather than cheap motel rooms. He parked his car for a second time, took his luggage out of the trunk of his *Ford Focus*, walked across the parking lot to Unit 150 and opened its door with the key attached to the red fish tag. He saw

Truscott owner and counter man Tom Heller waving to him from the office window. Mark thought; "All of this service plus a room for $110 a night."

Mark opened the door, stepped into the room, turned on the light, dropped his bag on the floor and stood immobile for a moment, staring at the bed like he had just been struck with a mallet. There, casually lounging on a blue floral bedspread underneath a small ceiling fan/ light, was a middle aged woman sporting too much make up, wearing a short green dress with a slit up one side and black high heeled shoes that seemed a little too high. She smiled casually and looked at Mark as if she had been expecting him. Still staring, Mark stepped back, one hand waving behind his back, searching for the door knob, as if he was trying to escape. The woman's nonchalant smile broke into a broad grin. She arose from the bed and took a step toward Mark.

Predictably, the woman spoke first. She had a cordial voice half way to sultry. "Don't be scared. I know it seems a little strange but I'm here as a kind of extra for staying here at the Truscott. I come with the place. My name is Daisy." She didn't think she had to explain that she was Buster's wife. For some reason, Mark already knew that.

Mark was still stunned. He hadn't even begun to start thinking about what to say to this woman standing there in his room. A story he had heard about doing business in some Asian countries immediately came to mind. He couldn't remember who told him about this curious business practice but it was memorable enough for Mark to recall it more than three decades after he had first heard it. According to whoever who had told him the tale in the first place, a government colleague no doubt, several businesses the man had been visiting were kind enough to ensure that when he checked into his hotels, local business girls would be waiting for him on the beds in his rooms, like a human variant of a welcoming bowl of fruit. In the most stimulating of his colleague's recollections, at least one of the girls was waiting for him in his room naked, a proposition that made it quite difficult for the man to eject her from his room without prompting unwanted attention. When questioned about the story by understandably curious colleagues, the man claimed that some of his fellow travelers naturally took advantage of the services. This was despite a constant order from the head of the delegation not to partake in any such activity. The men checking into the hotel rooms were left to expel the women themselves. Most simply telephoned down to the desk and had an amused hotel security official, many of whom might have taken advantage of the situation to escort the girl out of the buildings. Some did not. Mark's former colleagues never did say whether they themselves had telephoned down to the desks but only that they knew that some men had.

The woman was now standing in the middle of the room, one hand on her left hip and the other slowly running through her hair, almost theatrically seductive. She looked at him with a little cunning smile on her face. "As I said, Mr. Purchell, I don't want you to be afraid. I'm not here to frighten you. I'm here for...well, something else, that is if you're interested." She then took her hand out of her hair and waved it down the right side of her body, like she was making a turn on a fashion runway. Mark was still dumbfounded. It was like a scene out of some cheap amateur porno, something everyone, including Mark himself, had seen and never forgotten a long time ago. Maybe he should have looked for a camera.

Mark finally spoke, still standing with his back to the door. He had decided, at least momentarily, that the whole thing was probably some sort of joke. But the reason, if there was a reason, was completely elusive. Mark didn't know anyone in Truscott and no one in Truscott knew him. "This is a joke, right? You know like that old television show, you know the one....what the hell was it called?" He looked at Daisy who threw both hands up in supplication and then down again. She didn't know either. Mark briefly thought that it was possible that Daisy and her husband, Tom "Buster" Heller, may not have gotten that channel back when the show was playing. After all, the program was on a U.S network in the 1960s and it was likely that anyone in Truscott, Nova Scotia would have required a television antenna the size of a satellite dish to draw that network feed in back then.

Suddenly and surprisingly in view of the circumstances, Mark brightened. "*Candid Camera*, that's it, *Candid Camera* with that guy, what was his name ---Funt, Allen Funt."

Daisy's expression changed completely. No longer the beguiling vixen, she now had a vacant look on her face. "I don't remember that show. I don't think we ever got that show, not up here." She then sat down on the bed, her hands in her lap, and shrugged. "What kind of show was it anyway?"

Mark then exhaled, whatever anxious confusion that may have been percolating in his bloodstream --- it had been like a particularly belligerent barbiturate --- was dissipating. He explained the premise for *Candid Camera* to Daisy. She was now only a mystified middle aged woman in a short green dress with a slit up the side sitting on a bed in a motel room. The scene was no longer even remotely reminiscent of a pornographic clip.

Mrs. Heller shrugged her head. She now looked embarrassed, almost mortified. She seemed reluctant to say anything to explicate the situation in which she now found herself. She managed to suggest an explanation although Mark had already concluded that Daisy was accustomed to explaining herself in these circumstances. Now the conversation was drifting back to considerations of pornography. "It's embarrassing to explain but I would think that a smart city fella like you would have guessed by now."

Mark shrugged. Even though he was starting to figure things out, he still wasn't certain. "Maybe I'm not a smart city fella, if you know what I mean."

"It's obvious, isn't it?" asked Daisy, relaxing, a smile had reappeared on her face. "Do you think I dress like this to clean the rooms?" A substantive smile finally appeared. The two of them, Mark still standing by the door, Daisy sitting on the bed, were momentarily silent. Mark then tried to encourage Daisy to continue with her explanation. "No but I was wondering why you were dressed like that."

Daisy sat back on the edge of the bed. "Mr. Purchell, I'm dressed like this because....well because I like to party."

"Party?" asked Mark.

"Yes, Mr. Purchell, I like to party and when Buster spots someone who might be half decent, well he lets me know and I follow up."

Mark looked dumbfounded. "Come on, you have to be kidding."

"No, Mr. Purchell, I'm not kidding." replied Mrs. Heller. She was now resuming the role of the middle aged vixen from the sticks. "I like to party and poor old Buster hasn't been up to any partying for years. Nor is anyone else in this crummy little town, at least not anybody who's half way decent. And so he ..."

Mark finished her sentence. "So he spots someone who may be decent?"

Daisy smiled, nodded, stepped closer and put her right hand on Mark's left arm. Mark stepped back and shook his head. Daisy recognized someone declining her offer when she heard one. She smiled again, shrugged, stepped around Mark and was out the door, her inexpensive perfume hanging in the air. As Mark watched her leave, he noticed that Mrs. Daisy Heller had a fine rear end. Mark thought of Danny Beliveau for a moment. He would have been impressed. Even he probably didn't know too many couples where the husband was his wife's pimp. But knowing Danny, he would have wanted to.

Mark put his bag down, removed his shoes, sat down on the bed with a blue floral bedspread and contemplated the events of the past fifteen minutes or so. It was ten minutes after six o'clock in the evening, his first night in Truscott. He had arranged for five nights at The Truscott, five nights and he had already encountered behavior that he would ordinarily have only heard about on the internet or maybe in Jack's old neighborhood. He sat there staring at the blank television screen affixed on the wall above the chest of drawers at the end of the bed and wondered about dinner. He didn't consider it prudent to try the dining room associated with The Truscott. And he certainly didn't want to run into Daisy in the dining room, there was a possibility that Daisy might also assist her husband in operating the dining room by waiting tables as well as seducing or attempting to seduce its guests.

He checked the top drawer of the bedside table, predictably found a Gideon Bible and fortunately a regional telephone book, providing the telephone numbers for maybe a dozen local towns, including Truscott. He then found a list of about 20 local restaurants. Like the number of hotels that Truscott featured, Mark was surprised with the number of restaurants, suggesting somehow that Truscott was a popular vacation destination with a wide range of eating places. Many of them had interesting names: The Bell-Buoy-Blue, The Thistledown Pub, Sir Lobster, The Yellow Cello Cafe, The Bite Down House, The Bean There, Popsies, and a couple of Chinese joints, Fat Wong's and The Wang. Mark went with The Bell-Buoy-Blue, a restaurant that like most of the other places in town was seafood based. He was convinced that neither Daisy nor Tom would be dining there that evening. He didn't think he would need a reservation.

He unpacked his bag, a well worn imitation Louis Vuitton with black instead of tan trim, placed one dress shirt, two casual shirts, six pairs of underwear and four pairs of socks into the top drawer of the dresser underneath the plasma on the wall. He hung an extra pair of pants in the closet and set in the bathroom his shaving kit, another imitation Vuitton. Both that and his overnight bag were gifts from a woman with whom he had pursued a relationship between his first and second wives, a woman with occasional pretensions of wealth. On the bottom of the bag was a folded sheet of paper on which Mark had printed a number of establishments in the Truscott area, sources for his research of Jack's origins. He sat on the edge of bed and examined the paper, probably for tenth time. He re-examined the list, the result of his internet investigations: the Truscott Public Library, the Cape Breton Genealogy and Historical Association, three local schools, three local churches, the local legion, the local RCMP detachment, the town hall, and the humble post office. Mark wasn't sure whether any one of these institutions and agencies would be of use in finding any facts about his friend Jack's beginnings but so far, that was all he had. He decided that he would start at the top of the list, with the library on Chebucto Street. He had passed it on his way to the Truscott. He would visit there in the morning.

Sitting there, staring at the blank television screen, he suddenly remembered another avenue of inquiry that he had considered and then rejected. Using the internet, about which he had become quite adept, he had come across a number of websites offering a variety of adoption services, including the search for birth parents. Mark had decided to employ one of them, a company called OmniSearch. He had chosen it because it appeared to be the most professional of the companies that he had consulted, a well designed website with colorful graphics and easily understood directions the main attractions. Aside from undertaking to locate birth parents, it also promised to find lost family members, including not just birth parents but the children who had been adopted. Mark had never considered that any parent who had given up a child would actually want to search for the whereabouts of that child. Sure, Mark presumed that most adopted children, including Jack himself, were interested, if not in some cases obsessed with finding their birth parents. But the reverse, parents who had given up a child and then, years later, started to search for that child seemed strange. Mark was curious. He had never heard of or known anyone who had given up a child for adoption. Mark had dutifully filled in the electronic form that OmniSearch had provided but he declined to submit it when he realized there was likely a substantial fee attached to the service. Mark was not prepared to invest much money in something that seemed, at least to him, less than guaranteed.

He was later to reflect on the irony of having passed on the opportunity to use the services of OmniSearch for financial reasons after deciding to spend money on traveling to Truscott to investigate his friend Jack's adoption. He later concluded, after contemplating the question, that he was more attracted by the adventure of pursuing his own investigation than he was by sitting in front of a computer screen and waiting for an answer. Beyond being the end of a career within which he hadn't been doing much anyway, he was more than happy to occupy himself with something that seemed exciting. That ambition was also behind his quick dismissal of the thought of actually hiring a private detective to investigate Jack Quinn's adoption. The possibility of retaining such services was also advertised by OmniSearch.

Later that evening, having convinced himself that he was on the right track in his pursuit of his friend's early history, Mark walked into the Bell-Buoy-Blue, a tidy little dining room with twelve tables covered with pale blue table cloths and each decorated with a single maritime flag featuring some sort of family crest. Almost as soon as he sat down, a surprisingly spirited, pert, almost middle aged waitress wearing an inappropriately short skirt and a blond pony tail approached Mark's table and noticed him studying the flag. She leaned over and helpfully informed Mark that it was the flag of Nova Scotia, the Royal Standard of Scotland on the blue and white Saint Andrew Cross, details that he neither sought nor appreciated but she delivered anyway. In response to the blank look on his face, the waitress was remarkably understanding, even cheerful. She advised Mark that most people weren't that interested in the derivation of the province's emblem anyway. She emphasized this with a wink and indicated that the boss was always encouraging his employees to explain the table flags, even if the diners weren't interested. According to the pony tailed waitress --- she wore no name tag on her white blouse --- the boss was also a town counselor and potential Member of Parliament, which pretty well explained the compelled flag explanation. Mark recalled the obvious reference to patriotism being the last refuge of the scoundrel. She then asked for his drink order. He accepted her recommendation of a locally brewed craft beer called Big Bruce. She then recited, with memorized precision, a list of mainly seafood specials. Almost immediately, Mark selected the lobster risotto.

The waitress left and Mark noticed a copy of a local newspaper abandoned on a recently deserted table nearby. It was a bi-weekly called the *Victorian Scribe* and looked to be a couple of dozen pages of local news, classified ads, and commercial advertisements. Mark picked it up. He was not surprised with the headline on the front page complete with a picture above the fold: "Town Council Agrees to Fund Sidewalk Repair". Apparently, the issue of funding for municipal works, at least in this case, was quite contentious with three of the seven town counselors as well as the town's chief administrative officer opposing a financial outlay of $8,000 to fix the sidewalks on two of the major streets in Truscott. A second story concerned a recent function at the local Royal Canadian Legion which featured, among other things, an detailed description of entertainment provided by The Pirates, a three piece combo that apparently liked to play Celtic folk songs. There were several articles about other town events, including a car accident, an arrest, a wedding, an article about a rugby tournament and a death with an appropriate obituary. There were advertisements for local businesses, notices involving dairy quotas, the next town council meeting, and a two week weather forecast. In other words, a collection of small town cliches neatly packaged in two dozen broadsheets. Mark had finished his first glass of "Big Bruce" by the time he had completed reading the exciting events reported by *The Victorian Scribe*. He signaled for another beer and started to munch on one of the two dinner buns that the waitress had set down on his table. She nodded and was back at the table with another Big Bruce in moments.

She couldn't help but notice that Mark was perusing *The Victorian Scribe* and commented. "Nothing much in that paper," she observed, "You're probably better off with the Cape Breton rag but not by much mind you." She complimented a slight grin with a quick eye roll. Mark returned her expression. Her reference to the apparent absence of journalist value in *The Victorian Scribe* gave him an idea, an illumination that probably would have occurred to most people anyway. If his investigation of the possible origins of Jack Quinn proved pointless in Truscott, he could pursue his inquiry with the *Cape Breton Standard,* apparently a better source of infrormation. Among its reporters, which likely numbered more than the one that*The Victorian Scribe* employed, there could have been one who could provide some perspective about the humble history of the town of Truscott. He then thought about interviewing the waitress. After all, it could constitute a start.

The waitress, who seemed to be the only server operating in the dining room of the Bell-Buoy-Blue, arrived with the lobster risotto and a third Big Bruce, having anticipated his requirement for another beer with the supposition of a veteran gambler. After she placed the risotto and his third beer down on the table, Mark introduced himself and explained the purpose of his visit in very general terms, without identifying Jack Quinn. Looking a little stunned for a moment, as if unaccustomed to the refinement of a formal intro, the waitress identified herself as Elaine Butler, adding the title "server extraordinaire". She then smiled, seemingly a genuine grin this time.

Elaine Butler waited, as if expecting further comment. Mark obliged. "Do you think you could help me with a little information, you know on the town and some of the people who may live or may have lived here?" He thought that she might be able to save him some time, a more expedient method of research than exploring a library or a historical society. She was his first witness.

Elaine Butler took a quick look around for an assessment of the diners she was currently serving. Aside from Mark, there were only five other tables occupied: an elderly couple two tables over from Mark, gamely slurping down two clam chowders with two chardonnays; one table over was a young couple who did not seem the least bit interested in their fish and chip specials; off in one corner was a group of five, three bored looking teenage boys ignoring a conversation between two middle aged women; and two solitary men, one in denim overalls and the other a local real estate broker who apparently was a regular at the Bell-Buoy-Blue. Waitress Butler then concluded that she had a few minutes to talk to the curious diner Mark Purchell.

"Well, what exactly do you want to know?" she asked with a slight chortle in her whispering voice. Mark thought for a moment that waitress Butler was about to sit down but she didn't. She did, however, lean in a bit. She definitely seemed interested in either his story or him. He didn't know which. Mark stared up at her as if he was contemplating a flirtation.

Reluctant about being too candid, Mark generalized his explanation of his purpose in visiting Truscott. He also hoped that his intended explanation would make some sense or at least be believable. "Well, to be honest, I'm recently retired and I've decided to compile a history of the town."

"This town? Truscott? Why?" she asked, sounding curious but not particularly surprised. "I mean Truscott isn't the most glamorous place around. There are more interesting places in Cape Breton than this place. How about Sydney? Or Glace Bay? Or Baddeck? In fact, I've been in all three of those places, not to mention Halifax and I'd say that compared to them, Truscott might as well be one big retirement home."

With an opportunity to avoid a further explanation along that line, he had prepared some lame excuse about honoring a friend's memory, which was close to the truth when he thought about it, Mark then asked Elaine about her residence in the retirement home town of Truscott, Nova Scotia.

"If it is so bad, why are you living here?" inquired Mark. The question should have been anticipated by Elaine Butler, who seemed pretty sharp to Mark, at least based on their few minutes of conversation.

Elaine stood up straight and took a quick look around. "No time to talk right now. I'll be back." Elaine then turned toward the entrance. Apparently, she was the maitre 'd for the place as well. A couple was standing at the entrance. They were a comparably well dressed twosome in their forties ---- maybe they were visiting as well. Elaine conducted them to a table two down from Mark. He noticed that they didn't seem to be too happy. They weren't looking at each other, both their faces featuring frozen stares. Elaine handed them menus, skipped a recitation of the specials, which were included in a folder in the menu anyway, and walked away. The couple started to study the menus, both bringing them up to their faces so as to avoid looking at each other. It was a classic scene, right out of a situation comedy.

Within less than thirty minutes, Mark had finished his risotto and his third beer, had signaled for Elaine, had ordered a coffee and was waiting to resume his conversation with her. When she delivered his coffee, with a complimentary short bread cookie, Mark tried to re-engage Elaine in their conversation about her residence in Truscott. She said that she didn't really have the time, noting that at least two more tables had been occupied since Mark was seated although Mark had noted that three other tables had been abandoned in the same time period. She then suggested, with a pleasing smile that again seemed flirtatious in nature, that they could head over to the Thistledown Pub after the restaurant closed at ten o'clock. Mark replied by declaring it a date. He was embarrassed. Elaine smiled and agreed. It would be his first date in years. He headed back to The Truscott, hoping not to run into either Daisy Heller or her husband. As soon as he entered his room, he noticed there was a note taped to the television screen above the dresser. He walked over and pulled the note from the screen. In childish block script, the written message was simple and direct: "Turn on the DVD Player and play."

Of course, the missive was too intriguing to ignore. He picked up the remote for the television and pressed the power button. He then turned on the button for the DVD player and pressed play. A shadowy picture of Daisy appeared, wearing the same tawdry outfit in which she had greeted Mark earlier in the day. He adjusted the volume although there was no sound but for noise Mark assumed originated from outside the room. The camera work was terrible, shaky, full of shade and unwelcome light. The picture was frightening. Daisy looked like a shady vampire, like a middle aged woman dressing up for some sort of Halloween orgy. Her hands were on her hips, she was leaning forward to emphasize her breasts which he now noted were decorated with rose tattoos. The camera zoomed in to frame Daisy's face, which seemed to have been accentuated with another layer of blush from when he saw her earlier in the day. He did not, however, have any idea as to the timing of the video although he assumed that Mr and Mrs Heller could have filmed it after Mark passed up Daisy's first offer. She now made her second offer, suggesting, in a predictably breathless whisper, that she was still available if he changed his mind. She then held up, in a surprisingly theatrical move, a handwritten note that simply said Room 151, which was conveniently located right next door to Mark's room. The camera panned back to the full length revealing Daisy in a black brassiere and thong. As the screen was going blank, Daisy's parting words "I'm waiting" hung in the air, sounding more like a threat than an invitation.

Mark turned off the television. He stepped back from the screen and sat on the bed, stunned and a little frightened. It was clear to him that the Hellers were not exactly an innocuous couple. In fact, they could be dangerous, a notion that was reflected by an immediate and profound fear percolating in his stomach, like he was about to vomit. He sat there, wishing that he was still packing that little container of tranquilizers he used to carry. He needed one now, anything, Xanax, Ativan, Valium, Haldol, anything. After sitting there, still stunned, for maybe another five minutes, he decided to escape. He would simply check out immediately, leave the key on the desk and check in somewhere else. He did have a list of alternatives, including a place called the Dunlop Inn, which had been his first alternative selection. He had written down the address to the Dunlop Inn and several other hotel choices in Truscott. They were included on a list that was still sitting in his wallet. He checked the list and was reasonably certain that he could drive to the Dunlop Inn from Truscott without any guidance. It was also located on Turley Road. He had passed it when he was going west to The Truscott. He recalled there had been a red light sign notifying travelers of a vacancy standing in front of the Dunlop Inn. He hoped the light was still on.

He hurriedly packed, taking him less than five minutes to cram his clothes into his fake Vuitton, and was out the door of Room 150. He went to the main office, was relieved to see that Buster wasn't behind the counter, and gently placed the key to Room 150 on the counter. Mark then went out to his car and was on his way to the Dunlop Inn within minutes. The place was less than a kilometer away. He then remembered his date with Elaine

Butler. He had agreed to pick her up when she got off work at ten o'clock. It was almost nine o'clock. He could check in at the Dunlop and be back at the Bell-Buoy-Blue in time to keep his appointment with the friendly and hopefully talkative waitress.

THE FIRST EVENING IN TRUSCOTT

Mark was much relieved when it turned out that the Dunlop Inn, an old house converted into a three floor, eight room bed and breakfast turned out to have one vacancy. Mark was offered the largest suite in the place as he was enthusiastically informed by the clean cut young man behind the front counter. The lobby looked more like the parlor of an elegant boarding house than the lobby of a hotel. In short, Mark was relieved with the greeting and the person who issued it. The young man wasn't Tom "Buster" Heller and he seriously doubted that he had a wife or girlfriend waiting in his room. The young man behind the counter took his credit card information, handed him a key card to room six, asked him to leave his car where he had parked it, and then waved him to the staircase to his left. He apologized for the fact that room six was on the third floor and the Dunlop did not have an elevator, an inconvenience that the young man said the hotel's owners had been intending to rectify for years. He further explained that he could never figure out why the owners, a family that had purchased the place from the original residents, did not include an elevator in the eventual renovations that transforming the place into a hotel required. He then started to further explain the background to the place and the family that built it. Standing there listening to this young man explaining parts of the past of the Dunlop, Mark was worried that the young man would continue with his narrative history of the hotel. He had to meet Elaine Butler by ten o'clock. He checked his watch several times during his conversation with the young man. The kid wasn't taking the hint. Finally, he had no option but to insist. He had to go. Mark took his key card, picked up his bag and headed up to the third floor.

Room 106 was the much larger of the two rooms on the third floor of the Dunlop Inn. One of the last things the young man behind the counter had confided about the hotel was that it had taken the Dunlops several years to build it, an indication the young man said of its classic quality. Fortunately, the young man did not have enough time to comment on the details of the renovations. Mark opened the door, turned on the table lamp by the door, and stepped into the room. As advertised, the room was surprisingly impressive, at least to Mark, for a town like Truscott. It looked like it could have easily been featured in an architectural publication, perhaps in a story about hotel hospitality in the Gilded Age. He wondered why he had not made arrangements for the Dunlop before reserving at The Truscott.

The furniture in Dunlop's best suite was expensive antique with wine colored round tables and chairs with carved legs and padded, needlepoint seats. This was accompanied by a large dresser, a tall wardrobe, a roll desk, and three ornate table lamps. In the middle of the room was a large wooden bed with an elaborate leather headboard. There were also small footstools on both sides of the bed, presumably to assist weary travelers into bed. They were a convenience that to Mark only seemed to appear in old romance novels. He also noticed that the suite was not equipped with a television although there was a small sign on the dresser notifying occupants that television viewing was available in the lobby. Mark guessed that when the proprietors of the Dunlop Inn intended it to be some sort of reminder of the Gilded Age, they were quite serious about it.

It was almost ten o'clock, time to keep his appointment with Elaine Butler. Mark hurriedly unpacked his bag, put away his clothes in the dresser and hung his trousers in the wardrobe. He took a quick look around the room, turned off the table lamp and headed out the door. He rushed down the stairs, received a cheerful though perfunctory wave from the young man behind the counter in the lobby. He was noticed there was an elderly couple sitting on a couch in the lobby watching television. He was out the door into the parking lot, got into his *Ford* Focus, and was then turning left onto Turley Road. The Bell-Buoy-Blue was on Scott Street, two blocks to the right. He was in front of the restaurant in ten minutes. Elaine was just leaving when he pulled up, he stopped and waited, car still running. Elaine recognized Mark with a smile, opened the door and got into the car.

She greeted Mark with a curious comment, brash, sarcastic and perhaps a little cautious at the same time, "I hope you're not weird or anything."

That one sardonic comment from Elaine confirmed to Mark that his initial attraction to her in the restaurant was legitimate. She was cute, saucy, spunky, spirited, feisty, pick your adjective he thought. He immediately felt like he had developed or was developing a crush on Elaine Butler. He had not felt like that for years. Lost in reminiscence, he was taken aback a bit by her comment but recovered quickly enough to participate in the prospective repartee. He wanted to pursue the conversation, the first conversation he actually wanted to pursue with an actual woman in some time. She pursued it for him.

"Don't worry, I'm only kidding, at least I hope I'm only kidding." She then winked .

"I hope you are too." Mark replied, as close as he could come to a comment resembling wit. "I'm sure you can run into a lot of weird people in your line of work."

Elaine laughed. "Sure, Truscott is full of them."

"And you would know since a lot of them come into the Bell-Buoy-Blue, right?" Mark returned, the beginnings of authentic banter stirring.

"What I could tell you." an observation and then another light laugh. "You know how waitresses run into all sorts of people. That includes weird, even crazy people."

"But don't forget, I'm from out of town." said Mark.

Elaine turned out and started to look out the car window. "Well, I'm sure you have crazies where you live which is where?"

"Ottawa, I'm from Ottawa." answered Mark.

"Ottawa! Geez, talk about your crazies. That place is full of them but most are not dangerous types mind you.

186

They are mainly eccentric types but some of them, well some of the are nuttier than the proverbial fruitcake." commented Elaine.

Mark looked at Elaine, eyebrows purposefully raised: "You've spent time in Ottawa?"

Elaine nodded. "Yes, I lived in Ottawa with a husband and two sons for maybe twenty years. My husband and I moved there from Truscott just after we got married. I had met Chris in high school here in Truscott. He was the only decent guy in the town. In fact, he may have been the only decent guy in all of Cape Breton, not to mention the son of the richest. So it came as no surprise when I got pregnant by the end of the summer after graduation, my future was pretty set." She got a funny look on her face and appeared to want to start laughing. "There was no doubt that Chris was the father even though a lot of people thought there were other candidates, even one of the many losers in town." She shrugged and then giggled, in an adolescent sort of way.

"Anyway, just out of high school, Chris had already started working for his father in Ottawa and said that he could get me a job working there too. Chris's father, his name was Eugene Thompson, would be my father-in-law. He had owned and then sold a big dairy farm here in Truscott, probably the biggest. With the quota he had from the government, he was already a damn millionaire, even before he sold the farm. After that, he ran for office and eventually became the MP for Cape Breton and was appointed the Minister of Agriculture. He had the job for more than a decade. As you can imagine, the man had a lot of influence, both here and in Ottawa. So, it was obvious to me, and would have been obvious to almost anyone, that his son seemed not only the best bet but the only bet. So we got married and moved to Ottawa where we had Terrence, our first son."

Elaine, the memories shifting in her head, paused for a moment and looked at Mark intently, trying to remember her own history. She then took out a cigarette, lit it and took a slow drag, and continued her commentary. Her voice was suddenly lower, almost conspiratorial. "Anyway, Chris went to university in Ottawa while I stayed home with Terrence. A couple of years later, we had another boy, we named him Philip. Good old Minister Thompson was paying for pretty well everything."

Mark interjected, sensing that Elaine was fading somewhat and was in need of some encouragement to continue her story. He needed her to keep talking, hoping for some morsel of information that could help in his nascent search for the origins of Jack Quinn. Besides, sitting there in the car listening to Elaine was preferable to watching television in the lobby of the Dunlop Inn. For a moment, and a short moment it was, the thought of Mrs. Daisy Heller materialized in his mind like an specter. Maybe he should have remained a guest in The Truscott. But the thought faded as quickly as it had emerged. He turned to Elaine and commented. "It sounds like things were going pretty good."

Elaine shrugged and answered, her voice low, affecting the husky quality of someone who has smoked too many cigarettes and maybe too much to drink. Her eyes were more than halfway to shut, the long shift at the Bell–Buoy–Blue a likely explanation. After a minute or so, Mark reached out to tap her arm. He thought that she may have been drifting into dreamland. She then responded to his last comment. "I guess so. Yeah, things were going pretty good. By the time my youngest was about two years old, Chris and I were both working in the old man's department. Chris was climbing the ladder so to speak while I was sitting on the bottom rung. Not that I cared. I had a nice clerical job, everybody in the office was as congenial as hell." She looked over at Mark almost wistfully and then shrugged again. "I was happy there, for a good fifteen years or so, at least. By that time, we were living in this big house in this nice neighborhood of Ottawa called the Glebe."

"I know the Glebe." Mark pointed out.

Elaine nodded slowly. "Right, right, you're from Ottawa yourself."

Mark nodded sympathetically. "And then something happened I guess, something that changed things."

She paused again, staring strangely through the smoke, having already fired up another cigarette. She was continuing with her narrative. While there was a certain practiced cynicism in her recitation, like she had rehearsed it to herself many times, there was little hint of expected regret, and a little trance of bitterness. Sure, Elaine looked perturbed, slowly rolling her eyes and providing a practiced shrug. She had often reviewed the chronology of her journey from her home town of Truscott to an impressive residence in Ottawa and then back again to a one bedroom apartment in the rear of an old farm house in Truscott. Perhaps repeated recollections of her past had long smoothed the edges off her story. She had learned to live with her disappointments.

"So you had it pretty good." Mark repeated his earlier observation, not really knowing what else to say. He was showing interest, sympathy, understanding.

"Right, it was more than pretty good. We had this grand house in the Glebe. Chris eventually ended up a deputy minister in his father's old department and we had two great sons. They're both in university now, not that I've spoken to either of them in years. Then, one morning seven or eight years ago, presto, he and the boys were gone and I was left on my own....to end up back in the paradise of Truscott."

Mark didn't even bother to disguise a strange smile, a blank smile that he felt might be surfacing on his face having arrived. "So what happened?" Another thought of Daisy Heller crossed his mind.

"It was my ex, my damn ex-husband." Elaine paused and then suggested that they head over to the Thistledown Pub where she said she could continue with their conversation, specifically her history as well as Mark hoped the history of the town. The pub was over on Brock Street, less than three kilometers away from the restaurant where she worked. Mark assumed that Elaine was likely a regular patron of the Thistledown Pub. It was curious coincidence. They were almost there by the time Elaine proposed the destination. They had been traveling on Brock Street the whole time.

The place was a low square building that looked more like an abandoned warehouse than a drinking establishment. Above the front door was a small white wooden sign with faded green paint identifying it. Mark was frankly surprised with Elaine's suggestion of a destination. Despite her generally impertinent demeanor, Elaine Butler definitely did not look like she would frequent this kind of a place. Mark thought that bikers might well have felt right at home at the Thistledown Pub although he did not see any motorcycles parked anywhere around the place. The parking lot contained only pick up trucks and battered muscle cars. Mark's *Ford Focus* would doubtless stand out in that lot. As he pulled in, Mark looked at Elaine with a quietly dumbfounded look on his face. Elaine provided Mark with an understanding smile and a nod. He turned off the engine.

"Yeah, I know. The place does look like a dump. I started coming here because my ex-husband used to practically live here when he was growing up. They were serving him quarts of beer when he was only fourteen or so. I wouldn't be surprised if his old man, who was more of a drinker than his son, had something to do with that liberal policy. Both of them used to tell all sorts of stories about this place, some real dingers."

"Dingers! That's a strange expression. You mean humdingers, right?" noted Mark.

Elaine laughed. "Yeah, dingers! I couldn't help but pick it up growing up here." They were still sitting in the car. "Anyway, let's go in." She opened the car door and got out. Mark sat for a moment pondering. Why would a seemingly sophisticated woman like Elaine Butler end up back in a burg like Truscott, regardless of what happened to her marriage? He wondered.

Mark got out of the car and followed Elaine into the Thistledown Pub. They went up a couple of stairs, opened an old wooden door and were standing at the entrance of a dimly lit room with maybe twenty tables, some small and round, some larger and rectangular, scattered across a gray granite floor. The walls were a green gray pitted concrete material. The ceiling was equipped with a half dozen fluorescent lights hung from wooden beams. The place looked as decrepit internally as it did externally. To Mark, it looked like a prison lavatory. Most of the beer laden tables were occupied, mainly by a range of presumed locals of all ages, both men and women, many of whom looked to be playing cards. Elaine informed Mark that euchre was the preferred game. All that was missing from the scene was a cloud of cigarette smoke, a haze of nicotine effused fumes that undoubtedly used to be the chief characteristic of the place, that is until Truscott joined the rest of the civilized world and banned smoking. Mark mentioned that particular observation to Elaine who then related the brief history of the battle between the municipal politicos and every bar and restaurant in the town over the anti-smoking law. Elaine mentioned that during the last civic election, a local man named Campbell had tried unsuccessfully to get the smoking ban overturned through some sort of plebiscite. He was well known for such antics, having been arrested and fined countless times for smoking violations, including such outrages as smoking during church services and lighting up in city hall.

In any event, said Elaine, smoking regulations had been and still were a controversial issue in Truscott. It took years for the denizens of places like the Thistledown Pub to become accustomed to a smokeless world. In fact, there were reports, rumors actually, that many former clients of local drinking establishments took to ordering and consuming drinks in parking lots, sidewalks and building stoops. Truscott had yet to install patios to accommodate smokers who were no longer permitted to smoke inside. For reasons that Mark thought to investigate, Truscott did not seem to have any restaurants or bars that provided patios. It seemed curious. On the other hand, smoking would eventually be banned even on patios, even if they were any.

Elaine led Mark to one of the small, round tables in the middle of the room, nestled behind a stone pillar that was decorated with faded flyers advertising local concerts, flea markets, church socials, and other community events. They both sat down and were promptly approached by a young man, white shirt and black trousers. Not surprisingly, Elaine ordered a "Big Bruce", the same locally produced craft beer she had recommended to him at the Bell-Buoy-Blue. Mark shrugged and followed suit. Elaine laughed lightly and made a quick comment on his selection. "I told you it was worth ordering."

Mark shrugged again and agreed. He leaned back in his chair and looked around. "Nice place --- it kind of reminds me of a lot of places I've frequented."

Elaine nodded. "Oh, I'm sure it does. Truth is that this kind of place makes most people think of some other place." She paused and then added the obvious observation. "There must be hundreds of places like this, the same design, the same ..."

"The same delightful decor..." added Mark.

Elaine nodded, adding another reflection. "Yeah, it's an architectural marvel alright. I'm sure places like this are occasionally featured in those restaurant and bar magazines you see every now and then."

"Yeah, but every now and then in the 1950s." Mark agreed with a kind of sarcastic observation that her remark deserved.

Two quart bottles of Big Bruce arrived. The waiter asked if either of them wanted to see a menu, even though it was after ten o'clock in the evening. Both declined. Elaine smiled, picked up one of the bottles and poured some Big Bruce into both glasses. Mark remarked that the glasses, Pilzer glasses he thought they were called, always reminded him of the draft glasses that cost him a dime back in the old days. This was back when he was sixteen and he was visiting any tavern or other drinking establishment that would serve anyone who could show a phony ID that spelled the owner's name right. Sometimes, a lot of times actually, you didn't need to show an ID. He thought of retelling the story of frequently getting blind drunk after investing a dollar, enough for eight drafts of beer plus tip. But he thought better of it. Talk about a cliché. Elaine had almost certainly heard this kind of story before, probably a thousand times from a thousand different guys with a thousand identical experiences.

They both settled back and started on their beers. In less than a minute, Elaine had consumed half her quart before Mark had the opportunity to have two slugs of his beer, a boozing performance that reminded him of Jack in the old days. Mark could recall days, back when they were both working in the auto part plant, when Jack would polish off three quarts of Molson's Export. This would have been accompanied by a smoked meat sandwich, for lunch at Abby's Delicatessen, all in the forty five minutes they were permitted for lunch. Mark, who usually had a coke or a cup of coffee with his sandwich for lunch, often remarked that if he drank three quarts of beer at lunch, he would have to be hospitalized, either for intoxication or after some industrial accident. After a moment of rumination, Mark continued his inquiry about the circumstances that brought Elaine back to Truscott. Elaine demurred, protesting that Mark owed Elaine an explanation of the reasons for his visit to Truscott.

Elaine was right. He had another another few swallows while Elaine ordered another beer. He waited until the young waiter brought Elaine's second beer. Mark began his briefing by talking about Jack's last few months, his illness, his and Deborah's daily visits, the search for the safety deposit box and finally, the photograph and the letter he found in Jack's safety deposit box. Mark explained that the letter requested him to investigate the circumstances regarding Jack's adoption, the only clue being the letter, which claimed that Jack's adopted parents were supposedly born in Truscott. That was the reason, Mark said, for his visit to Truscott, to investigate the history of his friend's birth. He asked Elaine for her assistance in his search for the truth about the circumstances of Jack Quinn's birth. Elaine had almost finished her second beer while Mark was still enjoying his first. Elaine signaled for another beer as did Mark. Elaine took her first swallow from her third beer, leaned back and expressed a kind of facetious wonder with his story. "Wow, I think you may have quite a job ahead of you."

Mark handed Elaine the photograph of Jack the kid and his alleged father. She was examining and fondling the picture. She looked up at Mark and commented: "Cute kid, but you can't really tell whether he and the man are or aren't related. Not that that's much of a clue of anything. My youngest didn't look like me or my ex."

Mark shrugged again and then changed the subject, mentioning the various sources of potential information on local adoptions that he had located during his admittedly superficial investigation of the reference material available in Truscott. There was the Public Library, the Heritage and Archives Department of the Municipality of Victoria County, two churches, two schools, a Royal Canadian Mounted Police detachment, the post office, Royal Canadian Legion in Truscott. If he were to come up empty in Truscott, there was always the Cape Breton Genealogy and Historical Association and maybe even the Victoria County Memorial Hospital, both of which were located in Cape Breton. He did not mention his brief flirtation with the OmniSearch option, embarrassed as he was that she would think he was desperate enough to partake in what he had concluded may have been some sort of internet scam.

He did tell Elaine, however, that he hadn't decided on where to begin his research and asked her for suggestions. Elaine first provided Mark with a theatrical shrug, took another swig of her beer, and then seemed to have a brain storm, the index finger of her right hand suddenly up in the air like a sign. She almost came out of her chair, her beer spilling a bit. "Wait, wait, I think I have an idea." She paused and then blurted out a name, as if she had been keeping a secret. "Mr. Pictures."

Of course, Mark was amused. He snickered and smiled. "Mr. Pictures, you're kidding, right? Mr. Pictures, who's that? It sounds like a name that somebody just made up. Come on, it's got to be a joke, right?"

Elaine smiled back, leaned back, took a drink, put down the glass, then put both her elbows down on the table, paused, and looked up at Mark . "No joke, he's just an old guy who just likes to take and collect photographs. Maybe he took that old picture of your buddy. He's been taking them and collecting them for decades, used to run a local studio. He supposedly has thousands of them, most if not all of them local, some official, some professional, some casual. He might have photos of practically everyone who lives or has ever lived in this town, including as I say your friend when he was a kid. His father was supposedly a town photographer as well. Mr. Pictures probably has his own collection as well."

"Now that's interesting, very interesting." exclaimed Mark, genuinely fascinated. The story of Mr. Pictures suggested to Mark an avenue of investigation much more entertaining than the array of official institutions he had planned to probe.

Elaine continued her story about Mr. Pictures. "Now if you can charm the old guy, maybe he'll let you look at his photos. You might get lucky. You might find something about your friend, you know, like a clue."

"What's his real name?" asked Mark.

"His name is Ralph, Ralph Smithers. I think he has or had a wife named Joan. I think he lives out at the Lancaster Retirement Home." answered Elaine.

Mark answered with another question. "Do you know Mr. Smithers?"

Elaine explained. "No I don't, not personally anyway although, like everyone else in town, I give him a nod every time I see him. Everybody in town knows him or knows about him. Everybody in this town is familiar with the town's history and that sure as hell includes Mr. Pictures, both Junior and Senior. The plain fact is that I couldn't avoid knowing about him even if I wanted to, especially being in the restaurant business."

The two sat for a moment silently drinking. Mark watched Elaine drain her third beer. He could see that she was about to order another beer, a plan he interrupted by quarter filling her empty glass with beer from his own bottle of Big Bruce. She smiled. "Thanks, I think I should slow down anyway."

Mark figured that he wasn't going to get any more information from Elaine. He had already listed the sources of information in Truscott and environs that he had planned to investigate. She didn't make any comments about his plans nor did she make any recommendations of her own. But she had provided him with the enigmatic Mr. Pictures who, through local secrets to which he may have and may have had access, may provide invaluable hints in his hunt for the truth about the origins of Jack Quinn. As inviting as the thought of Mr. Pictures was to his project, he was reluctant about approaching him. He found himself staring at Elaine for a moment, thinking about his next move. She noticed his empty stare. She reached across the table and poured the rest of Mark's beer into her own glass. He didn't seem to notice. He looked to be in a momentary trance, lost in contemplation.

Elaine tapped the table with her glass which was now empty. Mark was startled awake from his musings. She asked if he intended to order another beer. He looked up at the clock on the gray green wall in the corner of the Thistledown Pub. It was almost one o'clock in the morning. Elaine caught him looking at the clock, advising him that most, if all the drinking establishments in Truscott seldom enforced any sort of closing time, preferring she said to leave closing times to the discretion of the waiters and eventually the patrons. Elaine let out a funny little laugh and signaled for one of the few waiters left on the premises, a paunchy middle aged man who could have played a bartender in the movies instead of real life. She held up a quart bottle and two fingers. Mark presumed that their original waiter, the young man with the white shirt and black trousers, had apparently punched out for the evening. The two quarts arrived promptly and Elaine thanked him by name. It was Tuck, short for Tucker Elaine informed him. Mark looked up, slowly shrugged and raised his eyebrows.

"I know a lot of people in this town, including most of the bartenders." Elaine explained. She poured herself a glass, drained it, and poured herself another. He hoped that she wasn't drunk. He wanted to keep her talking, about anything at this point. It was time to change the subject anyway. He wasn't going to get any further with Elaine about "Mr. Pictures" and his investigation of the origins of Jack. At least he didn't think so. Besides, he was now wide awake, surprisingly.

"So what's your story? How did you end up working back in Truscott anyway? You said that you were living in Ottawa for a long time and then you came back here." Elaine gave Mark a couple of quick nods and then went into the chronology of her last few years, from the acrimonious split from her husband through her return to her home town of Truscott to her current status as a middle age woman working in a small time restaurant with a weird name. In summary, the basic explanation for her manifestly woeful state was economic. According to Elaine, with Mark wondering about the accuracy of her account, her ex-husband, after accidentally discovering that she was conducting an affair with a much younger man in her office, immediately dumped her. His own affairs, which were multiple and constant, were irrelevant, at least in his mind, to any possible mitigation of her adultery. Her ex-husband had long resented her, the lack of appreciation for the quality of life he had provided to a woman he had always suspected of tricking him into marriage. Accordingly, he left her with nothing, the forces of one of the biggest and best law firms in the city of Ottawa too great to overcome with the inferior counsel she had managed to retain. Mark listened to her story like it was a soap opera, which it was.

He had the sense that she wasn't finished her story when Tuck approached their table, now the only one occupied in the Thistledown Pub. The waiter announced that it was time to go. Mark immediately pushed himself away from the table while Elaine looked up at Tuck, one hand over her eye, leaned back to her left and almost started to fall to the floor. She was drunk he guessed.

She then looked at her empty glass, shrugged in her chair and then put her head down on the table. Mark stood up and went to help Elaine to her feet. He put a five dollar bill down on the table and nodded to Tuck, wordlessly thanking him for his patience. It had been twenty minutes since he had had another customer, an elderly man who exited the premises after vomiting on his trousers. It was well after one o'clock in the morning and the rest of Elaine's life story was left hanging in the smokeless air of the Thistledown Pub.

He ushered her into the car and drove her home, after spending several minutes persuading a barely conscious Elaine to provide him with her address and the directions. Her place was close, only blocks away which was not a surprise in a town where every place is a few blocks away. It was a decaying, crumbling three story Victorian house with peeling paint, dirty windows, a roof with missing shingles and a crooked sign advertising a one bedroom apartment stuck in what little front lawn there was. Elaine's place was located at the side of the house toward the back. It was part of a two unit addition that someone had constructed maybe thirty or forty years ago, the comparative vintage of the materials an obvious indication.

Mark drove up to the door of her place and asked for the keys. She drunkenly laughed, shrugged and stumbled out of the car toward the door to her apartment, pushing it open. She looked at Mark and explained. "I've never lock the door to this dump." Of course, Mark immediately thought of his friend Jack Quinn. He never locked his apartment either. It was a dump as well, a kitchen, a bathroom, and a living room with a bed in the middle, a television and a small bedside table on which sat a lamp which Mark did not have to turn on. Elaine almost fell down entering the place. She flopped face first onto the bed, fully clothed. He appeared to be asleep within seconds. Her right arm fell off one side of the bed. Mark went to lift her arm to place it back on the bed. He noticed that Elaine had a jagged scar along the width of her right wrist. He quickly examined it. Elaine had obviously made an attempt to do herself in. Mark stood there for a moment, pondering the possible reason or reasons for Elaine's attempted suicide. He was reasonably certain that he had already been told about the background of Elaine's possible desperation: a regrettable divorce and an exile back home to an apartment no larger than one of the clothes closets in her previous home. Mark placed her arm on the bed and quietly backed out of the room, closed the door, left it unlocked, got into the car and headed back to the Dunlop Inn. He had to bang on the front door of the place until a man, who had not been on duty when Mark checked in, walked into the dark lobby and opened the front door. Understandably, the man had a scowl on his face, grumbled something, and disappeared into a room behind the front desk. Fortunately, Mark had kept his room card in his pocket.

He was certain that he would be speaking to Elaine again soon. He wondered about her suicide attempt.

THE SEARCH BEGINS

According to librarian Miss Blanche MacKillop, the Truscott Public Library was established in 1950. This was after years, if not decades of attempts to centralize the library services of several Cape Breton counties. Mark was able to glean this biographical knowledge when he picked up a copy of a brochure published by the Truscott town government in the lobby of the Dunlop Inn the next morning. Since Mark planned a visit to the library that day, his career as an amateur sleuth to formally begin, information on the history of the library was convenient, if not useful. At the least, it provided him with a name to whom he could refer when he visited. Blanche, Blanche MacKillop, it was obvious. Her name sounded like it had been appropriated from a Tennessee Williams play, not that Mark was particularly familiar with American playwrights but the idea had suddenly occurred to him, explanation unknown, that pretty well anyone with the given name of Blanche belonged in a drama by Tennesse Williams play.

The Truscott Public Library was situated in a one floor, low slung brick building on the corner of Main

Street and Brunswick Avenue. It was right in the heart of Truscott itself, diagonally across the street from the town hall with two churches, the union church of St. Augustine to the east and the Catholic Church, Our Lady of Fatima, to the west. It looked more like an elementary school than a library although that assessment was hardly unexpected, many civic buildings built in the era similar in design. Mark parked the car in the lot behind the library, walked to the front of the building, went up two steps, opened one of the two glass doors and casually ambled up to the front desk. Miss Blanche MacKillop stood behind the desk, as advertised. She looked like she had been waiting for him. It was fairly obvious that she hadn't been doing anything particularly important. She looked like she had been on guard.

It was curious. Going with the Tennessee Williams reference, he had hoped that Miss Blanche MacKillop would look a lot like Vivian Leigh or any other actress that may have or could have played Blanche Dubois. The Hollywood Blanche, the Broadway Blanche, every Blanche seemed to have a face framed by huge blond curls, a face with carefully arched eyebrows, an aquiline nose, and artfully applied ruby lipstick. She should have been wearing a loose fitting negligee, the term peignoir popped into his mind. She was the portrait of a star, a picture in a magazine from the 1950s, an anachronism from a black and white world long gone.

He had been imagining the whole scene, a notion that he doubtless formed after he first read her name in the brochure he had picked up in the lobby of the Dunlop Inn. As it turned out, Blanche MacKillop was definitely not that Blanche or any other Blanche he had had the occasion to envisage. Instead, she was a short, middle aged woman with silver hair twisted in a bun on the top of her head. She wore a beige cardigan over a white blouse with ivory buttons and a dark brown checked skirt. Although he couldn't see her shoes, she was likely wearing a utilitarian style, nun's shoes in the common vernacular. There was a severe look on a pudgy face belied by a surprisingly inviting smile. Despite her generally inviting look and the Blanche Dubois characterization, Mark still approached her like a penitent. Mitigating his anxiety was a hangover that was producing a light throb in his head like a radio signal. Although he was hardly a frequent denizen of libraries, he knew enough about the modern versions, with their pin numbers, book scans and technology, to realize that Blanche MacKillop was an anachronism, a librarian out of the 1950s.

"Good morning, sir. Can I help you?" Miss MacKillop asked, her voice soft, as decorous as a kindly kindergarten teacher.

Mark, momentarily tongue tied, first looked down at his feet and then looked up. There was a dark stained wood counter between the two of them. Mark studied the surface of the counter. It looked like it had been installed when the library was constructed in 1950. It was resplendent with pen marks, knife cuts and assorted unidentifiable ruts on the surface. He was standing there tranquilized, in some sort of trance, as Miss MacKillop repeated her offer to assist him for a second and then a third time. MacKillop had gradually developed that stern look that his own mother used to affect when she was annoyed, which was hardly infrequent. His mother's name was Martha, a name that could have easily been assigned to Miss MacKillop Mark came to attention, he was anxious for some reason. He finally introduced himself, almost trembling. He just went on to explain his purpose in visiting town, a recitation that required Miss MacKillop's rapt attention for a good ten minutes. Her irritation abated into something approaching actual interest. Mark inevitably asked her whether the library had information on provincial adoptions. She stared thoughtfully forward for a moment, a brief moment that seemed a lot longer as he continued to stand there, still a little nervous, likely due to the reminiscence of his mother. Miss McKillop gave him a curt nod and began to report on the relevant information that the library possessed on such matters.

"Well, Mr. Purchell," explained Miss MacKillop, "there are a broad range of information sources on adoptions. The internet is full of them but you probably already know that."

Mark smiled and provided a nod of his own. "I do. There are dozens of sites. The whole thing is quite confusing. I have investigated several of them without much success. I mean, some of them are testimonials, some of them are just listing of adoptees, birth mothers, birth fathers, siblings, other family members, even friends --- people like me --- looking for information on adoptions." Mark delayed for a moment and then proceeded with emphasis on a particular site. "One of them, something called *Adoption.Com* or *Adoption Exploration* and *Solutions* or *Adoption Trace*, I can't really remember which, even recorded a number of profiles and statistics about the site. They included the total number of profiles added in the past month, the number in the past week, the number in the past day, even the number of profiles put up in the past hour, the past hour for God's sake." Mark stopped again for a second and apologized for that last expression, thinking that referring to the divinity in the presence of Miss MacKillop was probably some sort of profanity. "Sorry. Anyway, that particular site had more than half a million profiles. That's a lot of profiles to go through."

Miss MacKillop offered a sympathetic smile. "I agree. That's a lot of names to go through."

"I know." replied Mark. "Do you have any sort of recommendation, the best site for somebody looking for an adoption?"

Miss MacKillop offered a gentle smile, a facial expression that would not have looked out of place in an exchange between a mother and a child. "The most dependable source of such information, at least as far as I'm concerned, is a website called the *Adoption Registry*. It's a fairly simple database that includes information provided by adoptees and birth parents. Even though the information database is pretty well worldwide, it can be accessed by country and province." Mark immediately stepped forward toward the counter, now almost leaning in. "Thanks so much. I'm surprised and pleased as hell." Miss MacKillop looked momentary taken aback, the use of a second minor profanity the likely explanation. Mark continued. "That's unbelievable. I couldn't have imagined that it could be that easy. Just look up my friend Jack's name and ....".

Miss MacKillop interrupted him "It won't be that easy. It won't be that easy at all."

Mark looked back at her with a momentarily blank look on his face. He then looked up and to the right, as if he was searching the ceiling for an answer to a question that he then quietly posed to Miss MacKillop, a little bewildered. "Not easy? How can you say that? I mean, this website looks like it might be a pretty good source for the kind of information I'm looking for, wouldn't it?"

Miss MacKillop smiled again, kindly, serenely. "Don't get me wrong, dearie.", the familial expression a surprise but then again, not really a surprise. "It's certainly a start but it may not be the panacea that it appears to be." Mark looked down from his consideration of the ceiling, a little surprised on hearing an unlikely word --- "panacea". It wasn't a term that he heard very often. The continuing sympathetic expression on Miss MacKillop's face suggested that she expected Mark to immediately accept the shortcomings of a website to which she had just referred. "It has certain limitations." she explained, her voice still as soft as that of a kindergarten teacher. She went on to describe the website as not providing comprehensive information, limited as it was to voluntary submissions, a defect of these types of sites. She further noted that only those individuals searching for the eventual destinations of children given up for adoption or children taken from them or lost children looking for birth parents provided information to the *Adoption Registry*. In addition, most of the information was in the form of inquiries by inquisitive parents or the curious adopted looking coincidentally for the same thing. Miss MacKillop then pointed out, her soft voice so quiet that Mark had to practically lean over the counter, that more detailed information, like names, locations, and the like may be available for a fee, a fact that she observed was predictable. "Nothing's free, you'll realize." she added.

"Let me show you," Miss MacKillop offered. She then turned to the computer monitor, gently typed in a short entry, and was handing Mark one page of names, obviously printed off the *Adoption Registry* website. At the top of the page, which was obviously the opening page to a specific section, there was a subtitle: "The Nova Scotia Register of Adoptions and Adoption Searches". In the lower right corner of each page was a space for an e-mail address for future notifications of new queries. Rather than print out the entire registry each time someone asked about it, Miss MacKillop kept one compendium of the entire registry under the counter, a sort of reference manual shackled together by block office clips. He thought she should have had the pages more elegantly bound.

Miss McKillop pulled the registry pages from under the counter and slid them across to Mark. He started to casually thumb through the stapled pages. There were hundreds of pages, a quick calculation suggested, several inches thick, all of which either announced or were searching for the facts of specific adoptions, of themselves or individuals to whom members of the registry may have been related. Aside from the sheer quantity of entries, which should not have surprised him, Mark also noticed that many of the entries, at least on the first few pages, identified the seekers as residents of Truscott. One conclusion seemed unavoidable. Truscott may have been inundated with people who were adopted, people who thought they were adopted, or strangely, people who wanted to be adopted. The latter group would seemingly be burdened with a pathology that was rarely reported but was a legitimate condition, bizarre psychological behavior that Mark having come across the description in the clinical literature.

After allowing Mark to examine the registry for several minutes, Miss MacKillop motioned him toward a long wooden table equipped with eight chairs and four table lamps. The lamps, antique devices that might well have graced libraries in the previous century, the sole illumination for rooms in the days when overheard lighting was limited to chandeliers equipped with candles.

"I suspect that you might want to be comfortable in order to study the document." opined Miss MacKillop. "I assume you would want to scrutinize it for more than a few minutes." She made the offer with a kind smile, knowing, given her experience with previous visitors to the library, that curious visitors with ambitions regarding the mysteries of adopted children needed reassurance.

Mark picked up the stapled papers, tucked them under his arm like he was about to attend class, and headed for the table with the antiquated lamps. "Thank you, Miss MacKillop. I imagine I will have to spend some time with, as you say, the document." As a matter of fact, I can't believe how fortunate I am to have approached you before pursuing some of the other avenues of research I have discovered." Miss MacKillop lightly laughed, the only kind of laugh that Mark thought she would be capable of. "Yes, of that I would be sure." she observed. Mark asked if others had been or were as interested in investigating such matters. He stared at her, waiting for her answer.

Miss MacKillop's smile faded, her gaze turned serious, as she was compelled to think about the answer. She explained, a quiet voice now diminished to almost a whisper, as if interest in the adoption registry was a secret. "Yes, there has always been an interest, a significant interest. I usually understand but not always."

Mark was surprised. He had generally considered his interest in adoptions relatively unique. Adoptions were uncommon these days, he thought, unless, it seemed, the adoption involved an orphan from another country. More than fifty years ago, an era in which everyone seemed to be familiar with the concept of an orphanage, the idea of adoption was still rare though less so. Fact was that the only adopted child Mark ever came across, or at least the only adopted child he ever knew about was Jack Quinn. But now, after becoming aware of the level of interest in adoption that was evident in Truscott, his investigation was now more than a retrospective promise to a dead friend. There was something fascinating about the issue, at least fascinating to him. His curiosity had grown. The search for Jack Quinn's origins had now developed into something more than a reluctant obligation to a dead friend. It had become almost an obsession. Somehow he had to know.

Mark took a seat at the table with the antique lamps and the stack of stapled papers from the *Adoption Registry*. Before he sat down, he remembered, the rather whimsical recommendation that Elaine had made to him the previous evening at the Thistledown Pub. He turned back to the library counter to again seek the counsel of Miss MacKillop who was back at the computer, presumably searching for a book for an elderly woman who had replaced Mark at counter. Again for reasons perhaps related to the ache warehousing in his forehead, Mark thought of the old card indexes that Miss MacKillop would have likely been looking through in response to such a request decades ago. He stood behind the elderly woman, waiting, holding the papers. He started to look through them when Miss MacKillop returned and pushed a small piece of paper, a yellow post-it note actually, across the counter to the elderly woman. She pointed over the lady's left shoulder toward the front door of the library.

The elderly woman turned and started toward the front of the library with the piece of paper in her hand. She took a couple of steps and then dropped the post-it note. Mark picked it up, noticed a eight numeral number on the note and handed it back to the elderly woman. She smiled through frightfully obviously false teeth and slouched towards her destination via the Dewey Decimal System. Mark turned back toward Miss MacKillop with a chagrined smile on his face, as if he was reconsidering his next approach to the librarian. To Mark, she looked like she was not looking forward to resuming their conversation. Maybe the old lady had annoyed her somehow although Mark did have a tendency to exaggerate unfortunate personal observations about other people. This was particularly true about people in authority, even about librarians named Blanche. Jack used to call the trait a kind of reverse paranoia although anytime he made the comment, he always amended it after the fact by saying that he didn't really know what the hell he was talking about. Miss MacKillop shifted her gaze from the old woman retreating and waited for another inquiry. Mark approached her cautiously, gingerly, still wearing an embarrassed look on his face. She quickly preempted him by posing the inevitable question.

"Can I help you....again?" asked Miss MacKillop. Affably stern was the closest description he could contrive regarding the expression on her face. For that instant, she now reminded Mark of his first grade teacher, Miss Helen McCarthy, who could console you with a pat on your shoulder one minute and then frighten the hell out of you with a swing of a yardstick the next. But Mark should not have been alarmed. She was neither looking nor sounding irritated. Mark still wasn't convinced, his curious neurosis about authority figures still lingering somewhere in the back of his mind. He was standing a couple of steps away from the counter and wanted to whisper but that wouldn't do. He may have to raise his voice, something that seemed ill-mannered somehow, something that no one would ever have the nerve to inflict on someone like Blanche MacKillop. So he took a couple of steps forward. He looked across over the counter at Miss MacKillop --- no reaction.

He asked another question. "Do you know a man called Mr. Pictures? He was supposedly the town photographer? A waitress I met in town mentioned him to me. She said he could be helpful in finding out about my adopted friend's parents. She said that he and his father were the town's unofficial historians, that they apparently knew everyone. They could have taken pictures of everyone who ever lived in Truscott over the past fifty or sixty years. The waitress told me his real name was Ralph Smithers. Do you know him?"

Miss MacKillop responded with another one of her soft little smiles. "Yes, I do. Everybody knows Mr. Smithers, known him for years. In fact, I knew about his father as well. He was called Mr. Pictures as well. I was an adolescent when he died." She was silent for a moment and resumed her commentary. "And you want to know if I believe that Ralph Smithers can help you in your quest?"

Mark nodded, an expression of anticipation on his face. "Yes. I'd like your opinion. I think it may be a little more credible than that of a waitress at a local restaurant."

"I wouldn't be too sure about that." replied Miss MacKillop. "People often sell waitresses short, particularly if they work in a small town like this one. They often know more about the people they serve than their friends do. They talk to them, they see the people they dine with, they overhear their conversations, they are aware of innuendo, town rumors, that sort of thing."

"So this Mr. Smithers probably would be a good source of information, you know about the town?" Mark observed.

"Without a doubt, Mr. Purchell." agreed Miss MacKillop. "Mr. Smithers used to come into the library, fairly often too. We used to talk about his collection of photographs. He said he had tens of thousands of them and that didn't include his father's collection, which he claimed was as large as his. I asked him more than once if he would donate some of his photos to the library."

Mark moved closer to the counter as he listened to Miss MacKillop. "Did he donate any pictures?"

Miss MacKillop shook her head, her silver hair stationary in its bun, her gentle smile almost contemplative now, her eyes narrowed, she was remembering something. "No, but it wasn't because of lack of trying. I tried to convince Mr. Smithers several times. I even managed to get the mayor involved. He offered to add a small wing on the library --- a sort of miniature museum to exhibit his pictures, to house them, to preserve them. But unfortunately, he wasn't interested. He just didn't want to share his pictures with the public. The town may end up with his photographs anyway, that is if we can find them." Mark looked puzzled. Miss MacKillop answered the unasked question. "You know, when he passes. Nobody thinks he has any heirs."

Mark shifted the conversation somewhat. He had to ask. "Have you seen any of his pictures? His or his father's for that matter."

She looked up. "Yes I have. Like almost every place in t he town, he has taken photographs here in the library on many occasions. I have seen most of them. He showed them to me. He had, and he presumably still has, hundreds of photographs taken here in the library. I offered to display them as well but, like his other photographs, he refused."

"So you haven't seen any of his other photographs?" asked Mark.

Again Miss MacKillop shook her head, in continued resignation it seemed. "Some of them, the ones that appeared in the newspaper."

"The newspaper?"

"Yes, the *Truscott News* --- it's a weekly with a small circulation, just here in town you'll understand." she explained and then let out a quiet, likely accidental titter. "It closed years ago."

"And Smithers worked for the paper?" Mark followed up.

"No, not really." she replied. "He occasionally worked for the paper, on consignment. If anything happened in town, anything that the paper wanted to report on --- things like accidents, any sort of crime, town council meetings, deaths --- Ralph Smithers would be called, to either ask him to take pictures or whether he had already taken pictures of whatever event the paper wanted to report on."

"So you could then say that Mr. Smithers was the paper's photographer." Mark thought for a moment that Miss MacKillop might think his observation a bit impertinent.

"No, not formally but in practice, you'd have to say that. He also worked for the *Chronicle Herald* in Halifax," she added.

As interesting as the information on Ralph Smithers' contributions to local journalism provided by Miss MacKillop had been, it was not really advancing Mark's ambitions regarding the adoption of Jack Quinn. Although he would doubtless keep" Mr. Pictures" in mind for further investigation, he did have to proceed with the examination of the entries in the *Adoption Registry*. As he had noted in the few minutes he had invested in inspecting the document as he stood before Miss MacKillop, there was no alphabetic or temporal listing of the adopted looking for lost birth parents, birth parents looking for children that they had given up, or relatives or friends of either category. Further, the level of detail provided in each entry was predictably basic: the date and location of birth, including invariably the name of the hospital, the name of either the adopting parents or the adopted, and sometimes the name of the social worker who handled the adoption. Sometimes Some entries included additional details, like birthmarks for example.

It was obvious to Mark that finding something useful in hundreds of pages of individual entries in the *Adoption Registry* would be fortunate to say the least, almost a fluke. Fact was that in order to properly pursue the search for Jack Quinn's birth parents, he would have to list Jack's profile, which was generally incomplete, limited to his name and the place and date of his birth, the latter two details hardly definite since they were based on Jack's assertions at one time or another. In that regard, Jack claimed that his birth certificate was based on a certificate of Catholic baptism. There were, however, a number of problems with Jack's report about any record of his birth. They were more like mysteries than simple bureaucratic errors, the most significant of which was the fact that Jack's birth certificate wasn't available for inspection. Mark wouldn't be surprised if Jack had either lost the certificate or never had it in the first place. Jack had also reported, during one of the few conversations they had had about his birth certificate, that the church issuing the certificate had burned to the ground more than fifty years ago. It had never been replaced. Jack also said that the date of issuance of the certificate was more than two years after the date of birth recorded on the document. Although he seldom discussed the matter, this fact was the basis for Jack's belief that he had been adopted by a local Catholic family two years or more after he was born. In any event, however, the accuracy of the dates was dubious.

He thought about these circumstances as he stared at page two of the stack of pages of the *Adoption Registry* he had borrowed from Miss MacKillop. At first, Mark had concluded that even if he chose to e-mail Jack's profile to the website, there would be substantive elements of the profile missing. After all, what clues could he offer in constructing a profile of Jack Quinn that could be considered unquestionable --- his name and maybe his place of birth, information that was provided by a presumable unassailable source, Jack Quinn himself. In looking through the first few pages of the *Adoption Registry,* he came across several entries that were similar in circumstances to those facing Mark. There were two of them in the first five pages.

> *<u>Bradley</u>: I am searching for my mother's birth parents or siblings. She was born Margaret Joyce Bradley in Sydney in 1966. Please take note that I am searching with her permission but for my own interests. She is not interested in any results.*

> *<u>Campbell</u>: My adopted name is Curtis Michael Campbell. To the best of my knowledge, I was born January 16, 1962 and was adopted*

in Halifax sometime in the spring of 1964
through the Catholic Charities by John and
April Campbell, both of whom are deceased. I
am interested to learn who my birth parents are
and any medical history that may be important.
I am also curious to know if I have any other
surviving family members and whatever I can
learn about my family history.

After reading the first five pages of the *Adoption Registry*, particularly the two entries that came to his specific attention, Mark had changed his mind about the efficacy of adding the limited data he had on Jack Quinn to the thousands of listings that were already sitting on the *Adoption Registry* site. Before he did change his mind, as he continued to look through the entries, he wondered how long each individual record stayed on the site and, more importantly, whether successful connections were recorded and publicized by the *Adoption Registry,* and whether such listings were removed from the site. He also noted that there were a number of so-called "commands" or services that potential clients could take advantage of once they submitted their registry biographies. These allowed clients, in order of importance, to correspond with the person providing the profile, post a new listing, view all listings provided by each submitter, edit the listing, and, surprisingly, an invitation for clients to report whether any profile is offensive. Mark was stunned by such an invitation, speculating about the criteria for defining offensive. He had no idea and he thought that maybe no one else did either although he did wonder whether profiling an adopted individual who had passed away might be considered offensive to those who were consulting the registry.

He had cleared his mind about the details of the listing protocol. It was worth a shot he figured. It was a little like entering the lottery except that it was free. Having definitely changed his mind about the entering it in the *The Nova Scotia Register of Adoptions and Adoption Searches,* he started to consider the wording of the profile of Jack Quinn. He considered the facts for the hundredth time. What did he really know? The source of the mystery that he was attempting to solve was that a close friend discovered shortly before his death that he had been adopted, a suspicion he had long held. Once more, he had been adopted, or so he had been told, by the two people that he thought were his birth parents. They were from the small town of Truscott, Nova Scotia. And finally, he understood that the adopted friend knew of only four people, aside of course from his parents, that knew the truth. Not much to go on but it was all he had.

He got up from his seat at the table, walked across the floor, got the attention of Miss MacKillop with a determined little wave and then asked her for pen and paper. Miss MacKillop nodded, held up a cautious finger, reached under the counter in front of her, and shuffled a single piece of paper and a pen across the surface of the counter toward him. The pen fell on the floor and she immediately apologized. Mark picked up the pen, thanked Miss MacKillop and then was surprised when she spoke to him.

"Have you found anything of interest?" asked Miss MacKillop.

Momentarily stunned, as if he didn't really hear her, Mark then attempted to recover with a weak, almost inaudible rejoinder. "Pardon me."

MacKillop leaned over the counter and replied to him --- she knew that he had said something because his lips had moved --- with an identical inquiry. Mark cleared his throat, a move that he hoped had not disturbed Miss MacKillop, and repeated his apology, in a higher decibel voice this time. Miss MacKillop smiled and then asked again in that smoothing kindergarten teacher voice. "Did you find anything of interest yet?"

"No, I'm just drafting an entry for the registry." Mark replied. "I want to get a notice on the list as soon as possible."

Miss MacKillop nodded and asked. "So are you hopeful?"

Mark responded with a smile of his own and a shake of the head. "Not really with a list like this." he said, motioning to the bound list of notices sitting on the table, "but it's still worth a try. After all, it won't cost me a cent."

Miss MacKillop smiled again and agreed. "Right, so why not?"

Mark returned her smile, took the pen and paper, and headed back to the table. He noted that the paper had her full name printed on the top of the page in bold italics ---- *Miss Blanche MacKillop*. The piece of paper was obviously a page from one of those personalized writing pads that accompanied charitable appeals. He sat down at the table and within several minutes, drafted something he thought would do, borrowing the wording from the examples he had come across. For a moment, he considered sharing the product with Miss MacKillop but then he didn't.

> *Quinn: I am searching for my recently deceased friend's birth parents and/or siblings. He was adopted by Robert and Eileen Quinn of Truscott, Nova Scotia sometime in the early to mid 1950's. His name was Jackson Quinn. Aside from his adopted parents Robert and Eileen Quinn, he had a cousin named Glen Quinn, and an aunt and uncle, also named Quinn. Please take note that I am searching further to the last wishes expressed by Jackson Quinn.*

Mark read and reread the notice and then, after an appropriate instance of reflection, e-mailed the final product from his laptop to the website provided by the registry. He had actually contemplated offering a reward for any pertinent information, just like a notice to a bounty hunter in an old postal office. He wanted to wait to examine the final text on the site but approximated, more like a guess, that it would probably take a day or so before it would appear on the site. Jack then went back to combing through the pages of the registry, reading through dozens of nearly identical stories. While most concerned people looking for their own birth parents, a sizable minority involved people looking for the birth parents of their mothers, their fathers, their brothers, their sisters, aunts, uncles, and, as was the case for Mark's investigation, friends. There were also some strange entries, people who were searching for the accurate dates of their births, the correct spelling of their adopted names, and more than one entry that were disputing the identities of their birth parents. In one almost hysterical account, the writer challenged the veracity of the names of the parents who did the adopting.

Many of the individual listings included references to other websites. Major examples included the ubiquitous *Ancestry.com*, the world's largest online resource, something called *Fold3*, a compendium of military and historical documents. There was GeneralBank, a collection of obituaries and death records which had appeared in newspapers. Some required fees, others did not. In addition, there were references to a host of other resources, most of which seemed to be provided by various government agencies. Then there were the various sources of reference material that he had already determined were available in Truscott: the library in which he was sitting, the municipal Heritage and Archives Department, the two churches, the two schools, the post office, the RCMP detachment, the local legion and even the Victorian County hospital. And then there was always Mr. Pictures.

His meeting with the head librarian ended with a final piece of advice from who he had started to regard as a town seer, a sort of small town oracle, at least as far as Truscott was concerned. Mrs. MacKillop suggested, as he was handing the *Ancestry.com* listings back to her, that he might want to investigate the province's orphanages, a history of which might be available on any number of websites, if he was inclined to look for them. She also suggested that the local Catholic Diocese could be a possible source of information. Mark thanked her for a final time and walked toward the door. He was ready to head back to the Dunlop Inn, perhaps for a quick nap, contemplation of his next move, and then dinner, hopefully at the Bell-Buoy-Blue with Elaine the waitress.

ANOTHER EVENING WITH ELAINE

Aside from meeting Miss Blanche MacKillop, someone who Mark thought might eventually turn out to be a valuable research assistant should his investigation hit an unexpected obstacle, his visit to the Truscott Public Library did result in one other success. While he was drifting through the *Adoption Registry*, he came across a peculiar entry that doubtless bore further investigation. It was on page 134 of 250, the total number of pages that had been produced by the library's printer. Mark briefly wondered about the total number of pages that the website could make available ---- 500, 1000, 5000? But he got as far as the page on which a man named Archibald John Stewart had recorded a unique plea for information about adoptions.

> *<u>Quinn:</u> My name is Archibald John Quinn. I have come to believe that my parents, Melvin and Edith Quinn of Baddeck, Nova Scotia, fostered two young children before I was born. I have come to believe that they were then abandoned before my twin brother, Hugh*

> *James, and I were born in 1949. I understand*
> *that their names were Allison and Beverly and*
> *they were five and four years old when they left*
> *my parents' care. My mother passed away three*
> *years ago, my father having died four years*
> *before that. I was then informed, through her*
> *will, of this fact. Like other siblings in similar*
> *circumstances I imagine, curiosity impels me*
> *to seek any information I can about children*
> *that my parents could have fostered. I would*
> *therefore appreciate any information anyone*
> *could provide about these girls.*

Predictably, Mark was immediately struck by the unique nature of Mr. Quinn's investigation into his history. He mulled over the circumstances of this search. He began to think of his pursuit into the past as a kind of family archaeology, just the kind of hobby that someone with nothing better to do might pursue. Searching for the identities of two women, who were released from one family's foster care almost seventy years ago seemed, at least on the surface, strange, if not a trifle bizarre. These women would be headed toward eighty years old now, that is if both were still around. Sitting on the edge of the bed in the Dunlop Inn, he pondered the possible reasons for such an ambition.

While such an investigation might seem interesting, if not startling, particularly if a discovery was made, it would likely be good for maybe five minutes of fascination, like unexpectedly coming across your name in a newspaper. Mark therefore questioned the utility of having, if not seeking such information. Aside from curiosity, Mark wondered why Mr. Quinn would want such information. If anyone happened to provide any useful information to Mr. Quinn, would he then attempt to seek them out and meet people to whom he would be a complete stranger? The women had departed their birth parents before he and his brother, were born, knowledge about these two foster children not evident until their former foster parents had died.

It struck Mark like that proverbial inspiration, as obvious as it was. However self-evident, he continued to think about it and then decided, after an interval that seemed to be a somewhat lengthy, to contact Mr. Quinn, if for no other reason than curiosity. Besides, he would be connecting with someone who had the same family name as the person for whom he was seeking an answer to a similar mystery. He took out his laptop, typed out a message to the doubtless inscrutable Archibald John Quinn, and sent it. Like a lot of the things he did, he almost immediately regretted it.

> Quinn to Quinn: *I read your current entry in The Nova Scotia Register of Adoptions and Adoption Searches. While I cannot provide you with any information that might be of helpful to you in your search for the children fostered by foster parents, I may have similar interests in investigating adoptions and related situations in the province of Nova Scotia. In that context then, I would like to meet with you as soon as possible. I think we may be able to help each other in our respective quests.*

Specifically, he thought the use of the word "quest" in his message to be inappropriate, almost antiquated, given the circumstances. But by the time he had come to that conclusion, the message was on its way and he was drifting into afternoon slumber. When he awoke, maybe two hours later, it was close to dinner hour. He thought of the Bell-Buoy-Blue. He wanted to see Elaine again. He wanted to speak with Elaine and hoped that he would arrive during her shift. But he needn't have worried. The previous evening, she had said that she worked a shift practically every day. He had forgotten she had said that.

The Bell-Buoy-Blue was less than half full when he arrived. It was a Tuesday evening. With no hostess to greet diners, the waitress closest to the entrance had the responsibility. Elaine Butler just happened to greet him, a big smile on her face.

"I didn't expect to see you so soon but I'm glad to see you." said Elaine as he handed him a menu and furnished him with a slight squeeze of his forearm.

Mark stood there, almost perplexed, almost scared by Elaine's enthusiasm. But he still recovered quickly enough to return her smile and her comment. "I'm glad too." He looked at her with a sincere, almost forlorn look on his face and stood there at the entrance like he was auditioning for a porter's job, waiting to carry someone's suitcase. He came up with something that was surprisingly flirtatious, even to himself. He didn't know how he managed it. "I was almost planning to came here all day, I mean for dinner." The smiles stayed on both their faces. And he almost, but didn't, hug her. Elaine escorted Mark to the same table, one of the tables with the little blue and white flags, the same table at which he had enjoyed dinner and a conversation with Elaine the previous evening.

Before he sat down, he ordered the fish and chip dinner and a draft of Big Bruce and handed the menu back to Elaine. When Mark handed back the menu, she gave him a copy of the November 15 copy of Halifax's *Herald Chronicle*. Mark thanked her and spread page one of the newspaper on the table with the little blue and white flags. He didn't recall seeing Elaine carrying the newspaper. He took a quick look at the paper and noted three headlines, all typical it seemed of the big deal/small time press:"Morgan To Serve Eight Years for Manslaughter", "Dealing With Vandalism At New Victoria Cemetery", and "Sydney's Peterson Recognized With Medal". At the bottom of the page, in a horizontal script, was an advertisement for something called Joe's Barnstorm. Even a picture of a horse standing in a corral wasn't much of a hint. He turned to page two and scanned the article about a man named Michael Morgan who killed a man named Douglas Turner in a bar after a Midget A hockey game in the small Cape Breton town of Baddeck. While there was a fair amount of crisply written prose about the Mr. Morgan's trial; a judge named Palmer, a prosecutor named Bailey, a defense attorney named Martin, the accused, the victim and a parade of witnesses all telling the same story about a dispute in a bar called The Green Hornet. Unfortunately, at least to Mark, there wasn't any commentary as to the basis for the argument that concluded in the death of a man named Turner.

And then, for reasons that should have been obvious given his current aspirations, Mark turned to the obituary page. There were five entries, three men and two women, only one of whom was younger than 80 years old, a man who died in his 59th year after a "brave battle" with brain cancer. For a moment, Mark wondered whether there was any other kind of battle or whether there was ever a battle at all. He thought of his own father, who drifted into his demise while continually yelling absurdities at the medical staff. Mark supposed that his father's behavior could have been so regarded as well although he didn't have cancer. He was just old, the onset of a little dementia a predictable consequence. Sitting there, he stared for another moment at the picture of the 58 year old man who had passed without any further explanation. He then moved on to the sports pages, where the main story concerned a volleyball team visiting from Yugoslavia. As weird as that was, he actually read the story.

He wished that Elaine would return with his order. He was bored. Even a couple of quick words from her, no matter how glib, would do. He was already starting to literally stare at the walls when Elaine arrived with his Big Bruce, remarking that his fish and chips would be "right up". He suddenly and surprisingly realized all of this scrutiny of the newspaper had probably taken up only five minutes of his less than precious time. He laughed to himself, thinking that it likely had taken about that length of time to put that day's edition together. Elaine heard his laugh and looked back at him. He noticed her butt. It wasn't the first time.

In what seemed to be a long wait, he continued to stare at the walls and think about the possibilities of an affair with Elaine. He was jolted out of his daydream when Elaine finally arrived with his fish and chips. She set the plate down in front of him, looked around for a moment, noting that none of her customers seemed to be in need, and initiated a conversation.

"Nothing in the paper of interest?" It seemed more like a statement than an inquiry. "Don't feel bad. There seldom is."

Mark looked up at her and shrugged. "I don't know. There could have been more details about the argument those two guys had at that hockey game."

Elaine almost laughed, more like a sinister snicker. "Well, you could guess. You know --- the usual craziness of a hockey game in a small town where there is little else to do, two drunken bozos who may or may not be fans of the opposing teams, and poof, you don't exactly have a hassle free evening."

"And sometimes somebody ends up dead." Mark exclaimed.

"Sometimes but not very often." replied Elaine, the whisper of a snicker now replaced with something approximately an actual laugh. Noticing that Mark's stunned expression was still on his face, Elaine pointed out, "I think the last time anyone actually died over there was probably three or four years ago."

Although he thought the question a little inappropriate, he offered Elaine a small smile and posed his inquiry anyway. "I wonder what they were fighting about."

"Nothing, probably like every other fight that happens at every small time bar on Cape Breton."

Mark just nodded and lamely commented, "I see. Not exactly like Ottawa."

"No, not exactly," Elaine said and then started to turn away and head for the kitchen. Before she took a step, Mark gently gripped her hand and blurted out a surprising proposal, at least to him but probably not to her. She had noticed the way he had regarded her, frequently.

"Maybe we can talk about it later tonight, you know, at the Thistledown Pub?" he asked, hopefully.

"Maybe".she answered. "Depends how I feel by ten o'clock".

Mark offered Elaine a big smile, picked up a fork and started into his fish and chips. He anxiously watched Elaine walk away. He wasn't sure that it was anxiety that accompanied his gaze. He was attracted to her and thought about doing what he could do to let her know that he was interested. Mark finished his fish and chip dinner, his second glass of Big Bruce, and waited for Elaine to bring him the bill. He glanced about the room, noticing the six other tables that were occupied by Tuesday night dinners. Two tables shared by two couples each, one with a single couple who seemed to be quietly discussing something confidential, if not romantic, and the remaining three tables inhabited by two lonely men and an elderly woman wearing a huge navy blue sweater with images of crocheted whales emblazoned on the sleeves and the back. She was in the process of attacking her lobster dinner, sitting like she was wielding a harpoon. She also seemed to be glancing at a magazine that was spread out in front of her. Mark was studying the sweater woman with increased interest --- he had seen her the night before sitting at the same table --- when Elaine arrived with the bill and a bit of often repeated advice.

Having noticed that Mark was staring at the sweater woman, Elaine slapped the bill on the table and softly nudged Mark with an elbow. "Don't go near her. She is a little eccentric, if you know what I mean."

"Yeah, that's pretty obvious," replied Mark with a deliberate smile and a nod. "Does she ever wear anything else?"

Elaine chuckled, placed the bill on the table, started to walk away and then turned back, leaned in and whispered a confidence. "No, I've never seen her wearing anything else and she comes in here for dinner maybe three or four times a week, always in that same blue sweater with the whales. I wouldn't be surprised if she wears that sweater to bed."

"And she's crazy too!" added Mark.

"Oh yeah, she's crazy as shit." Elaine agreed. She paused and then resumed her departure from the table. She stopped again and left Mark with an unexpected but welcome invitation. "And don't forget, I get off at 10:00. See you then." She turned and he watched her walk away. Mark thought of the word sashay, a word that his mother often used to describe girls of whom she disapproved.

Mark left two twenties on the table and headed for the door. He would be back to pick up Elaine in a couple of hours. He took one last look at Sweaters and left. He returned to the Dunlop Inn to consult his laptop for a message from Archibald John Quinn. There were three e-mails waiting for responses, none from Mr. Quinn. Two were from fellow Jack Quinn caregiver Deborah Inkster who, for reasons he understood but did not share, was still agonizing over the tragedy of Jack Quinn's death, if not his life. Every now and then, more now than then it seemed, Deborah would drop him a line to point out one or more unfortunate influences that led Jack to take a wrong turn at some point. This was an endless list: his mother, his father, his teachers, his damn hockey coaches, people at work, his friends, including Mark himself, his two wives, including Deborah herself, and whomever else she could remember who had made to cause him to take that wrong turn. Mark seldom responded to her depressing musings, hoping that she would just stop transmitting signs of her continuing lunacy. Fact was that it had grown quite annoying, most of his sympathy for her having evaporated over the few months since Jack had died. The other message concerned a Facebook post from a friend he barely knew. It concerned a recent news story regarding the reunion of two adopted brothers. It was the first Facebook post he had received in over six weeks. He immediately erased all three messages and realized that he wished he had never joined Facebook. Further, he had no idea as to how to discontinue his membership in Facebook. He had a brief thought of directly contacting Mr. Zuckerberg. It was a dream.

He then started to explore the various Nova Scotia websites he had identified in his initial research on provincial adoption. After discovering, much to his chagrin, that there were no results for adoption in the general Nova Scotia archives, the first useful site was entitled "Historical Vital Statistics". This potentially could provide birth registrations, marriages, and deaths divided into two eras for reasons unknown: specifically 1830-1915 and 1916-Present. He was of course particularly interested in the birth registration records, including a predictable array of information categories. Unfortunately, adoptions were not included in any of the records appearing in the "Historical Vital Statistics". He was disappointed but also relieved that he would not be compelled to spend hours searching through a morass of mostly meaningless minutiae looking for something that wasn't there.

After probing the archive for at least an hour, he came across Nova Scotia's Adoption Information Act, a statute that was created to assist people looking for members of their birth family. The introduction to the entitled "Adoption Disclosure" section did, however, emphasize that information will only be made available after both parties, the adopted and those who adopt, have consented. He checked his watch. He was to pick up Elaine at the restaurant in less than thirty minutes. He would start to read the summary of the Act tomorrow. He changed his clothes ---- he had been wearing the same shirt and trousers for two days. He thought Elaine might take note.

He didn't know why but he felt like smoking a cigarette as he sitting outside the Bell-Buoy-Blue in his rented *Ford Focus*. Perhaps it was the fact that the four people standing together in the parking lot were all smoking, a scene that was about as rare as it would have been common forty years ago. He actually considered getting out of the car, walking over to the happy quartet and asking for a smoke. As he was still pondering a return to nicotine, he noticed that one of the four was vaping, huge billowing clouds of counterfeit smoke drifting across the Bell-Buoy-Blue parking lot like a billboard that wasn't really there. For a moment, he thought he was smoking something beyond tobacco. It was a temporary image. Suddenly, Elaine was tapping on the window. She wasn't smoking although for that moment, he had wished she was.

She opened the door, got in the passenger side seat and brought the seat belt down across her chest. Mark noticed that her hair was somewhat disheveled and the top three buttons of her blouse were undone. He didn't say anything but was immediately reminded of Kate, a former work colleague who liked to show people in the office her underwear and in whom Mark had developed an infatuation that had lasted several months.

Mark greeted Elaine cheerfully, the thought of Kate continuing. "Hi," he said, "Looks like a tough night." She turned toward him and provided Mark with a wary, forced smile, as if she couldn't remember the reason for her smile. "Tough night? Yes, you can say that."

Mark moved closer and sympathetically replied, "Sorry to hear that." There was an odd silence for a moment. Elaine turned away from him and started to stare out the window. Mark elected to try a little humor, his usual alternative to any situation that was even remotely serious. "Did Sweaters finally change her top?"

"No. But it wasn't a great night," replied Elaine, turning back to look at Mark. He thought he detected the remnant of a tear in the corner of her left eye. She also moved closer to Mark. "What do you mean?" asked Mark, in almost a whisper.

Elaine looked up and told Mark that, toward the end of her shift, she had spilled coffee on an elderly man, a regular diner named Norman. Elaine explained that the event prompted considerable excitement, describing the entire scene as verging on hysteria, particularly from her boss, the owner of the Bell-Buoy-Blue, an unpleasant little toad of a man named George who usually supervised things from the kitchen. According to Elaine's narrative, George started yelling at Elaine, possibly thinking that Norman might use the opportunity to sue the restaurant for negligence, an experience that George, as the former owner of a convenience store, had previously endured. Elaine noted, however, that Norman, past 80 years old and generally feeble minded, was hardly astute enough to consider legal action, no matter what the result of a little coffee accidentally landing in his lap. Elaine finished her report by admitting that she thought for a few minutes that George would fire her for causing the mishap but forgot about the possibility, after remembering that George's wrath was usually short lived, not long enough for him to actually decide to terminate anyone.

Still, she reported, she was disturbed by the incident.

Elaine was now close enough for him to kiss. He did . She didn't seem surprised. It was a poignant kiss, almost feeling, at least to Mark, like a first kiss. She moved closer and placed her hand on his leg, a locale that had not been explored by any woman since a fellow commuter on a crowded city bus accidentally fondled his knee about a year ago or so. He remembered that the passenger in question, an attractive woman in her late middle age, offered an excessive apology, so much so that he thought, two minutes after she had disembarked, that he should have asked her out, or at least offered her something in the way of flirtatious banter. He actually thought about that woman as he accepted the move closer by Elaine, which now had crept dangerously close to his crotch. He was a trifle anxious. Elaine almost immediately sensed his discomfort and withdrew her hand. She wondered about the kiss as well. Perhaps it has been almost an adolescent reaction. He was wondering about it too.

Elaine spoke first, their faces still inches apart. She had a small earnest smile on her face. He was not smiling, he looked bewildered. "Well, that was strange." she said, neither of them sure whether she was referring to the kiss or his apparent reluctance to accept her further advances. He didn't answer so she continued with her analysis of the encounter so far. "I mean, I don't think I've run into anything like this for a while, certainly since my ex and I broke up. I don't really know what to do now." There may have been an unspoken and shared reference here, that the kiss was a sign of a fragment of a genuine romance and not the usual gymnastic groping that her hand on his thigh could have precipitated. Mark agreed with a murmured word, still considering his response to this sudden daydream. He then turned his eyes toward the windshield, put the car in gear and started toward the Thistledown Pub. He still had a blank look on his face. Elaine was still smiling, adding "Let's forget about that little situation, as weird as it was, until we've had a couple of beers." Then, she let out that cute little laugh of hers and turned forward to look through the windshield. Mark didn't think that a couple of Big Bruces would explain anything about what just happened between them. He also didn't think that he and Elaine would want to get into any sort of philosophical discussion about anything.

They rode in silence for several minutes until Mark managed, quite adroitly he thought, to change the subject. "With a boss like that, aren't you always worried about losing your job? I mean does that kind of thing happened often?" He turned to look at her. It was a serious question or at least he thought it was. Her smile evaporated as they were pulling into the parking lot of the Thistledown Pub. Her hand appeared again on his leg, her intention not in anyway libidinous. "Yes, all of the time. In fact, just last week, when I was on the morning shift, he yelled at me for ten minutes it seemed and at one of the cooks for poaching Mr. Jerome's eggs too damn hard." Mark parked the car, had the car door open, one leg on the ground, waiting.

"Poached eggs?" asked Mark, skeptically. This couldn't be serious he thought. "And who is Mr. Jerome?"

A smile re-emerged on Elaine's face ---- was it the thought of Mr. Jerome, whoever the hell he was, or the poached eggs that prompted the re-appearance of her grin? "Mr. Jerome is just an old guy who used to own the hardware store in town. He comes in every morning for poached eggs. The other three waitresses and I have been serving him bacon and two poached every morning for years and suddenly, one day last week he starts complaining about his damn poached eggs."

"And your boss starts to yell at you and the cook?" asked Mark, surprised but pleased that the subject had changed.

"Yes, and I thought George was going to have a heart attack." explained Elaine, that smile still affixed on her face like a cosmetic. "He demanded that I apologize to Mr. Jerome. I did, we gave him another plate, a free newspaper, and Mr. Jerome was out the door without another further trouble."

"And?" asked Mark.

Elaine shrugged. "And the next day, it was as if nothing had happened. Although the cook was asked to make sure they got the poached eggs right."

Mark smiled in response. "And did he?"

Elaine offered another smile and then a nod before she opened the car door. He guessed that he did.

They wondered carelessly into the rear of the room, passing the cement pillar with the posters plastered across every inch of its surface, and sat down in a shadowy corner, adjacent to the men's washroom on one side and an old fashioned telephone booth on the other. Mark commented on the telephone booth, noting that he hadn't seen one like that in over thirty years, recalling a similar antique convenience in a similar antique drinking establishment called the Glen Tavern, a dreary place that he and Jack had frequently patronized in their days of pointless assignation.

Elaine seemed interested, admitting with a casual smirk, that the Thistledown Pub was the only establishment that she frequented that was equipped with a telephone booth. She added that although she would be very surprised, even shocked perhaps, if anyone actually used the telephone booth in the Thistledown. Elaine then explained that most of the pub's patrons, including the older ones, were equipped with cellular telephones, making rotary telephones and telephone booths in which they were entombed profoundly redundant. Mark almost told Elaine about the several occasions when he and a female co-worker had had sex in a telephone booth located on the third floor of a decrepit office building where they were both worked for a bank. He still had an enduring recollection of both the woman and the relationship, particularly their telephone booth liaisons. As interesting as the story would have been, he never did mention it to Elaine, either then or any time after.

They had just sat down at the table in the shadowy corner when an older waiter approached them and asked for their pleasure. Elaine casually ordered two bottles of Big Bruce, just like she had the previous evening. For a fleeting moment, Mark thought of ordering a Stella Artois. This might well have have been seen as heresy in a place like the Thistledown Pub, that is until the place's new manager, who thought that the addition of foreign beers, including Stella, might add a certain zest to the place's menu. Ironically, Big Bruce was one of several locally crafted beers and was thought to have added zest when it was introduced to the menu a year or so ago. In any event, Mark did not say anything when Elaine went ahead with her order. She turned to Mark and pointed out that their waiter, the older man, was the father of the waiter who had served them the previous evening, the neatly attired and quietly efficient waiter named Tuck.

Mark was impressed, if not close to being kind of fascinated. Imagine, he thought, a family of waiters. "You're kidding, right?" he asked. He looked at Elaine with an amused look on his face. Elaine had already downed her first glass of Big Bruce when he turned toward Mark and looked through the glass as she was in the process of lowering it to the table. She smiled and started to pour herself more of her Big Bruce. She put down the bottle, nodded and replied in the affirmative. Elaine explained. "His name is Graham, Norm Graham, and I understand he has been waiting tables here for maybe forty years. So nobody is or was surprised when his son Tuck started working here. In fact, I'm told that Norm's wife, her name is Mary, worked here as well, back in the kitchen, until she had Tuck. And then, the place had to wait until Tuck was old enough to get a job here before another Graham took up a position at the Thistledown Pub. That was a couple of years ago."

Mark moved a little closer to the table, as if Elaine was about to share a secret. "Does that happen a lot here, you know here in Truscott?"

Elaine poured another glass of "Big Bruce", took a quick slip, and nodded again. "All the time I guess. I mean, it is after all, a pretty small town." Elaine shrugged. "I personally know of at least four father/son and mother/daughter combinations that are working in the same place."

Mark offered a light laugh, almost a snicker, and pointed out that he had once worked part time in the same department store as his father, a stint that lasted several months, at least until he got fired for running a refund scram with one of his felonious buddies. He also noted that a lot of his college friends were fortunate enough to obtain summer positions at their fathers' places of employment. But very few of them ended up working with their fathers beyond the summers. In fact, he could recall only one school friend that made a career at a company that also employed his father. Elaine concluded that part of the conversation by suggesting that things were different in small towns, where employment opportunities were not quite as abundant as they were in big cities.

Mark had to agree.

Elaine then asked about Mark's day of investigating the origin of Jack Quinn, specifically his day in the library and his conversations with the helpful Miss Blanche MacKillop. He mentioned his frustrations with the search for sites that could provide him with clues to the identity of Jack's natural parents. Elaine seemed to exhibit interest, sober enough interest despite the fact that she was already on the verge of finishing her second Big Bruce. She signaled to Norm Graham for another beer and then casually leaned across the table, putting her chin into her right hand. "Did any of the websites yield anything worthwhile?"

Mark nodded almost theatrically. "Oh yeah. I put an inquiry on the Registry of Adoptions and also replied to a notice on the same Registry that looks pretty interesting."

"What Registry?" asked Elaine, presumably unaware of the services available to inquisitive citizens. Norm brought another quart for Elaine and left. Mark noticed that, unlike his historical experience with other taverns, drinkers in Truscott, did not have have to pay for each beer as it was delivered. Perhaps it was the emergence of the use of credit and debit cards that prompted waiters and waitresses to wait until patrons were about to leave before asking for payment. Mark was transfixed for a moment, a flash of a memory of an old waiter in a tavern, the place may have been the immortal Glen Tavern. That waiter was a short, balding middle aged guy who would serve draft beers to any kid who could pay for them, a dime at a time, cash on delivery. Mark remembered that the waiter sported a leather fanny pack, a fashion accessory that was contemporary for the time. He remembered the scenes, a brief recollection of a group of high school classmates getting intoxicated in a working class tavern after investing a dollar on eight draft beers, servings of four at a time plus a dime gratuity. He then dropped the memory when Elaine asked again, "What Registry was that?"

Mark then answered Elaine. "It was the Nova Scotia Register of Adoptions and Adoption Searches."

"Sounds official, you know, kind of bureaucratic." observed Elaine. "Do you actually expect to get anything out of it." She smiled a little unwillingly, like she wasn't quite convinced she should have passed judgment on his choice of investigative direction. Mark shrugged. He wasn't sure that he would acquire anything of value from the day he had just spent interviewing Miss Blanche MacKillop and exploiting the resources of the Truscott Public Library. He explained. "Not sure, but it's probably worth a shot. I'll likely go back tomorrow to check out some other websites."

Elaine took the first gulp of her second Big Bruce and invited Mark to catch up, pointing to his beer, which had hardly been touched since it had arrived on the table. Mark nodded, poured himself a glass, took a quick sip, and continued his account of the websites he had already identified. This included sites devoted to births, deaths, and what appeared to be the most promising site of all, orphanages. He also recited a list of other possible sources of information about which he planned to become better acquainted in the next several days. He would visit the local detachment of the RCMP, the local Legion, two local churches, two local schools, and the Victorian County Hospital. Mark then said, with a wry little smile on his face, "And then maybe I'll have to consult with Mr. Pictures"." Mark then took another gulp of his beer.

Elaine grinned and looked impressed, commenting. "You're really are serious about this, aren't you?" Both of them drank in silence for a moment and then Elaine added another observation. "And if you're interested in seeking the advice of Mr. Pictures, one of his good friends is sitting in the corner over there, where a cigarette machine used to be." Elaine pointed across the room. Mark, who had no idea where the cigarette machine had been situated or why Elaine had mentioned a fact about which he couldn't be aware, looked around the room until Elaine apologized and pointed to a tall thin man wearing a straw hat, a blue blazer with a naval emblem on the breast pocket, and a striped rep necktie over an over sized white shirt. He was also sporting a pair of spectacle sun glasses. It must have been the fluorescent lights. Finally, Mark also noticed another detail, a silver cane hanging from the back of a chair at his table. The man was sitting alone behind a pint bottle of beer and a small shot glass. He was reading an electronic book.

"Really? Who is he?" asked Mark.

Elaine smiled. "His name is Andrew Ford, an old friend of Mr. Pictures. I have been told that the two of them have been close since both of them were in high school here in Truscott but not so much lately."

In an obvious piece of conjecture, Mark commented, "A falling out?"

Elaine shrugged. "I guess so but who knows."

Mark returned her shrug and asked. "Do you think he would be worth talking to and would he talk to me anyway? That is if all else fails."

"Worth talking to? Probably --- I mean, Mr. Ford was the guy's assistant for decades, even wrote the occasional press article as well. As far as whether he would be willing to talk to you. Sure, why not, guys that age, especially in the newspaper business, I think that they're always willing to talk about the the old days."

Mark looked at Mr. Ford and wondered. The man looked fashionably eccentric, a little like what he had imagined Mr. Pictures would look like. Mark had neither met nor seen the man but the two people who had recommended him insinuated that he was unconventional, maybe like the man he was staring at now. While Mark had hoped that his investigation of various websites and documents would produce results, credibility being the main reason, he was obviously interested in Mr. Pictures or his former friend. He had previously and presently pondered methods of approaching Mr. Pictures for information about the town's secrets, including adoptions he hoped. Now he had a second source of such information. Elaine poked Mark on the arm and pointed out that he had been staring at Mr. Ford. "As I'm sure you have already guessed, old man Ford is a little strange, a little unpredictable, just like his friend. They're both characters you know. Even so, he may not like someone staring at him."

Mark looked at Elaine, a little dumbfounded with Elaine's advice. "You'd think that the man would be used to being stared at. I mean, look at the way he's dressed --- elegant but a little unusual for this town, wouldn't you say?"

Elaine grinned and nodded. "Right....right. Some people call him the Ralph Lauren of Truscott, not that a lot of people in this town know who Ralph Lauren is."

Quiet for a moment, Mark then continued their consideration about Andrew Ford. "Aside from helping out Mr. Pictures occasionally, what did Mr. Ford do for a living? I mean, I'm assuming he's retired now."

Elaine smirked. "I'm surprised you haven't guessed. Andrew Ford used to own the only men's clothing store in the county. It's in Baddeck, which is about 50 kilometers from here, on the shore of the Bras d'Or Lake. Apparently, he inherited the store when his father passed away. His father was a dandy as well. The younger Mr. Ford moved from Truscott where he had worked with Mr. Pictures."

Mark was interested in Mr. Ford's biography. "So he was a news man and Mr. Pictures was a news photographer."

"That's right," said Elaine, "But their newspaper jobs were not their only occupations. Both pursued their artistic abilities on their own. Mr. Pictures sold a lot of his photographs to galleries around the island, though people have told me that he sold or even gave them away most of the them to individuals. After all, there aren't that many art galleries on the island or even in the whole province. On the other hand, he probably kept most of them himself, maybe thousands of photographs, enough to start his own museum I would guess. In fact, I heard he was planning one but but at his age he's probably running out of time. Fact is a lot of people would like to the family's pictures on display somewhere. I hear that the possibility has been discussed by the town council every now and then. But who knows?"

Mark asked again about Mr. Ford. "And what's the story with his friend Ford? What's he doing on the artistic side?"

Elaine gave Mark a knowing smile. "Oh, he writes books, mystery novels. I understand he publishes them himself and then hocks them in bookstores all over the island, even in Halifax. I doubt he makes any money, not too many sales even though I hear that the books are pretty good. I read his last one and I thought it was okay." Elaine paused for a moment and continued Mr. Ford's biography. "But he always needed the store to make a living."

As interesting as her report on Andrew Ford, he wasn't surprised. It seemed almost predictable. He thought of Ralph Smithers, i.e. Mr. Pictures, and wondered how he made a living. He doubted that selling photographs to local newspapers and to the region's art galleries, of which there were not many, was unlikely to support him. He had his wife and his two children. Blanche MacKillop had informed Mark that one of Mr. Picture's sons was a budding photographer, like his father and his grandfather. He then asked, as he had asked Miss MacKillop, whether he thought either Mr. Smithers or his friend Mr. Ford would be worthwhile sources of information in his search for the possible adoption of Jack Quinn. Elaine shrugged and observed that it would probably be worth a try, suggesting that Mark consider approaching Mr. Ford that evening, as he appeared to be in a good mood. Mark hesitated. He was being generally reluctant about approaching total strangers, particularly when they looked as unconventional as Andrew Ford. Elaine mentioned that he was available in the Thistledown Pub practically every evening.

After speculating about approaching Mr. Ford for Mark's investigation, Elaine asked about the basis for Mark's search for Jack's adoption. Just as she was raising the issue, two more quart bottles of Big Bruce arrived via waiter Norm Graham, her third, his second. For a moment, he caught himself staring at Elaine, realizing that any thought that Mark might have had of pursuing her intimately had almost evaporated with her declaration of curiosity in Mark's interest in his friend Jack's adoption.

"Tell me again, why go to all this trouble?" she asked in a low, almost conspiratorial voice. He might have thought it sultry if he had not discarded the whole idea of seducing her. She looked damn good, even after a twelve hour shift at the Bell–Buoy–Blue and sitting there in the dreadful artificial light of the back corner of the Thistledown Pub. For a moment, he thought of reconsidering the sudden disappearance of his temporary passion for Elaine.

It was tiresome. He thought, no in fact he knew, that he had already told Elaine the story of the search for Jack's real parents. Had she forgotten their conversation of the previous evening? Maybe four quarts of Big Bruce had something to do with it. Mark went ahead and rehearsed a reply to the question and repeated it endlessly in his head. "I told you, Elaine, remember? I was asked by a dead friend, a close friend, a guy who had recently been told he was adopted. So naturally, he was shocked and then wanted to know about his natural parents, you know, about his origins. And hell, it was his dying wish. I know it sounds strange but I felt that I had to at least try. Besides, I was curious, I have the time, and I really don't have anything better to do. It's like a vacation, an adventure. I thought it might be fun." A pause. "But I may have been about that."

For another moment, he thought of saying something flirtatious to Elaine but it passed. He worked up a look of sincerity, looked at Elaine squarely in the face, and then reached in his jacket pocket and produced a copy of Jack's last will and testament. He also took out his wallet and took out Jack's baby picture. Aside from Mark himself, Elaine Butler was the only other person to read the document that had initiated Jack's search. It was kind of like his Rosetta Stone.

Elaine took the single sheet of paper from Mark, carefully read its seven paragraphs, and looked up at Mark with a quizzical, almost skeptical look on her face. "Do you actually believe this?"

Mark shouldn't have been surprised but was anyway. Elaine's question seemed inappropriate, even rude, particularly given the circumstances of a grieving friend going to a lot of trouble to pursue the latter's dying request. "Yes, as a matter of fact, I do believe him, I believe the letter. I knew the guy for almost forty years and while he was quite the bullshit artist ----- he liked to use the word prevaricator ---- he considered himself a bit of a writer you see. He really wasn't, but he still liked to use unfamiliar words. In the end, I didn't think he would make up something like that, particularly in his so-called last will and testament." Elaine continued to have a slightly incredulous look on her face. "So you have no doubts about your friend Jack's story?"

Mark shook his head and softly smiled "Well, I wouldn't be here in your charming little town otherwise, meeting some of its charming people." He was trying to be slightly flirtatious rather than sarcastic. He still couldn't help responding to Elaine Butler in faintly licentious terms even though he had basically given up on actually approaching her in that regard.

The two of them sat in silence for a couple of minutes, seemingly contemplating their discussion while almost absentmindedly drinking their beers. Elaine then ordered another quart. Norm gestured toward Mark who declined the offer, he had almost a full bottle left. Elaine then resumed the conversation by raising the whole concept of adoption, which always seemed to interest, if not fascinate some people, if not a lot of people. "Do you know other people that have been or could have been adopted?" Her tone suggested that she was just making conversation.

"You mean aside from Jack?" Mark facetiously replied, a slight grin on his face to match the one on her face.

Elaine nodded laconically and moved toward him with her elbows now on the table, as if she was pretending to await a revelation of some significance, the grin on her face still affixed. Before Mark could answer --- he briefly wondered whether he was actually required to reply --- Norm showed up with Elaine's beer, forcing her to take her elbows off the table. She leaned back in the chair, spread her arms out briefly, returned them to the table and started to pour herself another beer.

Mark waited until she had taken her first swig of her third quart of Big Bruce. As she had the previous evening, Elaine was demonstrating her ability to consume alcohol with impressive alacrity. Coincidentally enough, this was a capability she shared with his old pal Jack Quinn. "Yeah, I had an childhood friend who was one of three kids adopted by the same family. It was well known around the neighborhood, everybody knew about it."

"Okay, so it was a neighborhood story, a little peculiar but why your continuing interest?" prompted Elaine.

"Well, Pete --- that was my friend's name, Pete --- talked about it. I don't know if his two adopted brothers talked about their adoption but Pete sure talked about it, especially when he got into his teens. He was weird about it. He started to use the adoption as some sort of excuse for anything, like he couldn't get a date or he was cut from a team or he had flunked history. He was neurotic about it."

Elaine asked the next question. "And how long did that last?"

Mark shrugged. "After a couple of years, he realized that the sympathy thing wasn't working, especially with the girls. And then, well then, he started talking about locating his real parents. He was always trying to convince his adopted brothers to help him though I don't think they ever did."

"What about his parents?" asked Elaine. "Were they aware of their son's curiosity with his origins? Did they try to help him, you know by giving him information about the circumstances of his adoption?"

Mark shrugged again. "As far as I know, no. I don't think they ever did, at least Pete never told me they did."

Elaine nodded, swallowed another swig of Big Bruce, and commented. "Well, I can understand that."

"Right, especially back then when adoption was a little more ......"

"Mysterious?" volunteered Elaine.

Mark nodded. "I guess so."

The two of them sat in silence, Elaine continuing to quaff her beer without apology while Mark stared at his beer, apparently disinterested about keeping up with Elaine. He concluded, after spending the preceding evening consuming Big Bruce with her, that she had an enormous advantage when it came to handling booze. Elaine ordered another beer, her fourth of the evening. Mark thought it excessive as he had previously. Interestingly enough, Mark suddenly thought, as he was sitting there watching Elaine drink, that she would have made a perfect partner for Jack Quinn. At least decades ago, Jack could have drunk pretty well anyone under the proverbial table. The two of them together could have financially supported the Thistledown Pub.

After several minutes of assumed contemplation, Elaine asked Mark about his thoughts about adoption in general, the conversation suddenly turning into something resembling one of those university bull sessions. It was not surprising that Elaine, who was well into her fourth beer, had turned philosophical. Again, it was reminiscent of university. All that was missing was the weed and the sincerity of the liberal arts.

"Why do you think that some people who are adopted are so interested in knowing who gave them up for adoption?" asked Elaine, her voice a little uneven. "I mean, I can understand it to a point, curiosity being normal I suppose, but to continue to search for a person's natural parents, like some people do, seems a little strange."

"I don't think it's strange." Mark answered. "If I were adopted, I would want to know, wouldn't you?"

"Maybe but I wouldn't obsess about it. I mean, don't you think it strange that your best friend asks you to find his birth parents after he's dead, even though he didn't even know he was actually adopted until he had only a couple of months to live." Elaine concluded her observation by taking another swig of Big Bruce.

Mark provided Elaine with another shrug, a shrug of finality it seemed. "Sure, I agree that it does seem a little weird but I'm also sure that some people who are adopted may be more interested than others in their roots, so to speak."

"I guess." replied Elaine."If I were adopted, I don't know to what lengths I would go to investigate my origins, so to speak."

"Me neither." admitted Mark.

It was a little after one o'clock in the morning when Norm Graham informed the two of them that it was closing time. Mark left his Big Bruce on the table half full while Elaine polished hers off as she was getting up from the table. They paid, Mark leaving $10 on the table as an additional gratuity. Elaine noticed, smiled, slowly shook her head and headed toward the door. They both got into Mark's *Ford Focus* without talking and were headed out to her three story Victorian dump several blocks away. Mark had long dropped any idea he may have had of seducing Elaine. For some reason, he was no longer interested, at all.

He drove up to her apartment and stopped the car. Before she got out and with the door partially open, she turned to Mark and asked about his next move in his search. Mark told her that he intended to start with the orphanages, having concluded that his investigation of various websites was unlikely to result in anything substantive. Before she continued into her apartment, she asked about whether he intended to seek the counsel from those improbable sources of information, Ralph Smithers and Andrew Ford.

Mark smiled and referred to the two as definitely his last resorts. Elaine Butler disappeared into her apartment without responding. For one brief moment, he thought of the scars on Elaine's wrists.

THE ORPHANAGE

Mark was awake until sometime around three o'clock Wednesday morning, contemplating or more precisely reconsidering his quest to find the natural parents of Jack Quinn. He still felt committed to the project but his ambition was fading. He had dedicated the better part of three days perusing various websites, speaking with head librarian Blanche MacKillop and with Elaine Butler. Both the librarian and Elaine seemed to be competent scholars regarding the chronicles of Truscott, both past and present. Again, he was also pondering his reluctance to pursue any sort of dalliance with Elaine. He had spent the next three hours staring at the ceiling of his room that night, wrestling with the pillows on his bed and having the occasional thought of Elaine and the last time he had sex, which was probably about two years ago. Aside from that recollection, he spent the rest of the time awaiting slumber and contemplating Jack Quinn's last wish.

Mark had reviewed his options almost constantly over the past several days, most particularly during that sleepless Tuesday night. He had concluded, after investing those sleepless hours, that his next move, on advice from

Blanche MacKillop, should be to visit the closest Catholic Diocese. This just happened to be located in Antigonish, 120 kilometers south of Truscott. According to Miss MacKillop, it was possible that the Catholic Church, which had historically, at least until quite recently, had operated the province's orphanages. Miss MacKillop suggested they may possess more direct information on adoptions than on any website that Mark may have been consulting. She explained that the Catholic Church was basically responsible for most of the province's adoptions until the entire process went secular sometime in the sixties. Appropriately enlightened, Mark consulted his laptop. He determined that the closest orphanage to Truscott and vicinity was Villa Notre-Dame, a building apparently overlooking the Bras d'Or Lake, less than a hundred kilometers from Truscott. According to Google, Villa Notre-Dame had been established by the Grey Nuns before Nova Scotia became one of the four provinces that formed the Canadian Confederation in 1867, back when it was still in a British colony. In 1963, the building was transferred from the Grey Nuns to the Diocese of Antigonish when responsibility for the care of orphans, the province's population of which was declining every year, was taken over by the Nova Scotia Department of Community Services. Since then, for more than five decades, the Diocese used the place to house addicts of various pedigrees, mainly drugs and alcohol. The place had been renamed the Villa Notre-Dame Renewal House. The website included a photograph of the building. It looked like a cross between an imitation Gothic cathedral and a prison. Mark thought it looked well maintained for a building that could have been almost 200 years old. He thought it might be worth visiting the Villa Notre-Dame Renewal House, an architectural interest added to the obvious pursuit. It was a little over a hundred kilometers away anyway.

Mark had managed to sleep for a few hours before a seven o'clock wake up call, the latter habit a holdover from his working career, which had ended several years ago. He could not explain, even to himself, his reasoning for continuing to ensure that he woke up at an early hour. It had also been his father's habit for his entire life, even into his nineties when his sleeping habits used to annoy the hell out of the staff at the Golden Lake Nursing Home. In any event, Mark got up that Wednesday with the full intention of driving to the Villa Notre-Dame Renewal House to see what information he could turn up on local adoptions circa the early 1950s. He got dressed, and stopped by a small diner he had previously noticed a block from the Dunlop Inn. He had picked up a copy of the weekly *Truscott News*, which was dated the previous Monday. He already had the opportunity to read this particular paper but had chosen it in favor of the daily *Halifax Chronicle Herald*. On this date, however, it was still too early in the day for the Halifax paper or even the *Globe and Mail*, both of which may have been available for diners who slept in.

The front page of the *Truscott News* featured a story about the possibility of the building of condominiums in nearby Port Hawkesbury, the first such development in the region. Also on the front page were references to stories about gas prices in Cape Breton, a federal prison sentence handed out to a Baddeck man, local hockey playoffs, and a musician from a town called Dundee joining a supposedly well known Halifax band. Mark had not heard of either the musician or the band. There was also a weather forecast for Cape Breton for the week. By the time Mark's sausage and two poached arrived, delivered by an elderly waitress who looked like she just didn't want to be there, he had read three of the stories on the inside of the paper. There was an interesting item about a Catholic church in Margaree Forks that burned down thirty years ago. According to the article, the former parish priest, who reportedly left the clergy after being elected town reeve several years ago, had announced an investigation into rumors that the blaze was the result of arson. This new allegation apparently emerged from a death bed assertion by a former church deacon whose name, ironically enough, was LaFlamme. Mark was predictably interested in the results of death bed admissions of any kind.

A copy of that day's *Chronicle Herald* was placed on his table as he was starting on his second coffee, the elderly waitress looking even more loath with her duties as she did when she took Mark's order. He scanned the front page, long enough to note several important stories, including the funerals of members of a recently murdered Halifax family, a million dollar boondoggle concerning the famed Bluenose schooner, the previous night's Golden Globe awards and, of course, the effects of the fentanyl crisis on the mean streets of Halifax. After paying for his breakfast, he left the dining room and went straight out the door to his *Ford Focus*, leaving that day's *Chronicle*

Herald on the table. He had previously confirmed with the concierge of Dunlop Inn the preferred route to the town of Little Bras d'Or.

During the drive to the Little Bras d'Or, Mark listened to CBC Radio One from Sydney. They were providing commentary about "your town, your province, and your country" on a show called "Information Morning" hosted by a man named Sutherland. The call-in show was highlighting several of the issues of which Mark was already aware from his quick examination of two local newspapers: the funerals of members of the murdered Halifax family, the fentanyl crisis and the implications of the ascension of Donald Trump on Canadian manufacturing. There were a variety of listeners commenting on the tragedy of the murdered Halifax family, many suggesting that Veteran Affairs was to blame for the actions of a man suffering from PTSD. Along similar lines, there was much hand wringing about the effects of fentanyl although less sympathetic listeners thought the crisis was somehow exaggerated. By far the more interesting dialogue was the discussion of Mr. Trump. Callers who reported owning businesses or working in manufacturing expressed the opinion that the Canadian government policies similar to those supported by Mr. Trump. Others expressed either fear, dismay or disgust regarding Trump and his views. In fact, the radio station had to bleep out every third or fourth word of some listeners who had called in, profanity coming from both sides of the Trump issue. Mark almost drove off the road several times listening to listeners spouting incendiary remarks about Mr. Trump or in support of him. Boy was he glad, he thought, that he was living in a civilized country. Fifty years ago, when Bobby Kennedy was his hero, he thought the United States was the greatest country in the world. Now, with a dangerous and seriously ignorant demagogue running the show, the United States was risking falling into the darkness of the 19th century. He was actually considering a letter to the editor, of which newspaper he was uncertain, but dropped the idea when a sign for Little Bras d'Or appeared. He made the turn onto what appeared to be a rarely used two lane blacktop, route 16 it was, and continued toward the Bras d'Or Lake and the Villa Notre-Dame Renewal House.

Within several minutes, a massive gray concrete building appeared in the windshield of his car. Mark had pulled images of the Villa Notre-Dame Renewal House from the internet, mainly black and white photographs but also some drawings. Most, if not all of them, regardless of format, looked like they were rendered in the serious past, maybe sixty or seventy years ago. This would have been the case when the building housed the region's orphans. Mark hoped that the Villa Notre-Dame Renewal House, which had abandoned the care of orphans for the treatment of alcoholics and dopers back in the early sixties, had kept documentation pertaining to the history of the orphanage that had preceded it. He parked his car in the lot. It was surprisingly empty. Mark also noticed that most of the cars in the parking lot looked like they belonged in an automotive graveyard, an array of jalopies that were likely to be driven, if they could be driven at all, by motorists who were hardly dependable. Mark got out of the car and walked toward the entrance, passing two men who looked elderly but probably weren't. One was attempting to light a cigarette while the other was helping him to stay erect.

The entrance to the building had two large brown oak doors held together by black cast iron brackets. Over the doors was a faded engraved stone sign identifying the building as the "Villa Notre-Dame Orphanage" with the year "1852" chiseled above it. A more recent sign was also affixed near the engraving on the stone. A blue on white plastic sign introduced the building as "The Villa Notre-Dame Renewal House". Mark went up three stone steps, pulled the left door open, climbed up six occasionally chipped marble steps anchored by brass handrails and found himself standing in the lobby. He looked down the hall. It was a long and narrow corridor disappearing into another oak door in the distance. It appeared to be the length of a football field, high ceilings with long slung fluorescent lights, pale pebbled walls which were decorated by a multitude of pictures. There were echoes of shoes walking in both directions in the hall. To the right, there was the office, up another couple of steps, so indicated by a small brass plaque. To the left was another hallway from which there were several small adjoining offices. Most of the foot traffic that was making all the noise was confined to that area of the first floor. Mark stepped up to the right and pushed the office door open where he was greeted by a young woman seated behind a large wooden desk. She was on the telephone. She held up an index finger with a chipped black painted fingernail and motioned Mark into an old fashioned wooden seat situated in front of her desk. It was a small room. He had trouble squeezing by the office receptionist to sit down. Her name was Janice McMahon or so said the name plate on her desk. She looked middle aged but was probably much younger. She had the look of a recovering addict. Her face was adorned with remnants of an array of facial jewelry, marks from removed rows of earrings in both ear lobes, in each eyebrow, two in the bridge of her nose, one in the right nostril, a fairly significant hoop that might have been attached to her upper lip, a smaller hoop in her lower lip, and a stud in her chin, all gone, all reminders of a life since abandoned. She still wore mascara although it was carelessly applied, almost like eye black down both cheeks, as if the woman was preparing for some sort of athletic contest. She was wearing a black sweater adorned with a red skull. She was chewing something. Mark didn`t think it was gum. Tobacco? He guessed that her position and surroundings had not exorcised all of her old bad habits.

Mark sat down and tried not to stare at or listen to Ms. McMahon . She was yelling into the telephone about something to do with her rent which, given the overall impression he had already developed about her. This may have been a fairly frequent occurrence. The conversation ended abruptly with her slamming the telephone down. Almost immediately, a cellphone erupted, the sound of an unidentifiable heavy metal song alerting the room. She took a quick look at the caller ID and immediately turned off the phone. Then, Ms. McMahon looked up at Mark and asked, in a predictably accusatory tone, how she could assist him. Mark was momentarily frightened. She asked again. Mark hesitated and then answered.

"I`m looking for some information about the orphanage" he said, in a low halting voice. She looked at him sternly and repeated her question. He repeated his answer.

"Orphanage, you're kidding, right?" replied Ms. McMahon, the stern look on her face now transfixed. "This is a treatment center, not an orphanage."

Mark tried to smile, a nervous smile. "I know but I understand that there used to be an orphanage here, right here in this building."

"An orphanage? I didn't know that." said Ms. McMahon, suddenly inquisitive, her voice less stringent than it was. He noticed that she had opened her desk drawer and removed a package of cigarettes on which she had started tapping her chipped black fingernails. Mark assumed she was anticipating a break.

He finally managed a smile. He was actually warming up to Ms. McMahon, at least he was feeling less inhibited by her. "Yes, this building was an orphanage until about fifty years ago. It was called Villa Notre-Dame. It was run by the Grey Nuns and was around for more than a hundred years before it became a treatment center."

Ms. McMahon didn't seem impressed by the history lesson and motioned rather casually over her left shoulder to the office over which she was standing guard. The inscription on the door to that office read "Director". "You might want to talk to Mr. Casey. He's been here for years. He could probably tell you something about the past. I think he used to be a priest."

"A priest?" exclaimed Mark, as if he had just stumbled on a serious clue. His excitement faded almost immediately. The phrase "so what" almost immediately crept into his head like a well known admonition.

Ms. McMahon then picked up the telephone and pressed a figure on the receiver. "Mr. Casey, are you available? There's someone out here that wants to speak to you." There was a delay. She looked at Mark for a moment. "No, I'm pretty sure that he's not a possible client; definitely not." She put down the telephone receiver down and informed Mark that Mr. Casey would be out to speak to him. She got out from behind the desk, picked up her cigarettes and headed out the door. Mark wasn't surprised with the rest of her outfit: a pathetically short skirt, her stockings and her cowboy boots, all colored black, were reminiscent of a life she was trying to leave behind. Mark started to investigate the surface of her desk when Director Casey opened his door, his hand outstretched. He was a tall lanky guy with a lantern jaw and a limp.

"Hello, I'm Ken Casey, how can I help you?" a sympathetic voice emitting from a kindly old wrinkled face that could have belonged to anyone, even a man of the cloth. Mark wondered about the man's age, which seemed ancient, perhaps in his eighties. He invited Mark into his office that looked like a railroad car, a narrow book lined room with a small window at one end. Mr. Casey motioned Mark to sit down in one of the two seats in the room. The chair was situated beside Mr. Casey's desk. There was no other space in the office.

Mark explained the importance of the history of the "Villa Notre-Dame Renewal House", or more specifically its predecessor, to his search for the identities of the actual parents of his friend, Jack Quinn. Mr. Casey seemed to be listening intently. Mark completed his presentation in less than five minutes. This was the third or forth time he had provided it to barely interested listeners. This proven to be an efficient practice, minimizing the length of the telling of the tale. Despite its shortcomings, his story was persuasive to seemingly secure Casey's full attention. Mark finalized what amounted to his pitch by speculating, if not suggesting, that Mr. Casey was sufficiently aware of the history of the building to know something about the orphanage. Casey started to comment. At first he was sort of muttering, as if he were trying to memorize something, like one of the sermons he may have given at one time. He then spoke slowly, almost as if he were coming out of anesthesia.

"You know, Mr. Purchell, Mark, I haven't thought about the old place for years. I think most people around here have forgotten about it. I was here when the place was an orphanage, back when I was a young priest." explained Casey. Mark wanted to inquire about his career as a member of the clergy but didn't. There might have been an interesting story behind his surrender of the collar. Casey continued. "Back then, even in the last few years that the place was actually an orphanage, we had maybe fifty kids, mostly boys but some girls. That was down from a peak of more than a hundred kids, all orphans.

"When was that?" asked Mark, the most obvious question he could muster.

"Probably in the thirties, during the depression when the place was full." replied Casey, a thoughtful look on his craggy face, his chin now in one hand. "It was almost the whole town back then. No, it was the town. Aside from the kids, fact was that everyone in the town either worked here or used to work here." Again, Ken Casey went contemplative, staring off through the office window.

Mark sat in silence, like he was in history class, it having come to him that Mr. Casey actually reminded him of Walter Wade, a Latin teacher he had in grade nine in the Jesuit high school he had attended. He hoped that Mr. Casey's memory could provide him with more specific information, the kind of information that could illuminate the trail to the secret of the orphan Jack Quinn. "Thanks, Mr. Casey, but do you have any information, you know, files, that sort of thing, about the kids who were there, I mean here? It looks like my friend might well have been here for a while, back in the fifties."

Casey looked a little uncomfortable, like he suddenly discovered that he had to use the restroom. He spread his hands out like he was about to offer Mark a blessing. "I'm sorry, Mark, but this place doesn't have the files, if anyone has any files, anywhere. When the place closed, when the province took over adoptions, back fifty years ago or so, the files, which by the way were probably not in very good order anyway, sort of disappeared." Casey paused and leaned forward, as if he was about to reveal something confidential. "You'll realize that I wasn't exactly familiar with the files. I didn't often consult them. All I know is that the files were taken away, never saw them again. Nobody did."

Mark was understandably excited. He was anticipating, perhaps unrealistically, waiting for the first real clue, a long shot at best. "Do you remember anybody's name, you know, like Quinn?" he asked, casually, almost whispering. He didn't want to spook Casey. Maybe he was reluctant, maybe he had a faulty memory, or maybe he didn't know anything.

Casey nodded. "You really can't expect me to remember any names. I mean, it was fifty years ago. Fact is that I don't remember. Besides, a lot of the files didn't have names, only case numbers." Casey then stood up, moved toward that tiny window at the end of the office, leaned on the window sill, lit a cigarette and blew a cloud of smoke out the window. He sadly shook his head and held up his cigarette. "I know, besides the damn no smoking regulations, it's a bad example, particularly for a treatment center."

Understandably disappointed, Mark then asked the obvious question. "Are the files still around, you know, maybe in the basement somewhere?" Casey blew another cloud of smoke out the window and beckoned toward Mark with a sad, resigned look on his face. "No, I'm sorry. Of course, we have files about our clients, both past and present, but they have nothing to do with the orphanage or the adoptions. Those files, the orphanage files....well, those files have disappeared.... they're just not here."

Mark asked another obvious question. "So where could they be, if in fact they're anywhere?"

Casey sort of shrugged and then made a suggestion. "Well, you can always try the Archdiocese."

"The Archdiocese?" asked Mark.

"The Archdiocese of Antigonish of course." answered Casey. "They could have been given the files from the orphanage when the province shut it down and transferred all fostering and adoptions to children's services. I can only guess that the church, which used to run the orphanage, would have received the files. Maybe they still have them.

ENTRIES FROM THE INTERNET

As he was returning from Little Bras d'Or to the Dunlop Inn, he had come to an obvious conclusion. He wouldn't have to be bothered with pondering his next move. His next decision would be evident to almost anyone. Mark had decided to contact the Diocese of Antigonish, which amazingly enough was in Antigonish, to determine whether the Diocese had inherited the files from the orphanage of Villa Notre-Dame. If so, more importantly, whether it still had possession of them. Mark was optimistic, more so than he was at any point during his investigation of Jack's adoption, including the day he located Jack's safety deposit box. By the time he drove into the parking lot of the Dunlop, he was looking forward to a nice seafood dinner, likely at the Bell-Buoy-Blue. Then, if he was in the mood for another fantasy dalliance with Elaine Butler and if she was doing her usual shift at the restaurant, it would be another evening drinking at the Thistledown Pub. On the other hand, feeling a little weary, the consequences of almost a week of investigating, Mark thought that he could just enjoy some supper at the

Dunlop Inn, check his e-mails, if he had received any, maybe watch television and get some sleep.

He checked into his room, got undressed, entertained himself in the shower for fifteen minutes or so. About an hour later, it was around six o'clock in the evening by then, he picked up his laptop, turned it on, and checked for e-mails. There were six. Four of them were from adoption websites with which Mark was not familiar, including two from an organization called *The Reunion of Families Canada* and two other websites; *The Parent Searches Group* and *National Parent Finders*, all three of them claiming to be nonprofit adoption support group offering to search for the birth parents of the adopted. The three sites included advice to adopted individuals and adoptive parents, a gallery of testimonials by people finding parents, parents finding children, and siblings finding each other. There was also references to books and movies about adoptions, relevant legislation, links to websites in other countries, recent postings by people using the services, and requests for donations. All of this was depressingly familiar to Mark. It was also obvious that he could expect further communications from similar groups in the future.

The other two e-mails were in responses to messages that he had posted on the *Nova Scotia Register of Adoptions and Adoption Searches*. Surprisingly enough, there was no message from Kevin John Quinn, to whom Mark had sent a specific message seeking a meeting. This action, upon reflection, may not have been worthwhile anyway. Give it time he thought. At any rate, the first message was from a fellow adoption detective named Wade whose missive was conversational and sympathetic. For a moment, Mark was pleased that he had decided to use Quinn as his posting name as opposed to his real name. He was still concerned about attracting the wrong element. In any event, Mr. Wade posted the following text.

> *<u>Wade to Quinn</u>: I read your recent post about your deceased friend's birth parents with profound interest. You have my sympathy. I have been in a similar situation for years. My best friend Joe, who was adopted when he was an infant, was long interested in knowing who his real parents were. He spoke about it frequently towards the end of his life and so when he was in the hospital the last time, the last few days before he passed away with cancer, he asked me to continue the search for his natural parents. I regret to say that I didn't do anything about his request for years. However, once I retired --- that was four years ago --- I began to seriously look into the question of Joe's real parents. I have likely done the same things you have, the same websites, the same social services, the same government agencies, and have probably encountered the same frustrations. While I have not been successful in my search, I encourage you to continue to pursue yours. I know I will although I am not certain as to where I will turn from this point forward.*

Even though he had long realized the fact, Mark was pleased, as loathed he was to admit it, even to himself, to be informed that other people were facing the same circumstances as he was. The message, which was more like a greeting, was also predictably depressing. Mark thought there were probably countless similar quandaries being faced by the adopted individuals all over the country. He wondered whether they too were or had been as ambitious as Mark was in pursuing the answers to questions about adoptions. In other words, did people looking for their or somebody else's birth parents or siblings go beyond the usual bureaucratic facilities? It also occurred to him, maybe for the first time that some parents were also looking for their natural children. The idea that parents who have given up their children for adoption would want to discover their whereabouts many years later should not have seemed that surprising to Mark but for some reason, it was. Fact was that Mark could not recall one such entry during his examination of the *Nova Scotia Register of Adoptions and Adoption Searches* although he might have ignored and possibly forgotten such notifications if in fact he had come across any such entries. In any event, he concluded that Mr. Wade's comforting message was still worthy of response.

The other message that had been directed to Mark was from somebody named Fraser who apparently, at least to Mark, was more interested in exchanging adoption rumors than actually finding a birth parent. When he was discussing his intention to search for Jackson Quinn's parents, somebody, perhaps Blanche MacKillop, perhaps Elaine Butler, perhaps Danny Belliveau, he couldn't remember who, suggested that some of the people who enrolled on the website were more interested in initiating conversations as opposed to looking for anybody's parents. It was like an "adoption lonely hearts" club based mainly on the destinies, both fortunate and otherwise, of people who were adopted, something like "Alcoholics Anonymous". Mr. Fraser's entry resembled an outline of an episode of a soap opera rather than a serious search for birth parents. He also thought of the entry by Archibald John Quinn who was looking for two children that were fostered and then abandoned by his parents before he was born.

> *Fraser to Quinn:* I read with great interest about your search for the birth parents of your friend who recently died. While I have come across similar cases in my experience with this and other websites concerning adoptions, there was something beguiling about your story. I can imagine the misgivings that some adopted individuals who may know they are adopted have. However, I cannot conceive of the feelings that finding out that one was adopted at the end of your life would prompt. As you may appreciate, I would like to share my thoughts with you on that tragic situation. Please get in touch.

Mark had never considered how discovering that you were adopted after thinking that your parents were your parents might have had on Jack. Aside from curiosity, which was obvious and understandable, he might have invested a fair amount of contemplation time about the situation. Did Robert and Eileen Quinn treat him any differently than they would have if he was their natural child? Who were his birth parents? What happened to them and what would have happened to Jack Quinn if he had not been orphaned? All these questions would have occurred to any adopted child but not suddenly toward the end of one's life. Mark imagined that most adoptees would have eventually forgotten or survived whatever neurosis they may have harbored about being adopted by the time they entered their adult years. To be introduced to the possibility that he may have been adopted when he himself was facing the end of his own life was something about which Mark could not understand. Mark had a lightening burst of inspiration. Perhaps Fraser's interest in Mark's pursuit of Jack's birth parents was academic in nature, as if he was working on some sort of university study. Mark recalled that he had known a woman in university who was working on a paper about adoptions for a sociology course. He couldn't remember whether she had ever completed the paper or whether, if she did, he had ever seen the paper.

Sitting there on the edge of the bed, staring at his laptop, he chose to respond to Mr. Wade, once he had decided not to follow up on his message to the other Mr. Quinn. It was obvious to Mark that Wade might well have had and was probably still having experiences that could educate him in his own search. In any event, aside from possibly picking up a hint or two, at least he would likely find a sympathetic ear in a person who could share his desperation. Sitting there, he composed the following note to Wade who, like most devotees of the register, had also supplied his e-mail address.

> *Quinn to Wade:* *Thank you for your note. Like you, I was surprised to hear that there were other people facing the same situation as I am, that is looking for the birth parents of relatives or friends. As we both know, it is difficult to find the birth parents of anyone who was born in this province and I would imagine any other province prior to the 1960s. This is particularly the case if you were Catholic, which applies in the case of my friend Jack and may well apply to your friend Joe. During my investigation, it quickly became evident to me that in those days adoptions by any Catholic were the responsibility of either the church or the orphanage in which the child was originally placed. Unfortunately, neither institution keeps easily accessible records. Accordingly, I am currently in the process of pursuing such records, if in fact they exist, first with the Villa Notre-Dame orphanage in Little Bras d'Or, where I was unsuccessful, and now with the Diocese of Antigonish, where I remain hopeful. I would appreciate any advice you can provide, particularly with respect to any endeavors you may have tried. While I hate to say it, this would be helpful in ensuring I don't waste my time with efforts that have wasted your time. I will keep you updated.*

Satisfied with his message to Mr. Wade, he pressed "Send", turned off his laptop, dressed and headed down to the dinner room of the Dunlop Inn, having definitely decided that he was just too damn tired to endure another evening at the Bell–Buoy–Blue and the Thistledown Pub, his waning interest in Elaine the other element of his reluctance. Mark was greeted at the entrance of the dinner area by a short thin man in a tuxedo, a surprising outfit for a relatively small hotel in a relatively small town. The dining area was an old fashioned baroque room decorated with a large chandelier and a dozen mahogany tables covered with linen table cloths, by a short thin man in a tuxedo,The supposed maitre d', who spoke in an almost theatrical tone, asked if he had a reservation, a strange request given that only three of the room's tables were currently occupied. When Mark said that he did not have a reservation, the tuxedo man asked if he was registered in the hotel. When Mark replied in the affirmative, volunteering Room 106, he immediately received an effusive apology from the tuxedo man and a table by the window. He was also handed copies of that day's *Globe and Mail* and the *Chronicle Herald*. Mark thanked the tuxedo man and handed back the copy of the *Chronicle Herald* as he had already read it.

A waitress, an older woman who was wearing a soiled white blouse, a navy blue skirt and basic nun's shoes, brusquely handed him a menu. Not surprisingly, she also looked like she was at the end of a twelve hour shift. She asked if he wanted to order a drink. He was tempted to order a "Big Bruce" but didn't, settling on a "Heineken" . She brought him his beer, pulled out a small pad and a pen, unnecessary equipment given there were only five other diners at the three other occupied tables, and asked for his dinner order. Mark ordered the special, Spaghetti Alfredo. The waitress took a quick note and seemed to smirk. He ordered another beer even though he was only halfway through his first, and turned away. He had started on the *Globe and Mail* when the maitre d' in the tuxedo approached Mark's table.

"Do you mind, Mr. Purchell?" asked the tuxedo man, gesturing toward the chair opposite Mark who put down the paper and nodded with a quizzical expression emerging on his face. The look was still there as his recently arrived visitor sat down. While he wondered how the tuxedo man knew his name, his curiosity was immediately quenched.

He introduced himself and put out his hand. "Sorry to bother you, sir. My name is John Gideon. I own the hotel, inherited it in fact, and I know pretty well everyone who visits us. You get to know people in a small place like this, six rooms, and as you can see." Mr. Gideon motioned toward the semi-deserted dining room and explained. "We're not busy right now." Mark shook his hand, nodded and smiled, took the final swig of his first bottle of his "Heineken", and started wondering how the hotel managed to stay in business. Mr. Gideon returned the smile and continued his introductory spiel. "Are you are wondering why I'm disturbing your dinner?" He seemed surprisingly sophisticated, at least for Truscott.

Mark replied. "I guess I am, yeah." and then leaned forward, waiting.

Mr. Gideon smiled and offered an explanation for the intrusion. "Well, I was just curious as to the purpose of your stay with us." stated Mr. Gideon, "I try to get to know everyone who stays with us, whether they're on business or just visiting."

Mark completed the thought. "And you're wondering why I'm visiting your town." Mark paused and sort of chuckled. "Are you doing some sort of a poll? Oh and by the way, care to join me." Mark lifted his glass. Mark was immediately tempted to relate to Mr. Gideon his experience with one of the town's other so-called resorts, the Truscott Bay Hotel and Resort and their X-rated proprietors, Tom and Daisy Heller. He also felt like asking about his tuxedo.

Mr. Gideon shared the chortle and shook his head. "No, no poll, let's just say I'm inquisitive. And no thanks to the drink, at least not at the moment."

In the meantime, the waitress arrived with a basket of dinner rolls. She acknowledged Mr. Gideon and he returned her greeting, calling her Arlene. She assured Mark that his dinner would be served shortly. It sounded like an apology.

Gideon watched Mark butter one of the buns and continued his prying. "So what does bring you to our town?"

"Business," answered Mark, curtly as he anticipated that he would have to expand on that explanation, as he had on several previous occasions during his stay in Truscott. Gideon nodded slowly and then made the obvious comment. "If you don't mind me asking, what kind of business are you in? As you've probably noticed over the past couple of days, there isn't much in the way of commerce in this town."

Mark smiled and nodded knowingly. "Yeah, I noticed. Aside from tourism, there doesn't really seem much going on here from the business perspective" They both paused as Arlene brought Mark another beer, motioned toward the entrance of the dining room and turned away without comment. Gideon looked up, smiled and excused himself. "Just a moment. I have to attend to some business." Mark looked up and saw a middle aged couple waiting for a table. He watched as Gideon greeted the couple, conducted a brief discussion, escorted them to a table across the room and then them menus. He then walked back to Mark's table, by which time Arlene had delivered his Spaghetti Alfredo.

Gideon returned to Mark's table as the latter had started in on his dinner. "Sorry, Mark, I still have duties. I play maitre d' most nights, I think it gives the place a little class, so to speak. Anyway, you were saying, you know, about your business here." Mark looked at Gideon, having hoped that he would have forgotten his interest in the objective of Mark's visit to Truscott. As reluctant as he was, Mark gave Gideon the summarized version of the purpose of his stay in Truscott and therefore his visit to Gideon's establishment. Gideon listened intently, as if Mark was spinning some sort of exhilarating narrative. It could have been that there weren't that many interesting stories in the "naked city" of Truscott. After ten minutes of discussion that seemed more like a script consultation than any other type of discourse, Mark ended his recitation with a tired, world weary story of his most recent internet exchanges with people with similar interests or anxieties regarding adoption.

Gideon, whose attention had seemed particularly diligent throughout their conversation, made a gesture of acknowledged sympathy, his arms posed as if in prayer. Mark then went back to this Spaghetti Alfredo, which he had hardly touched during the telling of the story of his investigation of the adoption of Jack Quinn. "What's your next move?" asked Gideon. The man had seemed honestly interested in Mark's dissertation and in his plans. Mark looked up from his plate and outlined his program for the next day. "I plan to head down to Antigonish to see if I can get any information from the Archdiocese, you know, files of past adoptions." He paused, took another helping of spaghetti, another swig of beer and continued to outline his intentions for the next day and the reasons for the trip. "I don't know if you know this but the Catholic Church was supposedly responsible for all Catholic adoptions until sometime in the sixties."

Gideon quietly interjected, "And you think they may have kept and may still have records on the adoptions they had arranged for Catholic parents from all over the island?" "Exactly, that's my hope." Gideon started to get up from the table and put out his hand. "Well, the best of luck." Then he stopped for a moment. "You know, you might also see whether they have any baptismal records."

"Thanks." replied Mark. He watched Mr. Gideon head out through the entrance of the dining room. He guessed that he wasn't expecting any more diners that night to greet. Mark was no more hopeful about his own plans.

THE DIOCESE OF ANTIGONISH I

The building in which the Catholic Diocese of Antigonish managed the activities of the Catholic churches, located in Cape Breton, looked like it had been recently constructed. It was strangely stark, presumably not at all like the churches they represented. To Mark, the building could easily have been mistaken for an elementary school or a recently designed warehouse. There was what looked to be a newly installed concrete cross positioned above the entrance as well as a temporary sign standing to its left. Its silver lettering on a black background announced the edifice as the "Chancery Office of the Diocese of Antigonish". The name, Bishop Brian Daniels, was under the sign. The Bishop was presumably the head of the diocese. The building was medium sized with two stories, hardly the kind of impressive and awe-inspiring architecture that one expects from a house of worship, no matter how small the town surrounding it. Mark was disappointed, particularly when he compared it to the Ville Notre-Dame Renewal House which, though generally unremarkable, at least had an implied ghostly grandeur that seemed consistent with its purpose.

It was almost 11 o'clock in the morning. Mark parked the rental car in front of the building and approached the entrance. He opened the door, held it for a moment for a priest who smiled and greeted him as he passed him on his way out. On his way into the lobby, Mark noticed the walls were framed black and white photographs of more than a dozen churches. He immediately assumed the pictures were of the churches that were responsible to the diocese. Above the pictures was a large silver crucifix which visitors were eventually told had previously graced the old diocese building, which was also portrayed in one of the pictures lining the wall. To the right of the lobby was a white haired woman sitting behind a small desk. She was wearing a light blue polyester top decorated with a large palm tree. There was something written over the right breast pocket. The shirt looked like it could have been a bowling shirt. She was knitting what appeared to be a pair of red socks or mittens.

When Mark approached her, she dropped her knitting needles and looked up with a pleasant, contented expression on her face. "Can I help you, sir?" she asked, looking up at him with an angelic smile on her face. Mark returned her expression with a grin of his own. He noticed a small brass plaque identifying the lady behind the desk as Sister Millicent Thomas. The lady was a nun for God's sake, a nun. He wondered about her shoes. He must have formulated a surprised expression on his face. Of course, Sister Thomas had noticed the expression on Mark's face and commented. "Yes, I'm a nun." She paused and explained the outfit with the tree. "I know what you're thinking. Everybody does. We don't have to wear the uniform anymore although I would probably agree with you if you think that my blouse is a little extreme." Mark nodded, his smile got a little wider.

She then tilted her head up and asked, "So how can I help you?"

"My name is Mark Purchell and I'm looking for the birth parents of a friend who was adopted by a couple named Quinn in Truscott back in the '50s." he explained, "I have been told the church arranged adoptions in those days and I thought that the church might have records of adoptions."

Sister Thomas rubbed her hands together, spread them out toward Mark and explained the unfortunate truth. "As you probably know, Mr. Purchell, the Diocese has archives on births, deaths, marriages, and adoptions. Most of them are available to the public but, unfortunately for you, the records on adoptions aren't open. But, if you are interested in perusing the records on adoptions, diocese staff can respond to inquiries and conduct brief searches on behalf of interested parties."

Of course, Mark looked disappointed and hopeful at the same time. "Can I ask the Diocese staff to search the records for me?"

Sister Thomas smiled and assured Mark with almost a whispered confidence. "Yes, we could do that but you must realize that we can't guarantee results, particularly if the search involves a lot of time and effort. And let's face it, anything from more than sixty years ago would definitely involve a lot of time and effort."

Mark's disappointment was obvious. He was planning to stay in Truscott until the end of the week. He could stay longer although, despite the relatively comfortable accommodations at the Dunlop Inn, the reasonable deal he got on the car rental, and the possibility of renewing his pursuit of Elaine Butler, he could hardly afford to stay longer, his monthly pension not enough to cover funding for a few more days in Truscott. He then had a thought which he shared with Sister Thomas. "Sister, can I volunteer to help your staff in the search? I have to tell you but this seems to be as close as I have come to finding my friend's birth parents. So you can see, I would be more than willing to help out. I'm asking you to please consider it."

Again, Sister Thomas smiled sympathetically and shook her head. "I can't let you do that. Only Chancery staff can search the archives. They are confidential. The Diocese can't allow people to search records that are as sensitive as adoptions. I'm sure you can understand that."

"I wouldn't tell anyone, promise." assured Mark, half hopeful, half facetious. He tried to look as sincere as possible. He quickly realized that Sister Thomas wasn't about to accept his appeal. She did, however, provide him with another beatific smile. The two sat in silence for a time, presumably waiting for the other to say something else.

Sister Thomas broke the quiet. "There is perhaps another option, Mr. Purchell."

"Another option?" asked Mark, hopeful again. He moved his chair closer to her desk. Sister Thomas, her hands clasped together, leaned forward and explained the other option. "You can always examine the baptismal records. It is not the same thing as adoption records you realize but you may be able to detect an adoption by finding any baptisms that were performed long after the birth date recorded on the baptismal certificate."

Mark suddenly developed a pleasantly stunned look on his face "What exactly do you mean? Does that happen often?"

"I don't know, Mr. Purchell, but it does happen." explained Sister Thomas in a voice that sounded, at least for a moment, like one of Mark's elementary school teachers. Either that or a character from *Sesame Street*. "You see, parents adopt a child and then have the child baptized. It is usually just after they bring the child home. And the children are almost always one or two years old when they are adopted. Hence, the difference in the dates of the birth and the baptism."

"What about the birth certificates?" asked Mark. "What happens to them?"

Sister Thomas smiled and explained. "Orphans were cared for by the Diocese...."

"You mean Ville Notre-Dame" interjected Mark.

Sister Thomas nodded. "Yes. I think that prior to the early 1960s, Catholic infants were not issued birth certificates, at least not in this province. Baptismal certificates were the only documents issued at the time of birth, at least I think so." A pause. "You'll understand that I wasn't in the...."

"You're weren't a nun back then," Mark helpfully suggested. "You certainly don't look old enough,", a comment, while inaccurate in any event, seemed inappropriate.

Sister Thomas didn't seem to take note of Mark's last comment, which in any other circumstance would appear to be almost flirtatious, even if the target of the remark was a middle aged woman wearing a bowling shirt. "No, I wasn't a nun but I am told that it was the procedure back then."

Mark then summarized the situation. "So what you are saying is that if an infant was adopted, the only proof of that infant's date of birth was a baptismal certificate issued one or two years after he or she was actually born."

Sister Thomas smiled and nodded emphatically. "That's right. I think you have a quite a search ahead of you, that is, if you still want to find you friend's birth parents."

"Well, I do," answered Mark, a slight misgiving starting to circulate in his mind. He already was wondering about proceeding with his investigation.

"It sure looks like you'll be looking through a lot of files." predicted Sister Thomas. "I suggest you talk to Father Nevin as he's in charge of baptismal records. He has an office in this building. I could get in touch with him right now, see if he's available." Sister Thomas picked up the telephone receiver on her desk and looked up.

Mark nodded. "Yes, I would appreciate that, if you could."

Sister Thomas pressed three numbers on the telephone and asked for Father Nevin. Mark listened to her explain Mark's story and his request for access to the baptismal records. Sister Thomas nodded and put down the receiver.

She looked up at Mark and relayed the result of her conversation with Father Nevin. "Father Nevin's office is located toward the end of the second floor, up those stairs." Sister Thomas pointed to the stairs. Mark did not see saw an elevator. "He's waiting for you. By the way,

Father Nevin is a trifle hard of hearing, so speak up. He's the oldest priest in the Diocese. Until a few years ago, he was the pastor at Holy Rosary, a small parish in a small town called Big Pond. He was there for thirty years."

Mark almost bowed to Sister Thomas in thanking her. He turned and walked to the foot of the stairs and then started to climb them. He arrived on the second floor where he noticed that there was a long empty corridor featuring three small signs advertising archive rooms for marriages, interments, and baptisms. He headed toward the archive room for baptisms, his steps echoing down the corridor, and stopped at the last room on the right, marked Baptisms. Sitting in front of the room, behind a small desk, was presumably Father Nevin, his head nestled in his arms. His eyes were closed. He was breathing deeply, breaths that sounded dangerously threatening to his health. His spectacles were resting on the top of his head, which was completely bereft of hair. He was dressed in a black cassock stained with nicotine with his white clerical collar loose. Mark crept close enough to Father Nevin to catch a significant whiff of tobacco and whiskey. For some reason, Mark had a fleeting thought of a scene in an old adventure novel he read as a kid, something about the ghost of an old ship's captain dying at the helm. He imagined Captain Ahab in priestly garb. He didn't know why he had conjured up such classic references. Perhaps he was experiencing some sort of drug flashback from forty years ago when such occurrences were commonplace in his then addled brain. After considering the move for a moment or two, he reached out to wake the slumbering reverend with a light poke of his upper arm.

Father Nevin stirred like he was emerging from a long slumber, rising up in his chair like he was taking in his first breath. He then started to stand up, wobbly, reaching back to hold on to both arms of his chair. It took him a minute or so to stand straight, at least as far as he was able to perform the movement, still unsteady but serviceable. He looked at Mark with a strange, almost frightened expression on his face, eyes wide open under white bushy brows, a curious juxtaposition considering his bald dome. He had something resembling a frown sculptured on a quivering liverish mouth.

Mark spoke to him, almost whispering, unsure as to whether the good father was fully awake. He placed his hand firmly on his forearm. "Father Nevin, can you hear me?" Initially there was no response from him, his eyes still spellbound, staring straight ahead. Mark spoke louder. "Father, are you awake? I'd like to speak to you?" He gave Father Nevin another shake of his arm. He started to rouse, his eyes eventually turned toward Mark, his craggy face tilting up. It suggested a scene of a confessor awaiting his next penitence.

"Do you want to speak to me? Who are you?" asked Father Nevin in a foggy voice, almost as if he was talking to himself.

Mark continued to communicate with the good father in a soft, quiet voice. "I'm sorry, Father, I apologize for waking you but I'd like to speak to you about your files. And oh yes, my name is Mark Purchell."

Father Nevin continued to rouse. He buried his chin into his chest and then brought it up again. "My files?"

"Your baptismal files." replied Mark.

"My baptismal files?" asked Father Nevin, in a shaky, hesitant voice, as if he was entirely uncertain about the reference. Mark thought for a brief moment that perhaps he was standing in front of the wrong office. He then noticed that there were double doors a couple of feet behind Father Nevin. Mark was now convinced there was a file room behind those doors. Mark found it difficult to believe that the Chancery would give Father Nevin responsibility for something as important as baptismal records. Father Nevin would likely be more suitable for taking care of the blue boxes.

Mark persisted, "Yes, Father, the baptismal files."

The good father now seemed more or less awake, or at least as awake as he was ever going to get. "The baptismal files?"

"Yes, father, the files with the records of baptisms." There was now a hint of irritation in Mark's voice, as if he had been talking to a distracted child.

After another minute of quiet, during which Father Nevin was rubbing his eyes, he was finally aroused enough to start making sense. "Who are you again?"

"My name is Mark Purchell and I'm looking for the Diocese's records of baptisms from the early 1950's. I was told that you are in charge of those records."

Father Nevin had discontinued fiddling with his eyes and finally provided Mark with a sensible answer to one of his questions. "Yes, Mr. Purchell, I am the custodian of those records." He paused and looked puzzled. "Are you looking for anyone in particular?"

Mark was tired of repeating the background story of his search for Jack Quinn's birth parents. So he didn't repeat it. He simply answered the question without providing further detail. "Well, I am looking for the baptism of a man named Jack Quinn, a friend who recently passed away." He then added another point, a point that he had not previously made to anyone who had ever asked or was told about his quest. "It's a legal matter."

The latter comment seemed to intensify Father Nevin's attention, insofar as he could pay attention to anything. He leaned across his desk, eyes quickly alert, and commented. "A legal matter ---- that's serious, isn't it?"

Mark nodded firmly in agreeing, even if the idea of possible legal implications was entirely fictitious. "Yes, it is serious," no hint of prevarication on his face or in the tone of his voice, not that it would have made any difference to Father Nevin. He was the kind of individual that Mark or almost any other rational person would think would believe anything.

The good father looked concerned, turned in his chair and pointed with a trembling finger to the double doors behind him. "I'll open the archive room for you." He stopped and then made an observation. "You know, I don't think I've opened these doors for weeks, if not months. Not much interest you'll understand, you know, in old baptisms."

Mark, relieved with the seeming progress, commented with a question. "Not too many baptisms lately either?" He immediately regretted making the remark. It was oddly sarcastic and obviously disrespectful. Sure he was a confused old man but he was still a priest, albeit with a dirty cassock and a badly discoloured clerical collar, but still a priest. "Sorry, Father, I didn't mean that." Father

Nevin did not react. He didn't seem to have heard any comment made by Mark.

Father Nevin had already started to extricate himself from his chair and turned toward the double doors. There was a combination lock on the doors, a puzzle with which Father Nevin predictably started to fiddle. He spun the wheel on the lock at least four times until he turned back to Mark with a curious stupefied look on his craggy face. "I don't think I can remember the numbers, you know the combination numbers. As I told you, I haven't opened the doors for weeks, maybe months." A contemplative look spread over his face like a sudden shadow. It was apparent that poor old Father Nevin wouldn't be opening those doors without help. Mark responded by asking Father Nevin if he needed assistance.

"Maybe you can ask Father Grady if he has a moment to help us," Father Nevin suggested. He had a hopeful look on his face, as if the idea of asking Father Grady to assist with the combination lock was cause for celebration. Father Nevin picked up the telephone and punched in three numbers. He spoke haltingly to Father Grady, hung up the telephone after writing six numbers down on a note pad. He turned back toward the twin doors and spun the wheel again, slowly. The lock opened, Father Nevin managed to push the doors open and produced a surprising and creepy little smile that would not have been out of place in a horror film. He then waved Mark into the room holding the Baptismal Archives. "Go ahead, the place is all yours. And now, if you don't mind, I'm going out for my unfortunate ritual", theatrically putting two fingers to his lips.

Mark walked into the room. It was filled with rows of gray file cabinets with three drawers each above which were hanging fluorescent lights. There were signs indicating each one of the fourteen church parishes which had baptized infants in the more than 120 years that the Diocese of Antigonish had kept records. In order to narrow his search --- it would be an enormous undertaking without any limits ---- Mark had reduced the number of specific files to four parishes, all four of which were located in and around Truscott, Nova Scotia. They were Saint Mary's of Frenchdale, Holy Rosary of Big Pond, Saint Joachim of Lakeside and Our Lady of Assumption of Truscott. Mark was completely relieved then when he discovered that the files were arranged by parish. In his less optimistic expectations of his particular search, he was worried he would have to look through hundreds of baptismal certificates without any further indications. Otherwise, he could see himself needing a sleeping bag to fully investigate the files in that room.

Mark walked to the first cabinet for the Holy Rosary parish. A small rectangular inscription on the front of the first of seven cabinets --- he had counted them before approaching them ---- read 1887-1919. The inscription on the fifth cabinet read 1947-1954. He opened the top drawer which held the files for the years 1947-1948. Mark started his search, looking through the second drawer of the cabinet which began with the baptisms in 1950. Although Mark could not remember whether Jack had ever told him his exact age, he had always thought they were that both of them were more or less the same age. He could therefore estimate that Jack was born in either

1950 or 1951. He started with the files in 1950, finding that the records were filed by month. He started to look through them, one page legal sized sheets that looked to be in pretty good shape considering their vintage. He examined them carefully, noting that all of the baptisms were recorded as being performed from one to three weeks after the dates of birth of the infants, no other official dates of birth being recorded anywhere, the Catholic Church being the sole registrar in the province of such milestones. Mark continued searching the records for the rest of the 1950, again not finding any baptisms that had been performed on infants long after they were actually born. In other words, infants who, once wards of the Catholic Church, were ultimately adopted by Catholic parents. It was a strange exploration, looking at those certificates, imagining infants with curious names, at least for the time, monikers like Paulette, Penelope, Nathaniel, Clarissa, Hector, Clifford, Jacob, Fagan and a lot of other names that probably belonged in Victorian novels more than they did in Nova Scotia in the 1950s.

In the third month for the year of 1951, Jack came across an adopted child who was baptized on March 20 of that year but was born on August 11, 1949, meaning that the child, whose name was Barbara, was eighteen months old when a priest poured holy water on her forehead. So it was possible, thought Mark, that baptismal records could identify children who were in fact adopted. While Mark was pleased, in fact more than pleased, that his plan was viable, he was a trifle disappointed that the first adopted child he found through his scheme was not Jack Quinn. Surprisingly enough, he found a second adopted child, this time it was a boy named Norman Richardson whose recorded date of birth was November 5, 1949. He was baptized at the age of nineteen months on June 6, 1951. Another disappointment and another promise of getting to the bottom of his quest for the true history of Jack Quinn. Mark finished looking through the remainder of the birth certificates for 1951 for the Holy Rosary Parish. There were more than a hundred documents. It took Mark over an hour to complete this part of his investigation.

Mark checked his watch and noted that it was almost one o'clock in the afternoon. Surprisingly enough, he wasn't hungry but he thought he might take in a little lunch anyway. He left the file room to return to the desk of Father Nevin. He was a bit surprised to find him awake at the desk, evidently reading a book. He looked up from his book, it looked to be a bible, when Mark appeared. He put the book down.

"Excuse me, Father, is there a nearby place where I can get something to eat?" Mark asked. Father Nevin smiled. "There is the sacristy in the rectory, where Bishop Daniels lives, that also serves as a cafeteria for the people who work for the diocese. You will meet a woman named Grace there. She runs the place." Mark nodded. He knew the rectory was the first building to the right of the Chancery and was between it and the Saint John the Baptist Cathedral, the theological jewel of the Diocese of Antigonish. Mark left the room, walked down the hall and then the stairs, and was then out the door of the Chancery headed for the rectory. It rectory was a remarkably pedestrian looking building, particularly when compared to the counterfeit majesty of the Cathedral, which was basically a large church with impressive looking spires and stained glass windows, at least for the bucolic environs of Cape Breton. It was built in 1932, the third and most recently constructed such edifice constructed in the entire province. Despite the feigned magnificence of the general architecture, the rectory portion looked like it could easily have been sold as a three or a four bedroom tract house in some suburb of Halifax.

Mark approached the door to the rectory and rang the doorbell. A pleasant looking middle aged woman, dressed in a white blouse, a black skirt, and a gray cardigan sweater, answered the door, and smiled. Mark asked for directions to the cafeteria. She waved him into the rectory and pointed down the corridor to the left. The woman stopped him before he started down the passageway and pointed out that visitors seldom dined in what she called the rectory dining hall. Mark, who had no idea as to the purpose of the woman's comment, thanked her and continued to the dining hall. He walked down the hall, noting the stained glass windows on both sides of the corridor. Mark sufficiently recalled his religious instruction to identify the scenes depicted on the windows as the Stations of the Cross. He was staring at the windows and listening to the echo the sounds of his footsteps made on the marble floor. At the end of the corridor were two tall maple wood doors with wrought iron rod inserts. The right door was open. He walked into the cafeteria. It was a little past one o'clock in the afternoon and the dining room was half full, maybe twenty diners, most of whom were clergy, predominantly priests but three or four nuns as well. While Mark could hear several quiet discussions, he noticed that the majority of the diners were reading.

The menu consisted of a daily special, it was a club sandwich on this date, as well as a small buffet, there being a selection of chicken fried rice, egg rolls, cottage cheese, three types of salads, some vegetables, and a pan of lasagna. There were also two sets of shelves on which there were a display of desserts and a glass cabinet full of sodas, juice, and milk. Coffee was also available. The woman who Mark assumed was Grace was manning the cash while two other women were working the kitchen behind her. Mark went to the buffet, picked up a plastic plate, selected two egg rolls, a little chicken fried rice and some cottage cheese. He picked up a Nestea and went to the cash where Grace asked him to place his plate on a scale. He paid and took a seat at a table near the one of the dining room windows, which looked out on woods behind the Chancery. He had picked up a copy of the "Diocese Courier" on his way to the table. It was a weekly periodical that seemed exclusively devoted to diocese and parish matters as well as the occasional article on theological issues. Mark couldn't imagine an increase in readership when the theological stories appeared.

Mark was partially through his lunch and an article about local parish funding when a nun, a predictably older nun, approached and asked him, in a subdued voice, if he was there to visit Father Nevin. She explained that people rarely inquire about old baptisms these days. She asked if he was doing historical research, observing that he was much too old to be a student, leaving her to speculate that he was either a historian or a journalist. Mark replied, "Neither, I'm here on a personal matter." The sister smiled, confiding that she was just curious, and scuttled off. Mark wondered whether many of the priests and nuns who worked for the Diocese were similarly curious. He watched her return to her table, whispered something to the other nun who was sitting at the table, and sat down. They both shrugged and went back to drinking their teas. A strange place, Mark thought.

Mark finished his lunch without speaking to anyone else and returned to the second floor and the baptismal certificates. He went to the top drawer of the second cabinet and started to look through the documents for the first few months of 1952. He must have examined over a hundred certificates without coming across anything worth pursuing further. He had started to flip through the files with expediency, the prospect of spending more than the rest of the day in this effort too daunting to consider. He had grown accustomed to checking the relevant sections of each form without dwelling on them. While it had taken Mark several minutes to inspect each certificate when he started investigating them, he had managed to cut the time down to less than a minute, quick looks at only the dates of birth and baptism sufficient for assessment. He went through the remainder of 1952 without finding any document worth examining further. He was through the entire year of 1952 without any success. While he was more or less convinced that the 1953 or 1954 files would not reveal anything worthwhile, he went through them anyway, noting that the number of baptisms had declined in the last two years, not significantly but fewer nevertheless. Once he finished, he checked the time. It was almost five o'clock. He was surprised that Father Nevin hadn't alerted him to closing time, which he had already noted was five o'clock, a sign on the wall in the lobby of the Chancery so informing him. It was time to go. He pushed the last drawer closed and headed out the door.

Father Nevin was still in place at his desk. He was slumped over, asleep. Mark stepped carefully around Father Nevin and started to head toward the stairwell. He then noticed that he had left the doors behind Father Nevin open. He returned to the doors, closed them, and spun the combination lock. As he was creeping around Father Nevin, he glanced at the crossword puzzle he had been working on and noticed that he had placed the letter A in every square in the puzzle. He wasn't surprised. Aside from his age, Mark speculated that maybe fifty years as a priest might have affected his psychology as well, one side effect being the development of a strange approach to crossword puzzles. After that rumination, he felt himself shrugging. Mark then headed back to the stairwell. He was out the front door, into his car in the parking lot, and on the road back to Truscott within minutes. He had been thinking of dinner at Bell–Buoy–Blue. Maybe Elaine Butler will be on shift.

Back in his room at the Dunlop Inn by seven o'clock, Mark changed clothes and was soon sitting at a table at the Bell–Buoy–Blue. He stood at the entrance to the restaurant reconnoitering, pleased to see that Elaine Butler was on duty. She gave him a little wave and pointed to a table.

She greeted him happily and handed him a menu. "Good to see you. I thought you'd have left town by now."

Mark smiled. "Well, I just couldn't bear to leave. Your town is just too charming."

Elaine laughed and responded in kind. "I once felt that way too and I've stayed here for almost six years. And by the way, the lobster mac and cheese is good tonight, highly I recommend it. How about that and a bottle of Big Bruce. She offered him a big smile and a beguiling look. Though a little stunned, Mark immediately agreed with Elaine's recommendation. Lobster mac and cheese and a Big Bruce it was. He watched her walk away. There was still an attraction there, at least from his perspective. He went to the washroom and on the way back to his table, picked up a copy of the *National Post,* having temporarily developed an interest in right wing madness, which occasionally overcame him when he was in need of perverse entertainment. Unfortunately, most of the front pages and the editorial section were devoted to tax reform and other uninspiring domestic issues, forcing him to turn instead to the sports pages. Elaine delivered his Big Bruce, she leaned over his table from behind him, and said that her team, which turned out to be the perpetual losers the Toronto Maple Leafs, was much improved this particular season.

Mark was barely able to agree, momentarily intoxicated with the scent of Elaine's perfume, prompted by proximity to her, a feeling that he hadn't recalled having for years, at least not until he met Elaine. He was tempted, like every other time he was anywhere near her, to start plotting her seduction. He imagined the scenario, as he had often recalled similar scenes from the past. Yes, a sophisticated evening at the Thistledown Pub quaffing quarts of Big Bruce, the drive home to that flat in which she was unfortunate enough to be living, and the pursuit of a great evening of sex for the first time in ages. He sat there wondering about such a prospect, sipping on his beer. By the time Elaine brought his lobster mac and cheese, however, he had mysteriously lost his ambition, temporary as he knew it was, and hoped that she did not continue to come on to him. He remembered the last time he had experienced any sort of brush with a woman. It occurred at a retirement party for an ex-colleague, five or six years ago. Her name was Carol, a woman with whom he had worked for maybe a year. She was frightfully inebriated. Carol had offered herself to Mark, tried to kiss him, and seemed to be quite disappointed when he declined. Fact was that he had to physically escape from her. He had no idea as to the basis for her pursuit of him. Nor did he have any idea as to his romantic reluctance at the time, either then or now, sitting there in the Bell-Buoy-Blue. He pondered his hesitancy, his unwillingness to allow himself to pursue an adventure that in decades past would have caused him to do cartwheels. But no more, for reasons that continued to elude him, even now when he appeared to have an amorous opportunity that did not usually present itself to him. Jack, in one of the few moments of elucidation he managed over the last few months of his life, had suggested performance anxiety, a condition he avoided until he ran into Carol. No matter the reason, he remained disappointed. Regarding Elaine, he knew that he would regret his reluctance, just like he had in the case of the temporarily licentious Carol.

He had just finished his entree when Elaine appeared and asked him if he was in the mood for dessert, the tone of her voice still threateningly inviting, at least to Mark. Perhaps it was paranoia but he thought that she had intended for Mark to consider her the dessert when she had made the offer. He declined the offer and asked for a cup of coffee, telling Elaine that he had a lot of work to do after dinner, going through records that he had copied earlier in the day. Mark feigned a look of disappointment. Elaine smiled, sympathetically. He drank his coffee, paid the bill, added a generous tip and was out the door.

THE DIOCESE OF ANTIGONISH II

Mark arrived in the parking lot of the Chancery Office of the Diocese of Antigonish the next day around nine o'clock, having awoken around six and taken breakfast in the dining room. It was too early he guessed for Mr. Gideon. Mark was out and on the road within the hour. He entered the building and was standing in front of Sister Thomas. She looked up at him and smiled. He immediately took notice of the fact that she wasn't knitting although he did notice that her knitting and sewing implements were sitting there on the desk. "I think I know why you're here." she observed.

"Yes, Sister, I still have some more records to go through. I may be here all day." answered Mark.

Sister Thomas nodded and motioned him to the stairs just behind her desk. "I guess I may see you at lunch." It was obvious that Sister Thomas was also a patron of the rectory dining room, which was hardly surprising since the closest dining hall was probably in a convent that looked to be about a mile away, behind the rectory building hidden behind a bunch of trees. Sister Thomas had identified the building the previous day when Mark had asked about it. He wondered about the population of nuns who resided in the convent. He almost asked Sister Thomas if the building was called a nunnery. Mark lightly tapped her desk and started toward the stairs to the second floor. He quickly regretted the gesture. Maybe she hadn't noticed.

Mark wasn't even remotely surprised when he found Father Nevin sound asleep at his post in front of the room holding the baptismal records. He stepped around Father Nevin and faced the twin doors protected by the combination lock that Father O'Grady had helped Father Nevin open the previous day. Fortunately for Mark, the combination numbers that Father O'Grady had provided had been written down on a notepad on Father Nevin's desk. The numbers were still there on the notepad. Mark used them to quietly open the doors. Mark entered the room and went straight to the cabinet containing the records for the parish of Saint Mary's, starting with the second drawer for the 1950 files. He pulled out the drawer and began with the records for the first quarter. His newly acquired investigative technique enabled him to get through the files in less than an hour, much less time than it had required him to get through the first quarter of 1950 in the cabinet containing the files for Holy Rosary. He managed to locate only one record that fit the criteria that he had set for identifying children who may have been adopted. The name was Charles Page who was baptized seventeen months after he was born. His recorded parents were George and Donna Page. He then moved on to the second quarter of 1950 where it took him less than twenty minutes to look through about two dozen records that did not reveal any appreciable disparity between dates of birth and baptism. He got the same negative results in his search of the records for the third and fourth quarters of 1950.

After not finding anything in his search of the files of Saint Mary's for the first and second quarters of 1951, Mark did come across something interesting in a third quarter file of that year. It was likely an adoption although the interval between birth and baptism was comparably brief, only three months. Fact was that he was lucky to have spotted the transaction. He had to examine the record carefully. As singular as the interval between birth and baptism was, the adoption was also unique in that there was only one adoptive parent, a woman named Linda Stephenson, indicated on the certificate. Although it was not relevant to his search, he initially thought of making a copy but didn't. It was strange he thought, a Catholic baptism of an adopted three month old infant by an apparently single woman. Mark thought that the Catholic church, Saint Mary's or any other specific parish for that matter, would not have allowed a single woman or a single man for that matter, to adopt a child. He also doubted whether social services or whatever other provincial agency was responsible for adoptions not arranged by the church would have permitted it either. He concluded, after considering the matter as he was leaning on the cabinet drawer for a few minutes, that there was the exception to every possible rule governing adoptions. For an instant, Mark thought of researching the possibility ---- it might be interesting ---- but he immediately dropped the idea when he realized that he was actually investigating something else. There was nothing else worth contemplating in the last two quarters of 1951.

It was in the 1952 files where Mark found two certificates which identified the adoptive parents as having the name of Quinn. The first certificate, which was mistakenly found filed in the first rather than the second quarter, recorded a baptism in Saint Mary's Parish on April 5, 1952 of a boy named Jackson Peter Quinn who was supposedly born on March 5, 1950. The parents were recorded as Richard and Eileen Quinn (nee Boggs). The other certificate, which was correctly found filed in the second quarter, recorded a baptism in the next month in Saint Mary's Parish, specifically on May 6, 1952 of a boy also named Jackson Peter Quinn who was also born on March 5, 1950. The parents were recorded as Robert and Eileen Quinn (nee Boggs). A burst of anxiety surged through Mark like he had just received an electric shock from a wall socket. He hadn't experienced anything resembling such a state since he was taking Prozac more than twenty years ago for an occasional nervous condition. Any idea that he may have had of celebrating when he found the first certificate had lingered for as long as it took him to find the second certificate. The second certificate was filed sequentially to the first, based he speculated on both showing the same date of birth. In fact, the two documents were almost stuck together. He could have easily missed the second certificate if he hadn't been cautious. It seems to have been filed out of order for a reason that seemed obvious once he examined the two documents.

He pulled both documents out of the drawer and placed them side-by-side on a small wooden table placed at the end of one of the shelves. He removed a pen and the small piece of paper on which Father Nevin had recorded the combination to the twin doors to the room. He wrote down the salient details from each of the two certificates on that page. Once finished, he stared at the two columns he had constructed.

Jackson Peter Quinn	Jackson Peter Quinn
Richard and Eileen Quinn (Turner)	Robert and Eileen Quinn (Turner)
Baptized April 5, 1952	Baptized August 11, 1952
Born March 5, 1950	Born March 5, 1950

Mark finished his research of the Baptismal Archives. He now had a significant part of the mystery unraveled. Three of the five elements of the baptismal certificates for comparison were identical: the name of the adopted boy (Jackson Peter Quinn – his deceased friend who had requested the investigation in the first place); the name of his adopting mother; and the date of the birth of the adopted (March 5, 1950). That left two of the five elements that were different: the names of the two adopting fathers and the dates of two baptisms.

There were two essential questions to ponder: who was Jackson Peter Quinn when he was born and who were his father and mother at that time? There was also collateral questions. Why two men, almost certainly brothers, had claimed to be his adopting father and why the boy was baptized twice, four months apart. He was staring at the piece of paper he was holding and started to ponder what his next move should be. He was now sure, or thought he was sure, that he had managed to confirm one thing he did not know before he opened that drawer: Jack's actual date of birth. One thing he already knew, the name of his adopted mother. He folded the piece of paper, put it in the front pocket of his pants, pushed the drawer of the Saint Mary's cabinet back into place, and headed out of the room. There was no sign of Father Nevin at his desk. Mark closed and locked the twin doors of the room holding the baptismal records.

He walked down to the first floor and encountered Sister Thomas who looked to be leaving for lunch, probably in the sacristy cafeteria. She called to him, gave him a friendly little smile and asked if he was planning to go to lunch in the cafeteria. She then asked if she could join him, a curious request but one he understood, almost by intuition. She was likely interested in the results of Mark's investigation of the baptismal records. He couldn't imagine that she would want to discuss anything else, that is of course if she wanted to discuss anything. Mark shrugged and smiled back. Why not he thought. He waited for her to collect her bag and come around from behind her desk. They started to walk down the corridor to the cafeteria, their footsteps echoing. He remarked on the stained glass Stations of the Cross windows. Sister Thomas reflexively commented, "They're beautiful, aren't they? We were all so proud when the project was completed. People come from all over the Cape just to look at the windows. The Premier came to the ceremony when Bishop Daniels unveiled the windows." For some reason, Mark started to think that

Jesus may have looked like a Disney character in some of the panels.

"When was that?" asked Mark.

"Well, I think it was a couple of years ago. It took the stained glass people more than a year to complete the windows. It was quite an accomplishment for the stained glass company that did the job. I understand that they're presently doing a job at All Saints in Halifax, the Anglican Cathedral. Once it is finished, I plan to visit." said Sister Thomas, explaining her admiration of stained glass artistry.

The two of them gravitated toward a table in the middle of the room. Sister Thomas nodded to several other diners, three nuns and two priests. Mark noticed Father Nevin slumped over at a table in the corner of the room. He was probably asleep, like always.

Sister Thomas saw Father Nevin as well and sort of let out a sigh, an understandable reaction. "Poor Father Nevin. The good father is elderly, I don't know how old he is but I am told that he's been a priest for over sixty years. Last year, we had a function to honor him but he fell asleep during the proceedings."

Mark smiled and asked. "Aside from guarding the baptismal records, does Father Nevin have any other functions around the chancery, you know as a priest?"

"No. Bishop Dolan won't let him even celebrate mass anymore. We all saw him fumble around during the recent masses he did say. The poor altar boys basically had to conduct the ceremony for him." replied Sister Thomas. "During the last few masses he celebrated, he didn't seem to notice that the boys were running things. I remember the boys had to steady his hand when he was giving communion. We all felt bad for him but, as I say, Father Nevin didn't seem to notice, didn't seem to be upset. For a time, the Bishop thought he was maybe facing a crisis of faith. The Bishop now lets him do odd jobs around the chancery, including sitting upstairs in front of one of the record rooms."

Not only was Mark sympathetic with Father Nevin's spiritual troubles but was also curious about his career as a priest. "Doesn't the Diocese have like retirement homes for elderly priests?" he asked. He had recalled that when he went to a Jesuit high school, he had heard that the older teachers were often retired to retreat or renewal centers where they could live out their final days in ascetic or theological contemplation.

Sister Thomas suggested that they visit the buffet before they continued their discussion. Mark nodded and followed her up to the food counter where he selected chopped salad, a butter tart, and some ice tea while Sister Thomas had chicken soup and a glass of water. When they sat down, Sister Thomas picked up on her narrative about the future history of Father Nevin. "I think the Diocese was seriously considering sending Father Nevin to the Manresa Renewal Center, a Jesuit respite place somewhere in Ontario."

"Is Father Nevin a Jesuit?" asked Mark.

Sister Thomas nodded. "Yes, I understand he was so ordained. Apparently, he used to teach Latin and Greek at Sacred Heart High School in Halifax. When he retired, they sent him here for a while." She paused and then changed the subject. "Enough about poor Father Nevin. How was your investigation of baptismal records? "Mark noticed that Sister Thomas was wearing rosary beads like a necklace.

"Well, I think I found something interesting, something very interesting. Two baptisms that involve the same adopted boy." explained Mark. Sister Thomas' eyes grew large. He noticed that she had suddenly started to nervously grasp her rosary bead necklace. "Two baptisms of the same child?" she exclaimed, as if she couldn't believe his statement or its meaning. "Two baptisms! I never heard of such a thing. It just can't happen." He understood her skepticism. He was initially incredulous himself and he could hardly be as familiar with church practice or doctrine as a nun. But he went ahead and explained the two certificates and the two differences in them: the names of the adopting fathers and the two dates of baptism, four months apart. Sister Thomas let her soup grow cold and allowed her face to develop a dumbfounded stare as Mark related the discovery of the two certificates in expanded detail. Once he was finished with his story, they both returned to their lunches although Sister Thomas took one spoonful of soup and gave it up. An uneasy silence descended over the table like they were participating in a religious service. Mark finished his lunch while Sister Thomas was staring into space like she was contemplating some liturgical mystery, such as the issuance of two baptismal certificates for one christened boy. Several minutes went by, the clatter of muffled conversations and shuffling dishes the only disruption to the eerie silence at Mark's table until Sister Thomas leaned forward as if she were about to initiate prayer, her grasp on the rosary around her neck tightening.

She then made a suggestion. "I think you should try and talk to anyone who was presiding over the parish of Saint Mary's back when your friend was baptized." She saw the look of disbelief on his face and offered an attempt at commiseration. "I know, it was a long time ago and there may not be anyone around who can tell you anything about the baptisms that were performed at Saint Mary's back then but...."

Mark smiled. "But it's worth a try." Mark observed. "Besides, there may not be any other possible avenue of, you know, inquiry." Mark also started to wonder whether Jack Quinn's cousin, Glen Quinn, the guy who precipitated the investigation into his adoption in the first place, could provide any relevant information. But how would he find Glen Quinn? Even if he was able to locate him, he may or may not know anything about the curious circumstances of Jack's birth and his subsequent baptisms. In addition, if he could find Glen Quinn, which was extremely doubtful, he would have to ascertain whether anyone in Saint Mary's had been around long enough to provide information on baptisms that were conducted more than sixty years ago. It was likely that he would be looking for someone of the vintage of poor old Father Nevin if such a person actually existed in Frenchdale or anywhere else for that matter.

Sister Thomas must have noticed the consternation on Mark's face and made another suggestion. "If I were you, I would talk to Marion Swift. She was the previous bishop's secretary, Bishop Fisher was his name. She worked for Saint Mary's before she worked for the Diocese. Anyway, I think she still lives in Frenchdale, in a retirement home."

Mark reacted hopefully, a smile coming across his face as he sipped on his ice tea. "And you know this woman?"

Sister Thomas returned the smile, now relaxed, no longer grasping her rosary necklace, and answered. "No but Bishop Dolan's current secretary, Monica Richards, knows her. I seem to recall that she worked with Marion Swift for a month when she first got the job. I would talk to Monica."

After finishing lunch, Mark walked Sister Thomas back to her desk and thanked her for the advice. She volunteered to call Monica Richards about Marion Swift. As grateful as he was with the offer, Mark had started to realize that he was growing weary of pursuing the seemingly endless string of characters that could help him with his search. Mark was simply tired of the idea of another meeting with another witness, particularly one who was certainly quite elderly. It was not to the point of declining her offer but it was disquieting nonetheless. Just consider, Mark thought, another witness in another small town to interview. He may have been running out of patience. Nevertheless, he hoped that Sister Thomas could arrange something through Monica Richards.

Sister Thomas motioned Mark to sit down on a chair adjacent to her desk while she made the telephone call to Monica Richards. It was obvious that Sister Thomas was fairly close to Ms. Richards, so affable was the tone during their conversation. After a ten minute conversation during which the two of them discussed the whereabouts of several former employees, including Marion Swift.

Marion was reportedly 90 years old and living in her home town of Frenchdale, in a retirement home called the Lakeview Retirement Home. After concluding the telephone call and relaying the information Ms. Richards had provided, Sister Thomas suggested that Mark would be well advised to take a chance and visit Marion Swift in Frenchdale, which she said was about a hundred kilometers away. "The woman is ninety years old. She's always at the home. I can give you the address in Frenchdale. You could probably see her this afternoon if you leave now." It was almost two o'clock in the afternoon.

After again thanking Sister Thomas for her assistance, he left the Chancery and was sitting in his rented *Ford Focus* several minutes later. He examined a map of the area to locate Frenchdale which, as suggested by the good Sister, appeared to be a little less than a hundred kilometers north on Route 104 past another small town, Big Pond which was another of the four parishes, Holy Rosary. Mark had originally planned to investigate the parish but it would no longer be needed. Fortunately, he had left his laptop in the glove compartment and so was able to find the Lakefront Retirement Home in Frenchdale. It was located on a Winchester Avenue just east of the town of Frenchdale.

The trip from Antigonish was uneventful except for a man hitchhiking with a dog who appeared on the side of the road just past Big Pond. Mark thought of stopping for a moment, the memory of an old hippie ragamuffin named Jake Fagan, who he had picked up on his trip from Halifax to Truscott, flashed through his mind. He hesitated for a moment, slowing down to check him out. He eventually passed him and his dog, the latter responding with a hearty bark while his owner didn't seem to notice the passing car.

As expected, Mark was turning into the parking lot of the Lakefront Retirement Home within the hour. It was a relatively modern two story building designed in a triangular shape. He parked the car, headed through the front door of the facility, and approached a counter behind which sat a middle aged woman, presumably the administrator. She greeted him, at the same time turning away from an individual talking nonsense about that day's breakfast menu. Mark immediately assumed that the newly neglected individual was a resident. He/she was bald, the gender seemingly indeterminate. He/she stepped away but continued talking, all the way to one of the empty sofas in the lobby where he/she sat down and then stretched out for a mid-afternoon slumber.

The administrator gently laughed and assured Mark that she was harmless and then asked if she could help him. Mark explained that he wanted to talk to a resident named Marion Swift, specifically about her work as a secretary for the bishop of the Diocese of Antigonish. Not surprisingly, the woman, who took a moment to introduce herself --- her name was Alice Lawrie ---- told Mark that Marion Swift was over 90 years old and may not be too useful in recalling her days as a secretary for the bishop, a fact of which she seemed to be aware. According to Alice Lawrie, Marion Swift liked to prattled on a lot about very little, predicting that it was doubtful that he would get anything useful from a conversation with her. Mark thought such behavior would be quite familiar to anyone who worked at any retirement home. Regardless, Mark shrugged and said that he still wanted to talk to her, adding that he had been referred to Marion Swift by the secretary to the current bishop. He did not give Alice Lawrie any further explanation as to the purpose of his visit. She nodded and told him that Marion was likely in her room, as she usually was. It was Room 212, which Alice contacted by telephone.

Mark listened to the Lawrie/Swift telephone call with a mixture of amusement and dread. He felt sorry for the poor administrator. It appeared from Lawrie's side of the conversation that she was simply fielding a series of complaints from resident Swift. Mark was pretty much able to determine the other side of the conversation given what Lawrie was saying. It was primarily about the food but also about the social activities of the retirement home, including the bingo games and the outings to shopping malls. Swift also complained about the crowded elevators, and most particularly, a Jamaican lady named Gertrude who apparently liked to dance during the entertainment activities. Administrator Lawrie looked routinely bored, like she had heard this conversation every day of the week for eons, which she may well have. She never raised her voice or got excited, seemingly answering each complaint with a strange serenity, as if she was somehow medicated. At one point, she covered the receiver with one hand and explained that it happened all the time, referring to the collection of complaints emitting from the other end of the line. Finally, she put down the telephone and assured Mark. "Why don't you go right up. She's in Room 212. The elevators are right around the corner to the left. They shouldn't too busy this time of day." She gave Mark an absentminded smile and Mark thanked her for her efforts.

Mark shared the ride up to the second floor with a man who had trouble maneuvering his motorized scooter into the elevator. He noticed that the man had a small dog in the scooter's basket. He identified it as a miniature Schnauzer. He knew that because one of his neighbors who was living in the same place, an old house which had been sub-divided into six separate apartments, also had a miniature Schnauzer. The neighbor was an old man who obviously liked to drink and occasionally carried the dog on their walks. On leaving the elevator, the man almost collided with Mark, brushing his knee as he turned to the left. The dog, which appeared to have been asleep, stirred but did not bark. His owner patted the dog on the head and offered Mark a gruff adieu. Directly across the elevator was a sign directing Mark to the right, to Room 212. Three doors down, past an internal balcony which overlooked the lobby was Room 212. He knocked on the door. Inside the room, he heard Marion Swift turning down the volume of the television, some paper shuffling, a minor profanity, and a shouted command to enter the room. This was one cranky woman, Mark thought. The door was open.

"Hello, Marion, my name is Mark Purchell and I would like to ask you some questions about your position as a secretary to Bishop Fisher at the Diocese of Antigonish.

Marion Swift was sitting on a lift-chair with a television converter in one hand and what looked like a coloring pencil in the other. There was a half colored picture in her lap. She examined at Mark with a bold, suspicious look on her face.

"You're here to fix the light in the bedroom, right?" she said, more a demand than a question. "I've been waiting for a week for someone to come here and fix that damn light." She was staring at him with a purposeful grimace on her face. Her expression reminded Mark of his second grade teacher, a frightening woman named Miss Fournier.

Mark offered her a sympathetic smile, the kind of grin that you'd give to a misbehaving child. "I'm sorry, Mrs. Swift, but I'm not here to fix the light. I'm here to ask you about your job with Bishop Fisher." He was worried that she would notice that he had just repeated himself, something to which a woman with her disposition might well react with anger. The bold, suspicious look on her face tightened. She turned down the volume on the television and put the converter and her coloring down on a small table beside her. She then softly tilted her chair forward and folded her hands in her lap.

There was a short awkward silence, during which time Mrs. Swift affected a pensive look on her face. "My old job with Bishop Fisher?" she exclaimed, "I haven't thought about him or that job for a long time." She paused for a moment and then asked. "Who told you about me and my old job?" He noticed that she was wearing hearing aids, large, unattractive hearing aids that gave her a faint alien look. Initially, she didn't seem to have any sort of hearing problem although he noted later in their conversation that she seemed to be speaking a trifle loudly, not often, but on occasion.

Mark smiled again. He seemed to be getting somewhere with Mrs. Swift, at least. "I heard about you from Monica Richards."

"Monica Richards? Who's that?" Mrs. Swift asked.

"She works for the current bishop, Bishop Dolan. She said that she worked with you for a brief time just before you retired." explained Mark, finally sitting down across from Mrs. Swift in a chair with a petite point cushion.

Mrs. Swift nodded a couple of times and replied. "Yes, yes, Monica Richards --- I remember her now, poor little girl, I think it may have been her first job, I stayed on for a while to train her. You know, being the bishop's secretary was more than just typing his letters. That job was more like being an assistant, arranging the bishop's affairs, running his office." Another pause. "So why are you here asking about my work with Bishop Fisher? Are you related to the bishop? I think he may have had a brother."

"Nothing like that, ma'am, nothing like that at all," Mark explained, using the appellation for the first time in their conversation. She didn't seem to notice. He continued. "I'm looking into a couple of baptisms that were conducted at Saint Mary's church, where I understand you worked before you worked for Bishop Fisher."

Marion Swift got a seriously blank look on her wrinkled face, as if she couldn't possibly know anything about two baptisms that supposedly took place at Saint Mary's sometime in the early 1950s. No surprise there. But Mark was hopeful that she, like a lot of elderly people, would be blessed with the ability to recall more distant memories. Simply put, thought Mark, people like Marian might well forget what they might have had for dinner two hours after they ate it, unless of course it contained something they couldn't abide. However, it was often possible that they could recollect with amazing accuracy events that happened fifty years ago. In fact, Mark himself often remembered his first day of school, the first time his old man hit him, the many times he shoplifted stuff, his first date and of course his first sexual experience. Oddly enough he recalled that event with more clarity than the last time he had sex, which wasn't that long ago. Mark sat across from Marion Swift waiting for her long term memory to kick in. He considered reminding her of his own experiences with remote memories.

She had put a couple of fingers of her right hand over her left eye. She sounded like she was moaning, rocking back and forth like she was having some sort of slow motion seizure. Maybe it was some sort of memory cue. Still, within a couple of minutes, during which time Mark had glanced at the headlines of several of the gossip magazines the woman had on display on the little table between her lift-chair and the sofa, she seemed to have regained her memory. Marion pressed a button on the chair converter that tilted it forward. She had removed her fingers from her eye and looked at him. "Now I remember, remember things from those days, when I was working for Father Conrad at Saint Mary's. It was my first job after I graduated high school in 1950. I was 17 years old. I think I was making about $30 a week, being his general secretary, taking care of some of the parish's business although not everything mind you. Father Conrad did the banking, dealt with the diocese, that sort of thing. I dealt with parish and parishioner events, counted the donations and scheduled things like marriages, funerals, and baptisms."

"You had a responsibility for baptisms?" asked Mark, momentarily hopeful. He moved to the edge of his chair.

"Yes, I was, or at least I think I was, but you can't expect me to remember who got baptized when. I mean, Saint Mary's used to baptize as many as four or five babies a month back when I was there."

"And when was that?" asked Mark, although he had a fairly good idea.

"Mainly in the 1950's but then baptisms slowed down in 1960's. And then, I left Saint Mary's in the late 1960's to work for Bishop Fisher," answered Marion, awaiting the next question, which was inevitable.

"So in all that time you were working in Saint Mary's, did you ever come across a situation where the same child --- and this child, a boy who would have been more than two years old --- was baptized more than once, a month apart?"

"Baptized more than once, you say?" Marion asked.

"Yes, more than once," answered Mark.

She affected a pensive look, like she was trying to retrieve another memory. She had again placed a couple fingers from her right hand over his left eye while she considered her memories. Mark picked up one of the gossip magazines and started to read an article about the current whereabouts of minor ex-television stars who have fallen on hard times. He was scanning a story about a man who used to have a part in an old western called *Wagon Train*. He finished the article and had started one about the guy who played the first captain on *M★A★S★H* when Marion brought both hands up to her cheeks and started to nod. She had remembered something.

"I think something like that happened in '51 or '52. I remember a time when Father Conrad didn't want to conduct a baptism because he thought the child had already been baptized." recalled Marion. "I seem to remember that while it was the same mother, there were two different fathers, that's right, two different fathers. Still I think the boy was in a state of grace." Her latter comment was so surprising that Mark almost interrupted her to seek clarification but he thought better of it. She then brought her hands down off her cheeks back to her lap, looking up like she was trying to access further reminiscence.

Mark prodded Marion for more, if there was more. "Do you remember anything else about those baptisms, anything at all?"

Marion looked thoughtful, staring and then added a further observation, a detail that more than aroused Mark's interest though he still tried to appear casual about it. He didn't want to spook Marion by pushing her to further revelations. "Well, I think the police were involved somehow, the RCMP." Eureka thought Mark. It was an extraordinary piece of information to say the least. Both of them looked at each other in silence. Marion concluded her testimony by firmly saying that she couldn't remember anything else about the curious baptisms. Mark had already come to the conclusion that he wouldn't be needing Marion's recollections anymore, even if she did have any further memories to share. With her information about the involvement of the police, Mark was now convinced that his best option would be to research local history, through either the files of the local RCMP detachment or the files of the *Chronicle Herald* or maybe some other newspaper, possibly the *Halifax Gazette*. He was fairly certain that any of the three sources, if not all of them would have information on an episode involving the RCMP and a church, even if it occurred 65 years ago.

Mark got up from the chair, took a couple of steps toward Marion, stood in front of her, bent down and grasped one of her hands. "Thank you so much for seeing me, Mrs. Swift. You have been very helpful." He offered her a grin.

She returned his grin with one of her own, displaying a mouth of predictably bad teeth, and then reached for the television converter. "Goodbye, sir. What is your name again?" The television was on again and she waved him out of the door to Room 212.

Mark proceeded to the elevator. There was no one else waiting, which was surprising since the crowd for the early bird dinner seating was expected shortly. After all, it was almost five o'clock in the afternoon. The elevator doors opened and he was in lobby waving a farewell to Alice Lawrie. He had decided that he would first approach the *Chronicle Herald* or the *Halifax Gazette* for information on Marion Swift's story of police involvement in the two baptisms of Jackson Peter Quinn in April and August of 1952. The RCMP, he surmised, may not be as forthcoming with their files as a newspaper. Besides, there was always Mr. Pictures and his friend to provide any further background information should Mark need it.

NEWSPAPER FILES

Mark passed an entirely uneventful evening after returning from his research adventures in Antigonish. He renewed acquaintances with the gracious Mr. Gideon when he chose to dine in the dining room at the Dunlop Inn. The place was about as crowded as it was the other time he had had supper there, four other tables with people grazing over their meals with a strange silence enveloping them. Mr. Gideon, attired in what he assumed to be his usual tuxedo, conducted him at the same table as he had occupied two evenings previously and handed him a menu with an almost theatrical flourish. Once he was seated, Gideon asked him about the progress into the search for the circumstances of the adoption of someone he referred to as "Whathisname". Mark referred to Jack by name and briefly summarized his day at the Diocese of Antigonish and the Lakefront Retirement Home, not in any great detail but general headlines, just like in the newspapers he intended to research shortly. Mr. Gideon seemed pleased with the report, observing that Mark had been right to seek the guidance of the church on matters of adoption. He recommended Mark order the baked fish, an entirely predictable menu item that Mr. Gideon acknowledged was perfected by any chef who worked in pretty well any decent restaurant in Cape Breton. Mark agreed with Gideon's advice, ordered the baked fish and a Heineken. Mr. Gideon waved the waitress over, the same woman with the nun shoes who had served him two days previously, relayed Mark's order and returned to his post as a maitre d' to an almost empty dining room.

Mark looked around the dining room like he was trying to memorize witnesses to a crime. He had forgotten to pick up a newspaper before entering the dining room. Accordingly, without anything to read, even one of the tourist pamphlets on display in the hotel lobby would have been sufficient. Mark was compelled to conduct surveillance to pass the time. He started to resume his role as a private detective, a character that he had been playing with various levels of enthusiasm and purpose since he first read the letter he found in his friend Jack Quinn's safety deposit box. He had developed impressions of his fellow diners, most of whom were probably not accurate. There was a group of elderly women, five ladies gabbing presumably about the daily activities of a retirement home, occasionally cackling like barnyard animals regarding the usual complaints and absurdities associated with residing in any retirement home. It would likely have been a litany of complaints Mark had surmised Mrs. Smith had described in her telephone conversation with the administrator, things like overcooked carrots at dinner, fellow residents who everyone apparently disliked, and the entertainment value, or lack thereof, of the weekly shows put on by the retirement home. Either that, or they were all widows who had recently and happily buried their better halves. One of the other tables had a middle age couple who were either unusually affectionate with each other or were having an affair. They were actually holding hands over the table. Then there were two apparently intoxicated couples sharing a table, laughing a little too loudly for the dining room of the Dunlop Inn. And finally, aside from himself, there was another solitary diner, an attractive woman in her mid-forties, presumably on business, just passing through. He found himself staring at the business woman, not thinking about her specifically but flashing momentarily on the image of Elaine Butler. It was an unwanted fantasy, a new experience for Mark.

He was therefore neither unhappy nor surprised when Mr. Gideon interrupted his enjoyment of the baked fish with another inquiry regarding the adoption of Jack Quinn. He was asking for further details about his search. Mark expanded on his previous and superficial report of his visits to the archives at the Diocese of Antigonish and the Lakefront Retirement Home. He provided further information about his plans to consult the files at the *Chronicle Herald* or the *Halifax Gazette* newspapers for possible stories regarding the two baptisms of Jackson Peter Quinn back in the spring of 1952, noting that he had been told there had been police interest. He also mentioned that he had considered and rejected, at least initially, the idea of contacting the RCMP about the two baptisms, suggesting to Gideon that he had been told that a newspaper would be more likely to volunteer information than the police would. He could not, however, be sure that either source would be reliable. Gideon expressed agreement with Mark's choice, adding that he knew the current editor of the *Chronicle Herald* if he ran into any trouble in gaining access to the newspaper files. Gideon told him that the editor's name was Donald McQuillan and he could be asked to help if Mark needed it. Gideon also mentioned that he didn't know anyone from the *Halifax Gazette*. Gideon also told him that the *Chronicle Herald's* participation in the online archive services was somewhat limited although he was not sure of the details.

By the time Mark finished poking at his baked fish dish, he decided that he would first consult the website of the *Chronicle Herald* regarding access to previous editions. Depending on his findings and the possibility that the material he was looking for wasn't available on-line, he had to be prepared to call on the *Chronicle Herald* in Halifax in the morning. It would be a Friday, the day on which he had originally planned to check out. Before Mr. Gideon could return to his duties, as meager as they may have been on a weekday evening, Mark asked him if he could stay a couple of additional days at the Dunlop. Gideon laughed, nodded his head vigorously and said "Stay as long as you like. Maybe it will take a few days to go through all those files at the *Herald* if the ones you're looking for aren't available electronically." Mr. Gideon then asked Mark if he cared for any dessert, having reported previously that they were featuring apple crisp that evening. Mark ordered the apple crisp and a cup of coffee. Again, Gideon turned the order over to the waitress and disappeared, likely for the night.

Mark returned to his room and started investigating the electronic availability of the newspaper files from the *Chronicle Herald*. According to their website, there was nothing on-line prior to August 16, 1999, and no explanation as to the reason for the limitation. Gideon had been right. It looked like he would be traveling to Halifax in the morning. He watched television for a while, paying $7 for a film entitled Nocturnal Animals, an advertised psychological thriller directed by a fashion designer named Tom Ford and starring two or three fairly well-known actors. Although he was entertained, he grew confused by the plot and basically stopped watching it. Instead, he begin to plan his journey to Halifax the next day, hoping that he would be able to arrange an appointment to research files relevant to the baptisms. As he took a refresher look over a map that he had used to drive from Halifax to Truscott almost a week ago now, he calculated that it would likely take him a little less time than it took to make the reverse drive, familiarity resolving any confusion. He realized it would probably require at least an entire day to drive to Halifax, study whatever files were made available, and return to Truscott. He thought of arranging a hotel reservation for a Halifax hotel and then driving back on Saturday morning. It would all depend on whether and when he could gain access to some files. He also thought of contacting the *Halifax Gazette* although he did not have a name of anyone at that particular paper. He would have to wait until the morning to make any calls.

Mark was on the phone at eight o'clock the next morning. He was happily surprised when he found himself on the line with Mr. Donald McQuillan, editor-in-chief of the *Chronicle Herald* of Halifax. Mark introduced himself and the purpose of his call. "Mr. McQuillan, my name is Mark Purchell. Your name was given to me by John Gideon, the man who runs the Dunlop Inn here in Truscott. He thought you could help me."

"Pleased to talk to you, Mr. Purchell. I haven't seen John for a while but he's a good man. So I'm more than happy to help you if I can."

Mark felt he had to introduce a little congeniality to the conversation but not too much. "By the way, how do you know Mr. Gideon? He never told me."

McQuillan replied with a little chuckle. "The guy used to run a diner here in Halifax. A small place, it was called *The Corner*. It had six stools at the counter, four or five tables, just down the block from the paper. I had lunch there practically every day. We got pretty friendly."

Mark inquired further. "When did he move to Truscott?"

"I can't remember exactly. It was probably more than ten years ago now."

It was time for Mark to get to the point. He told McQuillan the story in abbreviated form, concluding with the two baptisms and the supposed police interest. He did not identify any sources for most of the information although he did swear that he had copies of the two certificates he had found in the archives of the Diocese of Antigonish. He finally asked if he could look through the files that *Chronicle Herald* may have from 1952, hoping as he explained that he might find some news stories about police interest or involvement in the two baptisms of the same boy within months of each other during that year.

McQuillan predictably hesitated on his end, trying to recall the paper's filing system. Sure, over the last fifteen years or so, each edition of the paper was stored in an electronic repository, easily accessible. For some reason, however, most students of the newspaper's history surprisingly preferred the previous system. Each day's paper were carefully filed in chronological order in the basement of the *Chronicle Herald* building. Then he remembered, Mr. McQuillan said. Back when he first started at the *Chronicle Herald*, each edition of the paper was carefully folded, placed in a weekly hanging file and left in the basement. Apparently, the files went back to the First World War, or so McQuillan thought. He had never actually seen any of the basement files, having only asked one of the office clerks to locate a specific edition by date. McQuillan replied positively to Mark's request, suggesting that Mark was welcome to visit the paper that day. Mark enthusiastically agreed, thanking him and undertaking to be in McQuillan's office before lunch, if he could. McQuillan said that he usually went to lunch at 12:30.

Mark was in the car within fifteen minutes, dashing through the lobby like he was avoiding the bill. He got a glimpse of Mr. Gideon in the parking lot as he was leaving his car, a relatively new BMW, a dark blue color. He was dressed casually, attired in an expensive polo shirt, black slacks, and tan loafers. It was evident that he kept his tuxedo in his office at the Dunlop Inn. Mr. Gideon disappeared through the side door before Mark had a chance to acknowledge his presence. He would be taking Route 4 to Dundee, past newly familiar places like New Glasgow, Port Hawkesbury, Marble Mountain, and Whycocomagh, then Route 104 south to Truro and finally to Route 102 to Halifax. He was concerned that he would miss McQuillan before he went out for lunch.

No matter, he found Route 4 and then the local CBC station on the radio, the latter featuring a story about the opioid crisis in Halifax. At first, Mark listened intently to a series of observations by doctors, politicians, social workers, and street people. He really didn't understand the attention that the opioid issue was receiving in the media. It was a long time since Mark had dealt with anything to do with any type of drug, let alone something as dangerous as opioids. Listening to various commentaries, he briefly recalled the various pharmaceuticals he used to consume, mainly acid, mescaline, a little weed, and later Dexedrine, the occasional thrill of cocaine an added entertainment, none as hazardous as the current wave. Sitting behind the wheel of the car, he thought of the friends who had met or nearly met untimely ends following a career of the use of drugs and drink, including Jack Quinn. He even thought of Danny Beliveau. After an hour or so, he started looking for another radio station. He found, just as he had on the trip up to Truscott, an oldies station. Perhaps it was the same station. He wondered whether he would come across another Jake Fagan on the side of the road. He doubted whether he would pick that person up this time. Aside from his contemplation on drugs, it was a predictably uneventful drive, following the same route he had taken on the way to Truscott.

According to the map he had picked up at the gas station on the outskirts of the city, the newspaper's building was located on the Joseph Howe Drive in the Dartmouth area of Halifax. It was a relatively modern structure, a two story brick building with a large *Chronicle Herald* sign emblazoned over the entrance. Mark thought it strange. After all, the paper was almost 150 years old, the kind of history that suggested that it be housed in an edifice that looked more like a provincial parliament building than a shopping mall. He pulled into the parking lot and walked toward the entrance, which looked like it belonged to a bank. Interestingly enough, it was situated beside a Manulife Financial building, a huge glass structure that looked even more modern than the newspaper's building. The building's lobby was supervised by a lone security guard sitting behind a large counter with a marble top surface and a computer monitor. Mark walked up to the counter and inquired about the availability of Mr. McQuillan. The security guard, a man who looked like he had the shakes and was still recovering from some sort of hangover, nodded and reached for the telephone on the counter. Mark's experience with people like Jack and Danny Beliveau provided him with an insight into people so inflicted. The security guard almost whispered his inquiry into the receiver. He got a response, put down the receiver and informed Mark that McQuillan was out to lunch, a response that he had unfortunately expected. It was almost one o'clock in the afternoon.

"Can I speak to someone else?" asked Mark, almost leaning over the counter.

The security guard seemed a little stunned, as if he hadn't heard Mark. "What is that, sir?" he asked. Mark repeated his question. The guard then innocently asked whether he had anyone specific in mind. "No one in particular. I was talking to Mr. McQuillan about looking through the paper's archives." Mark explained.

"The archives?" questioned the guard.

"You know, the files in the basement." answered Mark, wondering why the security guard didn't seem to know what the archives were.

The security guard nodded slowly and suggested that he might want to talk to the office manager, someone named McPhee, Mary McPhee.

"Sure, thanks. Can you get her on the phone for me?" Mark asked. The security guard again nodded, picked up the phone again, and again whispered into the receiver. He nodded for probably the tenth time during their encounter, put down the receiver, and directed Mark to the elevator to the left and behind him. "Her desk is on the second floor, right in front of Mr. McQuillan's office. You can't miss her." Mark thanked him and headed for the elevator. He joined two other people waiting for the elevator, an older man who Mark thought may have been a reporter and a UPS guy carrying a small box.

The elevator came and the three of them entered, the older man hurrying into the car like he was about to introduce a breaking story to the city desk. The UPS guy almost dropped his parcel. Mark was last in. The three got out on the second floor --- there was no third floor --- in the same order in which they had entered. The security guard was correct. He couldn't miss Ms. McPhee and her desk. Surprisingly, the office manager looked to be in her mid-twenties, hardly the chronology one would expect in an office manager, the image of an aging spinster with a pencil stuck in her hair and a severe look on her face emerging. This office manager looked like she might more easily belong in front of a fashion photographer than a desk in a newspaper office. Even at his advanced age, Mark was still intimidated by the presence of an attractive woman, no matter how irrelevant that was supposed to be these days. A case of nerves was percolating in him like a sudden fever. He hadn't felt anxious for months but he felt it coming on. He crept up to and then stood in front of Ms. McPhee's office like he was about to apply for a job as her assistant or ask her out on a date, both of which could induce a panic attack.

Fortunately, Ms. McPhee had not been paying any attention to him standing in front of her desk which was long enough for his moment of anxiety to pass. She had been studying her computer screen. She looked up at him, smiled in an offhanded way and asked if she could help him.

"Hello, sorry to bother you," said Mark. He sounded embarrassingly timid, even to himself. He thought she was staring at him. "I was talking to Don McQuillan yesterday about the newspaper's archives."

"The paper's files --- you mean the ones that aren't on-line?" she asked, a little less casual this time. She actually seemed to be interested, or at least less disinterested. "Maybe you should wait for Mr. McQuillan."

Mark was surprised that a woman as apparently formidable as Ms. McPhee would actually be concerned with Mr. McQuillan's opinion or that of anyone else for that matter. She had briefly reminded Mark of a woman named Linda Richards who, despite a relatively lowly clerical position, had dominated an office in which he had worked many years ago, even the people, mostly men, who were her superiors. He wondered, standing there like a moron he thought, whatever became of Linda Richards. It was, however, more than thirty years ago.

Mark assured Ms. McPhee that Mr. McQuillan had agreed to allow Mark to access the archives. She looked a little dubious but then pushed herself away from the desk, pulled the top right drawer out, rooted around, and came up with a key. She then pushed the drawer back in, pushed her chair out a little further, and then got out from behind the desk. Mark's case of nerves returned for an instant. Mary McPhee was wearing a spectacularly short dress, short even by the standards of a fashion photographer. She held the key up and told him she would have to accompany him to the basement archive room, citing what she called the "house rules". As he followed her into the elevator, she told him that her boss, Mr. McQuillan, was a stickler for security. Mary sent on to say that there had been several break-ins at the paper over the last few years. She wondered aloud as to why anyone would want to rob a newspaper office. She said that no one seemed to have a clue. She then laughed, a subtle musical laugh.

The elevator reached the basement, they both got out, and they walked down a narrow corridor to a relatively small door in the middle of the floor. She opened the door, turned on the overhead lights, and waved him into the room. Before Mark was row after row of gray metal racks on which were stacked countless files. Unlike the archives at the Chancery Office of the Diocese of Antigonish, there weren't any title signs to identify the contents of individual racks. Mary offered Mark a sheepish look. "Sorry, the files are not well kept. You may have trouble finding anything." She then pointed to the back of the room and offered obvious advice. "The older files are back there, the more recent ones up front." Mark said that he was looking for articles from the first half of 1952. Mary shrugged her shoulders and left him with an admonition. "I have to go. I have to get back before Mr. McQuillan returns from lunch. Once you're finished, that is if you find anything, just lock the door and let me know if you need anything copied. We can't let you take any of the original files out of the building." She gave him a little wave and walked out. He couldn't help but stare, again.

Mark was looking at six rows of metal racks that extended from the front of the room, where he stood by the door, to the back of the room, which was maybe 10 meters deep. He started his exploration between the second and third set of racks on the left side of the room. He originally went straight to the back of the room where he had gone through a few files from the first decade of the 20th century. He removed several of those editions from their hanging files at random and spread them out on the concrete floor. The first edition was dated June 5, 1902 and featured front page coverage of the Ontario provincial election won by the Liberals under a man named Ross. The coverage also included an associated front page story about the congratulations offered by the sitting Nova Scotia Premier whose name was George

Henry something --- the page was faded and hard to read. He then moved across the room and read an edition from May 20, 1915 which reported stories about the arrival of the first Canadian infantry division in France and complaints about the quality of their rifles. The latter report reminded Mark of the misfortunes that one of his uncles, all of whom had enlisted during the Second World War, was injured when his rifle misfired and he shot himself in his foot. He also read parts of the sports section that featured, among other things, a portrayal of a man named Tom Trike, a Nova Scotia native who had recently played one game in the major leagues, at second base for the Boston Braves. It was an interesting story in which about a dozen minor league baseball teams were listed as having had Mr. Trike on the roster. The list included the Province Grays of Rhode Island, a team that had a pitching staff that included Babe Ruth, who often played a little outfield. Tom Trike was his teammate in 1914.

After reading the baseball story, he noticed that it was almost three. He thought Ms. McPhee had said that he had to get out of the place by six o'clock. He had better hurry. He moved on to 1939 out of interest, a pivotal year to say the least. The first front page story he came across reported the establishment by the federal Department of Labor of the Board of Wartime Prices and Trade Barriers, the purpose of which was to control inflation. It was announced two days after the declaration of war against Germany by Britain and a week before Canada would follow suit. He noted that over the next two weeks, almost every single edition seemed to be exclusively devoted to the war. There were prominent stories on a variety of related issues, special sessions of Parliament, the establishment of Canadian naval and air facilities, the landing of several infantry divisions in England, and the setting up of the Radio Canada services overseas. Mark sat there for more than fifteen minutes on the concrete floor thinking about all the war stories he had heard from his father in particular, many stories which had poured out of him with increasingly frequency the older he got. He remembered feeling guilty for his generally dismissive attitude at the old man's funeral home visitation when it seemed that practically every person who came by to pay respects mentioned his military service. Maybe he was feeling guilty about not having served himself, something that the old man occasionally brought up during his autumn years. But he never had any idea as to where he would have served, there being no world war in which to participate.

With time running out, Mark got serious about locating the newspapers for April and May of 1952, finding them two racks over, almost on the top shelf. He carefully pulled the papers for the two months out of the hanging files and spread them out on the floor. He immediately found the edition for Monday, April 7. It was two days after the initial baptism of Jackson Peter Quinn. He scanned the edition, checking the metro section in particular for any mention of police interest in a baptism at Saint Mary's church in Frenchdale. He went through the four subsequent editions of the *Chronicle Herald* before he came across a short article that was definitely relevant to his search. It was dated Friday, April 11, 1952.

Mike Robertson

Police Stumped So Far by Truscott Homicide

Officials of the Royal Canadian Mounted Police (RCMP) from the Antigonish detachment as well as local police have reported that the investigation of the murder of a Truscott man has yielded few clues as to a possible perpetrator. Richard Quinn was killed in the plain sight of a dozen customers and staff of the local Thistledown Pub late in the evening of Wednesday April 9. RCMP Sergeant Murphy as well as Officer Neeson of the Truscott Police were quoted as saying that according to all witnesses, Mr. Quinn was hit with two pistol shots by a short man dressed in black pants, a black sweatshirt, and black sneakers. The perpetrator was also wearing sunglasses. None of the witnesses could describe the killer's face. Again according to the witnesses, the man simply walked into the pub, pulled out a pistol, took two shots from about five feet away from the victim, and walked out of the building. Victim Quinn died immediately. Sergeant Murphy and Officer Neeson asked that anyone with any information on the murder contact the Antigonish detachment immediately.

The article also featured a photograph right out of one of those true crime magazines that he had heard about but had never actually seen, his knowledge of such publications based on the many films and television shows that had included them as part of the story. The photograph was a stark black and white rendering of the scene that night in the Thistledown Pub, Richard Quinn's body covered by a white sheet with four unnamed RCMP and Truscott Police officers, including Mark assumed Sergeant Murphy and Officer Neeson, standing over him. Mark also noted that the photograph was taken by Smithers, as identified in the lower right hand corner of the picture. So Mr. Pictures was actually the local crime photographer, even then.

After reading the article, Mark realized that it was highly likely that the same newspaper would also include an obituary of Richard Quinn. He immediately consulted the social section of the same paper and came across the following announcement.

Quinn, Richard (Truscott|) - *Died in tragic circumstances on Wednesday, April 9 at the age of 28 years old. Is survived by his parents Ernest and Irene Quinn of Frenchdale, his brothers Robert and James, his sister Susan, his wife Eileen and their recently adopted son Jackson. Friends will be received at the Churchill Funeral Home in Frenchdale from 3-6 PM on Friday April 11. The funeral will be held on Saturday April 12 at Saint Mary's Church in Frenchdale.*

Mark contemplated the information he had just collected. Aside from there being no explanation for the visitation and funeral being in Frenchdale rather than Truscott, he now had an explanation for the more important question regarding two adopting fathers: Richard the father was killed, a misfortune that apparently led to the introduction of the new father Robert. The mystery was the relatively brief interval between the two fathers and the two baptisms, the latter little more than four months apart. The most likely answer to the so-called mystery was also probably the most unlikely, it being too obvious to be true; in short, a Cain and Abel cliche. A simple narrative ---- as if Robert had killed his own brother

Richard in order to end up with his recently widowed wife and by extension her newly adopted son. If it was that simple, then the police would have Robert Quinn in custody rather than asking the public for information about his murder. He wished for one moment that Robert and Eileen Quinn were still around to ask.

As fascinating, if not exhilarating the discovery of the April 11 article was, it wasn't that relevant to the question of Jack's natural parents. Sure, it would appear that Jack's first adopted father may have been killed by his second but likely wasn't. This didn't provide any critical clues about Jack's birth parents. It was, however, intriguing. Jack would have been engrossed with the story. In fact, he may have been even more interested in the story of the slaying of his first adopted father than in the identification of his natural parents. Still, he would have to follow the story of the murdered Quinn to ascertain any further detail about the incident. He flipped through the next week's editions, finding another story about the murder investigation. The newspaper was dated Wednesday, April 16.

Police Claim Progress in Truscott Homicide

On April 15, officers of the Royal Canadian Mounted Police (RCMP) detachment from Antigonish and the Truscott Police held a briefing with the press regarding the status of the investigation into the murder of Richard Quinn, a Truscott man gunned down in a local pub on April 9. According to the officers, they have speculated that there may have been a romantic relationship between Eileen Quinn, the wife of the deceased, and the brother of the deceased, Robert Quinn also of Truscott.

Further, the adoption by the deceased and Eileen Quinn of a two year boy named Jackson Peter Quinn the previous month may have been another source of conflict between the two brothers. The police said that they plan to further investigate these two situations. When asked about any forensic evidence, the police said that the RCMP and the Truscott police are coordinating an investigation of locally registered 32-caliber handguns, the type of weapon already determined to have been used in the murder. Further, both police forces continue to interview local witnesses to the murder as well as other potential witnesses in the Truscott area.

Again, accompanying the story was a photograph by Smithers, a.k.a. Mr. Pictures. In fact, there were three passport type pictures, of the two Quinn brothers and Eileen Quinn. Interestingly, the Quinn brothers looked remarkably similar, like they could have been twins. Eileen Quinn was extremely plain looking, the chauvinist in him making it difficult to believe that the two brothers, in fact, any two individuals would fight over this woman. But who is to know what goes on in people's minds he thought. He recalled another plain looking woman, who had worked with Mark in another dismal office job. For reasons that eluded most observers, including Mark, the woman, whose name was Brenda something or other, was admired from afar by four or five colleagues, for reasons unknown. So it was possible he thought that Eileen could have been the source of discord between the two brothers. This again almost certainly supported the theory that Robert had been having an affair with his brother Richard's wife and killed him out of jealousy or romantic rage or a similar sentiment.

Mark continued to look through the April editions of *Chronicle Herald* until he came across another relevant article, this one a story of critical interest, if not importance. In fact, it initially seemed to be the end of the line for this part of his investigation. As he read the story, he started to wonder about his next move. Like the previous stories, this one did not contain any pivotal clue as to the identity of Jack's natural parents. It did however give him with another chapter in the fantasy novel that was developing in Jack's head.

Police Make An Arrest in Truscott Homicide

On April 30, officers of the Royal Canadian Mounted Police (RCMP) detachment from Antigonish and the Truscott Police arrested a Truscott man named William Boggs for the murder of Richard Quinn, also a Truscott man who was gunned down in a local pub on April 9. In commenting on the arrest, police spokesmen RCMP Sergeant Murphy and Truscott police officer Neeson said they have sufficient evidence of the guilt of Mr. Boggs to justify his arrest and bind him over for trial. The police would not reveal the evidence they had compiled regarding the guilt of Mr. Boggs. There have been rumors that Mr. Boggs, a longtime resident of Truscott, had been conducting an affair with Eileen Quinn, the victim's widow. Mr. Boggs, through Halifax attorney Lester Anderson, has denied the charges. A bail hearing will be held at the county courthouse in Antigonish next week.

Richard Quinn was killed in the plain sight of a dozen customers and staff of the local Thistledown Pub late in the evening of Wednesday April 9.

Mr. Smithers was also able to provide a photograph to accompany the article: Mr. Boggs being led into the country jail at Antigonish between Sergeant Murphy and Officer Neeson, both of whom were identified in the caption. Mark knew that Mr. Pictures would have spent a lot of time outside the court house in Antigonish once the trial began. Mark also wondered if there would be other photographers at the trial. He also pondered the possibility of a portrait artist following the action from inside the courthouse.

Having come across such a significant milestone in his search for clues to Jack's origins, he realized that he had probably exhausted the *Chronicle Herald* newspaper as a source for more information. He could continue to scan the editions of the paper, six days a week for maybe a year or more, a period of time he thought would cover the trial and eventual disposition of Mr. Boggs, his conviction, his acquittal, or some other adjudication. That meant approaching the police, either the RCMP or the Truscott police, for information on the eventual fate of William Boggs. Mark had initially chosen to avoid the police in conducting his research but he did not seem to have any choice at this point. He also wondered whether the RCMP or the Truscott police force kept records that went back that far and whether they would agree to share them with an amateur detective like Mark.

THE TRUSCOTT POLICE
SHARE HISTORY

Mark returned from Halifax around seven o'clock in the evening. It was Thursday, which meant he had originally scheduled himself to leave the next day. As soon as he entered the Dunlop, he arranged for another three day stay with the redoubtable Mr. Gideon who was kind enough to give him a reduced rate. Gideon asked about his day researching the files of the *Chronicle Herald*. Mark revealed that he had been enlightened by several interesting press articles he had come across in some 1952 editions. He continued advising Mr. Gideon of his research indicating that he was still stymied when it came to the mystery of Jack Quinn's natural parents. Gideon nodded sympathetically and suggested that he hoped the additional three day stay at the Dunlop would be sufficient. Surprisingly enough, Gideon did not offer advice as to any additional avenues Mark could pursue. He was strangely disappointed but he didn't know why. He returned to Room 106 and thought about the Bell-Buoy-Blue and, with understandable but minor reluctance, Elaine Butler.

He arrived at the Bell-Buoy-Blue and immediately spotted Elaine standing over a table at which three older women appeared to be debating their bills. He waited at the entrance until another waitress --- in fact it was a waiter --- greeted him. Mark asked that he be seated in Elaine's section, hoping to engage her in discussion about his planned pursuit of the local police department. He was confident that Elaine Butler, who seemed to be familiar with almost everyone and everything that went on in Truscott, would no doubt have some helpful information. The waiter handed Mark a menu and ushered him to a table right next to the women who had been discussing their bills and were now getting up from the table. Elaine turned her head, rendered an enigmatic smile and put up a finger. He sat down and waited for Elaine to come to his table. He noticed a copy of the *Globe and Mail* sitting on the table that had just been vacated by the deliberating women. He stood up and picked up the paper, sat down, opened it, and started to read it. It was yesterday's edition. He had just put it down and had started to consult the menu when Elaine arrived with a glass of water.

"Well, I haven't seen you in a while." she said, giving Mark another curious smile, simultaneously sarcastic and seductive. He returned the smile and replied, "It's only been a couple of days."

Elaine gave him a light laugh and asked with a little lilt in her voice, "So what have you been doing the last couple of days? Did you find anything useful, you know, for your project?" It was the first time anyone, including Mark himself, had referred to his quest for the identity of Jack Quinn's natural parents as a project. She then changed the subject by saying that she would be back to take his order. She then turned and walked away. Just like in a movie, he watched every step of her way back into the kitchen. He looked back to study the menu. He felt optimistic all of a sudden and decided on the lobster, the most expensive item on the menu. In addition, he decided on a Heineken rather than a Big Bruce although he had the intuition that he could be ordering a Big Bruce later that evening, specifically when he and Elaine would be sitting at one of those small tables in the Thistledown Pub. Somehow he knew. Besides, he needed her advice, again.

Elaine was back within minutes to take his order. She told him that they had run out of Heineken and quickly offering him a Big Bruce. He immediately agreed, suggesting that since he could be going to be drinking "Big Bruce" later in the evening anyway. Elaine smiled slyly and asked Mark if he was planning an after dinner arrangement. Mark thought he was being witty. "Yes, as a matter of fact." There was a slight pause and then he added the crucial element of his plan, which he hadn't realized he had concocted in the first place. "And I'd be pleased if you would join me for a Big Bruce at the Thistledown." Elaine almost immediately agreed to his proposal. "I'm off at ten o'clock but you already know that, don't you?" She smiled in that beguiling way of hers, assured him that she would be with his Big Bruce and disappeared again. Mark went back to yesterday's *Globe and Mail* and again watched her walked away. He had barely started on the main section of the *Globe and Mail* when she returned with his beer.

The rest of the evening was relatively uneventful though there seemed to be an ostensible tension between Mark and Elaine still simmering, at least as far as Mark was concerned. Mark had finished his lobster, his beer and was working on his second cup of coffee when Elaine arrived with the bill and informed him that she would be off in fifteen minutes, an hour early as it turned out. "Are we still going to the Thistledown?" she asked with her standard elan, like she already knew the answer. "Sure, I'll be waiting by the entrance for you, after I pay the bill of course." Elaine smiled. Mark looked at the bill and the question of the gratuity went through his mind. Too much would be inappropriate he thought, too little and he would look cheap. He decided on the standard 15 percent, which used to be 10 percent but somehow had increased over the past couple of years. Elaine handed him the machine, he gave her his debit card and they completed the transaction. Ten minutes later, they were leaving the Bell-Buoy-Blue and heading for the Thistledown Pub.

The two of them were soon sitting at one of those small tables under the strange florescent lighting of the Thistledown Pub. Waiter Tuck Graham, son of Norm, arrived to take their orders, which were, predictably enough, two quart bottles of Big Bruce. As efficient as ever, Tuck gave them a curt bow and had their bottles and glasses on the table in what seemed like less than a minute. Tuck knew what they were going to order. It was possible that everybody in the place ordered the same thing --- a damn "Big Bruce". Mark and Elaine had settled into their first beer, she more than him as usual. She leaned over with her elbows on the table, with a look of concentration in her eyes but equipped with that sneaky, perky smile of hers. "So what have you been able to find out about your friend's real parents? Any progress?"

Almost if he had rehearsed his story, he told Elaine about his adventures over the past couple of days, mentioning his visits to the former orphanage, the baptismal archives of the Diocese of Antigonish, a former secretary to Saint Mary's parish pastor, and the newspaper files of the *Chronicle Herald* in Halifax. He was excited to tell Elaine that the newspaper archives had fortunately featured articles about the murder of Richard Quinn and the complexities of the circumstances surrounding the two Quinn brothers, Eileen Quinn, the adoption of Jack Quinn and the arrest of a guy named William Boggs for the murder of Richard Quinn. Elaine seemed to be semi-interested although he was not sure whether she was pretending or just pretending to pretend, like she was going along with him so she would have someone with whom to drink. But he preferred to take her lukewarm interest seriously, finally asking her if she had any suggestions as to his next move, mentioning that he had already planned to contact the Truscott police. After ordering two more quarts of beer --- Mark had managed to keep pace with Elaine through their first beers --- they both paused for a moment until she leaned back in on the table, finally looking serious.

"Well, you may be able to get something from the locals. Not so much from their files but maybe from their memories. After serving cops in this town for years, I know they like to talk, especially about old cases." observed Elaine who then put her head back and took another slug of beer. Mark offered up a small grin, encouraged. "You really think so?" He also took another slug of beer. "So do you have any names of cops I could talk to?"

"Sure, that's easy. As you probably know, or could have guessed, I think the whole Truscott police force has six officers. Your best bet is either Bob Neeson or John McLeod. Both of them are veterans of the force. In fact, both had fathers who were cops --- I think that Neeson's father was on the Truscott force while McLeod's old man was on the RCMP up in Baddeck. Anyway, I've known the two of them for years, even since I came back. I used to serve them on occasion in the Bell and see them in this place. They're both good bets to talk history, you know, about the old days." Elaine took another drink and then leaned back.

"But we're talking about the real old days here, like 1952. Like I told you, the police stories I came across took place here in Truscott 65 years ago. I doubt that either of the two cops you mentioned could have had any firsthand knowledge of the incidents I mentioned." explained Mark, looking somewhat plaintively at Elaine. He sat there watching Elaine order another beer, her third and wondered again about his previous interest in Elaine's sexual proclivities. While he continued to be marginally tempted, his curiosity did not extend to the formulation of any plans that he might have contemplated about Elaine. He had just lost interest. He couldn't quite explain it. Four nights ago he was ambitiously plotting her seduction at virtually the same table in the Thistledown as he was sitting in now but now his only interest was in her advice.

She rebuked him gently about his dismissal of the memories of the local cops. Her voice lowered, she rebutted, "Hey, Truscott is a small place and there is a lot of nepotism when it comes to jobs, especially municipal jobs, like the police, the fire department, those sort of things. You see, people working in those jobs have a sort of institutional memory."

Mark interrupted. "I don't think I'm getting your point."

Elaine explained further. "Well, some jobs, in fact a lot of jobs in Truscott, are passed from father to son, you know like legacies. The two officers who I suggested you talk with --- Neeson and McLeod --- both had fathers on the force. So as you can see, if they can't help you with any information on the events you mentioned, maybe their fathers can fill in the blanks, that is if they're still around. And maybe Neeson and McLeod can recommend other former cops who may have some memories to offer."

They stopped talking while Tuck showed up with another two beers, the second for Mark and the third for Elaine. As soon as he left, Mark continued their discussion of the next act in the drama in which he seemed to have found himself. "What do you suggest I do --- just give them a call?" Maybe he thought he was being overly cautious.

Elaine gently snickered. "Well, if you worried about it, I'd be happy to give one or both of them a call. Personally, I suggest Officer Neeson. He's usually pretty talkative, at least anytime I spoke to him. Why don't I give him a call, you know, if you want? Sort of like a recommendation."

More than pleased, Mark downed almost half his second beer before responding to her offer. "Sure, that would be great. But you don't have to do that."

Elaine just smiled, a comforting smile. "I know but I'll give him a call anyway, just to let him know that you'll be contacting him." Mark then asked her, in the most courteous voice he could muster, if she could talk to them as soon as possible. She nodded and said that she understood. She finished off her third beer of the evening. He was relieved when she didn't immediately signal for a fourth. "Maybe we should get going." She then signaled to Tuck for the bill. Mark almost fell off his chair ensuring that he grabbed the bill. It was the least he could do. Elaine smiled and patted his hand.

Mark drove her to that dump she lived in a few blocks away. He recalled that four days ago, he was driving a drunken waitress home with lascivious intent on his mind, a plan that quickly faded once the intended had passed out, fortunately on her own bed, before he could initiate seduction. "Drop by at the Bell sometime and let me know what you find out," Elaine suggested as she got out of the car. "Thanks again," answered Mark. He drove off, feeling as optimistic as he had since arriving in Truscott.

THE NEESONS REMEMBER

The next day was a Friday, Mark got up around nine o'clock, late for him, particularly for most of the past week. He went down to the dining room for breakfast where he ordered pancakes and sausage. He picked up a copy of that day's *Chronicle Herald* and settled back to enjoy a leisurely breakfast. Before he went off to asleep the previous evening, he had decided to contact Officer Neeson of the Truscott Police to arrange for an interview. If he wasn't available or unwilling to talk to Mark, he could try Officer McLeod. He would wait a couple of hours before contacting anyone, hoping that Elaine would have had an opportunity to speak to either of the officers first thing in the morning. He did not see Mr. Gideon but the older waitress with the stained white blouse, the faded blue skirt and the nun's shoes was presiding over the dining room with another waitress who looked to be high school age.

So Mark spent a relaxing hour reading the *Chronicle Herald*, the *Globe and Mail* and then last week's edition of the *Victorian Scribe* that had been left on an adjacent table after its previous occupants had departed. He then returned to his room just as housekeeping was leaving. Having looked up the number on the internet the previous evening, he sat down to phone the Truscott police station. A women answered, a woman with a brittle edge to her voice, like she was on her way to anger.

"Hello, how can I help you?"

"Yes, yes, I would like to speak to Officer Neeson, Officer Bob Neeson."

"I already know Officer Neeson's Christian name, sir." he heard her expel a breath, like he was already running out of time on their telephone call. "Is this an emergency?"

"No, it isn't. I would just like to talk to Officer Neeson," Mark stated cautiously, like he was offering an apology.

"Is it business or personal?" the voice on the other end of the telephone asked.

"Well, it's sort of business, sort of personal." Mark answered.

"What is the nature of your business with Officer Neeson?" the edge of her voice turning harder.

Mark tried to stay calm. He was convinced that if he responded in kind to her, their conversation would be over. So he played it as honestly as he could. "To be completely honest, I'd like to speak to Officer Neeson about a past case."

"A past case?", surprise in her voice.

"Yes, a past case," he answered.

"Then it's business," she insisted.

"Well, my interest is personal, not business." he countered.

"If it's not current business, then it's personal," she observed.

"Okay, whatever you say," he resigned. "Can I speak to him now?" Mark felt like he should have gone back to bed.

She answered with a predictable curtness. "Well, he's not in right now."

"You're not serious?" he sarcastically commented, .

"Yes I am, sir, I suggest you try back after lunch," she concluded the conversation with as little grace as she could.

Mark hung up the phone without any further debate. He decided that he would simply show up at the station, hoping to catch either Officer Neeson or Officer McLeod in a better humor than the station's receptionist. That would be after lunch of course.

After eating at a place called McCurdy's, Mark drove to the police station on Turley Road. It was another low-slung warehouse type building, half brick, half aluminum with a flat roof. He parked in front and walked through the glass front doors on which was emblazoned Truscott Police in gold lettering. He was greeted by a stern looking woman wearing a ratty tan cable knit sweater over a navy blouse sitting behind a small desk. Was this the same woman with whom he had had that pointless conversation that morning? He hoped not although he thought that he should pretend that they had not had that conversation. She looked up with an almost accusatory expression on her face.

"Can I help you, sir?" Mark recognized her voice.

He stood mute for a moment and then mumbled something about speaking with Officer Neeson, trying to disguise his own voice. He looked beyond her desk at two men who appeared to be pretending to look through paperwork. One was a younger guy who couldn't have been either Officer Neeson or Officer McLeod. He got the impression from Elaine that the two of them just couldn't have been young, that they were veterans of the force, the type of individual officer who had experience and who liked to talk about those experiences. Therefore, he surmised, the young guy wasn't either Neeson or McLeod.

Mark awoke from his temporary repose. "Can I see Officer Neeson please?" The stern looking woman looked up, her expression softening a trifle, but she still replied officiously. "You mean Chief Neeson? He's here today." She glanced over her shoulder at the older man still flipping through a stack of papers, perhaps arrest reports, perhaps bank statements. Although he probably heard the stern looking woman confirm his presence in the office, he didn't look up.

"Can I speak to him please?" asked Mark, still standing in front of the stern looking woman, starting to shift from one foot to another, like he was in need of a washroom.

"Sure, just go over there and take a seat." she said with a wave of her hand and some sort of gesture. It could have been a smile.

Chief Neeson, an overweight man in his fifties, extended his hand. "Captain Bob Neeson, what can I do for you?"

Mark shook his hand and introduced himself. "My name is Mark Purchell. Maybe Elaine Butler spoke to you about me."

Chief Neeson nodded. "Yes, she did. She called me this morning, just twenty minutes ago. As she explained it to me, you're looking for information on an old murder case here in Truscott."

Mark was relieved to hear that Elaine had called. He didn't have to justify his visit, Elaine had already done that for him. "Yes, the murder of a man named Richard Quinn in 1952."

Captain Neeson smiled sympathetically. "Unfortunately, the force doesn't have any records that go back that far. Fact is that any such records, records going back to the 50s, either weren't kept, which I doubt, or were lost, which is likely. But I remember hearing about the case. My old man, who by the way was on the force before I was, joining just after the war, used to talk about that case. It was a huge case back then. In fact, it may have been the biggest case the force had ever seen. Either that, or the time the only bank in town was robbed and two of the tellers were shot by a guy wearing a clown mask." Neeson started to snicker. "Funny thing about the bank robbery was that we never caught the perpetrator although a kid was caught wearing the mask two weeks later. The kid said he found the mask in a school yard. We later found the gun too, in the same school yard."

"What about the guy who robbed the bank?" asked Mark.

"Never caught him. Just couldn't catch a break on that one." admitted Neeson. "The mayor, the city council, people in the town, they were all over us about that for months." Chief Neeson stared at Mark for a moment. "I think though we still have the mask and the gun in evidence storage if you're interested" Mark noticed that the Chief looked like he was pretending to smoke a cigarette.

Mark shook his head. Although somewhat entertained, Mark was still disappointed, his head bowed, his shoulders sagged, his arms started to come up to his face. Officer Neeson put his own hands up, like he was trying to placate Mark. "Don't worry, Mr. Purchell. You can talk to my old man. He was on the force back in the 50s. He's in his 80s now but I'm sure he'll remember the case. As I said, it was a huge case."

"Will he see me? Will he talk about it?" asked Mark, enthused as hell.

Chief Neeson produced a huge smile. "Sure he will. He likes to talk about his old cases, just like his son, right? Here, I'll give you his number. He still lives on his own which is kinda surprising. My mother's been gone for a couple of years and --- well, I thought he wouldn't adjust as well as he has." He wrote his father's phone number and address on the back of his business card and slid it across his desk to Mark. "I'll call to let him know you'll be in touch." The father's name was Robert as well.

Mark thanked Chief Neeson, shook his hand, and walked out the building, slipping by the woman at the front desk and into the parking lot. He was back in Room 106 of the Dunlop Inn. It was almost five o'clock in the evening. He watched CNN for a while, the continuing madness of so-called President Trump dominating everything but the commercials. Mark changed clothes, had a beer out of the mini-bar and went down to dinner. His old friend Gideon was standing by the entrance. He greeted him with his usual genteel enthusiasm, and conducted him to what had become his usual table. He handed Mark copies of the *Globe and Mail, the Chronicle Herald* and the menu, recommending the evening's special --- blackened catfish.

As expected, Mr. Gideon then asked about the day's activities. Mark told him about his encounter with Chief Neeson, who Mr. Gideon obviously and predictably knew, and about his plans to talk to his father about the old days on the force, specifically about a 1952 murder case. Gideon said he was happy to hear that Mark was still making progress. Mark ordered a beer and the special. Gideon smiled, nodded, and said he would pass his order along to the waitress, who surprisingly enough was not the woman with the faded blouse and the nun's shoes but a younger woman who he had seen that morning. He found himself ordering three more beers before he headed up to his room.

Apparently, Mark had had too many beers that evening, both in the dining room and then maybe later in the room. He woke up the next morning profoundly hungover and still dressed, something that hadn't befallen him for at least twenty years, back when he was seriously abusing himself in the company of his old pal Jack Quinn and others. He got out of bed, also falling down in the process. He noticed that he had soiled his trousers, some nice peninsula shaped stains evidence of last evening's inebriation. By the time he made it to the bathroom, he noticed it was almost ten o'clock in the morning.

After a spartan breakfast in the dining room, coffee and toast was all he could abide, he was back in his room, telephoning Bob Neeson the retired police officer. An elderly, shaky voice answered. He introduced himself. Bob Neeson Senior seemed to know who he was. Mark started to explain his purpose in calling when Mr. Neeson interrupted him to say that his son had called last night to let him know that Mark would be contacting him. He said he would be more than happy to help, boasting that his memory was pretty good for "an old guy". Mark asked if he could come over to talk to him, maybe take him out for lunch. Neeson immediately agreed, suggesting they meet at Thistledown Pub for a meatball sandwich and a brew. Mark managed to laugh and mentioned that he had spent several evenings there quaffing quarts of Big Bruce. Neeson let out what sounded like a whoop and said they could hit the Thistle within an hour or so. Mark offered to pick him up. Neeson agreed and gave him directions to his place on Shore Road. Mark said he would be by his place within the hour. The senior Neeson offered him a cheerful salutation and hung up.

Within less than an hour, Mark was parked in front of old man Neeson's place on Shore Road. It was a small Cape Cod style cottage. Neeson was waiting for him, standing in the doorway of his place, smoking a cigar and wearing a Boston Red Sox baseball cap. He opened the front door and stuck out his withered hand. Mark shook his hand and showed him into the car. They were sitting down in the Thistledown Pub within fifteen minutes. Mark didn't recognize any of the three waiters who were on duty although Neeson seemed to know all of them, cheerfully waving at them. One of them greeted him, a potbellied man with a bald dome and a mustache. Neeson introduced Mark to the waiter --- his name was Al Cross. They both ordered quarts of Big Bruce and meatball sandwiches, even though Mark suspected that his intestinal tract wasn't ready for such a lunch. Bob Neeson told Mark that Al Cross had been a waiter for almost thirty years, remarking that he was skinny when he first started serving beer in the Thistle. He also told him that Cross had worked at the Hornet, another Truscott tavern that had closed.

Mark asked Neeson about his tenure as a police officer, although he didn't specifically mention the murder of the man named Richard Quinn and his killer, William Boggs. The two of them exchanged pointless chatter, breaking the ice so to speak. The conversation focused on the history of Neeson's life in Truscott, his three kids, two of whom had joined a police force, his wife Barbara, who had passed away just last year and his fifty years living in that clapboard house on Shore Road. Mark enjoyed Neeson's recitation. It reminded him of his grandfather's stories being a cook in the First World War. Funny thing ---- he was never interested in his own father's war memories, even though it seemed that he repeated them endlessly. It was curious that Neeson never mentioned whether he had any war stories to relate. In any event, sitting there listening to Neeson was like watching a documentary unfolding on television.

Mr. Cross delivered two bottles of beer and two meat ball sandwiches. Chief Neeson immediately spilled part of his meatball sandwich on his sweater, laughed and rubbed the sauce into the sweater, which fortunately was a red color. They were halfway through their sandwiches when Mark raised the murder of Richard Quinn. Neeson smiled, Mark noticed for the first time that he was missing a front tooth. Mr. Neeson took a slug of his beer and started to talk. It sounded almost rehearsed. Mark was sure that this wasn't the first time he had been asked to tell, or more precisely, retell the story.

"Yeah, it was in the late winter, early spring of '52. Anyone who lived in Truscott back then knew about the case. It was a hell of a big deal. I remember getting the call one night from some waiter in the Thistle. It was a tavern in the center of town." Mark had nodded. "I guess you already know that. We got the call and rushed over there to find this man Quinn, Richard Quinn, lying dead in the middle of the place. He had been shot. I had never seen anyone who had been shot, even during the war although I was stationed in the Bahamas as a radio operator and never knew anyone who had ever seen anyone who had been shot. Anyway, this guy Quinn is lying there surrounded by a circle of customers, most of them still holding their beers. They were all witnesses and they all said the same thing --- that somebody dressed all in black had come in, fired two shots from a pistol at Quinn and skedaddled out of there before anybody could get any kind of good look at the guy."

From the *Chronicle Herald* articles he had already seen, Mark knew about those particular facts. He then asked about the basis for the arrest of Mr. Boggs, an arrest that was made on April 30, 1952 by a RCMP officer named Murphy and Neeson himself. He said that he had read the report on the arrest but he had no further information.

Neeson, who had just finished his meatball sandwich, put down his fork, took another swallow of beer and exhaled. "Well, to be honest, we had a tip." Mark had hardly touched his sandwich. He wondered if Neeson was going to ask him about his unfinished sandwich.

"You mean like an informant?" asked Mark.

"Yes, we did." replied Neeson, "A man named Turner, who was Eileen Quinn's brother. He knew everybody else concerned, the two Quinn brothers and Bill Boggs. According to Turner, Boggs was upset Richard Quinn and Eileen Turner were planning to marry and adopt a kid that was being raised by the nuns at the Villa Notre-Dame orphanage down in Little Bras d'Or. Anyway, that was the story. And since we found that Boggs actually owned a pistol that could have fired the bullets that killed Richard Quinn, we also found that he didn't have much of an alibi for the time when Quinn had been shot."

Mark took the explanation in and asked an obvious question. "What's the story about the adoption? I mean you basically had three potential fathers in the story: Mr. Boggs and the two Quinn brothers."

Neeson finished his beer and held up his arms in supplication. "To be honest, I don't know." Both of them sat in silence for a few minutes and ordered another beer. "Any suggestions?" asked Mark.

"Look, why don't you go back to the old newspapers." suggested Neeson. "The trial of Boggs went on for a few weeks. It wasn't the trial of the century mind you but the press, particularly the guys from the *Chronicle Herald*, must have written few stories about the trial and its aftermath."

"Do you remember their names?" asked Mark although he suspected he already knew them.

"Well, there was a guy named Ford --- he wrote the articles and this photographer/artist guy took pictures outside of the courthouse and drew pictures of people inside the courtroom. People called him Mr. Pictures. Those two were in the paper a lot back then. Come to think about it, that guy's kid is still around. I think they call him Mr.Pictures too," explained Neeson. Mark nodded, acknowledging that he indeed had heard of Mr. Pictures, both senior and junior.

Mark then asked about the trial. "How did the trial turn out?"

Neeson grimly smiled, his teeth clenched, as if transfixed in memory. "Well, this fellow Boggs was found guilty. He got life. Some people, me not so much, wanted the guy to hang --- this was before they outlawed capital punishment in Canada --- but the judge, a man named Bailey, gave him life in prison. You see, this guy Boggs got a lot of sympathy. I can't remember exactly why but a lot of people felt sorry for him. I suppose it had something to do with the kid that was being adopted."

Mark knew that he would be going back to search the files of the *Chronicle Herald* although he did, for a moment, reflect on the delightful prospect of seeing Ms. McPhee again. He then asked Mr. Neeson if Boggs was still in prison. "Oh no. He killed himself maybe six months after he was sent to prison. Couldn't take it, I guess. Funny thing though --- the prison where he was incarcerated,

Rockhead Prison near Halifax, an old, medieval looking place, was closed the next year. It was kind of …..."

"Ironic." suggested Mark.

Neeson nodded. "I was going to say strange." Or tragically ironic Mark thought.

THE NEWSPAPER FILES II

After spending much of that Saturday afternoon in the Thistledown interviewing and drinking with Bob Neeson, Mark returned to the Dunlop Inn just in time for dinner. He considered going to the Bell for dinner, feeling like he somehow owed Elaine Butler a report on his progress. He assumed she would be working even on the weekend. But first he had decided to take a quick nap, from which he awoke close to eight o'clock in the evening, too late, he thought, to drive to the Bell. So, as he had on several previous occasions over the past few days. Mark sat down for supper in the dining room of the Dunlop. As soon as he entered the room, he spotted Mr. Gideon presiding over its entrance with his usual gracious authority, appearing to chat amiably with an older couple on their way out. As soon as he saw him, Gideon gently excused himself from his conversation with the older couple and walked over to Mark, reaching out to place a hand on his arm. He asked about his day's activities. Mark was somewhat surprised that Gideon seemed to be aware of the fact that Mark had spoken to the Neeson officers, father and son. During their short conversation, Gideon informed Mark that he know both of them. Mark was not surprised.

Unlike previous times, during which the generally ostentatious Mr. Gideon seemed only superficially interested about Mark's efforts with respect to his friend Jack Quinn's natural parents, Gideon seemed sincerely curious. So Mark was comparatively receptive to Gideon's intrusions this evening. He related the main points of the elder Neeson's story, the murder of Richard Quinn, Jack Quinn's first adopting father, and the capture of a man named William Boggs for the murder of Richard Quinn. He told Gideon that he planned to return to Halifax to undertake further research about the history of the trial of William Boggs. He noted that he was hoping that any such press articles would provide further clues to the identity of Jack Quinn's parents. Gideon seemed to seriously consider Mark's story, nodding earnestly. He then escorted Mark to a table toward the rear of the restaurant, looked around for a moment, and then sat down at Mark's table, moving one of the chairs close to Mark. He asked if Mark wanted a drink. Mark agreed, even though he was still recovering from the afternoon's session with Neeson. Gideon held up his hand, the nun shoe waitress came over, handed him a menu, and took his drink order.

Gideon then pressed, in a low voice, almost a whisper, for additional details regarding the elder Neeson's testimony. Maybe the guy was simply bored. In any event, Mark said that he didn't have much more to say, repeating his plan to return to Halifax for further research in the newspaper archives. Gideon was then distracted by the entrance in the dining room of an attractive, well dressed middle aged woman in the company of an elderly man pushing a walker. Gideon immediately excused himself and returned to his post at the entrance to the dining room where he could be expected to demonstrate his usual charm.

Mark went to bed early that night, having decided to drive into Halifax the next day, a Sunday, stay over that night, and go directly to the *Halifax Chronicle Herald* the next morning. He would hopefully be able to complete his research of the press reports regarding the trial of Mr. Boggs in that one day. Mark reserved a room at the Haliburton Hotel on Morris Street, perhaps an unnecessarily expensive suite relative to the other hotels in Halifax. On the other hand, compared to Montreal, Toronto or even Ottawa, it was quite reasonable. Unfortunately, he had not brought an overnight bag with him, only the large suitcase sufficient for the planned five or six day stay in Truscott. Realizing that he could hardly bring a change of clothes in a plastic bag, he managed to return to the dining room to consult with his friend Gideon. Fortunately, it was just before the dining room was scheduled to close for the night. Gideon seemed to be more than happy to lend Mark an overnight bag, one of the many discarded valises he said were left in the hotel's Lost and Found, a service for which Mark was predictably grateful. Before he finally turned in on that Saturday night, he consulted a city map and noted that the Halifax hotel and the newspaper offices on Joseph Howe Drive in Dartmouth were barely two kilometers apart.

Mark departed for Halifax the next day at a relatively reasonable hour. He couldn't sleep and was compelled to stay up the previous evening until almost midnight watching the first two *Alien* films on television. He stopped for breakfast/lunch at a diner outside of Halifax, a prosaic looking place with six tables and a counter with four stools. All that was missing was a jukebox and a fat cook with a wedge cap and a dirty apron. Speaking of which, the cook was a rough looking younger man with arms covered in blue green tattoos. There were two waitresses, an older woman who was probably the owner and a much younger women who could have been her teenage daughter. Mark sat on one of the two stools that happened to be vacant. All the other chairs and stools in the place were occupied. He tried not to look at anyone although he did notice that the teenage waitress was wearing a nipple ring, having seen the outline through her blouse. He ordered a western omelet. It was pretty good. Mark never caught the name of the establishment.

Mark arrived at the Haliburton Hotel on Morris Street a little after noon and checked in. A charming young man in a maroon blazer took his credit card and assigned him a room on the third floor. He picked up a pamphlet from a wooden stall in the lobby explaining several of the tourist attractions in the area. By the time he had settled into Room 312, he had already decided he would spend the afternoon taking a tour of the Halifax harbor, having thought of little else to do. Unfortunately, as soon as he stepped into his room, he started to feel a little tired, opting then to catch some Z's rather than board a boat for the afternoon and early evening. By the time he awoke, it was six o'clock. He showered, scanned the internet for a list of local restaurants and was soon in his car with directions to the local "Keg". He choose a spot at the bar, his favorite perch at most restaurants, ordered a beer and was staring at the menu when an older man wearing a baseball cap with a *Mercedes Benz* emblem tapped him on his arm and asked him where he was from. Mark answered in an unfortunately curt tone and then went back to studying the menu. The man then volunteered that he had visited Ottawa several times, commenting that he had found the city quite pleasant despite, he said, the fact was "the place was full of government bureaucrats." Mark shrugged and agreed, wondering how the man knew he was from Ottawa. He wished he had something to read. Mark, who also seriously doubted whether the man owned a *Mercedes Benz,* happily received his beer and almost guzzled the entire bottle. The man took the hint and turned back to watching whatever games were showing on the hanging monitors. Although there were several games showing, he thought that he was looking at the game involving the Toronto Maple Leafs. Mark ordered another beer and the Thai bowl. He noticed there was a discarded newspaper on the other side of the bar. When the waitress, a young girl who was wearing, like every other female server in the place, a short black dress, brought him his second beer, he asked for the paper. She smiled and handed him the paper. It was the current day's *Chronicle Herald.*

He scanned the four stories featured on the front page, finally settling an article about a local man who had been killed when he was hit by a car on a highway near Sydney the previous Friday evening. The article, entitled "Few Clues in Tragic Hit and Run", was written like a cross between an editorial and a mystery story. It was full of breathless descriptions of a cold, dark night in which a speeding car, the identification of which there were no clues, apparently hit and killed a middle aged man named Tom Davis. Davis was apparently on his way home, which was strange the article noted since his home was nearly ten kilometers away from the accident site. The reporter penned a final paragraph in which the driver of the mystery car was described as fatally hitting Mr. Davis with intent but without remorse, an accusation that prompted the paper to ask the public for assistance in finding who the reporter referred to as "the highway perpetrator." Mark had wished the story had offered more detail. It was also obviously prescient of the newspaper stories he would be looking for tomorrow in the archives of the *Chronicle Herald*.

Mark also read front page stories about the possibility of a provincial election in the fall, a surge in cocoa production in Columbia, an odd choice for that page and the plan to use a small rural Nova Scotia community as a launch site for satellite-carrying rockets. In another spellbinding lead story, there was a report on a court victory for a rural couple who had been struggling for over a decade with contaminated water. By the time his entree arrived, Mark was reading a Canadian Press story about more than 250 skulls found in clandestine graves in the city of Veracruz in Mexico, a mass burial allegedly connected to a drug cartel. In addition, there were the inevitable stories about the U.S. Administration's intentions to renegotiate NAFTA and the efforts of the U.S. Congress to overhaul the American health care system. By the time his coffee arrived, Mark had pretty much read every story in the paper, including the letters to the editor, and maybe a dozen obituaries. He was back in his room at the Haliburton Hotel by nine o'clock and was asleep no more than an hour later.

Mark was awake by eight o'clock the next morning, having survived a dream involving being arrested for shoplifting in a pharmacy. The strange thing about the dream was that he was naked except for an unidentified baseball cap. He went down to the hotel restaurant for breakfast, ordering sausage and two from a young woman with a ponytail. She seemed to be a trifle harried, briefly and unnecessarily explaining that the other waitress scheduled to be on duty that day had telephoned in sick. He was therefore a little late getting on the road, which really didn't matter given the short distance to the paper. Mark was soon standing in the lobby of the *Chronicle Herald* facing the same security guard who had greeted him two days ago. Fortunately, he recognized Mark, assuring him that Ms. McPhee was at her desk on the second floor. He also alerted him that Mr. McQuillan was in his office if he wanted to talk to him. Mark thought about it for a moment for future reference he concluded. The security guard then waved him into the elevator. He was alone in the elevator.

Mark arrived on the second floor and turned immediately to Ms. McPhee's desk. She wasn't there. He stood there like he was some sort of penitent. A woman at an adjacent desk, an older woman who seemed, at least from the look on her face, to disapprove of Ms. McPhee, slowly shook her head. She informed Mark, in a voice barely below the decibel of a shout, that McPhee wouldn't be in that week. She sounded profoundly displeased, as if the mere thought of McPhee was enough to cause her annoyance. He was to explain his purpose in standing in front of McPhee's desk to a colleague who wasn't exactly a big fan.

"I was here on Friday. I spoke to Ms. McPhee about old editions of the *Chronicle Herald* going back more than sixty years," explained Mark, worried about not being given the same assistance as provided by McPhee. "You see, I'm researching a murder that happened in 1952." He stepped closer to the colleague's desk, close enough to read the name plaque on her desk --- Mrs. Strube. While waiting nervously for her response, he noticed that Mrs. Strube's facial expression had morphed into something approaching a scowl, maybe even a grimace.

She replied, her tone no less stern than the facial expression suggested. "And she allowed you into the basement archives?"

"She did. In fact, she escorted me down there herself." he replied, still anxious. He moved a little closer to Mrs. Strube's desk. She looked up at him as if she were suspecting him of something devious.

"Well, you may have to ask Mr. McQuillan if you want to see any files." informed Mrs. Strube, "As you may have guessed, Ms. McPhee did not have the authority to give you access to the newspaper files. And neither do I. You'll have to get Mr. McQuillan to agree."

Mark was ready to respond. "Well, I spoke to him last week as well. He said he would be happy to help me by allowing me to search the old newspapers."

Mrs. Strube almost allowed a funny smile to appear on her face. Mark presumed it was sarcastic. She pointed down the corridor where Mark knew McQuillan's office was located. "Well, you'll have to ask him again," she advised.

He gave her a curt wave and headed towards McQuillan's office. His office door was open. Mark knocked on the door and stood on the threshold to his office. Mr.McQuillan looked up and smiled. It was clear he recognized Mark.

"Can I help you?" he asked.

"Mr. McQuillan," you may remember me. My name is Mark Purchell. We spoke last week on the telephone. I asked you about the newspaper archives."

McQuillan nodded, got up from his chair, came around from behind his desk and shook Mark's offered hand. "Sure, I remember and please call me Don." he said with cheerful enthusiasm. "You're looking for press stories about a murder that was committed back in the 1950s, right?"

"Yes, a 1952 murder in Truscott," offered Mark.

On first impression, he seemed more like a car salesman than a newspaper editor. He was also too well dressed. Like a lot of people, Mark was under the impression that newspaper men, unlike their journalist cousins on television, were shabbily attired, rumpled, and fortunate to be sporting an old necktie and a well-used sports jacket.

"I was here last week, speaking to your office manager, Ms. McPhee." Mark assured him.

"Ms. McPhee," he murmured wistfully, "Ms. McPhee, now there's someone you can't forget." It would appear to Mark that his initial infatuation with, if not esteem for Ms. McPhee was shared. They exchanged slight eye rolling glances, as if they both knew something about Ms. McPhee that the other didn't. Then McQuillan smiled knowingly. "And I assume you had to deal with Mrs. Strube. She's a helluva delight, isn't she?" he said, his smile broadening, getting close to a chuckle.

"Yes, you could say that." answered Mark. "Anyway, she told me to speak to you." He delayed for a moment, leaning forward. "Ms. McPhee was very nice. She showed me down to the basement and the file room. She left and let me look through the old newspapers on my own. I found three articles about the murder. They were all dated in April 1952. Then, I locked up for the day."

"And I guess you're now looking for more articles from the same time period?" offered McQuillan.

"Yeah, there was a trial later that year. I'm looking for reports about that trial." agreed Mark. "I'm guessing the trial was over by the end of that year. I'm pretty sure that the *Chronicle Herald* will have a couple of reports about it."

"Happy to help." assured McQuillan. "Look, I'll have to take you down to the basement myself, if you're ready." He then escorted Mark out his office door, down the hall past the casually frowning Mrs. Strube, to whom he nodded briskly. He then turned and winked at Mark who almost laughed but managed to control himself. He did, however, contribute a smirk.

In the elevator down to the basement, McQuillan asked whether he was hopeful that press articles on the trial of William Boggs would help solve the mystery of the two baptisms he had mentioned during their original telephone conversation. "I hope so." admitted Mark. "Fact is that any press articles about the trial are basically my last hope. They may provide details that could shed some light on the baptisms." He didn't mention the ultimate objective of his pursuit of the details of the baptisms, the identity of the natural parents of Jack Quinn. On that, he still thought that there remained the possibility of discovering an accidental Rosetta Stone regarding the origins of Jack's birth; perhaps a newspaper story that would include a direct reference to, if not an explanation of the circumstances of Jack's birth, a reality that was plainly crucial to the murder case. McQuillan simply nodded as they exited the elevator into the basement. They walked to the door of the archive room. McQuillan unlocked the door, turned on the lights and ushered Mark into the room. Mark walked directly to the shelf that held the newspapers dated 1952. Mr. McQuillan then left, calling out to remind Mark to lock the door when he was finished.

THE TRIAL REPORTED

Mark started to carefully look through the newspapers, beginning with the editions from May 1952. It was curious but predictable. He noticed again that the old newspapers were yellowed and almost brittle. He had to continue to be careful handling each page of each newspaper he removed from the shelf. Within an hour of examining all editions of the Chronicle Herald for the months of May and June 1952, he had not found any reference to the trial of William Boggs. He was again tired of sitting on a concrete floor looking through old newspapers when another existential moment of doubt crept over him like a sudden fever. As had invariably occurred to him on many previous occasions, what the hell was he doing he thought, once again questioning his motivation in pursuing this treasure hunt, this investigation of a mystery that was more a curiosity to him than anything else. It was a curiosity that didn't really affect him, his deceased friend or anyone else for that matter. Still, as he had already concluded almost continually, he had invested too much time to simply abandon the search so close to a possible finale. It was like he was living a book that he was writing himself. He had to know how it would turn out, no matter how inconsequential. Despite the fact that it was unlikely that there were hidden inheritances or unknown relatives for a friend who would not be around to benefit even if there had been. He sat there, letting out an audible sigh and went back to his search.

It was the July 3, 1952 edition, the Thursday two days after Dominion Day as it was called then. On the front page, he found, among stories about continuing efforts to negotiate an armistice to the Korean War. It also contained an article about the recently introduced Old Age Security Act in Canada and a speech by the new Halifax mayor Donahoe, a man with the unusual Christian name of Alphonsus. But most important of all, at least to Mark, was an article on the opening of a murder trial in the small town of Truscott on Cape Breton. Mark read the article with considerable relief.

Murder Trial Opens in Truscott

Yesterday, the trial of a local man accused of homicide opened in Truscott, a small town on Cape Breton Island. William Boggs, a 24 year old carpenter, is charged with the killing of Richard Quinn, another local man. According to the Royal Canadian Mounted Police (RCMP) detachment from Antigonish and the Truscott Police, who arrested him on April 30, Mr. Boggs shot Mr. Quinn dead in the local Thistledown Pub in plain sight of a dozen customers and staff on the evening of Wednesday, April 9.

While police have not revealed any evidence of the possible motive for the murder, which appears to be the only question left with respect to the homicide itself, there have been stories that

Mr. Boggs had been conducting a romantic relationship with the victim's widow. Mrs. Quinn, the former Eileen Turner was another local resident. The two had apparently broken up after Mrs. Quinn had taken up with the murdered man, Richard Quinn, and then married him late last year. Several months later, on April 5, 1952, they then adopted a child, a two year old boy whom they named Jackson Peter Quinn. Four days later, Mr. Quinn was killed. It is expected therefore that the trial will hear a lot of interesting testimony, the apparent complexities of the personal relationships among the parties to the crime obvious fodder for speculation, innuendo, and outright gossip.

Judge Leonard Bailey is presiding over the trial, which for practical reasons is being held at the local elementary school, a much larger facility than the local courthouse. Dozens of potential spectators were not admitted to the proceedings, the high interest in the proceedings reflecting the notoriety of the murder. It is generally thought that Judge Bailey's chief responsibility will be to ensure that the proceedings are conducted in an orderly fashion. In the short term, however, the first order of business for the judge will be the selection of twelve jurors to consider the eventual fate of Mr. Boggs.

Like the three previous press articles he had found about the murder, Mr. Smithers supplied a photograph, this one a snap of the crowd eagerly awaiting entry into the school. Surprisingly, at least to Mark, there were no drawn sketches of the proceedings inside the improvised courtroom. He thought such art was a typical, if not an obligatory aspect of such trials. He also noticed that the authorship of the article was attributed to Mr. Andrew Ford who, as he already knew, seemed to be a partner of Smithers in such journalistic endeavors. He was eager to continue his search, fully expecting an article about the trial to appear in pretty well every subsequent daily edition of the *Chronicle Herald* for at least a couple of weeks. But, like his mistaken assumption about the prospect of an artist recording the legal proceedings in pen and ink, the trial was not to be like any trial he had every seen on television or in movies, the only references he had to go on.

For one thing, and most importantly given his preoccupation with the search for press articles about the trial, proceedings did not seem to be held every day. This was particularly true in the early stages of the trail when selecting a jury, twelve people and alternates supposedly chosen at random to consider the evidence and arrive at a verdict. Unlike his own experience in either being asked to serve on a jury or hearing about someone who had, he doubted any local adult asked to serve on the jury would find or invite reason to avoid it. Although he had never seen any reference anywhere in the press, at least not so far, to the Quinn murder being characterized as the "crime of the century",this would have been the usual appellation for such terrible crimes. He doubted therefore that any local citizens would decline to serve on a jury judging such a crime. In any event, he was soon to discover that it would take three days to actually choose a jury in the case. It was so reported by Ford in a *Chronicle Herald* article of Monday, July 7.

Jury Chosen in Truscott Murder Trial

On Friday, a jury was finalized after three days of questioning by Counsel for the Crown Andrew Stewart and Counsel for the

Defense Bryan Keller in the trial of William Boggs, a local Truscott man charged with killing another local man, Richard Quinn. Both Counsel Stewart and Counsel Keller said after the close of proceedings that, given the noteworthy, if not notorious nature of the case, special care had to be taken in selecting the jury. The jury that was eventually selected is composed of twelve local men, four farmers, three men employed at the local scrap yard, two fishermen, a bank clerk, a teacher from the local elementary school in which the trial is taking place, and an automobile mechanic. Throughout the three days of jury selection, a small group of women were outside the school singing songs and carrying signs in support of allowing women to serve on juries. Harold Ogilvy, the local member of the provincial legislature, also made an appearance in support of the campaign to allow women to serve on juries.

With the selection of the jury finalized, it is expected that the trial deliberations will begin in earnest this coming Wednesday with prosecuting Counsel Stewart to give his opening statement.

Not surprisingly, Mr. Smithers contributed his usual photograph to the report, this date's picture was a shot of the dozen or so citizens campaigning for women to be allowed to serve on juries. Sitting there in the archive room, Mark took a moment to consult the internet on his laptop and discovered that women were finally allowed to serve on juries in Nova Scotia by 1960. Given the efforts most people he knew, including himself, made to avoid jury duty, there was a certain retrospective irony to these efforts. In addition, artwork depicting both the prosecution and defense tables were included with the article.

Mark placed the newspaper back on the rack and enthusiastically pulled out the next five editions from the entire week. He found that two of the next three editions he consulted, dated July 9 and July 10, included stories on the trial. Both articles described in grim, gratuitous and ultimately redundant detail the shooting itself. The witnesses included six of the ten customers and two of the pub's waiters who were present in the Thistledown on the evening of April 9. Each gave basically the same testimony. Although the articles did not employ the term, Mark immediately thought that the reporter, specifically the intrepid Mr. Ford, might well have used the word "routine" in referring to these virtually identical stories. In the second of the two stories, Ford had included an semi-editorial reference to the likely tedium for jurors to be completely bored as they repeatedly listened to the same evidence. Mark himself thought that both stories could easily be substituted for each other, at least as far as the witness testimonies were concerned. The only difference between the two stories being the language used by RCMP Sergeant Murphy and Truscott police officer Neeson. Their reports included information about the technical aspects of the shootings, the identification of the gun belonging to William Boggs and the caliber of the bullets fired into Richard Quinn by that gun.

The only mystery left, as pointed out in the second press article, was the motive for the killing, hints of which had already been suggested to Mark by retired officer Neeson. Neeson was, of course, the same officer whose testimony in the Boggs trial that was included in the article from the July 10 edition of the *Chronicle Herald*.

Mark was looking forward to the continuation of the trial, more precisely the report on the next phase of the trial, likely to be reported in the July 15 edition, a Tuesday. Jack accidentally and fortunately came across the Saturday July 12 edition, that date's newspaper being misfiled. An article in this edition included an editorial supporting the candidacy of Crown Prosecutor Andrew Stewart to run for the Liberals in the next provincial election, which was scheduled for the next year. The article, which was the only missive on the editorial page, described Counselor Stewart as a man who "has been indispensable to the application of justice in Nova Scotia" and suggested that he would be an ideal candidate for the next Cabinet. As exciting as the article would be to political junkies, Mark wondered whether a recitation of the history of Stewart's successful prosecutions as well as a recommendation that he run for office was interesting to anyone else. Mark did, however, wonder about the timing of the article, a wonderfully cynical ploy in the middle of a trial in which Mr. Stewart was a playing a leading role. Mark also thought that if Stewart lost the trial, the *Chronicle Herald* editorial page would be unforgiving.

As expected, the July 15 edition of the *Chronicle Herald* included a story of the previous day's proceedings in the Truscott murder trial.

Truscott Murder Trial Hears Stunning Testimony

In a significant development, the Truscott murder trial heard testimony today from Eileen Quinn, the widow of the Richard Quinn, for whose murder defendant Williams Boggs is on trial.

Mrs. Quinn, who married the deceased a little more than a year ago, declared that she had had a romantic relationship with defendant Boggs that lasted several years but ended shortly before she married Mr. Quinn. Under unusually intense questioning from defense counsel Keller, Mrs. Quinn testified that she had grown up in Truscott with William Boggs as well as with the two Quinn brothers, Richard and Robert. In a tearful admission that drew audible gasps from the court, including the jury, Mrs. Quinn said that she had been romantically involved with the three men since they had been in high school. Of these three, one was dead and another was on trail for his murder. She also said, in an another emotional admission, that she plans to marry the decedent's brother Robert and that they plan to adopt the two year old boy Jack who had originally been adopted by Eileen and Richard Quinn only four days before the latter's murder.

In an unusual action and despite the objection of prosecutor Stewart, Judge Leonard Bailey asked Mrs. Quinn to explain specific parts of her testimony, including most particularly the complexities of interlocking affairs with these three local men, two of whom were brothers. In a halting, almost whispered voice that the court reporter was asked to repeat, she said that "To be honest, Truscott doesn't have many decent men you know. To be honest, Bill and the Quinn brothers were the best men available." The latter statement elicited intermittent laughter and muttering among the court, both the spectators, the jury, and the lawyers. Judge Bailey did not appear to be amused, using his gravel several times to quiet the room and then calling for a lunch break.

In a move seen by the reporter as an attempt to lay the foundation for a diminished capacity defense, Mrs. Quinn's testimony continued after lunch. She provided further testimony regarding the break up of her relationship with William Boggs and her subsequent liaison with Richard Quinn. Prosecutor Stewart renewed his previously overruled objection to what he termed "irrelevant and unfortunate personal details". With the courtroom seemingly on the edge of their seats, Mrs. Quinn made another shocking admission, telling the trial that she had become pregnant by Mr. Boggs when they were both 17 years old and still in high school. Although she was repeatedly and understandably evasive during the questioning, she testified that she quit school and was accepted into residence by the Christian Life Home, a maternity home for pregnant girls located in Little Bras d'Or, a small town located about 100 kilometers from Truscott. When asked about the fate of the infant boy who Keller noted was reportedly born on March 5, 1950, Mrs. Quinn testified that he was immediately taken into the care of Villa Notre-Dame, an orphanage established by the Grey Nuns in 1852, when Nova Scotia was still a British colony. Keller then introduced an exhibit, a Catholic Archdiocese of Antigonish affidavit that stated that most, if not all of the orphaned children in Cape Breton were adopted after a stay at and through Villa Notre-Dame.

Noting that it was past three o'clock in the afternoon and with the defendant William Boggs next scheduled to take the witness stand for what would likely be extensive testimony, Judge Bailey adjourned the proceedings until the next day.

He hardly glanced at, much less studied the usual Smithers photograph of the day. It was a trifle hazy exposure of a handcuffed Williams Boggs being escorted out of the back entrance of the school by a quartet of police officers. This had been common practice each day he appeared at the trial. The drawing that accompanied the article showed a mournful Eileen Quinn clutching a handkerchief on the witness stand. Mark Purchell sat on the concrete floor with the Tuesday, July 15, 1952 edition of the *Chronicle Herald* in his lap attempting to process the information that had been included in the article. His head hurt with hurried contemplation. Not expecting to have arrived so suddenly at a resolution to this mystery he had pursued almost religiously over the past several months so suddenly, he was pleasantly dumbfounded. He almost let out a shout, his heart was almost pounding. He wished he was still carrying a Xanax, an Ativan, some sort of tranquilizer. After all this time, he finally had the damn answer, all out of that day's court testimony, as strange as it turned out to be. Jack Quinn's birth mother was a teenage girl named Eileen Turner who had a baby boy with Jack Quinn's birth father, a local boy named William Boggs. Jack Quinn was born at the Christian Life Home, the unnamed infant being immediately taken into care by the Villa Notre-Dame orphanage just down the road in Little Bras d'Or, Nova Scotia. The orphan apparently stayed there until he was officially adopted by Eileen and Richard Quinn. The baptism was performed on April 5, 1952. He was adopted for the second time on August 11, 1952, again by Eileen and her new husband, Robert Quinn. He sat on that floor with the entire convoluted set of circumstances swirling in his head like a nimbus, the only mystery left being the reason for the unusually long stay of the orphaned boy in Villa Notre-Dame orphanage. He already knew that Mr. William Boggs was eventually convicted of the murder of Richard Quinn, having come across the relevant article in the Friday, July 18, 1952 edition of the *Chronicle Herald*. A follow-up article appeared in the edition that appeared on Wednesday, July 23, 1952, headlined "Boggs Gets Life". He did not have to look any further. As officer Robert Neeson the elder informed him at the Thistledown Pub, Boggs only lasted six months into his life sentence, eventually hanging himself in his cell at the Rockhead Prison.

THEN WHAT

Mark was safely back home in his dingy apartment by late Tuesday afternoon. He had departed the Dunlop Inn while it was still barely dark, driving from Truscott to Halifax in under four hours and managing, as planned, to board the one o'clock Halifax-Ottawa flight in plenty of time. Aside from an almost immediately regrettable decision not to contact Elaine Butler during his last evening in Truscott, the main subject of his ruminations during his drive along Route 104 and then Route 102 was the possible disposition of the facts that he had uncovered in the ten days. The person who petitioned him to pursue the mystery of his own origins was dead, the request being made from beyond the damn grave so to speak. There was only one person left alive to whom Mark could convey the information for which he had spent so much time collecting. That was the cousin Glen Quinn, the first and only person who had alerted Jack that he was adopted. But he had no idea where Glen Quinn lived or how to contact him and definitely did not have an appetite for initiating another investigation. Besides he concluded, Glen Quinn probably already knew, or could have guessed the information he had spent almost two weeks uncovering. Maybe he could give it six months and reconsider contacting Glen Quinn.

Mark then contemplated actually recording his findings, one paragraph would do he thought. He could then rent a safety deposit box, maybe the same one that Jack Quinn had leased, perhaps his lease was still current, into which he would place his paragraph until someone, the possibilities were hardly endless, would presumably access the box and its contents, i.e. the paragraph. As a symbolic gesture, he could bury the page on which the paragraph was printed under that disc at the Royal Cross Cemetery where Jackson Quinn was buried. He could seek the advice of the two other people with whom Jack Quinn was friendly: his ex-wife Deborah Inkster and his neighbor Danny Beliveau. He planned to inform them anyway but he doubted seeking their advice would result in anything more useful than he had already considered.

Before he finally found himself at home in that dingy apartment, noting that after almost two weeks of living in hotel rooms that were actually cleaned every day, the place depressed him more than it normally did. Mark thought of the observation that Jack Quinn had plagiarized from T.S. Eliot in one of his whimsical journal commentaries. "This is the way the world ends, not with a bang but with a whimper."

It seemed appropriate somehow.

Printed in the United States
By Bookmasters